The Revelations of Jude Connor

Books by Robin Reardon

A SECRET EDGE

THINKING STRAIGHT

A QUESTION OF MANHOOD

THE EVOLUTION OF ETHAN POE

THE REVELATIONS OF JUDE CONNOR

Published by Kensington Publishing Corporation

The Revelations of Jude Connor

Robin Reardon

KENSINGTON BOOKS
www.kensingtonbooks.com

All scriptural references in *The Revelations of Jude Connor* come directly from the World English Bible.

The following information about the World English Bible comes from eBible.org: "The World English Bible (WEB) is a Public Domain (no copyright) Modern English translation of the *Holy Bible*... The World English Bible is based on the American Standard Version of the Holy Bible first published in 1901, the Biblia Hebraica Stutgartensa Old Testament, and the Greek Majority Text New Testament."

KENSINGTON BOOKS are published by

Kensington Publishing Corp.
119 West 40th Street
New York, NY 10018

All Kensington titles, imprints, and distributed lines are available at special quantity discounts for bulk purchases for sales promotion, premiums, fund-raising, and educational or institutional use.

Special book excerpts or customized printings can also be created to fit specific needs. For details, write or phone the office of the Kensington Special Sales Manager: Kensington Publishing Corp., 119 West 40th Street, New York, NY 10018. Attn. Special Sales Department. Phone: 1-800-221-2647.

Kensington and the K logo Reg. U.S. Pat. & TM Off.

ISBN-13: 978-0-7582-8474-7
ISBN-10: 0-7582-8474-8
First Kensington Trade Paperback Printing: May 2013

eISBN-13: 978-0-7582-8475-4
eISBN-10: 0-7582-8475-6
First Kensington Electronic Edition: May 2013

10 9 8 7 6 5 4 3 2 1

Printed in the United States of America

They must find it hard to take Truth for Authority
who have so long mistaken Authority for Truth.

—Gerald Massey, poet (1828–1907)
"A Retort," *Gerald Massey's Lectures*

Don't trust the captain who is sailing in a straight line.

—Thea Gilmore, "Mainstream"

The Revelations of Jude Connor

In the Beginning:
Baptism of a Future Pastor

The water. The water will save me. Everyone has said so—Reverend James, my parents, the Bible—everyone.

Please, Jesus. Please, oh please take this burden away. Make me pure. Make me someone God can love. Do this, and I swear I will dedicate my life to you! I'll tell everyone what you did for me. I'll lead them all to you.

I'm stepping in, Jesus. Reverend James is in the water, his arms reaching out to me. I can't make out his features with the sun shining from behind him. It gives him a kind of halo. But I know he's smiling.

I look back at the shore, back at the life I'm leaving behind, for today I die. I'm buried. And then I'll be alive in Christ.

Everyone's gathered there, watching me in this sheet-thin, white, spirit-cloth, the baptism gown my mom made for me. She's smiling, my dad's arm on her shoulders. He looks proud.

The water is cold. Cold with snowmelt, even in May. But it's time. I'm fourteen, and it's time. My soul is in more jeopardy with every day I delay. I could have done this last year, but I wasn't ready. I wasn't ready to give up—well, to give up what I knew I had to. What I'm ready to give up now.

This is right. This is the answer.

Reverend James holds me, his right arm behind me and his

left hand crowning my head. I hold my nose. My head feels like it's going to explode, if my chest doesn't go first.

I'm under. The water makes rushing sounds in my ears, and the world disappears.

The World disappears! And all my sins, too. They're gone. The only things left are the water, my soul, my Savior, and the support of Reverend James's strong arm, like God's arm holding me and then pulling me into the Light.

Joy! Joy like I've never known, joy like I wanted to feel. Like I *knew* I'd feel.

I'm saved.

Chapter 1

Amos King was the most amazing preacher anybody ever heard. He could bounce you between the fires of Hell and the salvation of Heaven and make you be glad about both. I suspect now that one reason he kept his dark hair fairly long was so that he could fling it around as he preached, punctuating his exhortations with that dramatic visual aid.

I don't remember the first time I heard him. My mother started taking Lorne and me to church long before I was old enough to notice much, and eventually I came to take it for granted that every Sunday we would see him up there, his intense dark eyes narrowing in on first one congregant and then another.

In my teens I came to see that his clean, strong jaw, full mouth, and high cheekbones worked together to create a rather strikingly handsome face. But as a young child, despite the differences in their appearances, I think I confused Reverend King in my mind with my father, who'd left when I was four and my brother Lorne was twelve—a confusion possibly enhanced by the fact that my mother had given me the middle name of Amos, in honor of the pastor. When Lorne was named, Reverend King was not yet our pastor, so I got the honor. Over the years I discovered many other boys in the

Church who had the same middle name, for the same reason. The Reverend King was, indeed, revered.

Both men could yell, that was for sure. I don't remember much about my father, but Lorne had a few memories he shared with me. They weren't pleasant ones, and I came to understand why Lorne would flinch sometimes when Reverend King shouted or turned suddenly in our direction. My mother relinquished to me her memories of her husband rarely and parsimoniously, and without saying so in a direct way, she left me with the impression that our Church was too much for him. Whether that was her belief or the excuse he offered, I never knew.

It's true that the Grace of God Church might well have been a lot for someone not born into it, or reborn in it without real commitment. In fact, although the Church welcomed visitors gladly, after some number of visits, and some very specific attention by some number of us, they were expected to make a choice. Which is to say, take on the conversion process and be baptized, or experience having all the saints in the Body quite literally turn away all at once, suddenly and finally, by order of some authority that was never clear to me. We were a closed society. Saints, because we were true disciples of Christ. *Real* Christians. Pure. In the Body of Christ because of having died to the world and then being born again in him through the Holy Spirit. You were in, or you were out.

Maybe it was all the "fellowshipping" that got to my father. There was a lot of it, because even after dying and being raised again through baptism, we all knew we could fall again, back down into our sinful ways. We could lose our status in the saint-hood. We needed the constant presence, coaching, and prayers of our brothers and sisters to remain saved. Missing meetings of the Body was considered a danger sign. And there were so many meetings, designed to make sure we had little time to get into trouble. Church on Sunday was followed by fellowship time. There were Bible Studies during the week in people's homes; teens (aged eleven to eighteen) and adults were ex-pected to attend at least one. And often there was some group activity on Saturday that was not mandatory, but if you weren't there, people noticed.

Dad wasn't born in the Church, so he couldn't have married my mother—or, she wouldn't have married him—if he hadn't converted; but if she'd been the main reason he did it, that probably wouldn't have been enough to keep him. And she wasn't about to leave it. Not for him, not for anyone. Because what would that have meant, after all, but her eternal damnation? If he chose to be damned—although she would have done everything in her power to convince him to repent his doubt and rededicate himself—if Satan pulled him away, she would not, could not go with him.

The only thing of value that he left behind for me was his childhood bag of marbles.

Lorne was a wizard with engines. He'd started by working on the lawn mower. One memory that Lorne and I could both claim was that mowing the lawn was one of the things that enraged our father. We rented half of a big house that had been converted to shelter two families. The Christians who owned it gave us a break on the rent in exchange for some maintenance work, like mowing the lawn in warm weather and clearing snow in winter from both driveways—ours and that of our neighbors in the other half of the house, the McNultys. Snow removal was no small task in Idaho, where we lived.

My memory extends far enough back to let me recall the rickety mower, not quite red any longer, and the insecure sounds it made in its efforts to cut the grass over which my father would shove it. Every so often it would gasp, choke, exhale gas odors into the air, and sputter to a halt. In the silence, I'd cringe. Would Dad be able to get it started again, or would frustration send him over some edge? I shuddered with each rip of the cord as Dad tried to get the engine churning once more, and I'd breathe again if it caught and stayed on. Because if it didn't catch, I knew what would happen next. There would be a stream of language punctuated by blanks where a non-Christian would have inserted expletives, followed by a metallic clanging noise as he jerked the handle upward and let the machine crash back to earth, followed by the slam of a door that told me he was now inside the house and that shouting between him and my mother would begin. He seldom won these yelling matches, because she knew more scripture—and had loads more saintly patience—than he did. But if he couldn't win with her, he could win with Lorne or me. He never did more than yell, but it hurt just the same. And it sent a dense fog of depression and anxiety into the house, a palpable presence that fingered its way into everything I did or thought or dared to say.

At some point Lorne took on the job of lawn maintenance, possibly at least in part to eliminate anything he could that would send Dad into one of his furies. Part of the problem with this task was that the third-hand lawn mower someone had given us was not in good shape. I can picture Lorne sitting in our dirt driveway in the shade that big pine tree made, shaggy brown hair falling over his suntanned face, dirty rags and bits of lawnmower littered around him, and him intently tinkering and testing and greasing and cleaning and reconstituting the cantankerous old thing until his patience and technical intuition paid off. Now there isn't an engine that doesn't roll over and purr when he's done with it.

I'm not talking about just lawnmowers and cars, either. If there was one thing our community couldn't live without, it was engines. Trucks, tractors, backhoes, harvesters, diesel monsters—Lorne could fix anything. It was like he had some kind of sixth sense, a carbon-based dowsing rod, that would lead him to any problem and guide his greasy hands through the steps to make the world whole again. To stop the yelling. To hold the family together. People sometimes said it was a gift from God, and that Jesus himself would whisper instructions into Lorne's ear.

After Dad left, the money Lorne was bringing in when someone in the Church had an odd job for him to do didn't amount to much, and my mother had to find work. She wasn't trained to do anything, and her education had stopped when high school ended. But this is one thing that was great about our Church; we always took care of one another. One brother, Mr. Townsend, sold farm equipment. He had a bookkeeper, but he was planning to buy a few gas stations to add to his empire, so he offered to hire my mother as an assistant bookkeeper if she were willing to be trained. She was willing, and she worked there until she died.

I was eleven when Reverend King presided over my mother's funeral. She had gone pretty quickly; brain tumors can do that, especially if you don't catch them until you're nearly dead anyway. Mom was sick for months before she saw a doctor, with headaches that were so bad she cried. Many times she would go to work in the morning, looking drawn and exhausted, but she always said the pain would go away during the day. Sometimes it did, and sometimes it didn't. On the really bad days, Lorne would have to get a ride to where her car was so he could drive it home. And he drove us to church; Mom's vision was often too blurry to focus on the road. I came to depend on rides from others to get to my Bible Study meetings.

Finally one day when Mom had been driven home before lunch, Natalie King, the reverend's wife, stopped by. She was there when I got home from school, cleaning the kitchen sink. She greeted me like she'd been counting the minutes to my arrival, rinsing her hands and then drying them on the towel Mom kept on the oven door handle as she spoke. "Jude, sweetheart! It's so good to see you. How was school today?"

"Um, okay, I guess. Why are you here?" And suddenly I felt panic. "Is Mom okay?"

"She's resting, dear. Come sit at the table with me. I've got cookies and milk for you."

I sat and picked up a sugar cookie with green sprinkles, gnawing on it without any flavor registering in my mouth.

"Jude, I need to talk with you. You know your mother is very sick, don't you?"

I nodded; I wasn't sure what "sick" meant in this context, but I knew something was very wrong. I was also beginning to fear that all those prayers I'd prayed—that whatever was wrong would go away—were about to be denied. I didn't want Mrs. King to talk to me. I didn't want her to put into words that things weren't getting better. Words would make it real. I'd been keeping "real" at bay, leaning hard against a door behind which "real" was pressing to get in, and words would make the door evaporate suddenly, leaving me in a twisted heap on the floor and letting in the horror on the other side—a horror that had no name. As long as it had no name it couldn't get in. Mrs. King was about to give it a name. A name that started with the word "sick."

"She had to come home very early today, and Mr. Townsend called me. When I saw how much trouble she was in, Jude, I called Dr. Malcolm. He's given her something for the pain."

It was coming. I could feel the door getting thinner. My hand, still holding the cookie, began to shake. I set the sugary thing down and hid my hand in my lap.

Mrs. King's quiet voice got even softer. "I know this is very scary for you, Jude. I'm sure you've been praying your mother would get better. I'm sure you've asked God many times for that." The door was almost gone; Mrs. King had committed my own feelings to words almost as though I had told her. "But she needs help, Jude. We don't know exactly what's wrong, but Dr. Malcolm is setting up some appointments for her at the hospital, where they'll do some tests. Mrs. McNulty next door is going to make sure you and Lorne are all right while your mom is gone. She'll have to be in the hospital for a couple of days."

Mrs. King stopped talking and watched me, her face gentle and sad, and it was everything I could do not to cry. Perhaps she was waiting for me to say something, but I didn't trust my voice. Finally she went on. "What time will Lorne be home from work?"

I took a shaky breath. "Five thirty."

"Would you like to come with me until then? Aurora will be home from school by now, and I need to be there. You're in her class, I understand."

"Yes, ma'am. I mean, yes, she's in my class. But I want to stay here." There was a brief silence, and probably Mrs. King was contemplating whether to take me with her anyway. So I asked, "When will my mom go to the hospital?"

"Dr. Malcolm said he was hoping to have something arranged as early as tomorrow. He'll call a little later, after Lorne's home, to talk about what will happen." I looked down at my hands, sugar cookie crumbs still clinging to one of them. "Jude, I know you're a big boy, and you probably feel like you need to be brave. It's true that you need to be brave. But it's also all right to cry sometimes, too."

I couldn't speak, so I just shook my head, eyes still looking down so she wouldn't see the moisture that was starting to pool in them. I just wanted her to leave. If I could get rid of her, maybe I could get the door back in place again.

"Well, just remember what I said." She stood and moved behind my chair. Her hands on my shoulders calmed me somehow. "I'll let Mrs. McNulty know I'm leaving. Please ask Lorne to call me when he gets home, would you?" She didn't wait for an answer. She kissed the top of my head and left.

I watched at the living room window to make sure her car was going, and then I nearly ran, trying to be quiet, to my mother's room. She lay on her back under the covers, head turned in my direction, eyes more sunken shut than closed. I tiptoed forward, watching intently to make sure I wasn't disturbing her. She never moved. I watched the covers over her chest, but her breathing was so shallow and so infrequent it frightened me even more. Resting my body against the mattress, I leaned over to make sure she really was breathing. Then I turned and went into the corner, sat on the floor, and watched.

At some point I heard Mrs. McNulty call, "Hallooow!" I jumped to my feet, both afraid she would wake Mom up and wishing she would. It took me some time to convince Mrs. McNulty that I was fine, that I was doing homework in my room—a lie for which I half expected God would punish me on the spot.

"Is your mother still asleep, dear?" I nodded. "Is there anything I can get you? Are you hungry?"

"No, thank you, ma'am." The truth was that I didn't have a clue whether I was hungry or not. I just wanted her gone.

"Well . . . You let me know when Lorne gets home, will you?"

"Yes, ma'am." She left, and I went back to my anxious vigil.

Lorne headed upstairs before I could finish telling him what I knew, which wasn't much. Mom was still comatose. Lorne stood there, silent. Without looking away he reached an arm toward me, and we stood there together, his arm on my shoulders as they shook with fear and with my struggle not to bawl. Then Lorne called Mrs. King. He found out that Mom had collapsed at work, had fallen out of her chair and onto the floor, where she'd convulsed for a couple of minutes.

By now, there was nothing left of my door.

Mom never came home from the hospital. Lorne told me the tumor was so bad that surgery was deemed risky, but since it was the only hope it was tried anyway. It failed.

Neither Lorne nor I anticipated that my mother's absence would mean a change in our physical living arrangements. Lorne had shouldered a good deal of the responsibility by this time. He was bringing in a decent wage, working as a mechanic mostly for Mr. Townsend, and out on loan to other Christians, for extra money, when he wasn't busy. I was often directed by one saint or another to be amazed at how mature and conscientious he was.

And if it weren't enough to hear this praise from others, I can always call upon one memory I have of my mother that stands out for me above many. It was the way she praised him. She had taught me a lot about how to take care of the house, once she started working—how to do laundry, how to wash dishes, how to make beds and shake out the rugs and wash the floors. And she praised me when I did a good job or when I did something before I was told, but her praise for Lorne was different. Etched into my visual memory is the profile of Lorne, now tall and clean-shaven and strong, looking down at my mother, still almost a girl from the ponytail she always wore to the saddle shoes on her feet. Her hand is on his shoulder or the side of his face as she gazes up at him, saying, "I thank God above that we have you to be the man of the house."

So even after Mom died, we could feed ourselves, Lorne and I, although if we moved beyond the simplicity of cereal and peanut butter, our repertoire of comestibles was limited to a list including things like hot dogs, hamburgers, spaghetti with bottled sauce, iceberg lettuce and tomatoes, and almost anything out of a can. The casseroles and brownies brought by well-meaning women in the Church were welcome, but we wouldn't have starved without them.

We weren't sure how the social services in Boise heard about our situation; maybe someone at the hospital contacted them. At any rate, on an afternoon two days after the funeral—a quiet, low-key event as funerals typically were in our Church, even with Reverend King presiding—a social worker whose name I've forgotten stopped by the house before Lorne got home and found me eating a fluffernutter sandwich and watching television. She waited for Lorne to get home and told him she wanted to put me into foster care. He refused, insisting that he would not, by the love of God Almighty, let anyone break up what was left of our family. He pointed out that he was nineteen and gainfully employed. Hell, he'd been gainfully employed since before he'd finished high school, with part-time work before graduation and full-time now that he was out of school. Mrs. McNulty was there for me as well. The woman left looking unconvinced, but without evidence of neglect or worse there wasn't much she could do.

Perhaps standing up to social services helped prepare us to take a stand when Reverend King and his wife stopped by Saturday morning. Lorne had the metal parts of something spread over one side of the lawn, while I was inside, supposedly cleaning the bathroom but actually huddled in the corner of my mother's room, whimpering. I was committing everything within my vision to memory; Lorne had told me he was going to move into this room, and I knew that after that it would never look like this again. All traces of both my parents would be gone forever.

"No sense in lettin' the room go to waste, is there?" he had said when I shrieked "NO!" at him. "Plus, you'll have your own room now. You'll like that; trust me." By which I heard him to mean that he was sick and tired of sharing one with me.

Through my fog of self-pity that early June Saturday morning I heard voices from outside. At first I pretended to myself that I didn't care, that it was probably just someone come to talk with Lorne about fixing something. But then I heard the side door open, and I could tell one of the voices belonged to Reverend King. I swiped at my eyes, snuffled fiercely, and made my cautious way into the hall. I caught the sight of Lorne wiping his hands on something as he led the way into the living room ahead of the visitors. Mrs. King saw me cringing there. She smiled and moved slowly toward me, holding out a hand.

"Hello, Jude. It's good to see you. Shall I make you some chocolate milk?"

I shook my head. "We don't have any."

"No milk?"

"No chocolate to put in it." My eyes flicked toward the living room. Whatever was going on in there, it had to be important. Reverend King had been here once or twice in the past, and his wife once or twice, but they'd never come at the same time. And anything unusual that happened right now had to do with my mother's death; there was no doubt in my mind about that.

Mrs. King, it seemed, had been brought along to corral me and let Lorne and the reverend talk privately. I didn't want that. So I wasn't very cooperative when Mrs. King tried again. "Let's go see what you do have, and we'll fix something together. How does that sound?"

"No, thank you, ma'am." And I headed into the living room, Mrs. King on my heels and trying to reach one of my hands with hers, me doing my best to avoid her. For one thing, I was way too old to have my hand taken like that. For another, I wanted to know what was going on. Lorne seemed to take all this in pretty quickly. He patted the arm of the ancient over-stuffed chair he was sitting in.

The reverend evidently was in cahoots with the plan to keep me out. "Jude, why don't you go with Mrs. King? I'm sure the two of you will—"

"No, thank you, sir." I attached myself bodily to the arm of Lorne's chair.

Lorne's voice was quiet, his tone brooking no argument. "What concerns one of us concerns the other, Reverend."

There was a moment when the Kings looked at each other and at us and back at each other before the reverend said, "Very well. And you're right, what I've come to say does concern both of you." He gave his wife time to settle beside him on the couch. Then, "I know what a difficult time this is for you, because I've seen so many families go through something like it. But what you may not realize, and I do, is how difficult it's *going* to be. Lorne, you've been carrying nearly a man's burden for a few years now, and you've carried it well. It's time that load was lightened a little. It's time you were given some space to think about your own life. I believe you've decided not to go to college, and if that's the case, then it's time for you to move into your role as an adult brother in the Church. That will claim some of the time you've had to devote to taking care of Jude."

He stopped for a second or two, giving Lorne a chance to ask what that meant, but I knew Lorne wouldn't say anything. I knew he'd just let the reverend have his say, and then Lorne would let his position be known. And most likely, he wouldn't be budged.

The reverend took a breath and went on. "We want to help you do that, for your sake, for the Church's sake, and for Jude's. We want to free you from some of the responsibilities you've been meeting so well, and we want to help you begin to build a life for yourself." He laid his hands on his knees and straightened his arms, and his tone took on a note of finality. "Mrs. King and I would like Jude to come and live with us. We have a spare bedroom to give him, with Aurora being our only child, and we would provide for him as though he were ours. Then, to help you put some money away for your future life, the best thing would be either for you to move in with a brother close to your age, or for a brother to move in with you here, depending on what makes the most sense."

Again he waited. A few heartbeats went by, and in the silence I could almost hear my mother's voice, as I'd heard her say so many times, saying, "Thank the Lord for Reverend King!"

Finally Lorne said, "That's what you came to talk about?"

"Yes. How does that sound to you?"

I held my breath.

"I thank you both kindly. But I'm providing for Jude because he's mine. He's my family. So I'm already sharing living space with a brother."

"That's true, Lorne, and you're doing a fine job. But please remember that this job will get harder over time. Jude will need things as he grows that it will be harder and harder for you to provide for him. It's not good for him to spend a lot of time alone, and there are many things the two of you are unaccustomed to doing that are required for the maintenance of a household. And I know you want what's best for Jude."

"I'm not losing any more of my family," Lorne said, a slight threat in his tone now.

"Neither am I." I wanted to add whatever support I could, though speaking up to Reverend King like that exhausted my supply of bravado.

Reverend King sat back and let out a breath, staring at us thoughtfully.

"I have a suggestion." Mrs. King's gentle voice eased the tension with its tone alone. All eyes turned toward her, hoping for a workable compromise. "What if Jude were to come home with Aurora after school during the week? Then Lorne could come for supper, and he could take Jude home with him when he left. On Wednesdays, I can take both Jude and Aurora to Bible Study. That would leave the weekends for Lorne and Jude together to run any errands they have. One of us"—and she turned to her husband here—"could plan to drop by occasionally to make sure the boys aren't in need of any assistance here." She looked back at Lorne and me. "What do you think?"

Lorne turned to look at me, and I turned toward him. He said, "Do you see any flaws in that plan, Jude?"

Lots. For one thing, there was no way I was walking home with the pastor's daughter after school. And riding my bike wouldn't save me, because they hadn't figured out who kept slashing the tires of bikes left outside the school, so I didn't ride to school.

Before I could answer, and maybe because she was afraid of what I would say, Mrs. King added, "And Lorne, when you have a date, Jude can come to our house. You can pick him up on your way home." She beamed at him. "I know you and Clara Davenport have gone out several times, and I don't think you've had much time for dates lately."

So now if I made any objections, it was as though I didn't care whether my brother had time to lead his own life. He gave me a chance, though. "Jude?"

The only thing I could think of to say was, "Aurora doesn't like me."

"Oh, my," said Mrs. King, "I don't think that can be true. Besides, once she gets to know what a terrific boy you are, she will like you very much. You'll be like the brother she never had." Her voice sounded odd at the end, but I couldn't focus on that right now.

There was yet another silence, and before either of the Kings could apply any more pressure, Lorne stood and held his hand out to the reverend, who stood to take it. Lorne said, "I thank you both very much for these kind offers. Jude and I will think about them carefully, and I'll let you know what we decide very soon."

After they left—reluctantly, it seemed—Lorne said, "Come outside with me. I need to keep working, and we need to talk about this."

I sat in a patch of shade that fell onto the scrabbly grass, flicking ants off my sneakers and the legs of my jeans, and Lorne spoke haltingly, dividing his attention between the engrossing mechanical task and this difficult conversation.

"What do you think?" he asked me.

"I don't wanna spend all that time with Aurora."

Lorne nodded like he understood. "What's she like?"

I wasn't sure how to answer this. I didn't know her very well. She wasn't exactly a teacher's pet, but she was close to it. Smart, always paid attention in class. And of course she always understood scripture better than anyone else in Bible Study. But what was she like? "I guess she's okay, for a girl."

He worked in silence, possibly concentrating on his task, possibly giving me time to think some more about my answer, probably both. Then he said, "Do you want to know what I think?"

Immediately I felt ashamed. I wasn't the only one involved here, after all, and Lorne had stood up to Reverend King to let me be part of the discussion. "Sure."

He set down some metal object, picked up another, examined it, and said, "They're right about a few things. You shouldn't spend too much time alone here." I was about to protest, but he looked sharply at me and went on. "Social services backed off for now, but they said they'd be checking. If they think you're spending too much time alone, they'll push harder. Now, given the reverend's offer, they might place you there, but then you'd be out of here, no question." He set down the bits of greasy metal. "And Mrs. King was right about something else, too. If I'm leaving you alone all week until I get home from work, then I really shouldn't leave you alone on weekends. So I can't really go out on dates."

For people who don't know the Church's position on dating, the way we did things might sound a little backward. Even weird. Any saint who was sixteen or older and wasn't married was expected to date. Not *free* to date—*expected* to date. And dates are a regimented event. The dating couple is never alone; the minimum number of unmarried Christians on a date is four, or two couples. There's no driving down dark, deserted roads and making out. There's no going anywhere that isn't approved. Boys always ask girls, not the other way around, and they're expected to ask different girls. The idea is that until you've had a chance to get to know several people in dating circumstances, you won't know how you'll feel to be seen as a couple with a given person. The Church is big on not putting too much emphasis on the external characteristics of anyone. We're all expected to be neat and clean and well-groomed, but the Church wants all the girls to go on dates, not just the pretty ones, and it wants the boys to have a chance to get to see that looks don't always mean a girl is the right one. The reverse, of course, goes for girls, but I'm thinking about this from Lorne's viewpoint.

Lorne used to go out on dates, before Mom got sick. It had been a while, though, since his last one. And as I sat there not looking at him, watching for ants and trying hard to hang onto my wobbly branch of not wanting to spend enforced time with Aurora, I had to admit that the way things were, he'd never find a wife with me in his life, because he wouldn't have a chance to go out on enough dates. And Mrs. King had noticed that he and Clara had been together a lot. I hadn't noticed much of anything, and I was beginning to think I should have.

I was holding Lorne back, that's all there was to it, if I insisted that we maintain our status quo. But I needed to be sure. "Do you want to go out on dates?"

Lorne smiled and looked like he was trying not to laugh. "Yes, little brother, I do. I want to go out on dates with Clara. I think I want to marry her, and if I back out of the picture now, someone else could ask her first, and she might say yes if she thinks I can't get married for years."

This sounded like a solution to me. "Then why don't you ask her to marry you, and she can come live with us? Then I wouldn't have to go to the Kings' at all!"

Lorne did laugh now. "Not so fast, there! Gosh, Jude, it will be months—minimum—before I'm *sure* what I want, and Clara needs time, and then there's at least ten months of engagement to get through." He shook his head, smiling at me. "No, that's not an immediate solution."

I offered a few more half-hearted objections, desperate to avoid the inevitable. Mrs. King's offer would be accepted. But just because I couldn't avoid it didn't mean I had to like it. And Lorne's giving in to this plan, despite how sensible it was and how many problems it solved, felt—in my sulky self-pity—like he had given up on me, too. No father, no mother, and now no Lorne. It wasn't rational, but I was young for my years and no better than I needed to be. I was hurting and didn't want to admit it. I almost didn't want my problems solved.

I mumbled something about getting back to my chores, but actually I marched into the kitchen and made three fluffernutter sandwiches. I grabbed two cans of ginger ale and put them in the bottom of my school backpack, sandwiches on top. I grabbed my windbreaker and tied the sleeves around my waist. I got on my bike, the black one that had been Lorne's. And I ran away from home.

Chapter 2

Gregory Hart was a large man. Not fat, but he was tall, and he took up a lot of room. For all that, he was quiet and gentle. His voice was low and measured, though I don't remember ever having any trouble hearing his words, which always seemed deliberately selected. I had certainly seen him at Church, pushing his blind sister's wheelchair in, at which point one or two women—always different ones, as they seemed to take turns—would take over, and Gregory would be free to sit wherever he wanted. Sometimes he'd stay near his sister, and sometimes he'd be somewhere else entirely; I never saw a pattern. It was almost like he didn't want to be predictable. Didn't want people assuming they knew him so well they could tell what he'd do. I'd never thought of him as Gregory; he'd always been Mr. Hart. And I'd never spoken to him directly.

By about eight o'clock of the Saturday on which I'd left home provisioned with peanut butter and soda, it was starting to get dark. I'd managed to bicycle just far enough away from home for it to be a significant setback when a tire blew out. I'd decided to stay off the main roads, which is where I figured Lorne would look for me once he realized I was gone, and I had ended up on an old road whose once-paved surface was nearly corrugated with wear and frost heaves, open fields on either side and not a house in sight. My sandwiches were eaten, and I'd thought I had half a can of soda left until I felt the spilled contents dripping down my back side from within the pack I wore. That's about when the tire blew.

Angry at the bike, angry with Lorne and both my parents (dead or alive), angry with Aurora and all Kings everywhere, and angry with myself, I threw the pack off my back and sat down on the plowed earth along the verge of the road. Elbows on knees and hands clutching hair, with no one around, I cried. I moaned and wailed and sobbed until my throat was thick and I couldn't snuffle enough to clear my sinuses. I cried until the distraction of swatting at ravenous mosquitoes made it impossible to continue to wallow in this little corner of Hell I felt like I'd fallen into. Knowing I'd made everything worse made me slap harder at the biting bugs, and finally I started using words I barely knew, words I'd never used before, shouting these curses at the bugs. At myself. At God.

The tractor approaching me got fairly close before I heard it, I was that deep into my own valley, and when I finally looked up it was too late to avoid being seen. But I wasn't ready to be caught, and I felt fairly sure that whoever was driving would be someone who knew who I was. Leaving the useless bicycle where it lay in the dirt I turned and ran into the field, stumbling and tripping over the plowed furrows of earth, my desperate panting all I could hear. So the tractor driver had almost caught up with me before I heard him, and in a few steps his long legs overtook the remaining distance between us. His hand on my arm was strong and firm, forcing me to slow and then stop. We stood there almost facing each other, heaving breaths for a minute, his hand keeping me immobile despite a few feeble attempts on my part to free my arm.

In his low, quiet voice, Mr. Hart said, "Where you headed?"

If he'd shouted something like, "Where in tarnation d'you think you're goin', boy?" or "Just what d'you think you're doin'?" or something challenging like that, I was ready to throw some of those newfound words at him. But he asked me a real question, not a rhetorical one. And it was one I couldn't answer.

Where was I going? I didn't have a clue. I told him the only thing I could. "Away."

"Away from what?"

Another tough question. Or, it was the answer that was tough. So I said, "Everything."

He nodded, but he didn't let go of me. "So you're headed away from your home. Away from your brother. Away from your friends. Away from your chair at the kitchen table. Away from the tub your mother used to bathe you in. Away from your bed. Away from the place where you grew up, the only place you know. Have I got that right?"

By the time he stopped I was struggling with tears, even gasping a little for breath. Then I felt his other hand on my shoulder, and he pulled me to him. We stood there while I cried and he held me. I could almost see the red anger turn into blue sadness that flowed out of me and was absorbed into this strong man I barely knew. He held me until I was quiet except for catches in my breathing, and then without a word we both turned. He kept an arm on my shoulder as we walked back toward the road. I picked up the pack and he picked up the bike, which he latched onto his tractor using bungee cords, and we squeezed together into the tractor cab, him on the seat and me leaning against both the seat and the man for support. The engine literally roared as it got going again, and speech was not possible. I didn't know where he was taking me. I didn't care. Right then, I just wanted to stay with him.

I lost track of time, of direction, of anything other than the throbbing of the engine and the sensual, mesmerizing bouncing of our progress, a sensation deepened by the occasional touching of my body against his. These touches, innocent and unavoidable, sent thrills of something unrecognizable through me. For a while I tried to position myself so there would be more of them, but soon I realized that the pleasure was greater when I just relaxed, closed my eyes, and let them come to me.

When I felt the turn that would take us into his driveway, I was disappointed. It didn't help that the long, low house looked dark and unwelcoming in the heavy dusk. Like the large barn to the right, the building was not much more than a dark profile against the almost navy sky. But as soon as we got close to the house, one light after another began to glow, and by the time I scrambled off the tractor even the large outdoor spotlight on the side of the house was glaring, making the dark seem darker but the house more inviting.

We left the bike where it was, and Mr. Hart led me toward the house. As he opened the door he called out, "Home, Dolly." And then, "We have a visitor."

From somewhere inside I heard a woman's voice, no doubt his sister's, saying, "Goodness! A visitor? Who, Greg?"

Mr. Hart looked down at me, and I said, "It's Jude Connor, Miss Hart."

"Moira's baby?" In the kitchen doorway, her wheelchair appeared. "Sakes alive, you're a ways from home. Everything okay?"

Mr. Hart spoke up. "Young Jude's bicycle tire seems to have exploded. Left him stranded."

"Well, that's too bad." She got closer, and I could see her eyes—odd-looking, unfocused—moving around in their sockets a little. "Jude, you'll have supper with us before we figure out how to get you home. Mrs. Morgan brought over a chicken liver casserole, and I've got some zucchini chopped. Just need to do a little more and we'll be all set! And then there's most of that rhubarb strawberry pie that Mrs. Little brought yesterday."

"I think Jude needs to call home first and let them know he's all right. Jude, the phone's over there in the corner at the end of the sofa." He pushed me gently in that direction and went into the kitchen, helping his sister back in that direction as he went.

My fingers shaking, I punched the numbers of my home phone. A woman's voice answered. At first I thought I'd dialed wrong, and I was going to hang up, and then she said, "Jude? Is that you?"

"Yes."

"Thank the Lord! Where are you? Are you all right?"

I decided to pick up on Mr. Hart's story. "I was way out of town on my bike, and a tire blew. Mr. Hart gave me a ride in his tractor. I'm at his house now. Um, who is this? Where's Lorne?"

"This is Mrs. McNulty, dear. Um, Mr. Hart's sister is there, too, right?" She waited for me to say yes. "Lorne's out driving around, and so is my husband, looking for you. They're calling in whenever they get near a phone to see if you've called. I guess I'll tell Lorne to head out to the Harts', then, next time he calls. What's the number there?"

I looked at the phone and gave it to her, knowing as I did so that it was like giving up. Like there was no point in denying what life was going to be like from now on. And I had only my imagination to tell me what that was.

I hung up and went into the kitchen, only now beginning to take in how neatly everything was arranged, and how little furniture was in the room. The wheelchair needed space, and also Miss Hart was blind, so there couldn't be things in the way. Good thing they lived in this sprawling ranch house; no stairs for Dolly.

There was a place already laid for me at the table. It was a long room, the simple, round wooden table at the far right end, the working area and appliances at the left. A window over the sink, framed by yellow curtains flecked with tiny white dots, looked onto whatever was behind the house. Miss Hart's chair was at the table, facing in the general direction of the stove, where her brother was tending to something. Light from a copper-shaded lamp hanging over the table made the silver strands stand out in her reddish-brown hair, and the casserole steamed invitingly in front of her. She must have heard me approaching. "Sit here on my left, Jude. Were they relieved to hear from you at home?"

"My brother's out looking for me. So is our neighbor, Mr. McNulty. Mrs. McNulty was there. She answered the phone."

"So she's calling Lorne on his cell phone?"

This was an awkward moment. I studied the plate before me.

Pearl white, with dark green borders on the outside and the inside of the rim. "We, uh, we don't have a cell phone." The truth was we couldn't afford one. Neither could the McNultys.

"I see. So Lorne didn't know what direction you were going in?"

"No, ma'am." I didn't add that I hadn't known, myself, what direction I was going in.

Mr. Hart brought a bowl of steaming green zucchini circles glossed with butter and set it between the casserole and a basket of rolls. He poured milk into the glass at my place and filled the other two with water. By the time he scraped his chair toward the table and sat, Miss Hart's hands were extended, one toward him and one toward me. As we held hands, she said Grace. I bowed my head, but kept my eyes on Mr. Hart. He looked older than his sister, though that could be partly from spending so much time outdoors. The hair on his temples was gray, lines almost like pitchforks pointing away from the corners of his eyes, as though poised to lift the hair away from his head. His eyes were closed, his face relaxed. It was a gentle face, one that was easy to trust. Comforting. I watched it while Dolly prayed.

"Dearest Lord, we thank you for your abundance, for the love of others, and for the many ways they help you to provide for us. Thank you for sending Reverend King to guide us and help us understand your will. Thank you for bringing this young man to our house tonight, to share in your blessings. Thank you for keeping him safe and for allowing us the privilege of helping him in a time of need, so that we can return some of the goodness that you shower upon us. Amen."

Mr. Hart and I mumbled "Amen," and then Miss Hart's hand groped toward the bread basket on her right. I looked toward her brother, expecting him to help her, but he didn't. She managed to find the butter and her own knife without help, too, after she handed the basket to me. When she spooned zucchini slices onto her plate, though, one of them fell onto her place mat.

"Escapee, left," her brother said, and her fingers located and reclaimed the circlet.

For a few minutes there was only the sound of flatware on china, chewing, and swallowing. Then Miss Hart asked, "Do you and your brother have a plan for keeping the house now that you're on your own?"

At first I felt surprise that she would know about my situation; my family didn't mingle much with the Harts. But then I figured that the Church, while large, wasn't big enough to hide the fact that one if its saints had died, and certainly it had been no secret that my mother was failing. With a mental shrug, I described the situation that I knew now couldn't be avoided. She greeted this arrangement with enthusiasm, smiling and saying how marvelous it would be for me, to spend so much time with Reverend King and his family. I watched her brother's face when I could, and the only thing I saw in reaction to my news was a brief pause as he was lifting his fork from his plate.

The phone rang. Mr. Hart got up to answer it from the wall phone in the kitchen, and I could tell it was Lorne. "Yes, he's here, safe and sound. We've just started supper."

Miss Hart called to him to ask Lorne to join us, but Mr. Hart said nothing to Lorne about that. When he hung up the phone, he said, "He'll be here shortly, Dolly." He smiled at his sister, though of course she couldn't see that. "You can feed him then."

The casserole was better than it had sounded, so when Miss Hart asked if I was ready for more, I accepted. "Yes, please, Miss Hart."

"Help yourself, but leave some for Greg's seconds, and for Lorne. And Jude, please call me Dolly. It's short for Dolores. I probably shouldn't encourage the familiarity, but I can't abide the title. It makes me feel old!" She laughed lightly. "I'm getting there quite fast enough without the words to hurry me along."

We'd moved on to pie before I heard Lorne pulling Mom's car into the driveway, and I realized with a sinking feeling that it wasn't "Mom's car" anymore. It was Lorne's. Mr. Hart got up to let him in, and I stood, knowing I was already in trouble and it would only make matters worse if I looked as though I didn't know it.

But when Lorne came in he didn't yell at me. At first I thought maybe it was just that he wouldn't do that in front of the Harts, but after he'd looked at me a minute he hugged me. I felt his firm grip on the back of my head, but it wasn't hard and angry; it was solid, dependable. Loving. I held my breath so I wouldn't cry again. I was tired of crying.

Lorne accepted some supper gratefully and didn't say no when Mr. Hart got up to add to the basket of bread. Once Lorne had finished his pie, Mr. Hart cleared the table and stood at the sink.

"Jude, dear," Dolly prodded quietly, "why don't you help Mr. Hart with the dishes? You'll find a clean drying towel in the top drawer to the right of the stove. Look for the one that matches the dishcloth he's using; maybe I can't see them, but I take some pleasure in knowing they match!" She laughed sweetly, and I headed toward the drawer. I glanced around Mr. Hart's elbow into the sink to see what the dishcloth looked like, but when I pulled open the drawer I couldn't see any towel that matched it. I glanced up at Mr. Hart, who was looking at me. He winked and shook his head.

This tiny exchange warmed my heart. The trust he placed in me not to reveal the secret he kept, a secret intended to make his sister feel included in this chore she could not do herself, was like an exchange for the secret of mine he held. If I didn't tell Dolly her kitchen linens didn't match, he wouldn't spill the beans about how I had ended up stranded in the middle of nowhere.

The ride home with Lorne was silent for a couple of miles, except for the sounds the trunk hood made, bouncing onto the bike we'd tethered to the car with borrowed bungee cords while the spotlight between the house and the barn had thrown odd-shaped black forms around us. Finally, Lorne said,

"You didn't just happen to be way out here, did you." He wasn't asking; it was a statement.

I thought about sticking to Mr. Hart's story but decided against it. "No."

Another quarter of a mile later, Lorne said, "I just want you to know that I understand why you did it. But I want *you* to understand that it was wrong. It was wrong for so many reasons. Do you need me to tell you why?"

I took a deep breath. "It made everyone spend time looking for me."

"That's it? That's all you can come up with?" After several seconds of silence, he added, "How about that it didn't solve anything? How about that it wouldn't have solved anything if you hadn't had the flat? How about that you didn't have a clue where you were going? What did you think, that you'd eat berries and bark and trapped rabbits until you were old enough to get a job? What about clothes?"

I shrugged, which of course Lorne couldn't hear. His voice got louder suddenly. "How about you'd be leaving me alone, when I'm fighting anyone who wants to break us apart?"

At last, something I could respond to. "I thought you might be better off without me." Unfortunately, I couldn't keep the sulk out of my voice.

Lorne raised a hand and brought it down hard on the steering wheel. I jumped. He nearly shouted, "Are we better off without Mom?"

"No." My voice was tiny.

"Then how in blazes do you figure either of us is better without the other?"

I was fighting tears. Again. I hated this. And I loved this, because of what Lorne was telling me. We belonged together. "I guess we aren't."

Quieter now, he said, "You guess right." Then, "Don't do this again, Jude. Promise me you won't do this again."

"I promise."

"I know you don't want to do this thing with the Kings, but

you know it's what God wants or it wouldn't be such a good solution."

"Did God want Mom to die?" It was a question I'd been
aching to ask someone.

Lorne couldn't answer it. Or he didn't want to try. He
sighed. "That's a question you'll have to ask Reverend King. It's
all a mystery to me. I just take the pain and know that it will
help me be grateful for joy when it comes."

Lorne and I went to church the next morning, of course. I
didn't want to; I didn't want to face all those people who would
know that my mother had just died, many of whom had been to
the funeral and would be solicitous again anyway. But I was
more afraid of irritating Lorne again, after my self-indulgence
of the day before. Over our breakfast of cereal and orange juice
we agreed that after the service, during fellowship, we would let
Reverend King know that we'd take his family up on their offer
to let me go there after school. But we wouldn't have them
feeding us every night; that was too much. Tuesday through
Thursday, we decided, would be it.

This discussion didn't take much time, so we slurped and
swallowed without further conversation while I fought tears. It
seemed like forever since Mom had been at the breakfast table,
but I had been expecting that someday she would be there
again, as long as she was alive. There had been hope. Now
there was none.

I had spent a good part of the night sleepless, practically
shivering in fear. While it was true that Aurora King was a negative for me in this arrangement, I'd grabbed at that protest as a
smoke screen. What I really feared was her father. I had no reason to fear him personally. He'd never been mean to me, or
taken any particular notice of me as far as I could tell. Part of
my trepidation came from how intimidating his presence was
from the pulpit. But the bigger slice of fear came from the rev-
erence—pardon the pun—that my mother and all his other
congregants held for him.

He had come into our little community when Lorne was only

a few years old. From what I heard, he'd replaced a sweet but tired and uninspiring preacher who'd died rather suddenly of a heart attack. The elders—all men, of course—took turns leading the small family of worshippers until a replacement could be found. And from all accounts, Amos King might as well have ridden into town as a white knight on a silver steed, his adoring wife and daughter following demurely behind (sidesaddle, of course) on gentle mares. It hadn't taken long for news of his oratory powers to spread, and at first the congregation grew on the strength of that alone. But Reverend King was a true believer in witnessing. Before long he had everyone bringing friends, relatives, and total strangers to church so they could hear the Word of God and have their shot at salvation. All the saints were expected to witness, in casual conversation with the unsaved and in concerted efforts. Saints in their twenties often took teenaged saints with them into neighborhoods on Sunday afternoons, knocking on doors and inviting people not yet in the Body to experience the love and relief of turning their lives over to Jesus. This proselytizing was expected behavior in all our sister churches across the country, a collection of autonomous entities to which we were loosely connected. But some were more focused on it than others, and Reverend King's focus was laser-sharp. He held his saints accountable.

My mother had been one of his most ardent admirers, and she had transferred his expectations for right thinking and Christian behavior to Lorne and me. Probably transferred them to my father as well, or tried. Amos King was the example to follow. He was a courageous leader, marching in front and leading us all to Glory.

The idea of practically living in his house all week made my shoulders quiver and my intestines tie themselves into knots.

It had been only the previous afternoon that the Kings had come to our house to make their offer, but in my child's mind I believed that the sermon that day had been written with Lorne and me in mind. Everything began in the usual way, everybody milling around and smiling and talking. Lorne and I did our best to get there just in time for the service; it was a silent agreement, but it was understood all the same. In this way we kept to a minimum the sympathy and heartfelt hugs to which we knew we'd be subjected. I just wanted people to leave me alone, but I guess they couldn't help themselves. It was like they needed consoling, too, but it only made things harder for me. And, I think, for Lorne. Except when Clara came shyly toward us to tell Lorne how sorry she was. She didn't hug anyone, just stood there with her eyes looking down at her feet and up to Lorne's face and down again. Then she stroked my hair once and left. Lorne heaved a shaky sigh and watched Clara's retreating figure, her long, dark hair swaying gently.

We sat in as inconspicuous a place as possible, and the singing began almost immediately. The church had a small choir that relied on a pitch pipe to get them started, and then we would join in; we never used instruments, because the Bible never mentions the use of instruments and voices together in the making of joyful noises to the Lord.

When Reverend King stepped up into the pulpit, I remembered how he'd once said he didn't like it. He didn't want to fall into the trap of believing he was any different from any of the other saints, and he didn't want us thinking that either. At first he tried not to use it, but our congregation kept growing, and pretty soon he was using not just the pulpit, but also the microphone.

This Sunday—the first full service since my mother died, since I ran away from the offer Reverend King had made to me, since I'd tried to turn my back on my own brother who'd been almost a father to me—I waited with everyone else as the last echoes of our voices faded from a hymn. I watched as the reverend climbed into the pulpit, and I pressed against the hard wood of the pew in an effort to become small and avoid having those piercing dark eyes fall on me.

In silence as total as it can be in a church full of people, those eyes moved from saint to saint, around the room, and finally he bent his head forward. It hung there several seconds, and then suddenly it came up, eyes toward the beamed ceiling, and he backed just far enough away from the microphone so that he could shout one word: "Lost!"

He hung his head again. When he raised it, his face was sad. So sad. His voice, though quiet, could be heard everywhere. It was his quoting voice, the one he used when he was quoting scripture.

" 'Behold, the time is coming, yes, and has now come, that you will be scattered, everyone to his own place, and you will leave me alone.' " He paused, waiting for the effect to be felt. Then, in a harsh whisper, "Alone. Scattered. These are the words of our Lord Jesus as told in the Gospel of John. They cut into us now, even among the saints, because *we've been there.* We were lost; we were alone. We know all too well the feeling of isolation, of separation from the Light, from the Love that is God. And it's all too easy at this time of loss to let this feeling drag us down, down into the pit of unbelief, of doubt."

He looked around. Suddenly, his voice loud, he said, "Am I right?"

Responses popped up all over the place, different words at different times. "Amen." "Yes, brother." "Praise the Lord."

When the shouts and murmurs had died down again, he said, "We feel this today because our sister, Moira Connor, has been taken from us. We loved her, she loved us, and she is gone. I could tell you she's with God now, because she is. I could tell you she's looking down at us and sending us all the love of Heaven, because she is. But what do we feel?" A pause, then another shout, "What do we feel?"

"Lost!" came one response. "Alone!" came another.

"We're trapped here in this world," the reverend went on. "We're trapped here, and knowing sister Moira is in Heaven seems to make the gap between here and there seem like something we can't overcome. And you know what? We can't! We can't overcome it. We can't get there from here." Another pause. "We are lost!"

His face made it look as though he were about to cry. Certainly I was; a couple of tears had escaped my eyes and were making their slow, tickling way down my cheeks. I didn't wipe them away. I didn't want to call attention to myself, to my grief.

Now he was quiet, intense. "But our Lord Jesus knows the way out. For he said, 'Yet I am not alone, because the Father is with me. I have told you these things, that in me you may have peace.' " Both arms on the pulpit lectern, he leaned forward, head turning to take us all in. " 'I am not alone.' " His eyes moved to the doors we had come through earlier. In heavy, quiet tones, he said, "Sweet Jesus, show me the way."

We watched him in rapt silence as he straightened his body, still gazing toward the doors. His quoting voice was a little louder now. " 'I came out from the Father, and have come into the world. Again, I leave the world, and go to the Father.' " He sighed loudly. "Jesus, show me the way."

Louder still, " 'I have told you these things that in me you may have peace. In the world you have oppression; but cheer up! I have overcome the world.' " A few heartbeats went by. "Good Lord, show me the way."

His breaths came faster, as though he'd just climbed a flight of stairs too quickly. Nearly shouting, he said, "This is eternal life!" His arms flew up over his head, and his voice boomed, "Father! Show me the way!"

A gray-haired woman two pews ahead of me stood up. "Show me the way!" Then a young woman across the aisle: "Show me the way!" In twos and threes people stood up all around me, the same shout coming from all of them. "Show me the way!" "Show me the way!" The chanting got in synch, everyone shouting in unison, and the entire building pulsed with the rhythm. Something primal and ancient welled up inside me, frightening and enthralling at once. I wanted to believe it was the spirit of God, but my idea of God was as something separate from me. Something apart. And whatever this thing was, it captured my body and soul as it grew larger and larger. I didn't know whether I loved it or feared it more.

After a minute or so the chanting grew ragged, and someone shouted, "Halleluiah!" Everyone stood. There was no escape. Lorne pulled me up as he left his seat, and he wrapped his arms around me. I could feel his body shaking with sobs even though mine was doing the same.

When Lorne and I pulled apart, I saw that Reverend King was looking all around the room, tears streaming down his smiling face. Show me the way. He was following Jesus to Heaven, and I was to follow Reverend King to his home. He was showing me the way.

I barely heard him say, "May God grant you peace."

The closing song, "Farther Along," gives tune to that eternal human complaint: Why do bad things happen to good people? Which today, to me, meant, Why did my mother have to die? It says, down the road, we'll understand. We'll know. Have patience.

It didn't help.

Chapter 3

Lorne and I had Sunday supper with the Kings that night, sitting beside each other on one side of the rectangular dining room table. We all joined hands, and Reverend King said Grace before we started the meal, ending with: "May God grant us peace." This phrase punctuated not just his sermons, but also every Grace I heard him say.

I'd never even been in this house before, and starting tomorrow I would be here nearly every day. Lorne seemed to be doing his best to make polite conversation, though that wasn't his strong suit, while I mostly stared down at my plate and tried to remember everything I'd been told about "company" manners. Every so often I'd look up and see Aurora across from me, her eyes darting quickly away as though to deny that she'd been watching me.

There was strawberry shortcake for dessert, with real whipped cream. My mom had always used the stuff out of the can, and I was used to that, so the real whipped cream tasted odd. But the oddest thing during dessert was that although Mrs. King placed a regular portion at the reverend's place, and although he sat there with us the whole time we were eating, he didn't touch his shortcake. Didn't even pick up a berry. Every so often he lifted the plate and inhaled deeply, but each time he set it down untouched. This was a habit with him, as I came to know after having many meals there; he had dessert before him, he acknowledged it, even smelled it, but he didn't taste it.

After dessert, Mrs. King took Aurora into the kitchen, and Reverend King fetched a Bible. He read a few scripture selections to us, I guessed by way of comfort, and we talked—or, mostly, he talked—about each one and how it applied to us and our mother dying. Lorne and I mostly sat and listened, didn't offer much for him to work with. Finally he set the book aside, gazed intently at each of us, and asked if there was anything we wanted to say, or if we had any questions. I had the distinct impression that Lorne wanted this session to come to a close so we could go home and collapse out of anyone's sight. He said a quiet, "No, sir. Thank you."

I wasn't going to say anything. I really wasn't. And then I heard my voice ask the question that had been echoing in my brain for days. "Why did God make my mother die?"

I'll never forget his reply, because I puzzled over it for the longest time. I'm still not sure I understand it, really—at least not how to apply it in specific circumstances.

"I'm going to tell you a story, Jude." The reverend's voice was very gentle, and his speech slow and even. It was a little like when he preached and also not like it at all. I guess it was the same focus, just not the same delivery. "It's a story that took place long, long ago, but after Jesus had brought Light into the world. No one's really sure exactly where it took place, so we'll just say it was somewhere in Europe in the Middle Ages.

"A monk was on a pilgrimage through land that was very sparsely settled. As you know, monks don't have their own money, so this monk relied upon the kindness of others for food and shelter. At one point he had traveled for two days through the mountains without seeing anyone, so that when he came upon a poor farmer's house he was nearly fainting with hunger and exhaustion.

"The farmer and his wife took the monk into their home. They had very little, with their one cow being their only valuable possession, but they gave the monk water, milk, and food.

They washed his feet and gave him the softest, sweetest straw to sleep on. The next day they let him rest, feeding him the best food they had, including the freshest bread and the last cheese they had in store, eating very little themselves, for it was a strain on them to provide for another person.

"After a second night on the softest bed, the monk was refreshed and ready to go on his way. The farmer and his wife stood in front of their tiny house and were just about to wish him Godspeed on his journey, when the monk turned to their cow suddenly. He pointed to it, and it fell over, dead.

"The farmer cried out, 'How? How can you do such a thing? We need that cow! And we gave you the finest of everything we have!'

"Turning to the farmer, the monk said, 'I know. I'm very sorry. But Death was here and would not be denied. Death wanted your wife, but I bade him take the cow instead.' "

I probably just sat there, blinking, waiting for Reverend King to come to the point of the story. Finally he said, "You see, Jude, we can't always understand the reasons things happen the way they do. Until we're called to God ourselves, we probably won't know why your mother had to die now."

"Couldn't the monk have just sent Death on his way? Isn't God stronger than Death?"

Reverend King let a slow smile widen his face, and he said, "Death is just God's way of calling us to him. It's God's tool. Without Death, how could we hope to reach Heaven?"

This only confused me more. But when Reverend King asked if I understood, I nodded, afraid that if he explained anymore it would just get worse.

I remember lying awake that night wondering if someone had told Death to choose my mother over me. If she'd died so I wouldn't. If it was because of me that she was dead.

Lorne impressed upon me that I was to be on my best behavior whenever I was at the Kings', which to me meant that here was yet another reason why this wasn't such a great idea. The way my following of his instructions played out, Mrs. King and Aurora began to think I was too shy to talk.

I had the use of a spare bedroom upstairs for studying, and I used that space frequently as a safe base from an environment where I didn't feel comfortable being myself. From a place where I was afraid to say anything that might offend or do anything that might cause damage. It was a dark room, on the north side of the house, with a view of distant mountains and lots of evergreen forests. If I lay across the foot of the small bed, on my stomach with my jaw propped up on my hands, I could gaze into those hills for as long as I wanted, watching shadows change shape slowly or storm clouds soften the peaks. Or until Aurora was sent to knock on my door, instructed by her mother to see if I wanted to play a game—I always thanked her and always declined—or sometimes it was to tell me supper was nearly ready. Always I got the impression her mission was done out of pity and with some amount of reluctance.

The only bright spot in my change of circumstances was that my friend Tim Olsen lived closer to the Kings than he did to me. My house was in one direction from school, and the Kings' and Tim's were in the other.

Once school let out for the summer, which wasn't long after the funeral, the arrangement was that I would spend weekdays, while Lorne was at work, at the Kings'. At eleven I was deemed much too young to be left alone with only Mrs. McNulty next door to supervise my behavior. At first this arrangement infuriated me. But then Tim and I started phoning each other to get together, and it turned into the best summer of my young life.

Our first forays were fishing in the river, which neither of us really knew how to do, but we landed on that idea as a way to make our adventure sound unappealing to Aurora, just in case she expressed any interest in coming along. A couple of times Reverend King took us, and then Tim's dad taught us how to make our own flies. Eventually we were allowed to go alone.

Sometimes we actually caught something; most times we sat on large rocks in the sunshine at the edge of the river, dangling our lines aimlessly into the bluish, brownish water as it flowed by. Then one day we grew especially restless. We pulled in the lines, stashed our poles and bicycles in the underbrush, and headed for the woods on the far side of the tributary that joined the river, stepping gingerly as we made our way across the little sandy beach where baptisms took place in warm weather. Neither of us spoke, but I'm sure we both felt there was something sacred about this spot; it was almost like treading on a grave. We crossed by following a bar of rocks and sand that was about knee-deep for us, shoes and socks held high and pants legs—we refused to wear shorts—rolled up. Shoes back on, it was a short dash across a small meadow to get to the trees. We could have biked up the road about a mile to a bridge and walked downhill from there, but that would have been much less of a challenge. Not as much of an adventure, somehow.

The first time we ventured into the quiet gloom, my insides got all jittery—the kind of feeling you get when you're someplace you've never been, and it's all quiet, and you aren't at all sure what you're supposed to do. The effect on me was to make me feel like I had to stop and take a leak. Tim came up behind me while my stream was still going, pushed once on my back, and dashed off, his jungle cackle diminishing as he got farther away until I couldn't hear it anymore. I shook myself off, zipped up, and ran in the direction I thought he'd gone. Stopping every twenty steps or so to listen, focusing only on listening for sounds, I lost all sense of where I'd started, and eventually I heard nothing more. There I stood, in a small clearing, turning in circles.

"Tim!" No answer. I called again, two or three times, and suddenly he lunged at me from some leafy cover. He tackled me, and we rolled around the little clearing, laughing and tickling, until we'd laughed ourselves out and felt awkward that we were still practically hugging each other. We both stood quickly and busied ourselves brushing bits of forest floor from our clothes and hair, avoiding each other's eyes.

"Which way back?" I asked. He pointed over my right shoulder, and I turned that way. But he turned the other way and strode into the trees. "What are you doing?"

Over his shoulder he said, "I'm not ready to go back. Are you?"

I followed, not wanting to lose sight of him again. We walked single file in no particular direction that I could tell. He seemed to know where he wanted to go, so I just struggled through the underbrush, glancing up from time to time and catching occasional slants of sunlight flashing on his blond hair.

Finally he stopped. "I think back there, don't you?" I shrugged and shook my head; what was he talking about? "For our fort. There was a great spot back at that fallen hemlock. Let's go look."

I hadn't noticed it, particularly, and I hadn't even realized we were looking for a fort, but when we got back to it, he was right. It had been a tall tree, and about six feet above the ground the trunk had broken, probably in some winter storm a few months earlier. The upper part of the tree had landed on a boulder about four feet high, and the fern-shaped branches, dense with small fragrant needles, created a sheltered spot underneath. Tim walked around the fallen tree and finally selected what he must have deemed the best entryway. It was hidden by a few younger hemlocks. I followed him in.

We stood there for a few minutes, looking round, and then Tim began clearing the space of the debris that had collected there: lots of broken branches, small stones. We both began tearing off the branches still attached to the tree that broke up the sheltered space, and then we carried everything a good distance away. When we entered the space again, it seemed almost like a place you might want to move some furniture into. I also noticed that the sun had fallen behind the western hills, and the woods we were in had grown gloomy.

"We need to go now. It's getting late," I said, not wanting to leave but knowing it was necessary.

"Yeah. But we'll be back." He looked at me, waited until my

eyes locked with his, and held his hand out. We clasped finger-tips and squeezed, a kind of vow between us.

It was a summer of adventure and expanding horizons and creativity—all because of Tim and the fort. Tim's imagination inspired mine, and our fort was the heart and soul of all our stories. Sometimes it was an Indian teepee, sometimes a shelter from an imaginary blizzard. Sometimes we rescued young girls from the clutches of bad guys. Once we nursed a fictional lynx back to health after it had chewed off its own foot to escape a leghold trap.

I think our story with the lynx was my favorite, even though I loved huddling together with Tim for warmth (it actually was a chilly day) when we pretended to be snowbound by the blizzard. But nursing the wild cat, Tim revealed to me a side of him I don't think I would have seen otherwise. He had an immense capacity for tenderness, and once he had allowed that to show in himself—for the cat, to be sure—it felt safe for me to allow myself to follow suit. It's a bitter joy for me now, remembering how sweet that feeling was. The cat was a proxy: It was him; it was me; it was us.

Aurora kept her distance from me, which suited me just fine. She had her girlfriends, and when I got back to the Kings' from my times with Tim—which was almost always barely on time—she was usually putting away her tea set or some other feminine paraphernalia that I, as a boy who'd spent his afternoon rescuing a maiden from a bounty hunter who had kidnapped her to get to her falsely-accused father, viewed with disdain or ignored outright.

One Tuesday in late August I got there in time to hear most of a confrontation between Aurora and her mother over part of her back-to-school wardrobe.

"I may just as well take the whole outfit back!" was what I heard Aurora screech as I approached the back door after leaning my bike against the garage.

"Then, young lady, we'll just do that." Mrs. King's calm voice was a stark contrast to her daughter's preteen hysteria.

"That's not the point!" In my mind I could see Aurora's eyes flashing at her mother's calm face from beneath the eyebrows that were slightly darker than the sun-streaked auburn hair she was no doubt tossing back over her shoulder for emphasis. Her hair matched her mother's, but while Aurora had inherited her father's good looks, Natalie King's face was kind but unremarkable.

I stood on the back stoop, not sure whether to walk in on them or hang around outside until the storm passed. Just then I heard the reverend's voice.

"Aurora? Natalie? What's all this fuss? A man can't hear himself think."

"Daddy! Mom won't listen. She doesn't understand. This is important!"

I don't know what Mrs. King was doing. She didn't say a word that I could hear, just let her daughter make her case.

From the reverend, "What's important, Aurora?"

Aurora exhaled sharply as if to focus her thoughts, now that she had a new audience. "Look at this, Daddy," and I heard bags rustling; she must have pulled the outfit in question from the shopping bags. "Do you see the rust color in the pattern, just enough to make it really special?" He must have nodded. "This is the color that my shoes have to be. That will tie everything together. And I found the perfect pair. Perfect!"

There was a moment in which I imagined her father trying not to smile at the girl's intensity. "And you don't have any other shoes that color? You do have an awful lot of shoes, Aurora."

"But I don't have this color, Daddy! And this pair I saw would be *perfect*."

"What does your mother say?"

"She doesn't understand how important this very color is."

He prodded, "And she says . . ."

"She says I could wear my medium brown shoes."

His cough seemed to stifle a chuckle. "How many pairs of brown shoes do you have?"

"Four." There was no hesitation—Aurora no doubt knew exactly how many pairs of each color she had, and what the style was of each—but her voice was quiet, as though even she had to admit that four pairs of brown shoes was rather a lot.

"And how much do these perfect shoes cost?"

"That's not the point!"

Evidently her father couldn't keep his laughter contained any longer. Over Aurora's indignant "Daddy!" I heard him say, "You're right. That's not the point. Come with me."

"Where are we going?"

"We're going to talk about what the point is."

I hugged the side of the house, following the sounds of footfalls and Aurora's plaintive protests as father and daughter made their way into the living room. From my huddled position beneath a window I couldn't see where they sat, but I figured he'd take his favorite chair and she would sit at that end of the couch. They'd be close but not facing each other, as these two spots were at a right angle.

"The point," began the reverend, "is that you are the brightest spot in my life. You are my happiness, Aurora. Do you know how your name came to be Aurora?" This wasn't his preaching voice, and yet it carried a similar intensity. It was the sort of voice that zeroes in on you, that shuts out the rest of the world. Nearly hypnotic.

"No." Aurora's voice, still sulky, was beginning to show signs of giving in to reason.

"When your mother and I found out that God was going to bless us with a girl baby, I was the happiest person alive. And when you were born on Christmas day it was like the sun shone brighter than on any other day of my life, save one."

"When you married Mom?"

"That was a glorious day; it's true. But I was thinking of the day I was saved. The day of my baptism, the day that Jesus's Light gave me life. Gave me the life I will cherish until I'm called to Heaven. That light shone again because of you. Aurora means dawn. It means the return of the sun. It means glory and light and hope. To me, it means joy."

There was silence for several seconds, and then he spoke

again, so softly I could barely hear. "What is a pair of shoes to that? You are light itself, Aurora. You are beauty and joy and sunshine."

I heard, "Oh, Daddy," and then sounds that convinced me they were hugging.

Just then I heard the back door open and Mrs. King calling, "Jude?"

I pushed away from the house and ran closer to the door before I answered, not wanting anyone to know I'd been eavesdropping. "Yes, ma'am!"

"There you are! Wash your hands, please, and then set the table for supper."

I was quiet during the meal, wondering what it meant that the birth of his daughter meant more to Reverend King than his marriage.

Sunday's sermon that week, I was convinced, was inspired by Aurora and her shoes. We'd finished some hymn, Lorne sat down, and I looked around as I took my place next to him to see where Mr. Hart was today. Didn't see him, but I'd seen him earlier with Dolly, so I knew he was there someplace. Reverend King took his place in the pulpit and, as he usually did, he took a minute to look around the room, to make sure everyone was left with the feeling that he knew who was there. And maybe who was not. Then he spoke.

"Am I happy?" He looked around the room again, almost as though expecting an answer. "Are you?" Another pause. "How would you know?" He used his hands to push himself a little back from the microphone, a painfully puzzled expression on his face. The entire place was silent.

"Have I reached a place where my life is wonderful? In many ways, yes. Does everyone around me like and respect me? Not yet." Pause. "Am I happy?"

He ran a hand through his dark hair and stepped closer to the mike again. "Most people know better than to say that happiness is getting what you want. My mother used to tell me that it's wanting what you have, and certainly that belief will get you a long way toward it, but that feeling strikes me as closer to contentment.

"Here's the true measure. Happiness is not about having things. It's about how you feel. Getting something you want seldom gives you the same feeling as wanting it. Have you ever noticed that? Before you actually get it, there's anticipation, a desire, a longing that has its own charms. Then there's the intensity when it's nearly yours, and that great high you have when it becomes yours. And then?

"Did you think a certain piece of jewelry would make you more beautiful? What would that bring you? Be honest. Feeling attractive is just a way to get attention or make someone desire us. And if we get that? Will that make us happy?"

He looked around the room again, slowly, as if speaking to each person individually. "But what if someone would not have cared about you without the jewelry? What does that say about your own worth? And what if you lose the jewelry, or someone steals it from you? What then? So did the jewelry bring happiness? Or did it bring a short-lived, temporary feeling of elation that wasn't really happiness at all?

"Let's try it with something bigger. Let's say you're saving up for a new car that's faster and fancier than anything you've ever owned, than anything your friends own. As you're saving up, maybe for years, your anticipation grows. But what are you anticipating? You might think it's the car, but really what you can't deny yourself is the feeling you believe it will bring you. And what is that feeling? Do you think it's happiness?"

His voice began to grow louder, and he emphasized phrases by bringing a fist down on the pulpit. "Why was it important to have something better than what your friends have? Why would that make you happy? What does admiration or superiority have to do with happiness? What do worldly possessions have to do with God?"

He turned on his quoting voice. " 'Again I tell you, it is easier for a camel to go through a needle's eye, than for a rich man to enter the Kingdom of God.' " Pause. "Brothers and sisters, do not deceive yourselves! It is not only vast wealth that can keep you separated from God! It is not only rich men who need to beware!"

Reverend King leaned forward, intent, eyes boring into all of us. "What are you hiding? What are you hiding in your heart? In your dresser drawer? In your past? Is it something that's holding you back? Because I tell you, if you possess or desire anything that you feel you cannot, just cannot give up, or that you cannot confess, you are trapped in this physical world. You are caged. And you will be barred from the Kingdom."

He stood up, relaxing a little. "You may ask how you will know. How you will know what objects will trap you here, what possessions—what *ob*sessions will keep you out of the Kingdom. But only you and God know the answer. We must search our hearts, each of us, and we must be honest with God about what we would not give up to be with him."

He took a minute to look around, possibly wanting to see how many of us were hanging our heads, and how many were staring rigidly out of eyes that tried to deny that we had anything to hide, anything we wouldn't give up.

"If you possess or desire something so important to you that it traps you, you will have to keep it hidden. You must keep it from the Light and let it damn you. Or you must give it up and receive the Kingdom of God."

Very quietly, he said, "So what is happiness? It's not something that can be stolen from you or lost or destroyed. It doesn't come from money or possessions or admiration or even the fulfillment of desire.

"No! Happiness comes from being so deep into your relationship with God that the worthiness you seek is worthiness for his love. In true happiness there will be no barriers, nothing hidden. Happiness comes from knowing that the Lord of all things loves you. That he wants to take you to himself for eternity.

"*That,* brothers and sisters, is the Kingdom of God. *That* is happiness." He stepped backward, bowed his head, and said his usual benediction: "May God grant you peace."

I have to confess, this sermon really got to me. I didn't have much in the way of worldly goods. Would I give up my bike? My fluffernutters? My few comic books? Would I give up my marble collection, the one that had been my father's and that I treasured, even though I hadn't even opened the cracked leather bag in a year? Would I give up the only good picture of my mother that I had? I honestly believed that if God asked me to give up any of these things, I would do it. I might even have been willing to give up television, if I'd been convinced it was really God asking me to.

But I prayed that God would not ask me to give up my friendship with Tim.

Chapter 4

Lorne married Clara a year after Mom died. They wanted to start a family of their own, and with a teenager occupying the only other bedroom, things would get very crowded very quickly. Lorne still wouldn't hear of my living anywhere other than with him, so the money saving began as soon as they were engaged.

Clara had taken over my mom's bookkeeping job some time ago, and then of course after the wedding she moved into my mother's room with Lorne. At first, when she took the job, I wanted to hate her, or at least resent her. But she didn't upset our routines very much, and she was always very kind to me without making me feel like a stupid little kid. Plus, I could tell Lorne loved her. There was enough time, after she took the job, for me to get used to the idea of her being part of the family, so that Lorne's bringing her home as his wife felt like that was the way things had been ordained. And this is something else about our Church tradition, expectation, whatever, that made things work well, even though my parents' marriage failed. No one married in haste, and no one married without the general approval of the other saints. There was no committee or council or anything that had to give its permission, but Lorne's intentions were known well enough in advance so that anyone who felt so compelled could talk to Clara, to Lorne, to Clara's parents, whatever was necessary. By the time the ceremony got to the part that says, "If anyone present knows of a reason why these two should not be joined in marriage," you could be sure everyone present had already talked and talked about it. All bases had been covered—including Lorne's official asking of Mr. Davenport for his daughter's hand in marriage.

The wedding was in June, supposedly the perfect month for a wedding, although it did rain that day. I don't remember the weather making any difference to Lorne, who was more excited than I'd ever seen him. I remember two things in particular about the wedding. One was the way Lorne looked, standing in the church waiting for Clara to make her entrance—like he was a five-year-old on Christmas morning and he couldn't wait to see what Santa had brought him, knowing he was going to love it. The other thing I remember was the present Mr. Hart gave them: a year's worth of snowplowing.

Gregory Hart was one of the most useful people in our community, in or out of the Body. The tractor he'd been driving the day he plucked me out of my distress was only one of his machines. He also had a Bobcat, and he had a denim-blue pickup truck with a removable snowplow. He could drive all kinds of farm equipment and often helped neighbors and other saints with their chores for a token wage. If Lorne was the community fixer, Gregory Hart was the operator. People called him all the time when they needed help from someone who could handle big machinery, and I'd guess there weren't more than maybe two fields in our entire community he hadn't worked in at some point, moving earth or snow with metal monsters he turned into gentle giants in his own quiet way, by merging his gentleness with their power.

When I heard Lorne and Clara talking about his gift to them, I heard something I hadn't known: Mr. Hart used his Bobcat to plow the sidewalks of the older saints who shouldn't be shoveling, and he even did it for older folks who weren't in the Body. No charge to any of them. After that I started paying a little more attention to him on Sundays, watching where he'd go when Dolly had been wrapped in the attentions of whichever women were taking charge of her that day. My increased scrutiny didn't help me to see any more of a pattern than I'd ever seen before; he just wandered around vaguely and seemed to choose some brother to sit next to, always asking first.

The summer after the wedding, I still had to spend weekdays at the Kings', though Lorne no longer joined me there for supper. Both Lorne and Clara worked all day, and the idea of a twelve-year-old spending all that time on his own was not something anyone but me was happy with, anymore than they'd liked the idea when I'd been eleven. I consoled myself by anticipating spending time with Tim in the fort again. But that didn't happen quite the same as the year before.

We went out there a few times, but it felt like we were a little too old to be coming up with imaginary stories all the time. When we tried, they fell kind of flat. Plus it seemed to me that Tim was actually trying to avoid time in the fort, instead leading the way to wander around the woods aimlessly, lying down from time to time in sunny spots within clearings or along the river, talking sporadically about things in general.

One cloudy day in late July, for what turned out to be the last time, we went together to the fort, more to make sure it was still okay than anything else, and because there was no sun elsewhere to bask in. It had gotten a little messy, with twigs falling from the dying tree, still attached as it was to its trunk with corded twists of tortured wood. We cleaned it up, sort of for old times' sake, and then sat down with our backs to the boulder that the tree rested on.

Tim seemed restless in a way I couldn't fathom, and we didn't talk much. I stared ahead at dead needles and busied myself feeling around the dirt in the space between us for bits of twigs, small stones, whatever else my fingers came across. And I froze when what they came across was Tim's fingers.

He wrapped his hand around mine and squeezed. His breathing was odd, and when I looked at his face his eyes were shut, squeezing and relaxing and squeezing again. Then he looked at me and reached his other hand up to my face, my skin burning where his fingers touched me. I sat there, still paralyzed, not knowing what was happening but wanting to. Everything beyond his eyes was a blur.

Seconds later, an eternity later, he lunged to his feet and tore out of the fort.

By the time I caught up to him, he was at the river, shoes off, sitting there gazing at the other side where we'd left our bikes. He didn't acknowledge my arrival, and I hadn't a clue what to say to him. Lots of questions tumbled over each other in my mind. Like, *Are you okay? What was that all about? Why did you run? Why did you touch me like that, and why did you stop? Do you feel as confused as I do?* Somehow I knew he'd have no answers, and that he didn't want me to ask.

I didn't sleep well that night.

We never did talk about it. We didn't talk much at all after that. Things between us didn't feel good to me after that last fort day—no matter how much I wanted them to.

If anyone had asked me whether I looked for the Harts every week in church, I'd have said *No, of course not.* But one Sunday in August they weren't there. And I noticed right away. I said something to Clara, and during fellowship after the service she asked around and found out that Dolly wasn't well, and that Gregory had stayed home with her. Nothing serious, Clara was told, not to worry.

Over supper that night I asked Lorne if he knew why Mr. Hart had never married. Lorne shrugged and said, "I suppose it's because he has to take care of his sister."

"But you have to take care of me, and you got married."

"Then I don't exactly know, I guess." His discomfort was obvious and puzzling.

I pictured Dolly Hart and, for the first time, I realized that her blindness and her wheelchair weren't related. She had always seemed so dependent that I'd merged the two disabilities into one in my head. "What happened to his sister, anyway? Why is she blind *and* in a wheelchair?"

"That's an ugly story, Jude. You haven't heard it before?" I shook my head. He took a deep breath and let it out slowly. "She was born blind, I think. Never been sighted in her life. At any rate, she was blind when she was a girl. For some reason I don't know, she was outside in a snowstorm alone one winter. She was maybe ten or so. She wasn't far from home, and maybe she knew her way around when there was no weather, but the storm confused her, and she wandered into the road. There was a lot of snow in the air, and the snowplow driver didn't see her until it was too late. It broke her back. So now she can't move her legs."

"Geez." It was all I could think of to say.

"And now Gregory takes care of her. Can we stop talking about this now?"

I nodded like I understood, but I'm not sure it's possible to understand something like that. She always seemed so cheerful when I saw her, and ever since she'd fed me supper that time she'd been very friendly, always asking how I was, how school was, and when I might bike out to see her again. So the Saturday after the Harts hadn't been in church, over a year after my supper there of casserole and zucchini and pie, that's what I did.

I'd been feeling a little at large, wishing it wouldn't feel weird calling Tim and knowing it would, not wanting my holidays to end but not really knowing what to do with them. Clara, shelling peas on the side porch, saw me walking the bike into the driveway and called to me just as I was starting off.

"Where you off to, Jude?"

"Bit of a ride," I called over my shoulder, adding, "out toward the Harts'."

"What? Why?"

I stopped, turned, and looked at her; couldn't quite make

out the expression on her face—somewhere between surprise and concern. I wanted to shoot back, *Why not?* But instead I replied, "To visit Miss Hart. She's been sick."

There was a brief pause. Then, "You'll be back before supper?"

"Yes, ma'am." Lorne had insisted I call Clara ma'am, even though she still looked like a girl to me.

It was a good ten-minute ride, what with a few hills to get over, to the Harts'. I leaned my bike against the fence that lined the front yard along the driveway, walked up the ramp Gregory had probably built for his sister and onto the porch, and knocked on the front door. I figured it would take a minute or two for Dolly to get to the door, but it opened pretty quickly. It wasn't Dolly, however, who stood there. It was Tansy Thornton. Or, Pearl, as her mother had named her. "Tansy" was a nickname used by children. A very cruel nickname.

As I've said before, the saints need other saints to help keep them from doing things that would jeopardize their state of Grace. I couldn't help noticing, though, that at times it seemed like they didn't so much keep each other's heads above water (as it were) as much as they all kind of ducked down together and mucked about in a way I doubted the reverend would approve of. This was the approach they seemed to take when it came to plump, red-faced Belinda Thornton and her daughter, Pearl.

The Thorntons didn't come to church; they weren't in the Body, which of course all by itself would have been cause for judgment by some, and possibly even a little gossip that would be good for the saints' souls to confess and repent—gossiping more in the process of confession. But there was more to the Thorntons that inspired talk than not being in the Light. Rumor was that Belinda, who had never been married, had tried to rid herself of the fetus that got planted in her in a manner no one could explain. According to the stories, she'd never had a gentleman friend anybody had ever seen, and yet somehow she got "with child." And tried to get "without child" by drinking enormous amounts of tansy blossoms steeped in hot water. Tansy tea. It's a dangerous, risky method that can lead either to spontaneous abortion or to a disfigured infant.

Pearl's afflictions were a constant reminder of her mother's double sin, so town lore went. First was the sin of fornication, then of attempted murder. And when Pearl was born, her short and awkwardly formed body parts, slight harelip, and—Heavens above—her very dark complexion and tightly curled brown hair spoke worlds. It was obvious, wasn't it? It was like the scarlet letter that Hester Prynne was forced to wear. And naming the baby Pearl, something that should have been white, probably increased the scorn and condescension both mother and daughter received and might have prodded insensitive people to refer to the child as "Tansy." I don't remember a time when that name wasn't used.

For some amount of time after Pearl was born, none of the scandal stopped occasional attempts by some of the women in the Church to present the benefits of sainthood to Belinda, stopping by unannounced and interrupting her as she sat at home making sweaters on her knitting machine, the sale of these creations being her only source of income. But it was always to no avail. Eventually they stopped trying, although I occasionally would hear one of the saints cluck a tongue and say what an appropriate thing it was that both mother and child would be so constantly reminded that sin was wrong, usually polishing off the statement with, "And I mean that in the most Christian way!"

I remember forcing myself not to stare at Pearl in school. She was a year older than me but had been held back her first year in school for poor performance. Her face would have been pretty, if she'd worn a half-mask like cartoon Arabian princesses often wear, so just her eyes would show. Pearl's deep brown eyes were surrounded by long, curling lashes, and her skin was the shade of brown that you see on the backs of fawns.

I'd made the mistake once, when I was maybe nine, of trying to make friends with Pearl. I had a soft heart even then, and an imagination that allowed me to ache with her, to share a sense of isolation and rejection that she had done nothing to deserve. I wasn't old enough then to understand the things some of the grownups said about Pearl and her mother, but somehow I came to the conclusion that Pearl was being blamed for something that wasn't her fault, for being something she couldn't not be, and that wasn't fair. So one day I offered her one of my cookies.

Fourth graders can be cruel. Within minutes of my friendship offering to Pearl (which she refused), I was surrounded by some of my classmates. They bounced erratically around me, their singsong voices chanting without any music in the sound, "Jude and Tansy up in a tree, k-i-s-s-i-n-g. First comes love, then comes marriage, then comes Jude with a baby carriage!"

In my mortification, my empathy for Pearl evaporated. And only now that I'm recalling this scene does it dawn on me that there was a slap to her face in that taunt I didn't have the capacity to appreciate at the time. *After* marriage comes the baby. Didn't work that way for Pearl and her mother.

Slap in the face. Such an overused phrase, really. How often does anyone ever really get slapped in the face? Truth is, feeling like you've been slapped in the face is degrading and isolating. It mangles you emotionally, makes you feel like you're of no value at all.

But I felt what I could for Pearl, and it wasn't enough. Later I felt guilty that I hadn't felt more. All I'd had to endure was intense embarrassment for the remainder of recess, and a minor version of it for the rest of the day; she would be treated like this forever. Plus, she wasn't saved.

So when I saw her standing in the doorway to the Harts', I was doubly thrown. Not only did her being there surprise the heck out of me, but also there was a bucket-load of residual guilt and discomfort that I associated with her. I stared blankly at her.

"What do you want?" she asked impatiently, like I had some nerve just being there.

"I, uh, I came to see Dolly. Miss Hart."

"Wait here." And she shut the door in my face. I almost got back on my bike and rode away again. *Wait here?* Who did she think she was? I stepped off the porch, hands on hips, and turned around slowly, trying to decide how long I'd "wait here." Before I could quite make up my mind to leave, the door opened again.

"You're to come in." Pearl held the door open for me, though it seemed to me as though she were dying to add, "Although I can't think why." It was all very *Great Expectations,* Estella and Miss Havisham, it seems to me now. Though of course Dolly Hart was a wonderful woman.

Dolly was glad I was there, if her tone of voice was any indication. "Jude! This is such a treat." I could see her in the kitchen past Pearl's short and somewhat irregular frame, her eyes turned vacantly in my direction. "Pearl's just made us some cookies. I know you'll have some!"

This was a concept I had a hard time wrapping my mind around. I mean, I had offered her a cookie once, but if I'd given any thought to Pearl and what she might be doing at any given moment, it would not have been baking cookies. Nevertheless, there was the distinct smell of cooked peanut butter in the air and a plate of golden, crisscross-marked cookies on the table beside two glasses of milk. There was a school book, paper, and pencil there as well.

"Pearl, please pour a glass of milk for Jude, would you?"

"Yes, ma'am." Her voice seemed more compliant than the belligerent sideways look she threw at me.

"Jude, sit over here on my right and talk to me. I love visitors. It's hard for me to get out much, as you can imagine."

"Thank you, Miss Hart. Um, are you okay? You weren't in church last week."

"Now, didn't I tell you to call me Dolly? And aren't you a sweetheart to ask. It was just a bug or something, Jude. Nothing much." She beamed at me, her eyes vacant but her face tender and grateful all the same. I sat and glanced at the book. Math.

"How is Lorne?" she asked as soon as she heard my chair scrape on the floor. "And Clara? I'm so thrilled they got married. It seems as though they're just right for each other, though of course you'd know better than I would. How are things at home, Jude?"

"Great. They're great. Clara's—great." Pearl threw me a look of disgust as she took her chair, no doubt at my paltry command of adjectives. "They, uh, they seem really happy together. We make supper together, and we've been on lots of picnics with the Church. She's real nice to me. She smiles a lot."

"No news of a baby yet?" And Dolly giggled. "Sakes alive, that's not my business. When it's news, I'll hear it." But her head turned expectantly toward me as though she were hoping maybe it was news now.

"Not that I know of, but it's what they're hoping for." What I was hoping was that Pearl couldn't see me blush. I had some idea, at this point in my life, what had to happen in order for this news to be real, and talking about it with Dolly was a little embarrassing. Maybe it wouldn't have been, if Pearl hadn't been there.

"Pearl and I have been getting a head start on her math work."

"Dolly," Pearl interrupted, "do we have to talk about that?"

Dolly's face went a little blank, but she said, "No, dear, of course not. I just thought Jude might be able to help, too. Jude, are you good at math?"

I was, as it happened. "I can hold my own. I get good grades."

Dolly beamed. "I knew it. I love math. That surprises some people. They think because I'm blind that I can't work with numbers. I can't rightly say, but for some reason it's actually easier for me than working with letters and words. Maybe it's just that it takes fewer numbers to come up with something meaningful. Anyway, I do love it."

"My mom was a bookkeeper. And Clara has her job now."

"Yes, I know; I think that's marvelous!"

Pearl spoke up again. "Dolly, I've washed the dishes from the cookies. Bowls, pans, you know. So I'm going to head home, now."

"Oh, dear, do you have to? You can't stay and chat with Jude a little?"

"I'm sorry. If it's okay, I'll come back next weekend."

"Of course, dear. Now give me a hug, and you be very careful on your way home, do you hear?"

"Yes, ma'am." Pearl didn't have to lean over to hug the chair-bound woman. Then she uttered an obligatory "Bye, Jude," and headed out the back door. I heard the sounds of a bicycle pushing off; it must have been around the back, and I hadn't seen it.

"Help yourself to a cookie or three or four, Jude. Pearl makes the best peanut butter cookies I ever tasted."

"Thanks." They were good; it's true. I don't think I've tasted better since. "So, why is . . . Pearl working on math during school vacation?" I had nearly said "Tansy."

"She wanted to get a head start on the school year. It's not her favorite subject, and I offered to tutor her."

"Mmmm." I said, half to the cookie and half to acknowledge what Dolly said. At school, I hadn't paid much attention to Pearl's math work. Was it in need of tutoring? Probably.

Dolly said, "So you like math? Tell me what kind of work you like best."

We talked about math, about school in general, and about the Church, and I ate lots of cookies, until we heard her broth-er's truck pulling up to the barn.

"Gregory's been off harvesting for the Sandersons today. For a few days now, actually. They've got all that hay to do. He leaves his tractor there until he's done with their job. Then I think he'll just move it on to the Taylors'. Busy time of year."

The back door opened, and the space filled with the large frame of Gregory Hart. He blinked at me, letting the sun glare fade while his eyes adjusted, and then he said, "Jude Connor! How are you, boy? Don't think we've said two words since the wedding."

"I'm good, thanks."

He moved over to the sink and washed his hands and face. "Smells good in here, Dolly. Was Pearl here today?"

"She was. And if Jude hasn't eaten quite all her cookies, you might want to grab a few before he does!" I was getting used to

Dolly's laugh, and I liked it. It amazed me that someone in her situation could be so cheerful.

"You're not hammering at the boy about scripture, are you, little sister?"

Laughter, then, "No, Gregory, I am not. We've been talking mathematics, I'll have you know. Jude here is an excellent student."

"Is he, now? Glad to hear it. I was never very good with numbers, myself." He sat down across from Dolly, beside me, and reached for a cookie. The smell of sun and hay and sweat kept moving forward in a soft wave after he sat, and I breathed it in, feeling like it was the way things were supposed to be. It made me feel peaceful and awake at the same time. He smelled like a man. I couldn't remember my father smelling like anything other than aftershave, and Gregory's smell was good, healthy, right.

He swallowed his first mouthful and said, "Saw that bike of yours out front, Jude. Need a lift home?" He winked and took another bite of cookie.

"No, sir," I said, grinning. "I can get home on my own today, thanks. And I oughta do that. Clara wants me home for supper, and Lorne likes me to help get it ready."

"Then you get outta here, boy, and stop spoiling your appetite with Pearl's cookies!" He walked me to the front door. Holding it open for me he said, "You come back anytime, Jude. Dolly loves visitors. And we both love to see you."

As I passed by I leaned in a little for one more lungful of air that smelled like Man.

The next time I took a notion to visit the Harts was about a month later, though again Clara grilled me about it. I called first—ostensibly to make sure I wasn't putting them out in any way, but in truth so that I could avoid running into Pearl again. Great cookies or not, the girl made me uncomfortable.

I got there just as Gregory was about to leave, which disappointed me. I'd really hoped to have some time with him, too, not just Dolly. I couldn't stop myself asking, "Where are you going?"

At the truck, he opened the driver's door and looked at me from under the brim of his denim blue baseball hat that almost matched the color of the truck. "Mrs. Dillon needs a tree moved. Mr. Latimer volunteered his backhoe, but he couldn't spare a worker right now, so I said I'd do it." He swung his body into the cab and slammed the door. Through the open window he looked at me, my face no doubt giving away how forlorn and left out I felt. "D'you wanna come along?"

Did I! I let Dolly know where I was going and scrambled up onto the passenger seat. Neither of us spoke; Gregory Hart was not a talkative man, and I was too busy thinking about where we were going. I'd never seen a tree moved before. Questions formed in my mind, but I didn't let myself ask them right away. It was much too pleasant just sitting here beside this man, high up in the truck, feeling like maybe I owned just a little bit of my life.

Finally I couldn't stand it. "What kind of a tree is it? How big?"

Mr. Hart took a long breath in through his nose. "Not too big. It's a hemlock that Mr. Dillon planted several years ago, too close to the house. The roots are starting to damage the foundation. It's a beautiful tree, though, so Mrs. Dillon doesn't want to lose it. I'll just move it out into the side yard, far enough away from the winter road salt. Her neighbor will plant bulbs around it after we're done, while the earth is still nice and soft."

He'd said "after we're done." Him and me. Both of us, together. A tiny thrill went through me. And then the word "hemlock" sank in. We were moving a tree like the one Tim and I had as our fort. Or, that we used to have.

At the Dillons' there was a backhoe parked in the front left corner, just off the road, and to the right of the house was the tree. Hat in hand, Mr. Hart rang the doorbell. Mrs. Dillon must have heard us drive up; she was right there. "Well, hello there, Jude. Didn't know Gregory was bringing another worker with him today!"

Mr. Hart told her, "We'll get started, if you're ready. First I'm going to prepare the spot where it will go. Are we still aiming at that spot we talked about?"

"That's right. I've put a stick there with red yarn on it. You won't damage the house, will you?"

A gentle smile spread over his face. "With God's help, we'll be out of your way in no time, house intact."

"I'll be praying for you, then!" And she went back inside.

The stick was stabbed into end-of-season grass. Mr. Hart looked around, then at me. "Okay, Jude, now here's the deal. I can use your help when we're getting the tree uprooted, but while I'm on the backhoe I don't want to have to wonder where you are. So you need to stay over by the truck. I reckon you'll be able to see just fine from there. Do you understand?"

"Yes, sir. I promise."

He nodded and strode over to the earthmover while I trotted toward the truck. I watched as he climbed into the cab of the yellow monster and traded his baseball cap for a bright orange hard hat. Then he started the engine, worked the gears a little, and the thing lurched to life. It left chewed-up grid marks where it passed over the lawn; no help for that, I supposed. The bucket's prongs gouged the earth and brought up only a little at first, but once the hole was begun they could get a better grip, with the occasional screeching protest as the metal met with rocks. Each time Mr. Hart would pull back and gently work around the edges to see how big the rock was and, ultimately, to coax it out of its nest of brown earth.

The backhoe chewed more grid marks on its way over to the tree. Mr. Hart worked first on one side of the tree and then on the other, letting the heavy pronged bucket fall onto the earth as it dug in little by little. When he'd done about all he probably felt safe doing with the machine, he moved it away a little and got out, baseball cap back in place.

"You ready to do a little work, there, Jude?"

"Yes, sir!" I started to dash toward him, but he called to me to bring the tools and a length of rope from his truck bed.

We worked for—gosh, I don't know how long, him loosening

the dirt with the pitchfork, me tossing dirt away with the shovel, both of us getting in there elbow-deep to work the roots free with our hands. "We need to keep as many roots intact as possible," he told me between grunts of effort. "Otherwise we may as well just kill this tree and be done."

Finally we'd done all we could manually; we'd need the backhoe to finish the job. Using a rope and a pitchfork, between us we managed to coax the root ball well enough out of the earth for the backhoe to be able to pick it up. Mr. Hart sent me out of the way again and fired up the noisy monster, then eased the bucket down and under the tree's roots. He took so much time, and so much care, getting that root ball to sit just right, like that tree was the only valuable thing he had in this world.

When he got the tree over to the hole he'd dug, he didn't set it in. Instead, he got out, and on foot went back to the hole we'd taken the tree from, and he got into it. Then he went back to where the tree was and got into the new hole.

"Jude? Shovel, please, over here."

He shoveled and measured more than once. Only when the new hole was the same depth as the old one did he lower the hemlock into its new home, the surrounding earth softened by our work.

Using the rope again, we got the tree settled in its new home, then worked and patted dirt around its roots. I did my best to be as careful as Mr. Hart, but he outdid me. He approached the task with a tenderness that made me wish I were the tree.

He used Mrs. Dillon's garden hose to give the roots a little water before we finished filling in the hole. Not too much, though; he said that this late in the season, we didn't want to encourage the tree to start any new growth. And he said too much water right now would also be another shock to it.

"Shock?" I echoed.

"Sure. Wasn't it a shock for you when you started having to spend so much time at the Kings'?" He waited until I shrugged; he was right. "And you didn't actually move there. You just started spending regular time someplace other than home. So imagine what it's like for this tree. You know, trees, left alone, never move at all. And here we've changed everything it knows about what its world is like. It won't have the warmth of the house beside it all winter from now on. It's feeling fragile and vulnerable, and it's about to face a long, cold winter in an unfamiliar spot. Do you think maybe it's feeling a little shocked?"

I shrugged again. "Yes, sir. I guess so."

He grinned at me. "You guess so, indeed. But you and I know that the other choice was to take its life altogether, to hack it up into bits and carry it off to become landfill. So sometimes a shock is better than what else might happen."

On the drive back to his house, Mr. Hart asked me how things were going for me, being at the Kings' so much. I told him that I avoided Aurora as much as possible.

"Why is that?"

"*You* know. She's a girl. I don't have anything in common with her. Plus she hangs out with her girlfriends all the time."

"Do you think she avoids you, too?"

I hadn't really thought about that. "Don't know. I suppose so."

"She's pleasant enough, though, isn't she?"

"Sure. She's fine. We just like different things, that's all."

"So if you avoided her all summer, what did you do with yourself?"

I could feel my face get hot as an image flew into my brain: Tim's eyes claiming all my attention in our fort the day he'd touched my face. I shrugged to cover my embarrassment and gazed out the window. "Stuff. Fishing. Exploring the woods."

"All by yourself?"

"Sometimes with my friend Tim."

"Ever hiked up to Denmark Cliffs?"

"What's that?"

He chuckled. "Can't remember if it even has a real name. I've called it Denmark Cliffs ever since Mr. Denmark led me up it when we were about—oh, maybe sixteen, seventeen. The trailhead is just past the barn on the Johnson property."

Todd Denmark was a brother in the Church, and he and his wife had a boy who was twenty and still lived at home. Bruce.

He was mentally retarded, had a scrunched-up kind of face, and was generally unpleasant. I tried to avoid him, because we were supposed to be nice to everyone, and I didn't want to have to be nice to him. I said, "I think I know where that is. I walked partway in once."

"Well, if you go far enough, it gets quite steep. The trail crosses a few streams, and you get to this outcropping of rock face that looks northwest. Hawks and eagles nest there, and you can see them circling below."

"Cool!"

"Maybe you and your friend Tim would like to hike it with me one day after church, once the weather cools a little. What do you think?"

I could feel my pulse quicken at the thought of an outing like that. Mr. Hart, me, and Tim, all alone for the day. It sounded like just the thing to help mend that rip that seemed to exist in the fabric of my friendship with Tim. "Yes, sir! I'd really like to do that."

"I'll talk to Lorne about it at church tomorrow. Maybe he'd like to come, too. Just let me know if Tim is interested, and I can talk to his folks."

Lorne? I kind of doubted Lorne would want to come. Wasn't even sure I'd want him to. This was my adventure. Well, mine and Tim's and Mr. Hart's. But the point was, it shouldn't be a family affair. I decided I'd talk to Lorne about it myself at supper and slant the idea my way.

His answer, *no,* floored me. "What? Why not? Why can't I go?"

"Jude, just don't . . . don't press me on this."

"But—"

"Jude!" Lorne almost never shouted. Lord knows he'd done enough quiet things when he was younger to get our father to stop yelling, and it was completely out of character for Lorne. I shut up. But I wasn't happy. I didn't speak for the rest of the meal unless I had to, and as soon as I could I left the table and ran outside. I hadn't planned on leaving the yard, but once outside I didn't feel far enough away from Lorne yet, or from what

I saw as his unreasonable response to something I really, really wanted to do. So even though it would be dark in just over an hour, I took off for the meadow.

"Meadow" is a glamorous term for a large expanse of untended ground a few hundred yards through the woods behind our house. Huge metal towers supporting power lines and transformers marched their way through it, to the left and northeast up the mountainside, and to the right down into the valley—and, in fact, they were no doubt the reason it existed. But everyone who lived around it referred to it as "the meadow." Once in July and once in October industrial-sized mowers cut down the wild growth, and the place was otherwise ignored. Lorne had repaired the engines on some of those mowers. Before the first mow, the place was rampant with wild-flowers, otherwise known as weeds; by October it had become overgrown with wild carrot, curly dock, wild black-eyed Susans, purple loosestrife in the marshier areas, and clover everywhere.

Stomping with every footfall to express my fury at Lorne's unreasonableness, I headed that way and nearly broke an ankle about five times, stepping hard on uneven earth invisible beneath the wild growth, before calming down enough to be careful. The slope of the meadow went down to the right in the general direction of the setting sun. I sat in front of one of the towers, leaned my back against it, pulled up a few weeds to shred, and admired the red-orange glow in the sky left behind by the sinking sun.

The glow must have partially blinded me, because I didn't see Pearl Thornton approaching. Startled by the sounds she made as she came through the grasses, I sat very still to see what might be making the noise. She didn't see me at all. She was looking at the ground, peering in the gloom for the safest spots to plant her feet; she'd be even more at a disadvantage on this uneven ground than I was. Finally she scrambled up onto a large boulder, her comical body looking odder than usual in the effort. She was holding something, but in the dusky light I couldn't quite see what. It was in her arms, cradled. And then I heard her voice.

She was humming. Or singing; she wasn't close enough for me to be sure. It was a gentle, lilting tune that I didn't recognize. And as she sang, she gazed down at whatever she held. And I realized it was a doll. She was singing to a doll.

In terms of cognitive disconnect, baking peanut butter cookies was nothing compared to this. Singing to a doll? In the meadow? At sunset? *Tansy?* I had no idea what to make of this day. First Lorne shouts at me, then Pearl sings a lullaby to her doll.

I didn't want Pearl to know I'd been practically spying on her, so I figured I'd have to wait until she left and wondered how late that would be and how much trouble I'd get into. If I so much as shifted my leg position the rattling of the dry weeds would give me away. But she didn't stay long. Even so, it was dark by the time I got home.

The kitchen door had barely shut behind me when I heard Lorne say, "Jude Connor, where have you been?" He and Clara were at the table with some household paperwork.

"Out." I wanted to get through the room without further comment. Hopeless.

"Get over here."

I tried not to be defensive. After all, I was the injured party here. So I went to the table and stood there, hoping I looked as irritated as I felt. But when I got to the table, Clara picked up a Bible, opened it, and began to read.

" 'Let every soul be in subjection to the higher authorities, for there is no authority except from God, and those who exist are ordained by God. Therefore he who resists the authority withstands the ordinance of God; and those who withstand will receive to themselves judgment. For rulers are not a terror to the good work, but to the evil.' " And she set the book down again.

For the first time in my life, I believed that I had some idea how my father had felt. How caged. How fettered and controlled and emasculated. Hearing Clara quote scripture to me, scripture that was meant to tell me how wrong I was, brought back those days when my father would shout and my mother would fire bullets of scripture at him. The loud ringing in my ears nearly drowned out Lorne's words.

"Do you understand what this passage from Romans is saying, Jude?"

I couldn't answer. In truth, I didn't want to. But I couldn't. Not directly. Instead I asked, "Why won't you let me go hiking?"

Clara's voice again, no longer reading, quoting Ecclesiastes from memory: " 'For everything there is a season, and a time for every purpose under Heaven.' "

My jaw clenched to stop the screams pressing to come out of me. Finally, my teeth barely separating, I managed, "Stop it!" Lorne stood. I turned, ran from the room and up the stairs, and dashed for my bedroom like it was home base. But Lorne was on my heels and held the door when I tried to get it closed. Tried to slam it shut, really. When I failed, I threw myself on the bed, face down.

"Jude Amos Connor," my brother, my tormentor intoned heavily. "What do you mean by this behavior?" Face deep in the pillow, I tried to ignore him. But he would not be ignored. "Answer me." He didn't need to yell; his tone pierced my brain.

With my face lifted just high enough to enunciate, I said, "You aren't being reasonable. There's no good reason why Tim and I can't go hiking with Mr. Hart."

"Sit up. Look at me." I delayed my obedience as long as I could. "Do you think there are a few things in this world that I understand better than you do?"

He waited for my nearly silent *yes.*

"Do you believe and accept the word of God?"

Another whispered *yes.*

"God has put Clara and me in authority over you. It is your duty to accept that and obey us. In this particular case, there are things you don't yet understand. Things you'll understand later but can't yet. This is what Clara was trying to tell you."

"She's not my mother!" It was a stupid thing to say; of course she wasn't. But it had been screaming inside my head since I saw her lift that book off the table.

"She is in authority over you. She doesn't need to be your mother. And she's using the Word of God to help you see what you have to do."

"I don't want her to." I felt about five years old again, sulking and struggling against tears of frustration and thwarted fury.

"No one ever said that following authority is always easy. It isn't. But it's necessary. Now I don't want to hear one more word about this hike thing, and you're coming downstairs to apologize to Clara."

"Why?"

"She was doing God's work. You were disobedient and rude. Now get down there."

I couldn't remember that Lorne had ever struck me. And I didn't exactly get the sense that he'd do it now, if I refused. But I wasn't altogether sure he wouldn't. Even so, I tried one last volley. "I could leave here, y'know. I could go and live with the Kings." Playing in my ears was the conversation in which Reverend King had talked Aurora out of her shoe tantrum by telling her how much she meant to him. Lorne hadn't done that for me.

"And if you think they'd let you go on this hike, you're wrong. Now come downstairs and apologize to Clara."

Hating that I had no choice, I did as Lorne demanded. Clara seemed almost as uncomfortable as I felt. And then she hugged me. I nearly put my arms around her, too. I really wanted to. But I didn't.

The next day in church I watched for Mr. Hart, desperate to head him off before he approached Lorne. Maybe I wanted to spare his feelings. Or maybe I was hoping that at some future time the hike could take place after all, if I could keep Lorne from saying anything specific against it now. But as soon as Mr. Hart appeared, Lorne went over to him. Clara held my arm. I watched, feeling something near panic and not knowing why. I couldn't hear them above the din of the pre-service crowd, but I saw Mr. Hart's face. His expression went from curious to expectant and then turned to stone. Absolute stone. The kind of expression that's meant to subdue something so ugly that rock-like rigidity is necessary to keep it contained. He never said a word. Didn't even nod to Lorne. He just turned away.

I had to talk to him. I had to! But I wasn't going to get a chance now; Lorne and Clara kept me between them practically every minute until we got home again. That's when I decided I was going to have to lie.

A couple of hours before supper I told Clara I was going to my room to pray for a bit.

"I'm glad, Jude," she said, smiling sweetly as though in acceptance of some capitulation she believed I was making, some acknowledgment of my disobedience the night before. "About anything in particular?"

That was easy. "For forgiveness." I decided to leave it at that; let her think it was for last night. In reality it was for forgiveness for something I was about to do. And I did pray. I got down on my knees at the side of my bed and I begged God, through Jesus, to forgive the lie I was about to tell Clara.

Downstairs again I tossed a quick "Off to see Tim for a bit," over my shoulder as I made for my bike.

"Be home by six," I heard Lorne call from where he sat reading some book about how to be a good Christian father. I spared two seconds to wonder if there was a reason for this research before putting it out of my mind.

I made record time getting to the Harts'. Leaning my bike against the fence, I scoured the barn area. Would Mr. Hart be out here? I wanted to talk to him alone, if possible. But I didn't see him or his truck. That wasn't a good sign. I crept up toward the house to see if I could tell whether anyone was home at all. I heard music; someone was playing a CD or something. As I got closer to the open living room window, I heard something more. Someone crying quietly. A woman. It had to be Dolly. Over her soft sobs I heard a hymn, a gospel song called "Precious Lord." I'd heard this hymn before, many times. Reverend King had even quoted it in a sermon. "Precious Lord, take my hand." What I was hearing wasn't wildly different from the familiar version, but somehow this version—all women's voices, bittersweet, haunting—sounded more like the story Lorne had told me about what happened to Dolly: "... through the dark, through the storm ..." Take your child home.

Dolly, the blind child, caged in a wheelchair for life, was begging for freedom, for Jesus to take her to her real home. A home without pain, a home where she could be truly herself and not this maimed, deformed creature the world saw.

I think Dolly became real to me that day.

Chapter 5

By mid-October it had already snowed once, though not more than a couple of inches. It hadn't taken me long to get the snow off our driveway and the McNultys', so by the time Mr. Hart came by in his truck, plow attachment perched on the front and ready for the first installment of his wedding gift, I was already done and back inside. He just turned around in the driveway and went away. The next time I got to see either of the Harts it was because Dolly called Lorne.

Dolly's call came maybe a week later, one evening while Clara was at a women's Bible Study. I was doing homework at the kitchen table. Lorne answered the phone, and it took me a little while to figure out who he was talking to as I pretended not to listen. Couldn't tell much, but she was asking him something that he finally said he'd get back to her about. He hung up and came to sit at the table across from me.

"That was Miss Hart." I waited; that much I knew already. "She says you're good in math." I shrugged, deciding against telling him she preferred her first name. "I know your grades are always good, and I'm proud of you for that. Miss Hart thinks you're good enough to be helping another student."

Whatever I might have expected, this wasn't it. "Another student?" Please, God, don't let it be—

"Miss Hart says she's been working with Pearl Thornton, and she wants to continue, but she says it would be better if someone from Pearl's class helped, too, so she could be sure everything was in line with what the teacher is doing."

This sounded a little far-fetched to me. I wondered what Lorne thought. But I held my tongue; if this turned into a chance to spend time at the Harts', it might actually be worth putting up with Pearl.

"She's suggesting that the three of you work together, on Monday evenings, at the Harts'."

I figured it was time for me to speak. "Okay." That was noncommittal enough.

Lorne breathed out loudly through his nose and sat back in his chair, watching me intently for a few seconds. "Miss Hart thinks this would be good for you because she says teaching someone else something helps you learn it even better yourself. How much do you like math, Jude?"

We'd been getting into algebra. I'd enjoyed the class but hadn't given it much thought. "I like it a lot." As soon as I said that, I realized that I loved it. I loved how the answers to things could always be puzzled out. I loved figuring out the relationships between the variables and the constants. I loved algebra. This made Dolly's proposition that much more appealing.

Lorne obviously hadn't made a decision yet, though. "I'm a little concerned that you'd be seeing so much of Pearl. She's not in the Body, as you know."

I nodded. "Yeah, she's not my favorite person. I guess the good part would just be teaching somebody. Learning more that way." As soon as I realized I was echoing what Lorne had just told me, I shut up again. Let him make the decision; I had a feeling it was going my way. And with this thought, a rush almost like an epiphany went through me; was this a grown-up way to think? I had to refocus on Lorne.

"You'd be at the Harts'...." He let that trail off as though that were not a good thing. I hadn't quite forgiven Lorne for denying me that hike, and especially for not telling me why. And Mr. Hart's stony face when Lorne had approached him at church flashed into my brain. Did Lorne have a problem with the Harts themselves? Why? I waited, not knowing what words would push Lorne in one direction or the other.

"Getting you back and forth could be a problem."

"Could Mr. Hart—"

"No."

So the problem was with Mr. Hart, not with Dolly. "How does Pearl get there?"

"Miss Thornton. And Miss Hart says you could get a ride from her. But I'm not crazy about you riding back and forth with non-Christians. So what I'm going to do, if this is even something you'd be willing to do, is ask Reverend King what he thinks. Whether he sees a problem with you riding with Miss Thornton."

"Okay." Again, noncommittal, but willing. Eagerness to be at the Harts' was not something I wanted to show Lorne. I sent up a silent prayer to be forgiven for secrecy.

Reverend King, it seemed, thought this was a terrific idea. The way he put it to Lorne, this would be an opportunity for witnessing to Pearl. Dolly was known for her steadfast faith, and although Belinda Thornton had proved intractable, perhaps her daughter was not. I found myself wondering if Reverend King also thought that encouraging a connection between Dolly, a cripple of strong faith, and Pearl, a cripple of no faith, would help in this proselytizing effort. What didn't occur to me at the time, but has occurred to me since, is that he may also have been hoping that Pearl would be drawn toward the Church through a connection with me. Given how things eventually turned out, he should have applied Psalm 39, verse 6: "Surely every man walks like a shadow. Surely they busy themselves in vain. He heaps up, and doesn't know who shall gather."

* * *

The very next Monday, right after supper, Miss Thornton
pulled her car—too old for me to identify even the make without closer inspection—into our driveway and waited. No one
got out of the car and came to the door. No one honked, either. I grabbed my math book, a notebook, and a pencil, threw
my parka over an arm, and called "Good-bye" as I headed toward the door. No one said "Be home by..." I guess they
trusted Miss Hart.

Pearl got out to flip forward the seat so I could climb into
the back while her mother said, "Jude can sit in front with us,
honey."

I did not want to do that. "This is okay, Miss Thornton. I have
more room back here."

If I'd thought about Miss Thornton chatting with me during
the ride, I would have anticipated the types of questions most
adults ask most kids. But instead of how did I like school and
what was my favorite subject, she opened with, "Do you visit
your mom's grave very often, Jude?"

It was not an easy question to answer. Lorne and I had gone
quite a bit that first summer, then less once autumn and cold
weather set in. Now we went only on major dates like her birthday and Mother's Day. I did my best. "Sometimes."

"Is it in a pretty spot?"

"Yes, ma'am. It has a view of the mountains."

She laughed. "Jude, every spot around here has a view of the
mountains!"

She was right, of course, but her laughter embarrassed me,
and I clammed up until she asked another question. "Do you
know the Davenport family very well?"

"Some." How was I going to answer that one? How well could
a twelve-year-old boy know a family that had no kids in it anymore? Just because Lorne had married into it...

"Do you see very much of them?"

"Not really. Clara visits them."

It went on like this, almost as though she were chatting with an adult rather than a child. But if that surprised me, it was nothing to what happened when we got to the Harts'. Miss Thornton didn't drop Pearl and me off and leave. She stayed. In fact, before our tutoring session or whatever it was going to be got under way, Belinda came into the kitchen carrying a grocery bag. First out came chocolate cookies with chocolate chips in them, and next a folded sweater. Pearl arranged the cookies on a plate while Belinda made a show of giving Dolly the sweater.

"It's to thank you for helping Pearl," she said to the blind woman.

"Oh, you're so sweet to do this!" Dolly felt it carefully. "Oh, real wool. You shouldn't have, Belinda. What color is it?"

"It's varying shades of blues and greens, a sort of leaflike pattern, with a cream background. I used different weights of yarn, so you can feel the different textures. You can probably even tell where the leaves are by the way it feels."

Dolly oohed and aahed over the garment as though she could see it. I was fixated on the brilliance of knitting a recognizable pattern into the sweater using textures a blind person could follow when Dolly added, "I'll wear it to church this Sunday. Everyone will see how lovely it is, and they'll all want to buy them from you!"

Belinda beamed, so perhaps this was a reasonable hope. I was pretty sure that Belinda didn't sell her sweaters to anyone directly; that would have meant too much association with a non-Christian. But there were a couple of stores nearby where you could buy them, and later I found out that Belinda drove some distance in that ancient car to supply stores in other towns. It was how she made her living, after all.

She and Mr. Hart took a pot of tea and some cookies into the living room and talked. And laughed. And talked. I couldn't tell, working at the kitchen table with Dolly and Pearl, what they were talking and laughing about. Before long I stopped wondering anyway, because I got pretty engrossed in algebra. Dolly, as another surprise to me, got things started, but then she was mostly quiet, letting me lead Pearl through the exercises, occasionally prompting me to let Pearl work on something herself, or to give her more time with something. Pearl's mood changed, at least a little, from the initial sullen disdain she'd communicated to me in the car to a grudging admiration for my abilities and finally to a good working relationship, with math as the vehicle for our relative congeniality. This cheerfulness disappeared as soon as we moved on to the cookies and milk we got as a reward for our hard work. Pearl was once again haughty and taciturn, almost as though in retaliation for being forced to admit to my superiority in math.

Dolly, however, was full of praise for both of us. "I can't tell you children how delighted I am! I confess I had my doubts. I know you two are not the best of friends. But math has brought us all together." She beamed sightlessly at us, and I couldn't help wondering if sometime in the not-too-distant future she might hope it would be Jesus who would bring us together, and that we'd be studying scripture.

I was irritated that Miss Thornton was there at the end; I had been hoping to have a moment alone to let Mr. Hart know that I wasn't the one who didn't want to go hiking, and to ask if maybe someday we might go after all. As the four of us stood around Dolly in the living room, unnecessarily repeating our good-byes and reiterating when we'd see each other again, it occurred to me that since the Thorntons didn't ever talk to my family, I could say pretty much anything in their hearing. So I just launched in.

"I really wanted to go hiking. To Denmark Cliffs. I don't know why Lorne wouldn't let me go." Mr. Hart had a strange expression on his face, almost as though I'd thrown something at him. "Um, maybe in the spring? Maybe I can go then."

Dolly spoke up before anything else could be said about that. "It's time you were home, Jude Connor! Sakes alive, they'll wonder what's keeping you. Off you go!" She smiled broadly, and I think it was the first time I didn't believe her smile.

It was quiet in the car for the first mile or so. Then Pearl half turned toward the backseat and said, "You're so dumb."

"Pearl!" from her mother. From where I sat, in the middle of the seat, I could almost see flashes of fire between them.

"Well! He is! He didn't need to go reminding Gregory about that."

She called him Gregory? Why couldn't I? I blurted out, "About what?"

"Pearl, that's enough."

The girl sat straight forward again about as long as she could take it. Then she shot her words up at the car roof so they ricocheted back and struck me like arrows, tearing through me. "They're all terrified he's queer."

Queer. The word caught in my brain, in my throat, in my heart. It stopped my breathing. My face burned where Tim's fingers had touched it.

Miss Thornton steered the car to the side of the road and pulled the hand brake hard. "Young lady, when I say that's enough, that's enough." She turned to look at me where I sat, pinned against the back of the seat by Pearl's words. "Jude, dear, don't pay any attention to what Pearl said. Mr. Hart is a wonderful man and a faithful member of your Church. He's generous, and kind, and dutiful to his sister." She glared at Pearl.

In my stupor I barely took in Pearl's resentful posture as she threw herself into a new position, arms crossed and face turned to stare out the window. I barely remembered that Pearl had accused me of reminding him of something. All I'd done was mention hiking Denmark Cliffs. One thing that found its way through the shock was that this was probably why Lorne wouldn't let him take me hiking.

Only later, as I lay in bed reliving this scene, did I realize that Miss Thornton had said nothing that actually denied what Pearl had said. She hadn't assured me that no one thought that about Mr. Hart, and she hadn't said it wasn't true. She'd just said not to pay attention to Pearl.

And as for Pearl, who was—I knew—very fond of the Harts, why would she say a thing like that to me? Even if it were true; why say hurtful things about him to me? The only thing I could come up with was that she knew it would hurt *me,* and that was more important to her at that moment than protecting Mr. Hart. Gregory.

I thought about him differently after that. Usually it hurt.

Next Monday evening Pearl and I were back at the Harts' kitchen table, and Belinda and Gregory were in the living room again. I hadn't seen him when we arrived, and I didn't see where he came from, but I heard his voice and Belinda's in conversation, just like last time. It was distracting, trying to focus on math, when in the very next room Belinda Thornton—moral pariah—was chatting up a storm with Gregory Hart—sodomizer. I kept glancing at Dolly. Did she know? She seemed so religious, and she had a reputation for using scripture a lot, or at least of talking about God a lot. Though I didn't remember that she'd done that in my presence. But if she knew, how could she live with him?

What choice did she have? Was she trapped in *this* way, too?

Driving home that night, with everyone silent in the car this time, I felt an intense loss. I'd lost Gregory Hart. The man who had saved my skin when I'd tried to run away from home. The man who moved a tree like it was the most precious thing in the world. The man who smelled right and felt good to be around. The man who was kind to me, and gentle, and spoke to me like I mattered.

Lost. That word again.

Pearl brought peanut butter cookies to the next session. When I'd had these the first time, she'd made them not for me at all but for the Harts, so it surprised me that she would bring them when she knew I'd be consuming them. When I told

Clara, she made sure to send me off to the session after that with some of her own chocolate chip cookies.

Dolly sang their praises. "I've had Clara's casseroles and her apple crisp, so I'm not surprised these are delicious. Please thank her, Jude." She called into the living room, too. "Gregory? Belinda? You should try Clara's cookies. Come get yourselves some!"

Someone stirred in there, and I watched the door intently. Who would come through? Did I want to see Gregory? I did. And I didn't. But it was Belinda who came in, put several cookies on a plate, said "Thanks," and disappeared again.

Pearl, however, had none, despite Dolly's exhortations. She glared up at me at one point, as though I had committed some vile act merely by bringing them. She didn't do well with math that night, either.

Our treat for session number . . . five?—six? I forget—was Pearl's brownies. I loved brownies, but I was used to the kind from the box. Pearl's were different, and at first I was disappointed because they weren't familiar. If there was one treat I didn't think should be messed with, it was brownies. But being a growing and perennially hungry boy, I kept picking up another, and another, until finally I realized how good they were. What I'd been missing was that salty-sugary chemical taste; I was used to it, and I expected it. These didn't come from any box, and their moistness was from eggs, butter, and rich dark chocolate.

I capitulated. "These are great," I said, expecting Pearl to beam or express thanks or something. But no.

"I know."

It made Dolly laugh, anyway.

One thing that never happened in these sessions was Dolly even mentioning scripture. She never mentioned the Church. I had really thought she would, given her reputation and the fact that Pearl wasn't saved. Especially since Reverend King, from what Lorne had told me, was probably expecting it. It was as though Belinda had agreed Dolly and I could do Pearl this favor if we didn't impinge on their right to be heathens.

* * *

Sometime after Thanksgiving we had our first really big snowstorm. We'd had a few more little ones, and Lorne always made sure—partly through his efforts, partly through mine—that our driveway and the McNultys' were clear of snow before Gregory showed up with his plow. By this time I felt a certain solidarity with Lorne about the idea of having Gregory plow for us. The combination of discomfort and grief I felt about losing him, and why, had kept me from speaking to him since that first math session, and I understood why Lorne didn't want to be beholden to him.

But after that big storm Lorne and I were still out there, shoveling through nearly three feet of snow in our driveway, when Gregory came by. He cleared the McNultys' side first, expertly pushing the snow aside so that there was almost none that would need to be removed manually from behind the car, which was parked close to the house. Then, at our driveway, he cleared the berm at the end—that dirty, salty, icy wall that's hell to move by shovel and usually requires monstrous amounts of effort and time to shift—and waited, expecting Lorne and me to step out of the way so he could do our driveway. Looking at Lorne, I could tell he was of two minds. His chest was heaving from the effort he'd been exerting, and steam puffed out around his face as he stared at the salt-streaked blue truck, standing quietly, making his decision. Finally Lorne turned toward me, and we moved onto the stoop to watch as Gregory delivered the first installment of the wedding present he'd given Lorne and Clara. When he was finished he drove off as wordlessly as he had arrived.

I will always remember that winter. Not just for what happened, but also for what didn't. I didn't understand Pearl any better by the time we stopped our sessions in December. I didn't go and visit Dolly again after that for a long time. Gregory and I didn't break our silence. And Tim and I barely spoke. It was as though the day he'd run from our fort, after touching me the way he had, had created a barrier between us. We weren't enemies, but we were separate. Separated by what we felt, and maybe by what we wanted to feel. It was the opposite of that happiness Reverend King had told us about in his sermon. He'd said it wasn't just wealth that caused separation. He was right.

I saw Tim in my dreams, though. And I saw him in my mind sometimes, as I learned what it meant to waste my own seed.

Chapter 6

In the spring, Aurora King decided she had a crush on me. Following some progression that will always remain a mystery to me, she went from tolerating me to teasing me to giggling around me. Lorne told me it was a crush when I explained to him that she would watch me all the time, that she would smile at me whenever I looked her way.

"I'm not ready for a girlfriend," I told him. "I don't wanna get tied down."

He laughed. "Of course not, you dolt. Not yet. You'll date lots of girls. But if you start with the preacher's daughter, look out!" He laughed and winked at me, so I knew there was humor in what he said, but there was also truth. I would not start with the preacher's daughter. Who would? Who would be idiot enough to take that chance, to deliberately put himself under the scrutiny of that thunder-voiced interpreter of God's holy Word? Even spending all that time at Reverend King's house hadn't made me any less overwhelmed by him. And spending all that time at his house was another excellent reason not to be anything other than brotherly with his daughter.

In point of fact, I hadn't yet seen the girl I would "start with." Here I was, thirteen years old, and I hadn't had a crush on anyone yet. So at first, I have to admit now, the late spring resurrection of my quasi-relationship with Pearl was caused by my determination to avoid the preacher's daughter and her infatuation for me. And it was owed in part to whoever it was who kept slashing bike tires at the school; we couldn't afford to keep replacing them, so I walked to school. And to the Kings'.

I'd noticed that Pearl always walked too. Given her awkward gait, this was a project that took a lot more effort for her than it took me, and she'd probably have been much better off on a bike with its smooth, circular motion. One swelteringly hot Friday in May, as I left the school yard with my own books and school work in a backpack, I walked out of the school's front door and saw Aurora and a few of her girlfriends standing in a clutch nearby, more or less in the path I would have to take to get to the Kings'. More as a way to avoid looking at Aurora than anything else, I happened to look the other way, toward where Pearl was making her graceless way toward home. Watching her sent a pain through me, pulling at me, and I ran to catch up with her.

"Hey, Pearl."

She didn't even slow down, didn't look at me. "What do you want?"

What did I want? I hadn't got that far in my thinking. I said, "Can I carry your books for you?"

This brought her to a halt. She stared at me for an uncomfortable—to me—several seconds and then said, "Who put you up to this?"

"No one! Really. I just—" Okay, I couldn't exactly tell her that I felt sorry for her. "I thought they looked kind of heavy, that's all, and I'm trying to build up some muscle. You'd be doing me a favor."

It was true that I'd been trying to beef up a little. My scrawny child's body was grudgingly expanding into something that was beginning to look distinctly male, but I was impatient to get there. I wanted the world to look at me and think, "Wow. Now, *that's* a man!" I'd been looking for opportunities to increase my muscles, especially the ones that showed, like the ones in my upper arms.

But she wasn't buying it. "A favor? Get off it. How d'you fig-ure that, when you always go to Aurora's house after school, and I live across the meadow from *your* house? It's not the same direction at all. Why don't you carry *her* books?"

She was trying to sound like she couldn't care less about me, that I was some kind of idiot. But in those deep eyes I saw fear. It was like she couldn't think of one good reason why I'd make this offer, and she could think of several bad ones. I decided to give her a partially honest answer.

"Okay, it's not just the muscle building. There's someone I'm trying to avoid."

Pearl turned to look at Aurora, standing with her friends and watching my interchange with Pearl. Knowing that Aurora was watching made me a little frantic; seeing how quickly Pearl had understood it was Aurora I was avoiding made it worse. I was al-most ready to jettison the whole idea. I was trying to do Pearl a favor, for cripes' sake, and she was making things very unpleas-ant. "So do you want help with the books today or not?"

She turned back to me and shrugged out of her pack. "As long as it's not just my math book, sure." As soon as I'd taken her pack, she was off, leaving me to figure out how to carry two backpacks. I slung hers over one shoulder and then caught up to her. Immediately it struck me that here was something else I hadn't given any thought to: what, if anything, to talk about with her while we walked. We weren't exactly going to ex-change cookie recipes. For a good five minutes we said noth-ing, during which time I allowed myself to feel good that she seemed to walk more easily without the burden of books. Then she broke the silence.

"How come you spend so much time over there, anyway?"

"At the Kings'?"

"Yeah. It's gotta be pretty tough to avoid google eyes and gig-gles from Pretty Miss when you're practically living with her."

"I'm not! I'm not living there at all! I just go there after school. It's been since my mom died, 'cause Lorne and Clara both have to work."

"And you can't be trusted to be on your own till they get home?"

I shrugged. While it had occurred to me that they ought to trust me, it hadn't occurred to me to give voice to any objection. In the Body, one did what one was told. God decides which saints to put into authority over us, and we're expected to submit, just like that quote from Romans Clara had spouted at me when I'd chafed at not being able to go hiking with Gregory. To Pearl I said, "It's not just trust."

"What else, then?" She turned her half-pretty, half-ugly face toward me as she hobbled along.

"It's . . . you know. It's being around other"—I decided not to say saints at the last second—"other people in the Church, so we can help each other remember what's important."

"Ha! Ha, ha!" She shook her head and looked back toward the road ahead. "That's what I thought. You check up on each other. So it isn't just that the grownups don't trust you. It's that no one can be trusted to be on their own. Like the Heavens would come crashing down if one of you spent more time alone than it takes to say a prayer. My mom told me that, but I've never actually heard anyone in the Church say it."

"No, you're not getting it. We *help* each other. Wait—your mom? What does she know about the Church?"

"Oh, she used to be in it. She's told me some things."

Well, that sounded cryptic. "Yeah? Like what, for instance?"

"Things. Just things." Several steps went by while I tried to picture Belinda Thornton in the Body. Then, "How do you like the reverend?"

Truth was, I wasn't sure how I liked the reverend. We'd had several heart-to-heart conversations, just the two of us, in the weeks after my mother died. Remember that question I'd asked, about whether God had wanted my mother to die? That was the first. He'd always seemed well-intentioned, but always there was something uncomfortable between us. Looking back, I'd say that it was a gap between how I saw reality and how he seemed to see it. Like the world was this awful place, something to be got through; it made me feel sinful that I liked anything about life. And even when his gaze was focused directly on me, I felt as though he looked through me, not seeing me at all.

Pearl's question hung in the air unanswered a little too long. Finally I mumbled, "Fine. He's very good to me." This was true, after all; he'd never been anything other than patient and kind toward me, or toward his wife and daughter, either. He didn't haul out the fire and brimstone at home—just the Bible, along with that quiet, even tone of his that held my attention like he was a hypnotist.

"Does he know his daughter is crazy about you?"

"Okay, now I never said that. You're the only one who said that."

She shrugged and tilted her head to one side. "Fine. Whatever you say."

"Can we talk about something pleasant?"

"Can't we be honest?"

"What?"

"Why are you carrying my books?"

I came so close to letting her pack slide off my shoulder. I think I even lowered that side of my body a little. When I said nothing, she moved toward me and reached out her arm. "Give it to me. I don't need your pity. And it's safe to go back now; Aurora's most of the way home, so you can avoid walking with her."

I gritted my teeth, but I held onto the pack. "You could use my help, though." I looked down at her, reminding myself that she was fourteen already—a year ahead of me in age if not in school.

"And you're offering it now why, exactly?"

My eyes darted in several directions before landing back on hers. "We've got things in common."

"Such as?"

"I'm a orphan. You're . . ."

"Go ahead, say it. I'm a bastard." Hands on her hips, she stared at me, daring me to deny it or to agree with her.

"We're both different from the other kids."

"You're not different. Don't fool yourself. You're just like all the other clones in that Church. Cut from the same fake holy cloth."

"Why do you hate the Church so much?"

"Don't get me started. Now are you going to give me my pack or not?"

I hefted it up higher onto my shoulder. "I'm gonna carry it home for you, just like I promised."

She stared at me briefly and then turned and walked on. I'm not sure what I thought I'd won, but I felt like I'd won something. I followed.

It hadn't occurred to me to wonder where Pearl lived, exactly. I knew she and her mother lived on the other side of the meadow. If I'd pictured their house at all, it was as a kind of shack. What it turned out to be was a trailer—a mobile home permanently parked on a bed of cement, pine trees overshadowing one end and tall grasses and other nondescript plant growth crowding around the rest of it. There was no lawn, just a small plot of land populated by a mixture of clover and crabgrass, punctuated at random by other volunteer weeds. Their car stood at a rakish angle to the trailer. The positioning looked random, but there were track marks leading from the road to the car that had obviously been followed many times quite deliberately.

I almost missed the bicycle leaning against the end of the trailer; the whole scene was so busy. It was a peculiar contraption, proportioned oddly and painted an unlikely shade of yellow-orange. "What's with that?" I asked, pointing at it.

"My bicycle. Can I have my books now?"

As I let the pack slide down my arm I said, "It looks weird."

Her silence made me glance at her, and her eyes challenged me. "So do I."

I got it; the thing was as oddly proportioned as she was; they matched. "Where did you get a bike made like that?"

She grabbed her pack. "If you must know, Gregory made it for me. Well, that is, he adjusted a bike he found. He painted it, too."

That explained why it looked like it would be invisible alongside his tractor; it was the same color. The mention of Gregory Hart made me uncomfortable.

Miss Thornton appeared at the trailer door. "Pearl? Who've you brought home, sparrow? Oh, Jude! Why, hello. Haven't seen you in months. Are you two going to hang out for a while? Or would you like to come in for some cookies and milk?"

"No, Ma. Jude's got to get back to the Kings'. They'll send Gabriel himself out searching if he doesn't get there soon." I'd been thinking something along those lines myself, though Gabriel hadn't been in my image.

"Goodness, girl. They don't believe in archangels like that, do you, Jude?"

"No, ma'am. Not quite like that."

"Just regular angels, and saints, and things like that. But I reckon they would like to know you're safe." Miss Thornton laughed as though at a private joke. "And I expect they wouldn't be any too thrilled to hear you were at my house. Thanks for seeing Pearl home. You run along, then." And now it was "Pearl" again? What happened to "sparrow"?

Pearl picked up her book bag and headed for the door. Just before she went inside, she turned, looked at me, and raised her chin. Silent thanks, perhaps.

I hitched up my own pack and turned my steps toward the Kings', but before I'd gone ten paces I thought how silly that would be. I mean, I was so close to my own house at this point, and it was Friday, so I wouldn't even be having dinner with the Kings. Even after Lorne and Clara had gotten married, I still had supper with the Kings Tuesday through Thursday to give Lorne and Clara some time together, though I always went to the Kings' after school. But today, I didn't see any reason why I shouldn't just go home. I could call the Kings from there and let them know not to expect me at all today. I glanced at my Timex; yup, it was already four o'clock. What was the point of going all the way back to the Kings' just to turn around and come home again? This would save everyone a bunch of trouble, and me some walking on a hot day.

The quickest way home was across the meadow, of course,

not along the road that skirted all around. I waded into the underbrush that edged the road and out into the weeds that were growing longer every day as high summer approached; they hadn't mowed yet this season. The utility poles that marched away in both directions, up and down, almost seemed to be growing out of the ground themselves, embraced as they were by the undergrowth. But with their cables high overhead and humming lightly, they seemed above it all in more ways than physical distance. The tops were disconnected, in some psychic way, from everything that supported them. Or maybe it was a spiritual separation. Like, the tops, the important parts, depended on their supports, but the tops were the real reason the supports were there.

No one was home, of course; both Lorne and Clara were still at work. I dumped my books in my room and went to use the phone in the kitchen. "Mrs. King?"

"Jude, oh my goodness, is that you? Where are you? Are you all right?"

This was not the greeting I was expecting. "Yeah. I mean, yes, ma'am. I'm at home. I'm fine. I was—"

"Home? Oh, thank Heaven. Aurora said Pearl Thornton made you carry her books. What's going on?"

"Made me? No. No, she . . . I offered to. They were heavy. She has a hard time. . . ." I really didn't know how to say why I'd done what I'd done. "I just walked her home, and then since she lives so close to my house I came here. She didn't make me do anything."

There was a brief silence. "I see . . . Are you, um, where's Pearl now?"

"She's at her house. I mean, her trailer. That's where I walked her to."

"So you're at home. . . ."

I was sure I'd already established that. "Yes, ma'am. It seemed like it didn't make sense to go all the way back to your house and then come home again. Um, is that okay?" Her voice was carrying some element, some emotion I wasn't understanding. She didn't sound mad, exactly, but there was more than confusion. It hadn't occurred to me there would be a problem with my plan, but it seemed Mrs. King thought there was.

"Well, I suppose so, although it isn't what we agreed. Is Clara home?"

"No, ma'am. Not yet. But she will be, real soon. I, uh, I'll see you on Sunday. Okay?"

Another short silence. "Sure. Of course. Um, please have Lorne phone when he gets in, will you?"

My turn for silence. What on earth for? But I didn't feel I could ask. My next call was to Clara.

"Jude?" Her voice sounded worried. "Is everything okay?"

"Sure. I just wanted to see if you could get word to Lorne. I'm home, so he won't need to pick me up at the Kings' tonight."

"Home? You're at home? Why is that? Didn't you walk back with Aurora today?"

I'd had enough worried questions by this time. I was as brief as possible. And I never actually walked with Aurora, anyway. "There's no problem, honest. I'll be here when you get home. Thanks." And I hung up before she could ask anything else.

Friday night was pizza night. Clara kept frozen dough on hand and took out what we'd need on Friday morning so it could thaw, and we all had our own jobs to get the final product put together. My tasks were grating cheese and opening the can of tomato sauce. We didn't get the pre-grated mozzarella because it cost more, but I didn't mind. Tonight, though, before we did anything, Lorne called Mrs. King, and from what he said I figured he ended up talking with the reverend. After he hung up the phone, I followed him with my eyes to where he always stood to chop the pepperoni and bell peppers. He didn't say anything until he'd gotten started on his pile of thin meat circles.

Then, without looking at me, "Reverend King says it was a little upsetting that you didn't show up there after school."

"I called as soon as I got here," was my reply, uttered quickly to deflect any blame.

"I'm sure you did. But Mrs. King was worried, just the same."

"Why?"

He took a few seconds. "I'm sure you didn't think you were doing anything wrong, Jude, but she feels responsible for making sure you're okay. And she can't do that if you're not with her. And when you're not with her at a time when you've agreed to be, it makes her worry."

"She's not responsible for me."

"Well, actually, in a certain way, she is. She and her whole family took on the responsibility of making sure you'd be okay after Mom died, when I wasn't with you. I know you're not a troublemaker, Jude, but you need to understand how seriously adults take the job of making sure kids are all right. So you worried her. It would be better if you didn't do it again."

I set my grater down and looked at him. "You mean I can't ever not go there after school? Is that what you're saying? Doesn't she trust me? Don't you?" Pearl's words echoed in my brain.

Clara was paying very close attention to getting the tomato sauce spread really evenly over the dough she'd pressed into the pizza pan. Lorne looked up at me, a warning in his glance, and then back at his slicing. "Trust isn't the issue, Jude. There are lots of things that can happen to you in an hour or less. Things you might do that you don't know are wrong, or that you don't know will cause problems. Just look at today."

I went back to grating. "Today wouldn't have been a problem if you all trusted me."

"Reverend King says you walked Pearl Thornton home. Is that right?"

I was feeling a little defiant, but Lorne's tone was still even and almost casual. "Yes. She has a hard time walking because of her . . . problems. And it was super hot, and we have lots of homework, so her book bag was heavy." I was daring him to find a problem with that.

He nodded. "That's very Christian of you, Jude. And if you hadn't already had a commitment to Mrs. King, it might have been just fine. But you did." Carefully he wrapped up what was left of the pepperoni for next week. And then, a teasing note in his voice, he said, "Don't you think that's enough cheese now?"

He was right. The pile was huge. Clara smiled at me and took it away. Lorne washed his hands and then, towel still around one of them, he hugged me. "Little brother, just remember how many saints are helping us. And we need their help." He slapped my back gently and went to clean up the counter where he'd been working. "Being grateful to them is being grateful to God, because they're doing his work here on earth. The Kings have been very generous to us. In return, we need to be careful not to do anything that makes their work harder. Do you understand?"

"Yes."

He smiled at me. "I knew you would. Now, Clara, sweetheart, how long till supper?"

I wasn't altogether sure I understood what Lorne had wanted me to see, but I had gotten the message that I wasn't to break with tradition again. I chafed at these restraints, but I made no plans to do anything about it. At least, I figured, we were done discussing it. I was wrong.

Tuesday night at the Kings', after I'd helped dry and put away the supper dishes, Reverend King asked me to join him in the room he used as his office. I wasn't sure I wanted to go in there. "Lorne will be here any minute," I protested.

Reverend King held out an arm toward me. "This won't take long. Mrs. King will offer him a slice of pie if he gets here before we're done." I wondered if Lorne would get the piece the reverend had just inhaled from and hadn't touched.

His office was not a room I'd been in a lot. Even our conversation about the wandering monk who killed the cow had taken place in the dining room. In fact, I got the impression that no one spent a lot of time in here other than the reverend. I couldn't remember Aurora or Mrs. King being in here at all when I was in the house.

He closed the door and then sat behind the heavy, dark

wood desk, lowering himself into a leather chair on which I
could see white stuffing peeking out through a few cracks. I sat
on a small wooden chair with thin padding, gazing up and
around at the bookshelves that lined the small room, laden to
overflowing with books of all sizes and colors. A steady, low
hum came from the small room air conditioner that blocked
half the light from the only window, and I figured he'd been in
here for at least part of the afternoon. I looked at him atten-
tively across the uncluttered desktop, waiting for him to speak,
more than a little intimidated despite how gentle he always was
at home. He let his eyes rest on me long enough to make me
nervous before he spoke.

"Jude, do you know what it means to be saved?"

"Yes, sir. Only the saved will be with God when the Day of
Judgment comes."

"And you understand how dire the consequences are for
those who are not saved on that day?" I nodded. "Then why
aren't you saved?"

I blinked. Not saved? What could that mean? "I . . . I thought
I was."

He shook his head sadly. "Jude, how can you be saved if you
haven't died to the world and been given life again, been saved,
by the life that Jesus offers? You are not baptized, Jude. So you
are not saved."

I swallowed. He sat back in his chair, looking sad.

"I blame myself as much as anyone. Your mother would no
doubt have seen to this herself, if she were still with us, and
Lorne of course is still young and is starting his own life. It was
my dear wife, the helpmate God sent to me, who reminded me
of this oversight. And do you know how that came about?" Of
course I didn't. I shook my head. "It was Pearl Thornton. That
is, because of her. Because of the episode last week when you
disappeared."

I started to speak, but he held up his hand for silence.
"Whatever it seemed like to you, Jude, you disappeared. Mrs.
King and I take our responsibility of helping Lorne with your
care very seriously, and when you aren't where you have agreed

to be, where we expect you to be, you have essentially disappeared. And then we find that you disappeared with Pearl Thornton."

He rubbed his face and ran the fingers of one hand through his dark hair while I wracked my brain to make sense out of what he was saying. I failed.

"I'm going to ask you something very, very important, Jude, and your absolute honesty is vital." He paused to let that sink in. "While you were with Pearl, or after you left her before Clara and Lorne got home, did anything happen that you wouldn't want to tell me about? Anything that you think would sadden the heart of our Savior?"

"Like what?"

"Anything. Anything Jesus would not have done."

I shrugged and then regretted that casual gesture. What *had* I done, anyway? "I carried her books for her. Her mom came out of the trailer and offered us cookies, but I didn't have any. I went home and called Mrs. King and then Clara."

"And that's all?"

"Yes, sir." What was he asking? Did Pearl and I make out or something? Gross!

The reverend let out a long breath. "That's good, Jude. Very good. But that still leaves us with a problem. Is it safe to say that you did not invite her to church?" I nodded; should I have done that? I was feeling more and more confused. "All right. So you walked her home, you talked about—what? School?"

I couldn't remember much, except that she'd said some things about the Church that hadn't been particularly complimentary. So I just said, "And her bike. She has a bike that's, um, a little unusual." I was reluctant to drag Gregory into this discussion; I didn't know why we were having it or where it would go, so I didn't mention him.

Evidently the reverend had seen it. "Ah, yes. That yellow contraption. All right, so you talked about various things, you left her in her mother's care, and you went home alone. You didn't invite her to church. Are you aware, Jude"—and he leaned forward, arms on the desktop—"that the Thorntons are not saved? Are you aware that many attempts have been made to bring them into the Body and that they have refused? Did you know that Miss Thornton was once one of the saints and that she rejected that salvation?"

I hadn't known that until recently, but since Pearl had told me, I just nodded.

"Are you also aware that the saints do not throw pearls before swine? That we do not continue to spend time trying to coax the stubborn unsaved into the Body, beyond an occasional invitation just in case God has softened their hearts? Do you know this, Jude?"

"Yes, sir." The reference to actual pearls confused me for a second, and then I figured he'd given up on the "Tansy" Pearl after all; Dolly and I had failed.

"And do you also understand that it is actually harmful for saints to spend time in the company of the unsaved who have repeatedly scorned the offer of salvation? In his second letter to the Corinthians, Paul tells us, 'Don't be unequally yoked with unbelievers, for what fellowship have righteousness and iniquity? Or what communion has light with darkness?' " His voice got louder as he spoke. "Do you know that it can act as a temptation to spend less time in the Body, and that if we do that it becomes much harder to remain true to the path Jesus told us to follow? Do you understand that there is strength and safety in the Body but temptation and danger outside of it? Do you understand how much worse this danger is for someone like yourself who is not saved but wants to be?"

How was I going to say anything other than my meek "Yes, sir," to that?

He was quieter now. "Then you will understand why Mrs. King and I were concerned not just because you disappeared, but even more so because you disappeared with Pearl Thornton." Again, the pause for effect. It was almost like my own private sermon.

Like a fool, into the silence, I said, "But we didn't do anything we shouldn't."

He pounced. "You see, this is where it becomes so very obvi-

ous that you aren't saved. You haven't done the studies necessary to prepare you for baptism. Otherwise, you wouldn't even
need to be told that although this would be much worse if you
had done something wrong, it's plenty bad enough that you've
spent time with someone who won't be saved because she refuses to be. *And* that you weren't witnessing for Jesus during
that time." He spread his fingers apart and slapped both hands
down hard onto the desk. I jumped. "It's time you were saved."

I took a shaky breath, wondering how it could have escaped
my notice that without baptism, I was in peril. It's true that not
all kids get baptized at the same time, or at the same age, because it has to be something you're spiritually and mentally
ready for. So even though Aurora was already baptized, that was
to be expected of the preacher's daughter, so it hadn't raised
any red flags for me. But now? Now I was afraid. I was afraid for
my soul, and I knew that if I didn't get into Heaven then I really
would never see my mother again.

"Your friend Tim Olsen has just started meeting for lessons
with one of the elders, Mr. Voelker, along with a couple of boys
from another school." Something odd lurched somewhere
below my stomach. "I believe they're aiming for a July baptism.
I want you to join them. They meet every Thursday afternoon
at Mr. Voelker's house for a couple of hours. That's only about
a mile or so from here, so you could walk here afterward for
supper, so that part of our schedule doesn't change. You can
start this week. Be sure to bring your Bible and a notebook. I'll
speak with Mr. Voelker this evening."

He got up and moved toward the door, so I did, too, thinking
we were done, so I was surprised when he turned toward me
and wrapped me in his arms.

"Jude, I can't wait to welcome you into the Body. I can't wait
to share sainthood with you." He tightened his hold slightly
and then released me. "Send your brother in, will you? I'm
pretty sure I heard him arrive."

So Lorne had a turn in the office. I figured the reverend was
explaining to him about the baptism sessions. But he was in
there longer than I would have expected.

Shortly after Lorne and I got home, the reverend called me. "Great news, Jude. They've had only one baptism study session so far, and Mr. Voelker is delighted to have you join them. This Thursday, right after school. You can walk there with Tim Olsen."

"Yes, sir. Thank you." As I hung up I caught Lorne's eyes on me from where he sat at the kitchen table, a glass of iced tea and his folded hands in front of him. He nodded his head toward the chair facing him, and I sat down. Clara was nowhere in sight.

"I owe you an apology." His fingers twisted a little, knotting and releasing. "Reverend King has chastised me, and he was right to do so." I started to shake my head, but he wouldn't be interrupted. "No, he was right. I've neglected your spiritual needs. This is one of those things he meant, after Mom died, when he said there would be things I wasn't prepared to help you with."

He pinched the bridge of his nose a second. "Jude, if you had gotten much older before being saved, you would have been in very great danger. Every day a sinner goes unforgiven he's risking damnation. And the older we get, the farther into sin we're capable of getting."

"Why?"

His face told me he wasn't expecting to have to explain this. He took a deep breath. "Why," he echoed, and then paused. "Well, for two reasons, I think. One is that the older you get, the better you understand the difference between good and evil. It becomes clearer all the time what God is about, and the role that Satan plays to try and get our attention. So your own choices weigh heavier. The other reason"—he took a sip from his glass, and then another—"the other has to do with what happens inside you when you leave childhood. I'm talking about your body. God has a plan for your body, and this time of life for you is the time you need to let it grow into readiness. In time, God will make it known to you what plans he has. What you need to know now is that it involves marriage and children. But to prepare you, to let your body grow into its—um, to get ready, you need to go through a time of growth. And Jude"—he looked down at his hands, around the glass dripping with condensation—"during this time it is so easy—so very easy—to stray."

I had some idea where he was going, despite his halting embarrassment. "You're crazy if you think I'd do anything with Tansy Thornton."

Lorne glared at the use of that nickname, then sat back and let out a shaky breath. "You were pretty irritated when you thought we didn't trust you. Remember?" I nodded. "Trust is something you earn. You've earned trust from us in lots of ways, but you haven't yet been tested in this one. So for now the way you must behave is to be on the lookout for even the possibility of something wrong. Of doing anything that might make people wonder if you're doing something wrong. Over time, they'll trust you."

"I don't get it."

"Okay, well, think of Reverend King, then. Can you imagine in your wildest dreams that he would do something wrong with another woman?" I shook my head. "Why not?"

"Because . . . well, because he just never would, that's all."

"How can you be sure?"

"Because . . . I don't know! How would I know that?"

"Maybe it's because you trust him. Maybe it's because of the life he leads, the life he's been leading as long as you've known him. You trust him, because he's known for righteous behavior. So for you, this means that even though we trust you in lots of ways, you need to establish yourself in this area. And you do that by never doing anything that makes people wonder. This trust doesn't come quickly. It can't. And this time of your life, while your body is preparing for the destiny God has in mind for you, it would be very easy to make a mistake, and so it would be easy for other people to imagine you making a mistake." Another pause. "Do you understand?"

He looked almost desperate for me to understand, and I guess I knew he didn't want to have to talk about this anymore. By this point, it was pretty clear to me what everyone thought was such a problem. So I could have just nodded and that would have been it. But I was still irritated, and I was still chafing at all the scrutiny. So I said, "But you're making it sound like I have to account for every second of my day. Like I have to *prove* that I haven't done anything wrong by having someone there watching me all the time."

Lorne looked even more uncomfortable, his head shrinking down into his shoulders a little. "Well . . . it's not quite that bad. But, Jude, here's the thing. You were expected at the Kings' after school. You don't show up, which causes Mrs. King to worry. Then we find out you spent some amount of time alone with a girl. And it's even worse that she isn't in the Body. No one was with you, so for all we know Satan was tempting not only your body but also your soul. And, Jude, you're not saved."

That again. "I will be. I'm starting baptism study on Thursday."

"Yes. Thank the Lord. And thank Reverend King. But you'll still have to be on the lookout for times when your behavior—"

"I know, I know." If he was tired of it, I was exhausted. "Can I go do my homework now?" I barely waited for his nod and got away from that table as fast as I could.

In my room, pretending to focus on schoolwork, my mind moved like metal to a magnet with thoughts about Tim, and about how we'd be studying together, even if it was at Mr. Voelker's house. Thoughts of studying for baptism with Tim and about my body growing into readiness for God's plan for it weaved their way in and out of my brain, kind of like how thoughts do right before you fall asleep.

Eyes closed, I touched my face where Tim's fingers had left a permanent sensation, invisible burn marks. With my other hand I sought out that part of my body that seemed to be growing ready for manhood faster than the rest of me. I knew that what Reverend King and Lorne had in mind when they worried about Satan tempting our bodies had more to do with Pearl than with Tim. But it wasn't Pearl's face—not even her lovely eyes—that were in my mind. It wasn't Aurora. It wasn't anything female.

Through no conscious thought on my part, the fingers touching my face became Tim's. The hand wrapped around my dick was his. In vain some voice in the back of my mind protested that this was evil, this was wrong, this was unsaintly. But the voice faded and faded as Tim's hand on that growing male part of me squeezed and pulled and rubbed in a way that only a male hand would know how to do, and that hand was Tim's. The hand on my face moved to cover my mouth, and then to hold a pillow over it, stifling the sounds of painful ecstasy Tim wrung from deep inside me.

I wasted a lot of seed that night. And afterward I prayed. I knelt on the floor, leaned my arms on the bed and my head on my arms, and I prayed. I begged God to forgive me. I begged Jesus to keep Tim from committing the same sin, and especially from thinking of me the way I'd been thinking of him. I begged again for forgiveness, tears squeezing out from under my eyelids.

I felt a hand on my shoulder. It was so real I gasped and turned, expecting to find Lorne. But no one was there. No one visible. With a deep, shuddering breath, I accepted forgiveness.

Chapter 7

Thursday, I thought school would never end. If there was a bright spot, it was that Aurora seemed to have cooled toward me. Maybe my little indiscretion-that-wasn't with Pearl had made her think again. Or maybe, although this didn't occur to me at the time, the way Aurora had exaggerated the manner in which I'd walked off with Pearl—saying she had made me carry her books—had alerted the parental Kings to their daughter's interest, which of course they would want to discourage. Our age was an issue, as was the fact that I was in the house so often that there might be opportunities to—how was it Lorne had put it?—allow Satan to tempt our bodies.

Whatever the reason, it was a relief. And it left me free to speculate about the afternoon session at Mr. Voelker's. I steeled myself against rejection and then caught up with Tim at lunch to ask if he wanted to walk over together. To my delight and amazement he said "Sure," and I spent the afternoon day-dreaming about that half hour when we'd be free to talk about whatever we wanted. Or not to talk at all.

We met, at the end of that long day, in the same place where I'd asked Pearl about carrying her books. Hands in his pockets, leaning against the building, army green messenger bag slung across his body, Tim tilted his head down and a little sideways when he saw me, looking at me from the sides of his eyes. I lifted my chin in acknowledgment and moved toward him, self-consciously aware of the battered backpack I'd had for years and was still using. Tim's family was better off than mine, which wasn't difficult; but beyond that, I'd begun to notice that Tim seemed to have a knack for dressing in a way that suited him. Like he knew exactly what he looked like, it was deliberate, and it worked. Even his hair cooperated, or maybe he did something to it to make it cooperate, but it was that light-on-the-ends and dark-near-the-scalp color, strategically tousled to seem casual while probably quite purposefully positioned. That I noticed his appearance so specifically was a sign of our changed relationship. Once upon a time, I wouldn't have noticed if his pants had been torn at the knees.

He had always waited for me to speak first. "Hey," I said, trying to hide my secret delight, trying to seem like I didn't especially care that he was there waiting for me.

"Hey, yourself. Ready to get wet?"

This comment had an odd effect on me. My head knew this was his way of alluding to baptism, even though of course we wouldn't actually be immersed for weeks. Some other part of me gave a pleasant lurch, and I chuckled to cover that, feeling awkward and thrilled at the same time. "You bet."

We said little on our brief trek. I felt awkward; don't know whether he did. He gave no indication of being aware that our strides were nearly identical and that our footfalls were in synch, and I was hoping he couldn't tell how aware of it I was. But I *was* aware.

I did feel the need to have a little advance notice of what to expect. So I asked, "Who are these other guys who will be there? Reverend King says they aren't from our school."

"No. You mighta met them at church. Their folks have been dragging them to services since January. It's Larry and Bill Schumacher."

"But—they're old! I mean, they're older than us." I had seen them, though I hadn't paid much attention to them. Bill was around sixteen, and Larry maybe a year younger, but they both acted more worldly than the guys I knew who were saints in the Church, which made them seem even older than they probably were.

"Yeah. They think they know everything. We'll just see if they get saved."

"We will, though."

Tim shrugged. And we both fell back into our companionable silence while I mulled over this information and Tim's assessment.

Mr. Voelker and his family lived in a big, old, Victorian-style house, curlicues around the porch ceiling and about five different colors of paint highlighting the fussy woodwork. It had always struck me as kind of like a gingerbread house, and I loved it. I couldn't remember ever having been in it, so meeting here would be a bit of a treat all by itself.

Mrs. Voelker let us in, a flowered apron in various shades of pink covering her from neck to knees, a big smile on her broad face, and what must have been very long hair that was once all dark piled in an old-fashioned way on the top of her head. "Boys, boys, come in! Come in. Mr. Voelker will be here any minute now, and so will Larry and Bill. Why don't you go into the dining room? There's a snack in there for you. Help yourselves, but remember there will be others to share with."

I chose a chair and dumped my pack onto the floor, leaning over to dig out my Bible and hoping Tim would sit near me. He didn't; he sat across the table and down one, so we were diagonally positioned to each other. He kept looking at me, though, and then dropping his eyes, which left me feeling kind of on edge but in a good way. There were family photographs hanging on the walls and set on the sideboard behind Tim, and as I reached for a cupcake I pretended I was looking at them when his eyes flicked my way. I asked, "Don't the Voelkers have a daughter? I don't see her anywhere, just their son."

Tim's lips barely moved. "Keep your voice down, will ya? She left. Got kicked out, really. Veronica. Said she was a lezzie and wouldn't repent."

Nearly whispering, I asked, "What's a lezzie?"

"Lesbian. You know. Homo."

I nearly dropped my cupcake. "No way! Are you serious? When did she leave?"

"About a year ago, I think. Something like that."

As I scanned the photos again, verifying for myself that she was in none of them, I tried to wrap my mind around what this would mean. Of course my mind went first to the sexual aspect of it, picturing two girls together, and this sickish feeling of something weird and unnatural came over me. So I moved on to the evidence before me. Veronica had been cut out of the *family*, not just the picture frames. She didn't exist. She'd left the Body and wouldn't come back, so she didn't exist. The Voelkers now had only a son.

I tried to imagine what it would be like to be cut out of my own family. If Lorne and Clara pretended I wasn't alive anymore. If all my things that I couldn't take with me got trashed, ritually burned—I didn't have a clue what this process would look like, but I created some unpleasant and even improbable scenes for myself as we waited.

Tim opened his Bible. "Jude? You, uh, you oughta be looking over what we did last week. We read . . . hang on . . ." He opened a notebook, flipped a few pages, and ran his finger across as he read haltingly to interpret his scribbles. "Here. We read the second letter to Timothy, three sixteen and seventeen. It's about using scripture. Mr. Voelker said—here's a Latin term you need to know—*sola scriptura*, or scripture alone, is the basis for understanding God. Not like in the Catholic Church, where only ordained people are supposed to be able to understand it. And in the Body we're supposed to read it to each other and talk about it to make sure everyone understands it the same way. Did you write that down?"

I'd gotten some of it. "You didn't give me time to get my notebook out. Say it again?"

He sighed and read his notes again and then went on. "Matthew, seven thirteen and fourteen, about the gate to righteousness being narrow and the gate to destruction wide and easy to get through. Few people find the narrow way, and all others go to destruction. Got that?"

I nodded, saying, "This isn't new stuff, though."

"No, but you're gonna be asked where to find it before we get baptized. So learn it. Besides, Mr. Voelker made a real point that we're gonna be expected to use this stuff when we talk to non-Christians. Okay, next is some stuff about who Jesus was, why he was here, and how we have to try and be like him. Here." He pushed his notebook across the table toward me.

I could barely make out his notes, but I jotted down chapter and verse references. Then I made out, *Catholicism is for people who like mystery, people who don't want to know but thats not enough for us we want certainty.* His lined page was blank after that. I asked, "No more from last week?"

"Look at the beginning. There was some homework he gave us before we even started."

There were a few references from Acts there, which I jotted down. I pushed Tim's notebook back his way, watching his hand take it, and then looked up the references in my Bible. It was mostly people like Peter telling other people to repent and be baptized. I shut the book, reached for another cupcake, and tried to pretend I was looking at a picture behind Tim's shoulder. Both of us turned as we heard a car drive around to the back of the house, and then the engine cut and three doors opened and slammed shut. I returned my eyes to my Bible, Tim looked down at his notes, and we waited silently through the sounds of footsteps approaching and then coming through the back door into the kitchen. Mr. Voelker called to his wife that he was home, and Larry and Bill came through the doorway into the dining room. Larry sat across from me and Bill beside me, each landing hard in his chair so the room bounced with the force of their obvious reluctance to be here. Bibles landed slap, thud on the wooden table, then notebooks beside them, and finally pens that clattered, rolled, and had to be captured. Their moves were so much alike they seemed choreographed.

I looked up at Larry. "Hi," I said, for want of anything better to say. "I'm Jude Connor."

He didn't look at me. "Ask me if I care."

I glanced at Tim, who just shook his head slightly at me. So I gave up trying to be friendly, wishing yet again that Tim had sat across from me. As it was, I was stuck with nothing to look at but Larry's sullen, pimply face, topped with almost nothing but the scalp showing through what looked like light brown hair so short it stuck up. At least Bill had some hair on his head, even if it was kind of shapeless.

Mr. Voelker didn't leave us alone very long. Within a couple of minutes he came into the room, sat at the head of the table beside me, and smiled at all of us. The room felt better already.

His eyes fell full on me. "Jude Connor"—and he held out his hand for me to shake—"welcome. I'll be calling you 'brother' before the summer is out!"

His Bible before him, he sat quietly for several seconds. Then, "What is baptism?" No one said anything, so he said, "Tim?"

"Um, being immersed into water, dying to sin, and being saved."

"What must you do before you go into the water?"

"Repent."

"What does that word mean?" Silence. I actually knew, but I was afraid of saying anything. Didn't want to stick my neck out. Then he said, "Jude, do you know?"

"It means to change your path. Stop doing what you've confessed. Stop doing whatever that sin was."

"Very good. So, Tim, you're not wrong, but the process goes like this: hearing and understanding the Word of God, confession of ways in which you were not living according to his Word, repentance, immersion and spiritual death, and being reborn into the Spirit of Jesus Christ. Then, rejoicing."

He looked around, and I snuck a peek at the others. Tim was looking at him, but Bill and Larry were both pretending they were interested in something else.

Mr. Voelker spoke again. "Bill, once you are saved, can you be lost again?"

"I'm never lost. I've lived here all my life." A snort came from Larry that was probably supposed to be a chuckle.

Mr. Voelker let some time go by and then said, "Jude?"

"Yes. You can fall."

"Anyone can fall from Grace, no matter who they are, no matter how deeply they repented at one time. Repentance doesn't count if you go back to a sinful life. Will just one sin do it?"

Tim said, "No."

"Why not?"

"Well . . ." and Tim fell silent.

"As saints, we live in the Body of Jesus Christ, right here on earth, in preparation for God's Kingdom. Our brothers and sisters love us and support us, and when one of us sins—which is something that happens from time to time, despite our best intentions—they let us know they have seen it, if we don't confess it first, and then we repent. Sometimes it's necessary, if things have gotten really bad, to be baptized again. But to really fall from Grace, you would have to leave the Body. You would have to turn your back on God's Word and on his direction for our lives. It would have to be deliberate. But if a saint chastises you for a sin and you don't confess and repent it, you have begun your fall. Questions?" No one said anything. Not even about Veronica. "Why do we get baptized?"

Tim was quick with his response. "For the remission of sins."

"Who may be baptized?" Silence. "Can infants be baptized?"

"No." Tim again.

"Why not?"

"They can't understand the Word of God. They can't confess or repent."

"That's right. We can see more specifically how this happens by reading the Bible where baptism is discussed. I gave you a few references last time. Here are some additional ones, and you should be able to summarize what they mean by the time we meet next week." He rattled off several things, and I scribbled them down.

Mr. Voelker did his best to get Larry and Bill involved as he went over some verses from Isaiah about how sin separates us from God and makes it impossible to have a relationship with him, but they sat there, silent and sullen. He got a little more pointed with a verse from the first letter of Peter about how everyone is either in darkness or light, that we can't hang out in a middle ground for very long without things getting darker and darker for us. Jesus brings the light, which makes the dark darker, and if we don't turn toward the light we'll be lost in darkness. We'll be destroyed. It was pretty grim stuff. At first it scared me a little, but then I decided he was just trying to convince Larry and Bill. But then I got scared again. If I didn't get baptized, I would be like Larry and Bill, who really didn't look like they were headed for immersion anytime soon.

After an hour and a half, Mr. Voelker ended the session. "Next time we'll talk about who has sinned, what sin is, and what the consequences of sin are." He rattled off a few more references, and I thought we were done. But before he stood, he looked at each one of us in turn. Then he said, "As you go over the material for next week's discussion, I want you to keep one question for yourself in the back of your mind: Are you afraid to die?"

I was still sitting there, mouth hanging open a little, eyes still glued to Mr. Voelker's face, after everyone else stood. He smiled at me and said, "I'm going to drive Larry and Bill home now. Anyone else need a ride?"

"No, thank you, sir," I mumbled, breaking the spell and looking at Tim, who said something similar. Good; we could walk partway together before I had to turn toward the Kings'.

But as we walked I was still a little overwhelmed by the boldness with which Mr. Voelker had asked that question. Part of my mind wanted to be angry with him for having the nerve to ask it. But most of me was expending a good deal of energy to try and pretend it wasn't affecting me, and this kept me too busy to think of anything to say to Tim until he broke with tradition and spoke first.

"You got some boning up to do, Jude. I didn't think I knew scripture better than anybody, but I think I got you beat."

I wanted to deny this, but there had been several times during the course of the session that he'd known things, that he'd been able to dredge up quotes and references that escaped me completely. Plus, he made it okay that I needed help when he added, "We oughta get together sometime, maybe over the weekend, and work. D'you wanna come over on Saturday for supper and then work on this stuff for a while? Then maybe we could, you know, watch TV or something."

I did. I very much did. This was the breakthrough I'd been— well, not praying for, exactly, because somehow it didn't feel like something that God would want to get involved in. But I'd sure been hoping. "I'll have to check, but I think so. Can I let you know tomorrow?"

"Sure. Just need time to break the news to my mom!" His laugh made me smile. "If supper won't work, maybe we could still study after."

"You're on," I said in a voice calculated to hide the energy rushing through me. We walked twenty paces or so in silence, and then I asked, "So, what's with Bill and Larry? They don't seem that anxious to get baptized."

"Nah. Their folks are making them do it. The parents got baptized recently, don't you remember?"

"Sort of. I guess. So now they're trying to get their kids to convert?"

"Yup. Looks like a lost cause to me. I'm trying to pretend those jerks aren't there."

I nodded; seemed like a good approach. "Um, d'you think Mr. Voelker's gonna want an answer to that question he asked at the end?"

"The one about being afraid to die? Doubt it. He ended last week's session with it, too. I think he's just trying to remind us that if we die without being saved, we go to Hell."

I kicked at a small stone and missed. "Do you think about that?"

He shrugged, looking down at his feet. "Not really. Not until I have to. You?"

"Well . . . you know my mom died a couple of years ago? She was saved and all, so she's in Heaven. But she wasn't that old. So, I guess it could happen to anyone. It could happen to me. And this kinda snuck up on me. Getting baptized, I mean. Why haven't you done it before now?"

Another shrug. "Guess I wasn't ready. My dad asked me once or twice last year, then he asked me again after the Schumachers did it, and I figured it was time. I mean, I believe, and all. I just wasn't quite ready before."

I considered this for several paces. "I hadn't even thought about it." I kicked at another stone. Missed again. "My brother feels like he should have had me do it sooner." I wanted to bring up some of what Lorne had said about our bodies getting ready for God's destiny, but I could already see the intersection where I'd have to split from Tim's direction. I punched him on the shoulder and dashed ahead. As I veered off, I turned and waved. "See you in school tomorrow."

He saluted, his head cocked, half smiling. I wanted to watch him disappear down the road, but somehow I knew I shouldn't do that.

I had no trouble getting permission to have Saturday supper at the Olsens'; I think Lorne and Clara were glad to have the house to themselves for the evening. I'd been to Tim's house once or twice the first summer I spent at the Kings', including a few suppers, but not since then. No one seemed to think this was odd; no comments about it, even from his little sister Nancy, who was a pain in the neck.

I'd been hoping we'd go to Tim's room to study, but he led the way into the living room. His sister and mom went into the family room to watch an ancient Disney DVD. *Dumbo.* I remember thinking that I'd even be willing to watch something old and stupid like that if we even had a DVD player at my house. Mr. Olsen came with Tim and me and sat reading something in a chair across the room while Tim and I sat on the floor, the coffee table between us. Tim was about in the middle on his side, and I was at one end on mine. At one point I moved a little closer to the middle, pretending to stretch my legs and change positions. Almost immediately Tim moved farther along his side, away from me. I didn't try getting closer again.

Somewhere between Romans three twenty-three (everyone has sinned, no exceptions) and Galatians five twelve to twenty-one (descriptions of what sin is, such as lustfulness and sexual immorality), my attention wandered away from the tender way Tim's head bent over his work and the soft curve of his fingers on his pen, and toward the strains of music coming from the next room, where *Dumbo* was playing. I heard a woman's voice singing a lilting melody that sounded unaccountably familiar. I caught just a few of the words—something about not letting what other people say make you cry. It seemed like a lullaby, and I heard the phrase "baby mine" over and over.

By the time Mr. Olsen drove me home I had made a lot of progress on my baptism studies. But in terms of my friendship with Tim, I felt as though we had taken a few steps back. Sure, we were speaking again, and we were studying together. But he wouldn't let me touch him. Because of the forgiveness I'd been given that night I had masturbated with Tim's imaginary hand on me, I chose to believe friendship was all I wanted to give him, or to get from him. But there was something between us. I could feel it, almost touch it. I just couldn't shift it.

By the middle of July it was evident that Tim and I would be the only ones being baptized that month. Twice Mr. Voelker was late arriving, and when he came into the dining room he was alone. I heard him tell his wife that Bill and Larry had not been where they were supposed to wait for their ride.

I loved the sessions without the Schumacher troublemakers. It was just Mr. Voelker, Tim, and me in the warm room, talking about really important things, being open and honest and hopeful and afraid together. Sometimes it was so heady I felt a little dizzy and weak, but in a very pleasant way. It was all the more poignant because I realized I *was* afraid to die. And all the photographs around me, Veronica Voelker conspicuously absent from all of them, reminded me that there was more than one way to die.

Our immersion was set for after the service on the last Sunday in July. On the Thursday before, our last session felt disappointing. I'd expected to feel anticipation, excitement, maybe even a little joy. But it was heavy, dull, subdued.

Reverend King was waiting for me in front of the Voelkers', watching from the air conditioning of his four-wheel-drive Jeep, a vehicle I'd heard him express thanks for on several occasions when he had to get through bad weather to church or to some saint's house. I hadn't expected him to pick me up. Mr. Voelker had walked Tim and me to his front door, a hand on each of our shoulders. When I saw the Jeep I felt his hand tighten slightly. I looked behind me, up at his face, and it looked tense, ready for something unpleasant. Then I noticed that Tim's head was down, like he didn't want to look at me. This felt wrong, or like something bad was going to happen. I stopped moving. But Mr. Voelker's hand on my shoulder pressed me forward.

Odd things flashed through my mind. Had everyone hidden things from me? Was there some bizarre preparation, an initiation or something, that Tim knew about and I didn't, that was about to happen? Feeling deep trepidation I opened the passenger side of the Jeep and got in. I wanted to wave to Tim. I wanted to call, "See you." But this thing that I couldn't identify was too oppressive.

A minute or so after Reverend King put the car in motion, his voice sounding strained in a weird way, like he was trying too hard to sound casual, he said, "How was your last session, Jude? Are you ready to join the Body?"

"Yes, sir. I'm ready. Tim and I—"

"I'm not asking about Tim, Jude. Just you. You have to do this alone. You understand that, don't you? This is *your* work, *your* critical moment, *your* personal relationship with God. You must take this step as though no one existed in the world but you." He waited through my silence and then gave up. "Jude?"

"Yes, sir. Between me and God. Yes. I know." What was he telling me? I felt like there was some secret hidden between his words, and I struggled to decipher it. In vain.

We drove in silence to the house and then he told me to come with him into his office. Maybe he was just going to test me? To be sure I'd learned what I was supposed to? Even though Mr. Voelker had done that, did Reverend King feel a sense of commitment to me because of how I nearly lived here, like Pearl had said? I had more thoughts bounce through my brain than there were steps between the Jeep and the chair in that office.

It was cool, at least, with that window air conditioner humming away. Reverend King lowered himself slowly, deliberately, into his chair behind the desk and laid his arms on the uncluttered top. And he stared at me. I looked back at him, expectantly, anxiously, eyes darting from his to some mindless spot and back again, wondering what on earth he wanted me to do. Finally he spoke.

"I have spoken with Tim." He waited. And waited.

I gave up. "About what?" What kind of a test was this?

"About you."

I shook my head vaguely, fought the urge to shrug. "Why?"

He sat back, watching my face closely. "Are you a liar, Jude?"

My turn to sit forward. "No sir! Why would you ask that?"

Leaning toward me suddenly, his voice a hoarse whisper, he said, "What is Tim to you? How do you feel about him? How do you think of him?"

I'm sure I blushed. I fought to quell images that had come into my head at night, alone in my bed. "He's my friend. I've known him all my life."

"You haven't answered my question. How do you *feel* about him?"

I went for the rote response. "He'll be my brother in the Body of Christ. I love him."

"Would it surprise you to learn that he has impure thoughts about you?"

Now *that* did surprise me. Despite that touch a year ago in our fort, I had come to the conclusion that Tim was not thinking of me the way I was thinking of him. If he were, how could he be so remote? For a whole year? Truthfully, I answered, "Yes, sir. It would."

What had Tim said? What was I to him? How much trouble had he got us both into? This wasn't fair! I'd never said a word to anyone about *him!* I grew angrier by the second.

"What are you feeling right now, Jude?"

I took a deep, shaky breath. "Anger. I'm angry at Tim. I can't believe he would say that. Especially right now!"

"Why right now?"

"We're—I'm about to get baptized! I have to have a *pure* and loving heart to do that and do it right; Mr. Voelker said so, and I know what he means. My heart was pure and loving. Now I'm angry." Tears stung my eyes, born of fury and betrayal. How could he do this to me? "What did he say?"

"Never mind the specifics. What we need to do right now, you and I, is to make sure that your love for him is saintly. That it's God's love, shared among Christians. Do you understand what I mean when I say impure thoughts?"

My breathing was thick, heavy. "Yes, sir."

"Tell me."

"It means thoughts that . . . that aren't pure. Um, thoughts that have something other than"—and I used a form of his own word here—"saintliness in them. Thoughts that are inappropriate."

"It means that and more, Jude. What you've described could be said to happen between a boy and a girl. What we're talking about is much, much worse. Do you understand how God views homosexuality?"

"It's a sin."

"It's a huge sin. It separates you from God, from your family, from all the other saints like few other sins can do. It brings isolation and evil into your life and prompts you to involve others,

to drag them down with you. It *will* not, *cannot* be tolerated."
He paused, eyes searing into me. "What have you got to say
about this situation?"

"I'm not a homosexual." A lie, though I didn't know it at the
time. I hardly knew what it meant to be homosexual. And then
came a lie I *did* know was a lie: "I never think about him like
that."

Reverend King sat back and rubbed his face, ran a hand
through his hair. He looked like he was in pain. "I believe you
think you're telling the truth. And maybe you are. But I need to
warn you that if you have even one shred of this unnatural feeling in your heart on Sunday, your baptism will fail. Even if you
and God are the only ones who know, no matter how thoroughly you're immersed or what I say as I plunge you under the
water, it will fail. You will be condemned to everlasting Hell.
You might lie to me and get away with it, but you cannot lie to
God. He knows what's in your heart, better than you do, yourself. So. I'm going to ask you again. And remember that if you
need more time, we can help you through a time of trouble.
This is not hopeless. But redemption comes only with honesty,
Jude. So. Are you hiding even a shred of this feeling in your
heart?"

I was going to Hell. There was no way around it. And then I
remembered something Mr. Voelker had said, about how a second baptism was an option. And a plan occurred to me, in
which I would get baptized on Sunday after making an agreement with God that I would do it again sometime in the future
when I'd worked this thing out. There was no way—in Hell or
anywhere else—I was going to have Lorne know that I har-
bored these very feelings Reverend King had just called evil
and unnatural anywhere inside me. No way. Plus, at this point,
I didn't want to give that traitor Tim the satisfaction. I even
managed—and all this in the span of a few nanoseconds—to
decide that since Tim had betrayed me and had essentially lied
to me all year, I didn't feel about him the way I used to, it wasn't
even really a lie, and maybe I didn't really have any evil shreds
hiding in the inner recesses of my heart after all.

"I'm not hiding anything. I have nothing to hide. I might need your help to forgive Tim for putting me in this position, but I have nothing evil in my heart."

Reverend King opened a drawer, pulled out a yellow paper tri-folded like a brochure, and handed it to me. It looked like something he'd probably printed out on his own printer. On the top fold it said, **Homosexuality = Sexual Immorality.** Inside the fold was a list of scriptural references. Six of them.

"You have one more assignment, Jude. One more before you can die in Christ and be resurrected through his love. Before the service on Sunday, you and I will step into the antechamber together, alone, and you will recite all the verses in these scriptures. By heart. And you will have one more chance to ask for help. If you convince me that you need no help, and we go forward with your baptism, it will be a joy like no other for you if all is well in your heart. It will be as bitter and black and painful as anything you will ever do if you are lying to me, because you cannot lie to God. Do you understand?"

"Yes, sir."

He never did tell me exactly what Tim had said, but he said that he and Mr. Voelker felt that Tim was not yet ready to give up what he knew he would have to give up in order to be saved. Those words echoed in my head for a long time: what he knew he would have to give up. Was that me?

So Tim would not be baptized on Sunday with me. I really would be alone. I guessed he had some more work to do, to get over those impure thoughts about me. The reverend and I sat for about an hour, missing the start of supper, as he went over those six scriptures, and then he helped me learn to forgive Tim. Or I let him think he did.

Driving home with Lorne that night, I found out that he'd been told about this revelation. He broke the ice, though I could tell he didn't want to. "You've sorted out this, uh, this thing with Tim. You and the reverend."

"Yes." I truly didn't know what else to say.

"And you're going forward? With your baptism?"

"Yes."

"Do you want to talk about any of it?"

"Not really. There's nothing to talk about."

I heard him sigh deeply, and his hands on the wheel relaxed. "I'm glad." And that was it. Except that I'd lied to Reverend King and now I'd lied to Lorne. Maybe I didn't think of what was in my heart as evil, but I knew everyone else would. So on the brink of my baptism, I began my fall.

I worked and worked on those six verses to make sure I knew them cold, until the words themselves ceased to have any meaning. I had expected it might be difficult; I had expected they'd make me think of Tim. They didn't. They had nothing to do with how people *feel* about each other. And in spite of my anger and his betrayal, on some level Tim was still Tim to me, and these verses had nothing to do with how I felt.

Even so, I lost some sleep thinking about some verses that did seem pertinent to my life—the ones from Isaiah that we'd studied in baptism prep about how sin separates us from God. How it puts up a barrier. Right about now I felt like there was a barrier between me and everybody. I felt isolated from Reverend King and from Lorne, and nothing with Tim would ever be right again. I had no one. Maybe I would have had Gregory, but Pearl's arrow words had lodged in me. If Gregory was a homosexual, or even if it was just that people thought he was, I couldn't afford the association.

I was more alone than I'd ever been. Even when my mom had been sick, I'd had Lorne. Now I had no one. The only thing I could conclude was that homosexuality was where the sin came from—just like the Bible said. Just like Reverend King said. That must mean that what I was hiding, and the act of hiding it, were sin. So as Sunday approached I was terrified. I feared that God, knowing what was in my heart, would not let me come up out of the water. I would drown, die for real, go straight to Hell, and never be with my mother again.

I went round and round trying to decide whether I should come clean, tell Reverend King that I felt about Tim the same way he felt about me. He'd said there would be help. But what kept coming back to me was that those six verses didn't seem like me at all, didn't seem to be condemning anything about me. So what was the good of "help"? What was the point of further struggle? And then, as I'd already figured out, if I got to the other side of this baptism and still felt like there was something wrong, I could confess then, repent then, and get baptized again. It was the best plan I had.

On Sunday I recited the verses to Reverend King. Somehow I got through them.

After the service I got into my spirit cloth in the bathroom and tossed my clothes into the trunk of Lorne's car. Clara made me sit in front; it was my day, she said. Other cars followed us to the spot we used on the river for warm-weather baptisms.

Lorne and Clara stood on the river bank with the other saints, smiling, looking much happier than I felt. Everyone started singing "Down to the River to Pray" while they clapped in rhythm. As inconspicuously as possible, I looked for Tim. He wasn't there.

It was overcast but not raining. Reverend King, also in white, waded into the water ahead of me and beckoned me to follow. One hand on my shoulder, in loud, round tones he said, "Jude Amos Connor, do you accept the Lord Jesus as your Savior?"

"I do."

"Have you confessed and repented your sins, and have you been as honest with your brothers and sisters and with God as you know how to be?"

"I have."

"Are you afraid to die?"

I tried not to gasp. I'd attended many baptisms, and I'd never heard this question asked at one before. I reminded myself that I was about to die to the world, and that Mr. Voelker had done his best to prepare me for this. But it was still unexpected. And I was half afraid of actually dying right here, today. What was the correct response? The others had been standard formula. Finally I managed, "No, for I will rise again in Jesus."

"Then come, die to the world, and live again in the Body of Christ Jesus."

The hand on my shoulder moved behind my head, his other arm wrapped around my back, and—as Mr. Voelker had instructed—I held my nose with one hand and folded both elbows against my waist.

It's an odd feeling, being totally helpless in the arms of a man to whom you've lied. A man whose own righteousness is without flaw, a man whose love and trust you have just violated. Whose love and trust you believe you've lost, because you're not worthy of it. Because you've willfully, knowingly, turned your back on it.

He held me under for maybe three seconds to be sure I was completely immersed, and then he pulled me up and wrapped me fully in his arms, laughing and saying, "Oh, brother Jude! Welcome to the Body! Welcome to God!"

There were shouts of "Halleluiah!" from the crowd, and more singing. I felt like crying. But at least I didn't really die.

Tim and I barely spoke after that. He must have managed to convince himself I was out of his system, though it took a while—all the way to January; I tried not to feel gratified. I attended his baptism and stood with the other saints in the damp, blue-and-gold-tiled, echoing baptism room, swaying with the rhythm of the hymn everyone was singing, clapping along with them, shouting when appropriate. Lying, again. Lying, still.

Chapter 8

Becoming friends, real friends, with Aurora King was not something I would have predicted. Nor would she have, I dare say. We both turned fourteen before Tim's baptism—me in November and Aurora in December. Christmas day. And for a gift that year, Aurora got a computer. That was the start.

No one at the Kings' house knew much about computers. The reverend had one in his office, but it was hardly state-of-the-art. Dennis Tillman, a brother who owned a computer sales and service place, had donated it years ago, and it's possible he set it up with all the bells and whistles of the day. But all the reverend needed it for was churning out sermons, so as long as the word processing program and the printer could keep talking to each other, that was enough.

Aurora got a laptop with purple on its casing, and purple on the extra screen to use when she was at her desk, plus her own printer. Dennis set everything up including Internet access, which was new to that house. It was new to me. I had no computer. Even so, when Aurora began to bog down figuring out how to use it, she came to me.

"I don't know anything about computers," I told her from where I lay sprawled on the bed in the room I used in that house, reading an assignment for school, trying not to glare and willing her go away. "You should ask your father to get Mr. Tillman back."

She leaned against the doorjamb, her face morphing into something that looked both coy and helpless. If I hadn't been absolutely convinced that she'd outgrown that crush she once had on me, I'd have been worried. Just as I turned my eyes back to my book, hoping to give her a hint, she said, "I can't. I told Daddy I already knew how to use a computer."

My eyes jerked up to hers. She had lied to her father? *To Reverend King?* I'd thought I must be the only person on earth who would be stupid enough to do that. And here was his daughter, his morning sun, telling me we had this in common. I sat up. To gain time, to decide how to approach this new landscape, I said, "What'd you do that for?"

She must have sensed an opening, because she came to sit on the edge of the bed. "When I asked him for a computer, he said no because I didn't know how to use one, and he said I'd never use it. He's not very with it on these types of things, you know. So I . . . well, I lied, I guess."

"I guess you did." That was when I began to take her a little more seriously. "What kind of help do you need?"

Growing more animated as she talked, she told me about her e-mail account, and how some friend had sent her a link she couldn't open. She was embarrassed to admit to her friend that she didn't know what to do. I had some idea what e-mail was, but beyond knowing that things called "sites" existed on the Internet, my knowledge didn't go very deep. All I could do was repeat that I didn't know anything about it. She pleaded, "Couldn't you just come and look? Couldn't you try? Maybe together we could figure it out."

I watched her face for a few seconds, making sure she wasn't just pulling my leg. Then I followed her into her room, where I'd never been. I'd walked past it and had been so overwhelmed with the color combination that I hadn't wanted to look closer. There was lots of white and splashes of purple, blue, and orange. A poster of some Christian rock band was over her desk, where the computer sat waiting for its secrets to be revealed.

Not knowing what I would do first, I sat at the desk. Aurora told me in about five sentences the extent of her understanding, and I followed her instructions using the mouse and the keyboard. Pretty soon I was clicking all over the place, experimenting with what would happen.

"Stop!" Aurora shrieked. "What are you doing?"

"Trying to figure this out. Have you tried this? Or this?" And I clicked again and again.

"Don't hurt anything!"

"I won't." Yeah, right; like I had any idea whether I could "hurt" anything or not. As far as I knew, I didn't hurt anything that day, or any of the other days she let me come in to play around on the thing. Allowing me to use it was my reward for getting her link working and then finding another site for her to send back to her friend. She was thrilled.

The computer was like our facilitator. Our moderator. And it built a bridge between us, or at least gave us the raw materials. I played around to discover how things worked and what else could be done, and I taught her. It was just like Dolly had said: Teaching Aurora helped deepen my own understanding.

By March, I had figured out how to do research for school-work, which was a huge win; it helped Aurora add some special touches to a paper she had written on the life of Martin Luther, which netted her an A grade on it. I had just arrived at the Kings' after school the day she got the graded paper back—our friendship did not replace the connection she had with her girlfriends, and we still walked separately to her house after school—when she came dancing in and presented the paper to her mother. In response to Mrs. King's praise, Aurora surprised me with her generosity by saying, "I couldn't have done so well if Jude hadn't found some really cool Internet sites for me."

Mrs. King turned to where I stood frozen in the doorway from the kitchen, about to head upstairs, and she smiled. It was a big, warm, motherly smile, and it had in it all the tenderness I could have hoped for from my own mother. I nodded—embarrassed, pleased, hurting—and bounded upstairs.

On the drive home that night, I asked Lorne if he thought I might be able to get a computer of my own. I was hooked, and this was the proof; I'd never asked for anything expensive in my life. Not even a new bicycle.

He contemplated this for a minute and then asked, "What would you do with it?"

"For one thing, schoolwork. I helped Aurora with some research that helped her get an A, and I'm getting real good at using the Internet."

He nodded slowly, then said, "So you're using hers. Why do you need one, when you're there as much as you are?"

I blinked. Was he crazy? And then I realized it was just that he'd never used one. "Well, it's hers, not mine. Two people can't use the same computer to do research on different things at the same time. If she's doing her stuff, I can't use it at all. Besides, I need my own e-mail address."

"Your own e-mail? Why?"

I let a lungful of air out loudly. "It's how you communicate on the Internet." I watched his face as well as I could in the dark car. I knew there would be no point in rushing him.

Finally he said, "Well, Jude, actually I have to talk to you about something. It's sort of related. . . . It's Clara. I mean, Clara and me. We're going to have a baby."

My brain felt foggy; where was this coming from? I gave up trying to figure out what it had to do with computers and, like most teenagers, started wondering how it would mess up my life. I barely remembered to say, "Wow! That's great."

He was smiling now, a huge smile. "Yeah. It is. It really is. We didn't want to say anything too soon. They tell you to wait until after the first trimester in case something goes wrong. So come September, you'll have a niece or a nephew."

"Wow." I knew I was repeating myself, but I really didn't know what else to say. I let a little time go by, struggling not to dwell on details like where the baby would sleep, and how soon

I'd be kicked out of my room. When I felt enough time had gone by I brought up the computer again. "Um, so, what does this have to do with the computer?"

"Ah. Yes. Well, Jude, you may not realize this yet, but babies are very expensive. We'd been kind of hoping to get into a bigger place before Clara got pregnant, but we haven't been able to save as much as we'd hoped. So there's no money for things like computers." In the silence of the next several seconds, my heart fell about to my knees, and I began to associate unpleasant thoughts with this baby. Lorne added, "I'm sorry."

I forced myself to say, "That's okay. The baby is more important." He went on about telling her folks next, and how much a baby shower would help with what they'd need.

Just before we pulled into our driveway I got up the guts to ask, "Where will it sleep?"

"We'll have a crib in our room so Clara can feed him at night, and so we'll know right away if there's a problem."

I decided not to ask how long that would last.

My new friendship with Aurora encountered a few bumps in the road, as I wanted to spend more and more time on her computer, in her room. Not only did she also want to use it, but when her girlfriends came over after school, they all wanted to hang out in her room. I offered them my room, but they just laughed. I could have taken the laptop into my room, but there was no Internet access in there; wireless connectivity had not been part of the installation.

Then one Tuesday afternoon when Aurora and a couple of her friends were hogging her room and, probably, the computer, too, Reverend King came to find me. I was sprawled on the bed upstairs as usual; I used the desk sometimes, but I liked sprawling. I was glad I had remembered to take my shoes off as soon as I saw the reverend appear in the doorway. I sat up straight.

He glanced around the room, nodded once or twice, smiled, and said, "I hear you've been helping Aurora with schoolwork."

"Yes, sir. Well, that is, I've helped her do some research, a few times. She did the work." I figured that was the safe thing to say. And it was true.

He nodded a few more times, and I started to wonder if he had a problem with my being in her room. But then he said, "I've asked Brother Dennis to have an Internet connection put into my office. I'll need a newer computer." He moved into the room, pulled the wooden chair away from the desk and sat with his legs on either side of the back, facing me. "He'll get me all set up, but I gotta tell you, I'm sure as heck going to need some help when he's gone. I'd like to count on you for that, Jude."

Well, this certainly wasn't anything I had expected. "Oh. Well, sure. I mean, I'm no expert, but I can show you a few things."

A few more nods, and then, "I reckon I'll get the basics all right, but I'm doing this so I can do research. Find some Christian sites. And I want to set up some connections with other Churches, share experiences. Do you think the Internet can help me do that?"

"Yes, sir. That's exactly what it does, as far as I can see. You might need a site for our Church. . . ."

"Brother Dennis says he'll put me in touch with someone who'll donate Web design. Does that make sense to you?"

I wanted to ask him what made him think I'd know. But if Mr. Tillman had recommended it, I'd go along. "Yes, sir. It does."

He turned and gazed at the mostly empty desk for a few seconds. "Seems to me"—and he turned back toward me again—"that there's room right here for a computer."

He must have seen my eyes widen; his smile did the same. I couldn't bring myself to believe this! A computer, right here? But—"There's no Internet connection here."

"There will be, son." He stood up and held out his hand, and I got to my feet like lightning. "I'll make a bargain with you. If you'll help me with my work, and if you take a solemn vow not to use the computer or the Internet for anything Jesus wouldn't do, you can have your own connection, computer and all, right here. What do you say?" His warm hand was still in mine, and I pumped it. He closed his other hand over mine and shook it once or twice, grinning at me.

"Thank you, sir! Thank you so much! I really appreciate it. And I'll help you whenever you need it. Weekends, even."

"We'll see, Jude. We'll see."

He let my hand go but stood there. I felt like I needed to say something, to make it clear that depending on the kindness of others wasn't the only way I tried to help myself. "I, uh, I did ask Lorne if maybe we could get one. . . ."

"Yes, I know. He mentioned it to me. He's not at all clear on what you'd do with it, but he felt real sorry that he couldn't get one for you since you seemed to want one so badly. He's worried that you're going to feel a little left out, with the baby coming. Babies are attention magnets, Jude, and they tend to yank it away from everything else without meaning to. They just can't help it." My turn to nod. "Are you worried about that?"

"The baby?" I half shrugged. "I guess I'm kind of wondering what it will be like, having it in the house. They'll have a crib in their room at first, but that can't last forever."

Reverend King sat down again. "I haven't talked with Lorne about his finances in any great detail. There will be help from the Body for them in terms of caring for the baby, if they want it, but perhaps Clara would rather stay home with the child for a time. That would mean no salary."

"So, no saving for a new house."

"That's what I'm thinking. Mind you, I don't know. But the reason I'm bringing this up now is that I want you to know what I told Lorne, and that is that our offer still stands. If it works out best for everyone, you could come live here. This would be your room."

I looked around with new eyes. With a computer and the Internet, this small, impersonal, unremarkable room could be a haven. The computer screen, I had begun to realize, was a portal to the world, and it had no boundaries.

Reverend King laughed softly and slapped my shoulder. "We'll see how things go, Jude. Meanwhile, it will be here whenever you need it. Now, supper's almost ready."

He left, and I began automatically to collect my things. With my pack still open and the last book in my hand, I stopped and looked around again. If this were my room, I wouldn't need to pack everything up when supper was ready. I could have my own stuff here. I could fall asleep at night in this bed and then watch the morning sunlight creep up the sides of the mountains.

Then I realized what I wouldn't have. No more listening to Clara sing hymns as she got breakfast ready. No more Friday pizza nights. No more Lorne in my life, really. I'd have lost my family. What was left of it.

I shoved that last book into the pack, hefted it, turned the light out, and went down to have supper with this family that wasn't mine.

Driving home with Lorne later, I told him about the computer Reverend King was putting into the room I used. His voice sounded like he was trying to convince me he thought that was great. Then, silence. I turned in the seat to watch his face. "Would it be easier for you and Clara if I weren't there? In the house?"

His head snapped in my direction and then back to the road. "No, Jude. It wouldn't be easier. We're your family. It's your home. I know Reverend King's offer is still open, and maybe you want to take him up on it, but that's not what Clara and I want." He breathed audibly for a few seconds. "Do you remember what we talked about after you ran away on your bike?"

"Yes."

"Tell me."

I took a deep breath. He'd said exactly what I'd wanted him to say. But now that he'd said it, I wasn't quite as sure. "That we wouldn't be better apart. That we'd stay together."

"And you promised not to run away again."

"But going to the Kings' wouldn't be running away!"

"Not exactly, no. But if you decide to do that, it should be for the right reasons. I don't know what those reasons would be, but I do know that your leaving is not what Clara and I want." He glanced at me again, and away. "What do you want?"

"I want to stay with you." Once I'd said it, I believed it. Lorne was right; we were *not* better off without each other, and it *was* my home. Gregory Hart's words to me as we had stood in that plowed field years ago came back to me and brought tears to my eyes.

So you're headed away from your home. Away from your brother. Away from your chair at the kitchen table. Away from the tub your mother used to bathe you in. Away from your bed. Away from the place where you grew up, the only place you know.

The computer at the Kings' would be there for me, whenever.

Lorne nodded his head once, emphatically. "Then that's settled."

Silently, I added, *At least for now.*

Chapter 9

Just before the end of March, the music teacher—Miss Chatham—asked Aurora and me to meet her in her classroom after school. I wondered vaguely whether Aurora's friends would wait for her or leave her behind. It looked as though she and I might walk home together for maybe the first time. But what was really on my mind was that Mr. Tillman was supposed to have gotten everything all set up at the Kings', in terms of two new computers and Internet access in Reverend King's office and in "my" room—and that's where I wanted to be, as quickly as possible.

Miss Chatham was new this year, and not in the Body, although she was certainly being encouraged by a number of saints—including some ambitious students. Not by me, but for all I knew, Aurora had invited her to Church. She was young and unmarried, so there would be no recalcitrant husband to cajole, and she'd be a great catch.

"Please, sit down," she said to us.

She leaned against her desk, distributing a broad smile between us, while we took a chair each, not knowing what to expect. "I believe you are both in the Grace of God Church, is that right? And the minister is your father, Aurora, and Jude I believe you're close to the family." We nodded. "I know there are a lot of students and teachers here who are in your church, and I want to respect your traditions. I had an idea that I thought might be something that you could guide a group of us through, to make sure it was authentic and—oh, I don't know, compliant, I guess—with what would seem right to everyone." She paused for effect. "I want to put on a historically accurate Easter pageant. What do you think?"

My eyes shifted sideways to Aurora, who was looking full at me, alarm on her face. The Body would not condone such a thing. Easter was Easter, and the holiest of days, for it's when Jesus rose into Heaven to be with God after his crucifixion, leaving his disciples with orders to spread the gospel. We gave the day due honor, to be sure, but it was not in the popish ways that most other churches would do. Pomp and circumstance were anathema to our beliefs, and the word "pageant" brought both of them to mind.

I looked back at Miss Chatham. "Um, I'm not too sure. Aurora's father would be the one to talk to."

"Yes, I know about Reverend King. That's why it was the two of you I asked to meet with. But now I'm a little confused. You don't think it's a good idea?"

Aurora found her voice. "It's just that we don't do a lot of that stuff. Like, for Christmas, or Easter, or anything. We celebrate through worship every day, because every day is a holy day, and we do it with the other Christians."

Miss Chatham scowled in confusion. "But—most of the children and teachers in the school are Christian. You would be—"

Aurora was shaking her head. "No, I mean the *true* Christians. The ones who belong to our Church. We worship with *them*. We celebrate with *them*."

I saw Miss Chatham's entire body pull back slightly, as though to distance herself from us. "I see." Her voice was no longer enthusiastic. She stood, and so did we. "Thank you, both of you, for helping me to understand. If I have any other questions, I'll be sure to speak with your father, Aurora." She smiled again, but it looked like a cover-up. "I'll let you get on home, then. See you tomorrow."

Outside the room, Aurora and I struggled to keep our laughter in until we were far enough away that we wouldn't be heard. Barely able to speak, Aurora said, "An Easter pageant? What was she *thinking?*"

"I *know*. But—really, she doesn't know much about us."

"Or about Christians. The real ones, I mean."

By the time we got outside the laughter had nearly subsided, but we were whispering together like conspirators about the re-action Reverend King might have to that suggestion. I barely noticed Pearl Thornton, who hobbled out the door a little be-hind us and went the other direction from us, no doubt toward her home. I remember thinking, uncharitably, that she'd prob-ably been held after for a bad math test score or something.

Aurora and I were maybe a hundred yards from the school when a car drove toward us from Pearl's direction, going too fast. We might not have noticed it, except that it squealed to a halt and then backed up, tires complaining again, then drew up beside us. Bill Schumacher was at the wheel, leaning toward the passenger window, out of which Larry's freckled arm hung. Smoke curled up from the cigarette in Larry's fingers.

I hadn't heard Larry's voice since last summer. It was a little deeper now. "Well, if it ain't Baptism Boy. Jude, right? Who's your girlfriend?"

I wanted so much to hurl words at him that would sting, that would make him think twice about taunting me, but all that came out was, "She's not my girlfriend."

Larry cocked his head at Aurora. "No? Whose girl are ya, then?"

Aurora lifted her chin, but she was afraid. So was I. "Come on, Jude. Let's get home."

We turned our backs on the car. With every nerve on edge, I listened helplessly to the sound of a car door opening. I grabbed Aurora's arm, trying to hurry her along, but a second car door opened before we could get very far away from these delinquents. Suddenly they were in front of us, blocking our way. I glanced frantically around. Was there anyone nearby who could help us? Just before Larry grabbed my arms and held them behind me, I saw Pearl at the school door, moving as quickly as I think she could, and I caught her eye. She nodded once and went inside.

Bill, meanwhile, had taken hold of Aurora's upper arm with one hand while he wrapped his other arm behind her. His head bending to get close to her face, he said, "You're a pretty little thing, aren't you? Don't have a boyfriend?" I saw his hand move from her shoulder to stroke the side of her face. She struggled to free herself, and I kicked madly behind me hoping to catch a shin, but neither of us had any effect.

"Let her go!" I managed through gritted teeth, and Larry yanked me sideways, twisting my shoulders. I cried out in pain but kept struggling.

"Shut up, shithead, or I'll really hurt you."

It seemed like an eternity, but it must have been less than a minute before Mr. Lincoln himself—the school principal— came thundering out of the school, shouting. "You hooligans get out of here! Leave those children alone!"

I heard Larry mumble, "It was that fucking little midget. I saw her." He pushed me away from him as Bill did the same to Aurora. Scrambling back into the car, Larry looked past Mr. Lincoln toward the school where I'm sure he couldn't actually see Pearl and shouted, "Hey, midget! Little Miss Tansy! Ugly as roadkill! You're gonna be crow food!"

The car streaked away, leaving black marks on the road and a burnt smell in the air. I went to Aurora, who looked like she was about to collapse. "Are you okay?"

She nodded. "You?"

"I'll live."

Mr. Lincoln shepherded us inside, where he called the Kings. "I don't think you two should walk home right now. There's no telling if those hoodlums will be back."

Pearl was in the office, perched awkwardly on an orange

plastic chair, feet dangling a little above the floor. I went over to her. "Thanks, Pearl. Thanks for . . . you know."

"Saving your skin?"

I tried to chuckle, but it came out more like a snort. "Yeah. Saving our skin."

All three of us sat in a row on those ugly chairs, waiting for our rides. Miss Thornton showed up first, and Mr. Lincoln went over the incident again.

Belinda Thornton beamed down at her daughter, stroking that wiry hair. "I'm so proud of you, sparrow." There was that nickname again.

Sparrow hopped down from her chair and threw a backward glance at us as they left, nearly bumping into Mrs. King and the reverend. Mrs. King hugged Aurora, who was trying not to cry.

"Young Jude was putting up quite a fight, Reverend," Mr. Lincoln told him. "That other boy was just too big."

"The Schumachers, was it? I'll have to pay a visit to their parents."

"Yes indeed. They're nothing but trouble."

"It was Pearl who helped," I said, puzzled that her name had not been mentioned. "She saw what was going on, and she came in to tell Mr. Lincoln."

Mrs. King looked up from where she was bent over Aurora's head. "Is that right? We'll have to thank her."

And she did. The next day she drove out to the Thorntons' trailer with fresh fruit and flowers. I couldn't have said why, but I didn't think either Belinda or Pearl would be especially thrilled. Belinda would be polite, I felt sure, but that was all. I wondered if Mrs. King witnessed for the Lord—if she shared God's Word—when she delivered her gifts.

Every night that week, on the edge of sleep, I relived the confrontation with Bill and Larry—what I did, what I might have done, what might have happened if it had gone on much longer. And each time I came to the conclusion that despite how awful it had seemed at the time, our tormentors were not likely to have done anything really harmful there in full view of anybody anywhere nearby. We hadn't been in any real danger.

And yet Pearl, who had already started down the road toward home, turned around and came back to find someone who could help in a way that she could not. She had risked being seen, and she *had* been seen. She'd put herself in danger for us.

That Saturday I decided to thank Pearl better than I had. Knowing that I'd be chastised or worse for doing so if I were caught, I shrugged into my jacket in mid-afternoon and told Clara I was going to the meadow for a bit. It was a difficult trek across that marshy expanse, squishy with spring snowmelt, toward the Thornton's trailer. I had to pay such close attention to where I stepped that I didn't see the motionless girl where she sat wrapped in an old, ragged afghan, faded swirls of blue and beige around her huddled shape. She was on top of that flat boulder where I'd seen her in the past, on the opposite side of the utility right-of-way from my house, at the edge of a short expanse of woods between the meadow and the road on the other side. I was practically at the boulder, still unaware of her, when I heard her speak.

"What are you doing here?"

I heard myself gasp, smelled the sharp scent of my own fear, and then shrugged as soon as I could manage it, trying to pretend I wasn't startled. Somewhere between my fright and her antagonistic tone I lost sight of why I'd come. Pearl seemed to bring out the worst in people. So I said, "I have as much right to be here as you. This isn't your yard, y'know."

Angry, she bit back. "You've got the whole world! Leave me this little piece of it."

I blinked stupidly. "What whole world?"

She was sulky, now. "Everywhere. You, Aurora, all your little friends, even those poor excuses for humanity who attacked you. All of you can do whatever you want, go wherever you want. And you don't give two hoots about the likes of me."

"That's not true!"

"What's not? Which part?"

"I . . . I can't do whatever I want. I shouldn't even be here talking to you."

"See? See?"

"No, stop it. Listen. I came to thank you for what you did. And to let you know that they saw you. You shouldn't get anywhere near them."

Her expression had changed from a pout to something like quiet terror, and her voice was tentative. "They saw me?"

"When Mr. Lincoln came out and yelled at them, Larry said that he'd seen you." I opted against repeating the insulting words he'd used: *roadkill . . . crow food.* And *Tansy.*

She banged the heels of her hands against her forehead several times, punctuating each strike with "Shit. Shit. Shit."

I couldn't remember anyone saying that word in front of me, aside from the occasional epithet from the Schumachers or one of the non-Christian boys at school, and there weren't many of them. It took me so by surprise that I couldn't speak for several seconds. Then, "Maybe they'll forget about this whole thing in a week or so."

Something slipped off the rock and dropped to the ground, and Pearl nearly fell trying to grab it. "Give her to me!"

Wordlessly obedient, I bent over and picked up a cloth doll. It had brown skin and curly, black yarn hair, and I had to stop myself from dropping it again, its looks were so unexpected. Plus, what was a fifteen-year-old girl doing with a doll, anyway? Gingerly I handed it up to her, and she snatched it from my hand and brushed the moisture and bits of plant from the face, hair, and clothing. It looked like someone had made it by hand. I wondered if this were the doll Pearl had been singing to the first time I'd seen her out here. Then I began to notice a sound, rather strangled and muffled, coming from Pearl. She was trying not to cry.

Maybe the doll was torn? I asked, "She's okay, isn't she?"

"*I* am not okay! I am *never* going to be okay! And those shit-heads are going to make sure. They're always after me, just for the obvious reasons those fuckers would be after anyone like me. But now they've got a real reason!" She turned on the boulder and began to struggle down the opposite side from me. One corner of the afghan was the last to disappear.

I don't know why it occurred to me; I must have been out of my mind. I said, "I could walk you to school in the mornings. Maybe your mom could—"

Her scorn was evident despite her awkward landing out of my sight. "You! You couldn't even help Aurora, and all they wanted to do was tease her. They want to *hurt* me. Don't you get it? What could *you* do? Go away! Leave me alone!" She hobbled into the woods toward the road and, no doubt, her trailer. I watched her go, over burdened by the huge lump of blue and beige yarn, my mind forming options for keeping her safe. Maybe her mom could drive her to and from school? Then I had a brainstorm.

I turned and ran back across the meadow, stepping in mud and water and nearly spraining an ankle before I got home. I opened the back door just long enough to yell, "Off on my bike for a bit!" There was some distant response that I couldn't quite hear.

Pedaling fast, partly due to being cold and wet and partly to this burning idea, I headed for the Harts'. Gregory might not be there, which would actually be better from my point of view; I'd prefer not to have to talk with him, as long as I could get Dolly to see what he needed to do.

I nearly threw my bike against the fence and thundered up the steps, pounding on the door. By the time Dolly opened it, Gregory had stepped out from the barn where he must have been working on some piece of equipment. He came nearly at a trot and got to the front steps just as Dolly was saying, "Goodness, Jude! Whatever's the matter? You're acting like the hounds of Hell are after you!"

I looked from her to her brother behind me, a smear of grease on the side of his face, concern in his gray eyes. His voice even and calm, he said, "Is everything all right, Jude?"

Still panting a little, I managed, "I need to talk to you. Both of you. It's about Pearl." Then hastily I added, "She's okay. For now."

I was ushered into the kitchen, where I sat at the same chair where I'd eaten casserole and pie on my first visit. No one offered food this time. Still wiping grease off his fingers with an old flannel rag, Gregory took over. "Jude, start at the beginning, and don't leave out anything important."

So I told them about what had happened and how upset Pearl had been once she knew she'd been seen. I finished with, "So I guess someone who looks like they mean it has to take those two aside. They aren't afraid of Pearl or her mother. Reverend King talked to their parents, but I think someone needs to let them know that if anything happens to Pearl, we'll all know it was them." I looked expectantly at Gregory. "Someone like you, who could hurt them. Not that I'm saying you should . . ."

Dolly's empty eyes moved from my direction to her brother's. "Gregory? What can you do? Can you help her?"

He sat there quietly, eyes staring at nothing much, for too long. I tried to shame him. "I offered to walk her to school if her mom could pick her up after, but that's not enough." I felt Dolly's hand on my arm, fumbling for my hand. I touched her fingers with mine, and she grasped my hand.

"You are a wonderful, brave boy, Jude." Dolly squeezed my hand. "But I don't think that would be allowed."

"What? Why not?"

"Never mind," Gregory said. "It won't be necessary. I'll take care of this, Jude. Don't you fret over it anymore." He let out a long breath and smiled at me. "We haven't seen you out here for months. Why don't you sit and chat with Dolly until it's time for you to get on home? I have an errand to run." He stood, and I felt his warm hand on my shoulder. He squeezed firmly and left. In spite of what I'd heard about him, it felt good. I liked it.

"Will he talk to them?" I asked Dolly. "Do you think that's where he's going?"

She nodded, her eyes watering. "I do. He's a good man,

Jude, and he's always had a soft spot in his heart for that poor little girl." She found my arm again and laid her hand gently on it. "And I think you know that, or you wouldn't be here now."

I shrugged automatically; she couldn't see it, of course. "I know he made a special bicycle for her. I've seen it."

She nodded and sniffled once. Then, "I think there's a few cookies left in the tin on the counter. Why don't you get yourself a glass of milk and tell me everything that's going on? I was so thrilled when you were baptized last summer! You're a full brother now, Jude. *And*"—this last word was emphatic—"I know there's a baby in your house, to be born in September! I want you to tell me all about that, all the preparations. It's so exciting! Do Lorne and Clara have names picked out yet?"

I got only a glass of water for myself, sat down, and told her what little I knew about the baby, and then I talked about my computer, all the while trying not to be angry that she'd echoed the constraint placed on me about spending time alone with Pearl. For crying out loud, Dolly was the one who had us both here doing math! She was fascinated with what I told her about the computer, though, and I spent a long time explaining the Internet to her. She was very grateful.

"Jude, I can't tell you how much it pleases me to have you tell me about this phenomenon! You know, I think most people just talk to me because they feel sorry for me. They shouldn't, for I have a wonderful, rich life in Jesus, but it's like they think I can't understand things just because I can't see them. Thank you for not being that way."

I saw an opening. "Pearl isn't that way either."

"No, thank the good Lord, she's not. She's a dear, dear friend to me. It breaks my heart that she can't find her way to the light. There's so much love here, if she could just believe in it."

"Her mother was in the Body once."

She nodded. "Yes, that's right."

"Um, who's Pearl's father?"

"Now, child, if I knew that, I wouldn't tell you. It's not my place."

I was tempted to ask for her explanation about why I shouldn't walk Pearl to school. But I was sure her answer would be something along the lines of what Reverend King and Lorne had already said, and that would be disappointing. I wanted Dolly and Gregory to be more flexible, but I couldn't count on it. And I didn't want the disappointment. I said, "It's getting late. Um, tomorrow in church, will you tell me what Mr. Hart did?"

She smiled, a little sadly it seemed. "Probably not, Jude. I think it's better if you don't know. This way you're not involved, and no one can claim you had anything to do with it."

If I wanted to know what was being done about the Schumachers, and what information Pearl had been given about it, one person I might be able to ask was Reverend King. I'd never phoned him before, but after supper I girded my proverbial loins and called. Aurora answered.

"Daddy's not home right now, Jude."

"Will he be there soon?"

"I doubt it. This is one of his Boise nights."

I had no idea what she was talking about. One of his Boise nights? She made it sound like something I should know about. "What does that mean?"

"You know. If there's no Church activity on Saturday evening that he needs to attend, he goes down to the city to look for lost souls. He says there are lots of them down there."

This made no sense. "How would I know that? I'm never there on Saturday. What does he do with them when he finds them?"

"Well . . . I mean, he tells them about Jesus, and he invites them to Church. Just like we're all supposed to do with the unsaved."

"Why does he go all the way down there? We have unsaved souls right here."

"Jude, honestly! I don't know. Why don't you ask him?"

I went to bed that night feeling like I'd swung hard at something and missed.

Sunday was worse. Reverend King looked like death warmed over. He gave a short sermon, full of doom and gloom, about sin and sinning and what happens when you consider only your own desires. I had kind of hoped that he'd rant and rave about something that sounded like the Schumacher boys' trespasses, but no. By the end he got almost weepy, and his closer—usually either wildly uplifting or thunderously scary—kind of petered out when he mumbled something about how sin starts to take hold in you when you start telling lies to yourself, because of course God knows they're lies, and so would you if you were searching your heart and doing only things that Jesus would do. Even his usual punctuation, "May God grant you peace," was missing. Afterward he disappeared, so I couldn't talk to him.

Back at the house again I wanted to take matters into my own hands, but Lorne heard me tell Clara I was going out for a bit—my plan was to go to the Thorntons' and talk to them—and he stopped me.

"You were out yesterday, Jude, twice, and you weren't very forthcoming about where." He was reading something in the living room. I moved only as close as I had to.

"I told you I went to talk with Dolly Hart!"

"Yes, and I checked with her today, and she did tell me you were there. But—"

"You did *what?* You're checking up on me?" Furious. I was furious.

"I was about to say, but you disappeared before that, too. Where did you go?"

Struggling to keep my voice even, I said, "I was in the meadow. I told Clara."

"That's part of my point. You didn't ask permission for that, or to go to the Harts'. You just told." He was turned in his chair to look at me, his neck straining a little.

My fists were starting to clench. "Why do I need permission to go to the meadow?"

"Come over here where I can see you." I moved, but I didn't want to. "This may be difficult for you to believe, little brother, but Clara and I care about you. We want you to be safe, and you don't always know what's unsafe. And for your part, you need to remember that all of us are asking permission all the time. God has put someone in authority over each of us, and it's our duty to obey. We don't always like it."

"You didn't obey when Reverend King wanted to break our family apart."

"He didn't tell us what to do. He made a suggestion, and we took the one his wife offered. And I was a few years younger then, myself. So you see, I understand not wanting to obey. I know what it feels like. But it's my job to see to the safety of your body and, as much as I can, your soul."

I'd managed to calm down a little as he talked, and I knew I'd never get out if I made a scene. "All right. I get your point. Now I'm asking. May I go to the meadow?"

"Why do you want to go out there? It's cold, and it might snow."

I don't know where this came from, but it came very quickly. "I'm studying the plants. Which ones come up first, when the first flowers open, what stays green in winter, that sort of thing."

Lorne blinked at me, genuinely puzzled. So was I. He asked, "Why?"

"I'm interested, that's all. I study the plants, and I'm going to figure out what they are, and I'll look them up on the Internet. You never know; I might need a project in science. Besides, I like the meadow. I feel close to Jesus there." Lie after lie after lie.

"They'll mow out there in July."

"So I'll see which ones grow back fastest!" He was pushing me, and I was afraid I'd run out of replies. He scowled like he was thinking. I didn't want to give him time to come up with a reason to deny my request. "So may I go?"

He took a few seconds anyway. "For a little while. And I'll want to know what you find."

Whatever. I yanked my jacket off the hook near the door and made a huge effort not to slam the door. All this trouble just to talk to someone I wasn't supposed to talk to, for no good reason. I stepped carefully, avoiding puddles and mud this time, but also watching to see if Pearl was already there; I didn't want her scaring me again. But I didn't see her.

At the trailer, I heard laughter. I knocked on the door, and Belinda Thornton opened it.

"Well, I'll be! What on earth are you doing here, Jude Connor?"

From farther in, I heard Pearl say, "Jude? What's he doing here?" She appeared behind her mother.

"Come in, boy, come in. You're lettin' out all the heat." I stepped up and into the narrow space and saw a checkerboard set up in the living room area to the right. The place was crowded, but it would have been tough for it not to be. It was the first time I'd seen the inside, and I looked in vain for the knitting machine. Mrs. Thornton said, "Sit."

Heel, I wanted to reply, but I sat on a footstool on the far side of the game. Pearl plopped onto the floor by the game board, and Belinda sat on the small couch. "What can we do for you, Jude?"

"It's about what happened last week. I don't know if anyone told you"—I made a snap decision not to say Pearl knew—"but Larry and Bill know Pearl was the one who went in to get Mr. Lincoln. Larry said he would get her for it." From the look on Belinda's face, I guessed Pearl had shared this news. Even so, Pearl's eyes were shooting darts at me. I plunged ahead. "Reverend King spoke to their parents, but I don't know if he talked to Bill or Larry. I decided someone had to talk to *them,* so I told Mr. Hart about it. I think he talked to them." I paused, and the silence nearly knocked me over. "So I don't think Pearl will have to worry about them." More silence. Belinda's face looked blank. "I thought you should know. Just in case."

"In case what?"

"In case you already knew that Larry knows it was Pearl, and you might be worried."

Belinda looked at me hard. "You've gone to a bit of trouble, haven't you, Jude?"

I shrugged. "Pearl went to some trouble for me. She didn't have to go back and get Mr. Lincoln. She could have just left."

"That's true." Belinda turned toward her daughter and smiled. "She's a brave girl." Facing me again, she said, "Do you know what Mr. Hart did or said?"

I shook my head. "Dolly—Miss Hart said it would be better if I didn't know, so I wouldn't be involved, in case Bill and Larry found out I told Mr. Hart."

Belinda's laughter started quiet but grew to fill the small room. She leaned against the back of the couch, threw her head back, and howled. It was contagious. I began to chuckle, almost against my will, and even glum Pearl grinned and chuckled grudgingly. Finally, wiping her eyes, Belinda said, "This is one ridiculous situation. I'm sorry, Jude. I don't mean to belittle what you've done, and I'm very grateful for all your efforts. But this chain of if one person knows another person knows something, then someone else needs to know that they know . . ." Her words trailed off into more laughter, quieter this time. "It's too much. It sounds too funny." She leaned forward and placed one hand on each jean-covered thigh. "Can I offer you anything? A soda? Cookies?"

I stood. "No, thank you, ma'am. I have to get to the meadow and collect plants." I stopped, not wanting to go into this lie for a second time, knowing that I was going to have to put in at least a token effort that Lorne could see.

"Plants, is it? Pearl here is an expert. She can tell you about anything that grows out there. Sparrow, why don't you get on your mud boots and go help Jude with his task."

"Ma!" Pearl protested.

"Get on, now. It's the least you can do after he went to such trouble for you."

I trudged slowly behind her from the trailer back through the woods, past the boulder where she'd dropped her doll, mostly in silence. At one point she asked, "What do you want plants for?"

"I'm trying to see if it would make an interesting science project." I didn't quite trust her with the truth.

She turned and looked up at me. "You looking for poisonous plants?"

I blinked. "Really? Are there poisonous plants here?"

She rolled her eyes Heavenward as though I were the stupidest person on earth. Then she walked forward again, heading toward a small copse of young trees that the mowers must have decided wasn't worth cutting when they were younger. She pushed aside some dead grasses with fingers swathed in what looked like homemade gloves—multicolored yarn knitted together, in no discernible pattern, that was probably left over from other projects. Bent over, there was almost no height to her at all.

"Look here." She held dead growth away from some dark green leaves on reddish-brown stems, decorated with small yellow buds, still tight shut. "It's called sagebrush buttercup. A member of the Ranunculus family." I was looking hard at the plant, committing its appearance to memory so I could find it again, and I didn't notice that Pearl was working a stem free between her thumb and forefinger. In a sudden motion she whipped her hand toward my face and brushed my cheek with the broken stem.

"Hey!" I swiped at my face with my hand, feeling the spot begin to sting.

"Don't worry; it won't kill you that way. You'd have to eat it to get really sick."

Rubbing my face I asked, "So it wouldn't kill you? I mean, someone?"

She shrugged. "Make you wish it would, maybe. If you want to kill someone, wait for the death camas to come out. They'll be in the marshy areas."

"I'm not looking to kill anything. What else can you show me today, without rubbing my nose in it?" My face was stinging more and more. "And do I need to put anything on this?"

"When you get home, maybe some baking soda mixed with water. It might blister, but you'll be okay. Don't be such a baby. Come over here." She moved uphill a little and back toward the woods, along a small stream that was barely flowing for all the grass. Bending again, she scoured up and down the water flow for a good four minutes.

"What are you looking for?"

"Wake-robin," she mumbled.

"What?"

"Trillium." She moved hunched over like a very old woman whose bones won't let her straighten up. "Ha! Here it is. Come look, and don't pick it."

I bent over. "What am I looking at?"

Gently she touched a stem with three leaves on it. "It hasn't bloomed yet. Soon. White, three petals. It's lovely. And you mustn't pick it."

"Why not? Is it poisonous?"

"Do you always need a bad reason? Don't pick it, because it's beautiful and there aren't a lot of them anymore." She straightened up to her full height and glared at me. "Don't make me wish I hadn't shown you."

"All right, all right. I won't pick it. I'll come back and look next weekend. What else?"

"Greedy, aren't you?"

"I need to have a few things to get started."

"It's really too early. I mean, I can show you the plants, but they don't look like much yet." She headed away from me again, following the water into the edge of the woods. The stream was a little deeper here, moving among rocks and tree roots. Clumsily, Pearl moved to the water's edge toward some intensely green plants. She leaned over and came up with a yellow flower bud on a thick stem. "Here." She handed it to me. I was a little tentative after the buttercup. "It won't hurt you. It has a nice smell."

I took it, lifted it to my nose, and then turned away with a jerk. "Peeew! This stinks! It smells like . . . skunk?"

She laughed. "Skunk cabbage. Take it home with you. But don't eat it raw, or the insides of your mouth will burn."

"You said it wouldn't hurt me!"

"Are you even tempted to take a bite?"

I glared at her. "What else?"

"Fine. One more lesson today, and I'm going back. My feet are cold." She trudged back up the gentle slope and led me into a small area of pine trees farther uphill, coming to a stop beside an unimpressive shrubby thing maybe a foot high. "We have here a member of the heath family. It's called pipsissewa. Or prince's pine. There'll be little flowers on it in June. It contains an ingredient used in root beer. How's that for a smattering of wood lore?"

I squatted down beside it and fingered the waxy, dark green leaves. "Are they pretty flowers?"

"No. Does that make them worthless?"

"That's not what I meant. I was just wondering."

"If you want to see something special, look for a dogtooth violet. They aren't blooming now—not till sometime in May. I haven't seen any in this area in the past two years, though." She looked around, almost as though for a sign that pointed out where these special flowers would be. Then, "I'm going back now. Hope you have what you need."

"For now." She turned and started to walk away. "Pearl?" She stopped but didn't turn around. "Thanks. For the lesson. And for saving my skin the other day."

She raised an arm and waved a few colorful fingers. Watching her small, ungainly body get smaller as she moved farther away, I tried to make sense out of the odd things I knew about her. She baked fantastic cookies. She played checkers. She carried a doll around and sang to it. And she knew about poisonous and useful wild plants. What else was there about her that I didn't know?

I turned toward home, thinking that between the skunk cabbage and this messy patch on my face, I'd be able to prove to Lorne that I hadn't lied. I made a mental note to come back in time for the trillium flower. Just before I got back to the house I wondered whether there were any tansy plants in the meadow.

Chapter 10

There was no Easter pageant, of course. And I don't recall ever seeing Miss Chatham at church. I did see a lot more of the inside of Reverend King's office, though. He called upstairs to me the week after I harvested my meadow plants, and when I appeared at the top of the stairs he asked me to come with him.

He had me sit in his leather chair so I could work the keyboard and mouse while he watched. He asked me to explain as much as I could—which wasn't a lot, since my knowledge was a compendium of experience gained from just trying everything—as he sat on the hard chair, pulled up close to me so he could see what I was doing. Alternately he'd watch, ask questions, and scribble notes for himself. I did some searches for him, and he had me bookmark a few of the sites I found.

What stays with me the most about this quasi training session was the way I felt sitting there so close to him. It was like I was mesmerized or something. It was different from how it had been riding with Gregory in his tractor, because other than one hug the day he told me I had to get baptized, and again when he immersed me, and maybe a handshake or two, Reverend King and I had never touched at all.

I think I wouldn't have noticed his scrupulous avoidance of any touch during this first session if it hadn't been for that time he reached for the mouse a little too soon. He was eager to learn what I was showing him, and his eyes were on the screen when his hand landed on mine. As though I had screamed, he jerked his hand back, shot a look at me and then back to the screen, and pointed to something he saw there.

"Click on that, would you?"

Afterward I became hyperaware of his physical presence. I could feel the heat of his body. I knew when he had shifted positions more by the change in proximity to me, the change in the energy, than by the sounds he made doing it.

This first session lasted about ninety minutes. He didn't ask for help again until he needed to incorporate some material from a Web site into a word processing file. He kept taking notes, so I figured that he wasn't looking for me to do his work for him. I wouldn't have wanted that; I wanted to spend time doing my own Internet work.

I used my computer (I began calling it mine very quickly) to augment almost every homework assignment I was given. I used it to chat with people all over the country who called themselves Christian—or, mostly, to watch them chat with each other. I used it to try and find my father, to no avail. Mostly I used it to fill the gulf I felt widening between me and the rest of the world. I hadn't ever reassessed my need for confession, repentance, and re-baptism. That didn't mean that it wasn't hanging over my head; it was. And, like Isaiah said, it made me feel separated.

The Internet was also useful to look up Idaho wildflowers. And maybe the way the Internet made me feel—connected to the world—transferred to this particular project, or maybe there was something else going on; whichever, once I started researching about local plants I got hooked. Mildly, anyway.

I forgot to go back for the trillium bloom in time, but I managed to find pictures of it on the 'Net. The next time I went to the meadow was a Sunday afternoon in late April. I was armed with printouts from my Internet searches—including one of the dogtooth violet, just in case—along with a trowel from Mrs. King's garden tool set and a paper grocery bag.

My printout photos were black and white, so I wasn't prepared for the grass widows. Almost as soon as I'd stepped into the opening from the woods on my side of the meadow, a soft haze of light purple up the hill caught my attention. I headed up and soon found that I had to pick my steps carefully to avoid treading on tufts of the little things. Why had I never noticed them before? They must have been here every spring. The thickest swaths of color moved along in an irregular, winding pattern that I eventually figured out was following the flow of snowmelt—a purple snake climbing the hill.

The striking effect of the grass widow nearly caused me to miss the western springbeauty flower, clusters of tiny, white-petaled, open flowers and soft pink buds. My printout on these told me they were edible; the raw greens were supposed to taste like radish and the boiled tubers like potatoes. As I dug up a few of the pretty plants I imagined the scene at the supper table tonight. "I've been hunting and gathering," I'd tell Lorne and Clara. "And look: radishes and potatoes!"

I'd been hoping to find a shooting star—I kind of liked the name—but either they hadn't started blooming yet, or they didn't grow in my meadow. But as a consolation, Lorne was sufficiently impressed with my harvest of springbeauties, although Clara read through my printout a few times to make sure they were safe. In the end, she decided not to eat anything she didn't know was safe because of the baby.

There have been a few times in my life when I've eaten something that's supposed to taste like something else. Carob instead of chocolate; Postum instead of coffee; xylitol instead of sugar. Each time something's been introduced to me that way, that it's "like" something else, I've been disappointed. That's how it was with my springbeauties. I wished that the printout hadn't told me what to expect.

In early May I began to wonder where else I might find wildflowers, and it occurred to me that I could look in our woods. I mean, Tim's and mine. Tim wouldn't be there, of course; I was sure he'd never go anywhere near there again. But that didn't mean I couldn't. I'd established some credibility with Lorne on this topic by now, so he didn't protest when I said I was going hunting and gathering near the river.

At the baptism bank, I left my bike locked to a tree, hidden behind it, and crossed where Tim and I used to. The water was higher, what with the melting snow water, and freezing cold, but once I was across and into the edge of the woods I was glad I'd come. First, there were shooting stars in a long wave on the very edge of the woods. Just under the first trees I found the soft blue clusters of trumpet-shaped wild hyacinth, which I gathered, risking another disappointment, because of the nut-like flavor they were supposed to have. Then there was a whole field of arrowleaf balsamroot, the tall stems topped proudly by large yellow heads that mirrored the sun overhead. I gathered some of the immature flower stems, the insides of which were supposed to be good raw.

Deeper and deeper into the woods I went, finally having to admit I was no longer scouring the forest floor for wildflowers. I was headed for the fort.

It was there. It didn't look as though anyone had visited it since Tim ran away from it and from me, nearly two years ago now. I crawled inside with my bag of harvested groceries and sat where I'd been the day Tim touched my face, my back against the cold, rough boulder the tree trunk also leaned on. A few deep breaths fought their way into my chest, each one trembling more than the last. I couldn't have said, and still can't, whether I missed Tim or Jesus more, but I felt separated from both. And it was my feelings about Tim that troubled my relationship with Jesus. Knees up, arms folded over them, head on my wrists, I breathed deeply, fighting tears.

I felt heavy and profoundly sad when I finally left the fort and started back, my progress slow as I watched one foot land, and then the next. At one point I nearly swore, stepping inadvertently into mud, and I almost fell getting my foot away from its vacuum grip. I caught myself by grasping the trunk of a tall pine, looking down to assess the amount of wet earth that had attached itself to my shoe. And there, huddled into the moss at the base of the tree, was a flower I had not expected to see. It stood alone, nearly invisible against the green ground cover surrounding it. A dogtooth violet.

Six or seven inches tall, the filament-thin stem rose straight up from leaves that lay nearly on the ground. But the stem curled at the top, so that its crown—the flower—hung face down: six small, pointed petals, a yellow color that was almost green, and the sharp point of a stamen cluster pointing back down toward the earth. It looked demure. And, as Pearl had said, special. I reached down to pluck it, but at the last second I didn't. I almost heard the flower ask sweetly not to be disturbed.

The next day in school I watched for Pearl. My approach couldn't look deliberate; I'd had enough of being told I shouldn't associate with non-Christians. It wasn't until before my last class that I saw her with no one else around, at her locker. I walked casually behind where she stood and dropped a folded piece of paper as inconspicuously as possible, so that when I picked it up and handed it to her, it would look as though I was merely retrieving for her something she dropped, herself.

She started a little when I held it in front of her, looked at me oddly. "What?"

"For you. A special flower." I kept my voice low.

Tentatively she took the paper, watching my face, caution on hers. I smiled, nodded once, and walked away.

I nearly skipped all the way to the Kings' that day, loving that I'd pulled something over on Pearl, that her aloof, superior attitude would be punctured at least a little. The note had said, "Dogtooth violet. Ask me where."

Later, up in the room I called mine, doing some Internet research for a homework assignment, I was irritated when Aurora appeared in the doorway.

Our friendship, still in its early stages, had barely survived my acquisition of a computer to use for myself, and at this point in time it consisted mostly of her coming into my room to talk when I just wanted to surf the 'Net. She usually complained about her friends, how they were petty or jealous or vain or conceited or self-righteous. That's what she did today, sitting on the end of the bed with legs stretched out onto the floor and arms propping her up from behind. It was a flirtatious pose, but I didn't take it personally.

I grew weary of the sniping quickly today. "Why do you hang out with them, then?"

She shrugged. "They're my friends. And, you know, we can't have any friends who aren't Christians."

"So, do you complain to your friends about me?" I really wanted to know. I'd never had the kind of friendship she seemed to have with these girls.

"No, silly! I don't talk about you. Not really. Or, if I do, it's just about what you show me on the Internet."

"But you complain to *me* about *them*."

She laughed prettily. "You're not exactly going to tell them what I said, are you?"

I tried not to smile; she was right. I was a safe audience.

Pearl must have thought I was safe, too, because in school the next day she marched right up to me. "So where did you find it?"

Not playing coy today, I thought. Imperious, today. Hardly out of character, though. "There's a great patch of woods just across the water from our baptism bank," I told her, wondering if she'd know where that was.

She searched my face, assessing. "Across? How do you get across?"

"Wade. Very cold, just now, and well up over my knees on the sandbar."

"So I could go up to the bridge past the bank and walk in from there. Right?"

Feeling awkward, I said, "Probably. Or use a boat." That wasn't likely, though.

She didn't seem fazed. "And you're at the Kings' every school day." She waited for me to nod, and I wondered where she'd go next. "So, would you show me on Sunday morning?"

"Sunday?" I'm sure I sounded aghast.

Pearl laughed. "Kidding. What about Saturday afternoon, if it doesn't rain?"

Now, I'd never said I would show her. But it would probably have been useless to pretend that I'd given her that note for any other reason. "I guess. I'm not supposed to—"

"Oh, I know. So let's say I'll bike on my own to your sacred spot, and if you're not there by two I'll assume you're chained to your bed. I'll be there by quarter of. Then we can bike up to the bridge and figure out how to get back down to where you saw the flower."

"I saw lots of flowers. Shooting stars, wild hyacinth—"

"You can show me Saturday. Now get along before someone hogties you and makes you say half a bazillion Hail Marys."

"We don't—"

"You think I don't know that? Get a sense of humor, Jude. Honestly." And she left me standing there watching her hobble away.

As I approached the river that damp Saturday at about one fifty-five, I'd been mentally flagellating myself for the entire ride. Lying to Lorne and Clara was getting easier, and I both hated that and didn't care. I tried to tell myself I wasn't actually lying; I mean, I'd told them why I was going to the woods across the river. I just hadn't mentioned Pearl.

But I was shaken out of my self-indulgent ruminations rather suddenly. I could see from a distance that same car Bill and Larry had been in the day they tormented Aurora and me. Exhaust from the idling engine condensed in the cool, moist air. Just beyond the car the bright orange-yellow of Pearl's bicycle nearly glowed, starkly visible on this cloudy day. She was poised on it as though to take off quickly if necessary, though what good that would have done wasn't clear. She saw me approaching and relaxed visibly, though I grew tenser as Larry's words grew clearer.

"You know why they won't baptize you, don't you? You're a monster. A freak."

Just then Bill, behind the wheel, caught sight of me, pedaling hard in their direction. He slugged Larry's arm, I heard Larry cackle, and the car peeled away.

"Assholes!" Pearl yelled after them, as if they could hear. It was a word I'd love to have dared use from time to time.

I asked, "Did they hurt you?" She shook her head. "Threaten you?"

"Can we get a move on? Nothing happened." And she took off up the road. I followed, thinking that at least the "assholes" hadn't stayed to torment me. Maybe Gregory's efforts had paid off enough to make them leery of taunting Pearl when a witness was near.

I didn't come out this way very often. Not past the baptism bank, anyway. If we'd stayed on the road we'd have come to the Denmarks' house in half a mile. Todd Denmark was the one with the retarded son, Bruce, and Todd was the guy who'd shown Gregory the cliffs as a teenager. I wondered vaguely if I'd ever hike up to those cliffs, see those raptors, feel the peace the image haunted me with. It wouldn't be with Tim, that was one thing I knew now.

We ended up chaining our bikes to the railing on the far side of the bridge; we'd have to walk downhill from there, approaching the flower from the opposite direction than if we'd come my usual way. Pearl wasn't quick on her feet, but all that treading through the meadow must have prepared her for this terrain, and she hardly slowed me down. We approached the woods from the other side, and I was a little worried I wouldn't be able to find the flower again. Something else I hadn't counted on, in terms of locating something very small in a complex and uncharted environment, was that the lack of sunshine today made a huge difference. It had been a bright, sunny day before, and the total lack of shadows now was disorienting. We were coming up to where the fort was before I knew it, and I had to make an effort not to let it pull me toward it, not to acknowledge it in any way.

I was sure I had found the patch of mud I'd stepped into, though I couldn't find my tracks and I couldn't find the flower. Pearl wasn't dismayed. "If we don't find that one, we'll find another. The one proves they grow here, and it's the perfect environment for them."

Head down, she moved slowly and unevenly between trees, navigating tree roots and muddy spots, moving away from where I stood. She disappeared behind a large pine, and then I heard, "Eureka!"

I hurried over, and sure enough, right under where she stooped was the dogtooth. One of her fingers gently lifted the yellow-green face upward as though to invite its gaze, to capture its attention in return for the homage she paid it. Releasing the face, Pearl fingered the leaves, examining how they attached to the stem at ground level. Not looking away from the small object of her worship, she said, "Isn't it beautiful?"

Now, I'd allowed myself to get sucked into the hunt and the satisfaction of discovery, but as much fun as that was, I wouldn't have called this flower beautiful. I wasn't even sure why it was such a big deal for her, unless maybe it was that it was hard to find and unusual-looking. Kind of like her. Rather than say anything hurtful or dismissive, I responded, "You said it was special. You were right."

She looked at me and smiled. I'd never seen her smile. Laugh at me, yes; but that wasn't the same. It was so unexpected that my first impulse was to pull away; the malformation of the lower half of her face looked more pronounced in its otherness when she smiled. But her eyes, those lovely eyes, sparkled with a deep, simple pleasure that I wanted to share. So instead of recoiling, I smiled back.

I showed her my other treasures: the shooting stars and the wild hyacinth, their purple colors looking deeper in today's gloom; and the arrowleaf balsamroot, bringing sunshine up from the earth itself in resplendent, silent laughter. Pearl picked her way carefully into the middle of the spread of yellow and then turned around slowly, letting the visual warmth surround her. We picked nothing.

Walking back through the woods I couldn't help compare how I felt today with how I had felt covering this very same ground with Tim. Especially that first summer, when each time we were here alone together the air itself sparkled with possibility, with the promise of fascination. That promise had been fulfilled in so many unanticipated ways. The emotional intimacy of creating stories together was still rich and deep inside me, but each time I allowed myself to sink into it, I was roused by the flashbulb memory of him touching my face and then running from me.

With Pearl, I felt—unsettled, I guess, though that wasn't the most important aspect. There was intimacy here, too, from sharing something entirely different: this obsession with wildflowers, and this secret meeting, for which I would get into serious trouble if it were known. If she revealed it. She would not suffer at all—or, at least, not any more than she generally did anyway. So that intimacy also came from trust.

By the time we reached the fort on our return trip, I didn't feel the same urge to ignore it. Almost by surprise, I stopped and gazed at it fondly.

"What're you stopping for? It's just an old tree that fell, like, years ago."

I shook my head. "No. It's a secret place. A hidden place." I wanted to add, *A place where you can create stories and imagine things.*

I felt rather than saw her turn to face me, and then she moved slowly around to the other side of the fallen hemlock, to where the doorway was. Trying to pierce through the boughs with my eyes, I watched as she gently parted the bits that partially hid the entrance, and then she moved inside. Something tingled all through me, as though I'd allowed someone to come inside me. My body. My mind.

Then I heard, "This is cool! Are you coming in?"

Hesitantly I made my way around, parting the branches at the entrance with a certain trepidation. It wouldn't be Tim in there this time. It wouldn't even be empty.

"How long have you been coming here?" Pearl demanded immediately.

I shrugged, trying to hide the place's importance. "A couple of years, but not that often. It's not far from the Kings'."

"It's like some kind of woodland temple. Like, Druid. Pagan."

This shocked me, and so did the loudness of my voice. "Pagan?"

"Sure. Pagans get to what's holy by observing nature. By having it show them where the guideposts are between the physical and the spiritual. Kind of like the Holy Spirit in Christianity."

"That's God's love. It's got nothing to do with nature."

She laughed. "You Christians are so narrow-minded. Don't limit God like that."

"I'm not limiting God! I'm telling you what it says in the Bible!"

"Then the Bible is limiting God. It doesn't matter; neither of us is going to convert the other today, and that's for sure."

Another surprise. "What would you convert me to? If you could?"

Her glance at me was not one anyone but Aurora had ever given me. It was coy. It was teasing. So was her voice. "Pagan?"

Brain cells collided with each other, many of them screaming *Reverend King was right! I shouldn't talk to her!* I fought to draw breath. "Is that what you are? Pagan?"

Another laugh. "Will you calm down? I told you. I'm not trying to convince you of anything. You can have whatever religion you want, as long as you don't try to beat me up with it." She sat on the ground, carefully, awkwardly, right where Tim had sat the day he touched me, and leaned back. "This is a great place."

"Yeah." I was at a loss. I sat on the ground, almost but not quite facing Pearl.

"D'you always come here alone?"

Should I tell her? What harm could it do? "Tim Olsen . . ." My throat closed just long enough to prevent me from finishing, from saying he had discovered it.

"Ah, yes. Tim." Her smile was odd. "You guys don't ever hang out anymore."

I cleared my throat. "No."

"Anything to do with his delayed baptism?"

Panic made my voice squeak. "What? What do you know about that?"

"Oh, I hear things. You'd be surprised. It's like people think because I'm odd, because I'm outside of things, I'm not really there. Like I'm not really a person. And they say things in my hearing they wouldn't say in yours. Or Aurora's. So, yeah, I know. Makes you nervous, does it?"

"Nervous?"

"That someone might figure out that he's not the only one who was feeling like that?"

My ears rang. "I don't know what you're talking about."

"Fine. I guess you need to stick to that story. But you know, it doesn't matter to me. I couldn't care less. In fact, I feel more comfortable around you. Has Aurora figured it out?"

I nearly shouted. "What? Figured what out?"

"Calm down! I'm telling you, it doesn't matter. Figured out that you and Tim could have been like Gregory and Todd Denmark, if Tim hadn't panicked." She shrugged. "Maybe someday you will be."

I shook my head so hard my neck hurt. And I grabbed first at what was easiest to prove wrong. "Todd Denmark is married!"

"So?"

"*So?* So he can't be . . . he couldn't be like that with Gregory! And as for me, well, you'd just better believe that I'm *not* like that."

She shrugged again. "Look, I'm sorry I brought it up. If you don't see yourself that way, fine. I'm just telling you what I see."

I wanted to say more, to protest more, but something told me to shut up. So I pointed the conversation away from me, even if I wasn't ready to leave the subject altogether. "Are you sure about Gregory?"

She looked hard at me. "You know, I told you that when I was really pissed at you. I can't remember now why, but I hated your guts. I just wanted to show you that not everyone in your precious Church is a saint. And I knew you'd be grossed out." She sat up a little, her gaze still very intent. "But it's much worse for

him when people talk about it. You'd better keep your mouth
shut. Or I'll tell everyone you dragged me out here to have
your way with me."

I drew back a few inches. "Hey, look, don't threaten me!
What am I gonna say, anyway? How would I tell them I know?
'Pearl told me' isn't exactly going to wash. But see here"—and
I leaned forward again—"don't you go talking about me to any-
one. Don't you say those things about *me*. They aren't true.
D'you hear?"

We stared at each other, our breathing audible, for several
seconds. Then she said, "Okay. I'm sorry. If you aren't gay, fine.
Just don't go saying anything about Gregory. They all think he,
y'know, put it behind him."

"Who? Who thinks that?" Was he still acting on this sin? I didn't
even want to know.

Another shrug. "The elders, I guess. Reverend King, for
sure. I don't know if anyone knows about Todd, but a number
of them know about Gregory."

"You're crazy. I don't believe you."

"Oh, yeah? Where do you think Gregory was the day Dolly
was hit by that plow?"

I felt the blood drain from my head. "Where?" It was nearly a
whisper.

"He was with Todd. I don't think they know it was Todd, because Gregory wouldn't tell them. But he was supposed to be
watching her." A nearby cricket made me jump. "Look, Jude . . .
I've done it again. You pushed my buttons, and I ran off at the
mouth. I shouldn't have told you any of that stuff. And I'm not
threatening, okay? But, really, you can't repeat that." Her eyes
narrowed. "If I think you have, I'll—"

"How do you know all this? Who told you?"

She breathed in audibly and looked at me, assessing. "My
mom knows. She and Gregory are good friends, and I've heard
them talk sometimes."

I stood, wincing as my shoulder collided painfully with the
tree trunk. I'd grown taller in the two years since Tim and I had

found this spot. "Stop it. Just stop it. I don't believe any of that, so I'm certainly not going to tell anyone. I think we'd better go."

She stood, brushed off her clothes, and said, "I'm sorry. I've kind of ruined this little adventure. I—I don't get a lot of practice talking to people."

"It's just that you said things that aren't true! They can't be."

She looked at me a minute, obviously struggling not to say what she wanted to say. Then, "Yeah. All right. Let's go." It sounded like a concession, but it didn't feel like one.

The rest of the walk took longer than getting in; we had to climb uphill, which was tough for Pearl, and there were spots where I had to help her. Finally I saw the bridge and then the bright color of her bicycle cutting through the dull atmosphere. But when we got to our bikes, I felt thrown into yet another surreal situation. Our tires were slashed.

"Fuck!" Pearl shouted, and I jumped.

Although I was dying to shout it myself, I just stared in horror at the mess for several seconds. Then, "This isn't supposed to happen except at school!"

Pearl's look was disdainful. "Jude, this isn't *supposed* to happen anyplace. But I should have known. We should have hidden the bikes."

"Why should you have known?"

"Because of who's doing it." She bent over her front tire as if making sure it was dead.

I blinked. "Who's doing it? I thought no one knew."

She stood, looked around, and turned to me. "It's Bruce Denmark. The retarded kid. The Denmarks live just up the hill that way." And she pointed.

"But . . . why hasn't anyone done something about it?"

"They have. They've told everyone not to ride their bikes to school."

"But . . ."

"Jude, knock it off. What are they going to do, arrest a retard?"

I sighed heavily and looked around helplessly. How the

Hell—and I cringed at even this silent use of a word like that; I was defying authority and God all over the place today—was it that Pearl knew so much more than I did about people I should know better? I shook myself a little and turned my mind to what we were going to have to do about this. In a pinch, I could walk home, though it would be a long walk. But Pearl didn't have that option. However, she did come up with the solution.

"Listen. You go up to the Denmarks' and tell them you need to use their phone because your tires got slashed. Don't say who did it; they'll know, and they'll let you do whatever. Then call my mom—she knows I was meeting you—and tell her to come, but don't let the Denmarks know who you're talking to, and don't mention my name. Come back here, and we'll drive you someplace else where you can stop and call your house. Then they can come and get you. Can't have your precious Church know you've been into the woods with me." She looked at me, defying me to come up with something better. I couldn't. She told me her telephone number and I trudged uphill, reciting it the whole way.

Mrs. Denmark answered the door. With Pearl's revelations—if that's really what they were—in mind, I looked at Todd's wife through new eyes. She was almost pretty, blond with pale blue eyes and nearly white lashes, a faded look to her. She shrank inward a little when I told her my plight, so maybe Pearl was right about Bruce. I chose my words carefully on the phone so that no one listening would know precisely whom I was talking to, and then I went back downhill.

Pearl and I waited in silence for a time, watching the road. I hid once or twice when a car went by so no one would see me with Pearl. During a car-less stretch of time, eyes searching the distance, she said, "Listen, Jude, I really am sorry I blabbered on. Part of it is what I said, that I don't talk to a lot of people. But part of it . . ." She paused, sighed, and went on. "Part of it is that I don't know why you talk to me at all. I mean, no one else does. Especially not anyone in your Church. So I don't know how to trust you. And that means I say things that I know will upset you."

I had no clue how to respond to that. "It's okay," seemed insipid, but it's what I said. Why *did* I talk to her, anyway? Why had I told her about the flower I'd discovered, knowing there'd be a good chance she'd want to see it? Why, really, had I carried her books home last summer? Why was I risking being chastised again for consorting with a non-Christian, when a second trespass would be considered much worse than the first, baptized or not? Why had I felt so protective of her that I enlisted Gregory Hart's help to keep Bill and Larry away from her?

Most important, why was I risking my soul consorting with a pagan, heaping disobedience and defiance on top of my inability to confess the truth about my feelings for Tim to Reverend King before I was baptized? It was Satan. It had to be.

I decided to stop spending time with Pearl. My slashed tires, and the fact that I had to be deceitful to get out of this situation, were a sign from God that he was watching me, that he knew all the bad stuff I was doing. And thinking. I didn't want to end up like my father, an outcast, literally Hell-bent. It was time to rededicate myself. And maybe it was time to prove I wasn't gay.

But it wouldn't start today. I'd just managed to get Pearl's bike roped precariously into the trunk of Miss Thornton's car and was about to pile mine on top of it when Gregory Hart's blue truck approached us from up the hill. At first I felt panic; no one could see me here with the Thorntons. I tried to duck, but the truck slowed and stopped. Gregory called to Miss Thornton.

"Looks like you could use some help." He didn't wait for an answer, just pulled to the side of the road and got out. In very little time, he had tied Pearl's bike more securely into the car trunk and then hefted mine into his truck bed. I didn't quite know how to tell him I didn't want his help, so in the end I had little choice but to climb into the cab with him, edgy, nervous, pressed against the door on my side. The contrast with how it felt now to ride with him, compared to the day we had moved the hemlock, was like day versus night. Light versus darkness.

Good versus evil. It barely sank in that this was the second time he'd helped me with a wounded bicycle.

He asked what we'd been doing there, and I answered him as briefly as possible, adding that I thought Lorne would rather not know I had been hunting for anything in the woods with Pearl. Gregory nodded like he knew what I was asking and then was silent.

About a quarter mile from my house I asked him to let me out, saying I'd walk the bike home from there. As he pulled to the side he said, "What for?"

There was no other way to say it, so I was as honest and as brief as possible. "I don't think they'd want me riding alone with you."

He didn't get out of the truck to help me lift my bike out. I didn't blame him.

Chapter 11

That year I was especially anxious for summer to arrive. Or, that is, for school to be over. It would mean more time that I could spend on my computer, because I expected this summer to be a repeat of the last two—at least in terms of being at the Kings', if not in terms of my time with Tim. The rededication of my life would, I believed, be assisted considerably by spending more time in the company of Reverend King and his family.

But Clara's baby got in the way. Lorne sat me down at the kitchen table one Sunday afternoon just before school let out.

"Jude, Clara and I need your help," he began. "And I know you never wanted to spend lots of time away from home before, so I hope this will work out for all of us. It's harder and harder for Clara to do the housework, and she's been having trouble sleeping. I can help only so much, working all week. But you'll have lots of time." He must have seen the look on my face; he held up a hand. "Now, don't panic. We don't expect you to spend every waking minute doing chores. But I've asked Clara to make up a list of things she needs help with, and how often, and you know we can't afford to hire anyone to come in. So." He pushed a lined pad of paper closer to me on the tabletop. "Here's the list."

There was dishwashing; Clara's back hurt when she stood at

the sink for very long, and of course her growing belly got in the way. There was mopping the kitchen floor. There was vacuuming. There was cleaning the bathroom—the tub being particularly difficult for a pregnant woman. My muscles wound tighter with each new task as it was heaped onto me. I hated that it was all reasonable, and that not wanting to do it was like saying I didn't care what happened to Clara or the baby. "So will I have *any* time for myself?" The tone of my voice made me wince.

Lorne looked surprised, whether at my tone or my words or both, I wasn't sure. "Jude, you've done almost none of this work since I married Clara. She's been doing most of it, on top of her full-time job."

"I do the dishes! I vacuum sometimes! And I've been at school all week and at the Kings' most evenings!"

He paused, eyes boring into me. I slumped and waited. Then, "And in the summer, there's no school, and Clara's going to stop working in the afternoons so she can rest. You'll be at the Kings' in the mornings, and you can do these chores in the afternoon. For the rest of the summer, we need your help around here. And Jude"—his face grew even more stern—"once the baby is born, we'll still need your help. We don't know yet how soon Clara will be back to work afterward, but she won't have a lot of time to do housework. She may not need quite as much help, but she'll need some. We'll work that out in September."

So I'd have mornings, at least, when I could bike over to the Kings' and use the computer. And maybe ... I decided to ask: "So, can we get Internet access here? That way I can bring the laptop home sometimes."

He started shaking his head before I'd finished. "We can't afford it, Jude. You can see that. With Clara working only part-time for the summer and not at all for some time after the baby? How could we do that? If we have any money to spend, it will be on a cell phone in case Clara needs it for emergencies. But we haven't even decided about that."

Oh, sure, I thought; more and more and more things for Clara and "the baby." I crossed my arms over my chest.

Lorne took in an audible breath and exhaled. "Are we clear on this?"

"I guess."

"Jude." He waited until I looked up. "I have to say I'm disappointed by your attitude. I'd have thought you'd be glad to help out if you could, or at least that you'd see it makes sense and you'd do it with love. Clara loves you, you know. Don't you love her?"

Stifling the urge to repeat, "I guess," I responded instead, "Yes."

"Then help her. Help me. Help our family. Be glad you can. Now, bow your head." I did, and he did. "Dearest Lord, I ask that you soften Jude's heart so that the love he has for me, for Clara, for the baby, and for you can find its way in. Help him to see that by helping his family, he's doing your work. Give him understanding and patience to help him keep his own spirit alive and grateful. I ask this in Jesus's name. Amen."

I echoed his "Amen." But I felt no patience, just resentment and frustration.

So my summer didn't turn out quite like I'd hoped. I biked to the Kings' as early as was reasonable so I'd have some time on the computer, and then back in the afternoons to do my chores and help Clara with whatever she needed. Sometimes in the afternoons she'd try to take a nap, but she seldom slept, and her face took on a sunken look.

She did a lot of sewing, some things for her as she grew larger, but mostly for the baby. She and Lorne didn't want to know the sex of the child until it was born, so she avoided pink and blue. One of the sisters gave her an old crib that needed refinishing, so she asked me to sand it down and paint it. I actually kind of liked doing that. Lorne and I moved furniture around in their room to make room for it, and his bureau had to take up residence in my room, leaving me to wonder how soon other things would follow and there wouldn't be room for me anymore.

My mornings were sacred to me. Aurora would sometimes intrude, asking for help with something or just wanting to chat, but I actually began to enjoy her company, as long as I could still worship at my computer screen most of the time. One day in July she started talking about Andy Bruckner, in another Bible Study from ours.

"You don't mind, do you Jude? If I talk to you about him?" I shrugged and gazed up at the mountains. We were in the backyard in the shade—a break from my computer time—sitting in lawn chairs, glasses of lemonade screwed into the grass to keep them from tipping. "If you do, just let me know."

"I don't mind. But don't you talk to your girlfriends about him?"

"I want your opinion as a boy about some things. Plus, I'm not sure they get how hard it is for me, with my dad being the pastor. You know?"

I sipped from my glass and nodded. I did get it. Lorne had even cautioned me once, I remembered. "Yeah, it must be tough to find a guy who's even brave enough to be interested in the preacher's daughter."

She sat up straight. "That's it, exactly! Oh, I'm so glad you understand." She sighed, and then she looked intently at me. "Jude? You're not . . . I mean, you don't feel . . ."

I shook my head, puzzled. "What?"

"You don't like me that way, do you?"

There was a moment of panic; was she, too, going to tell me I was gay? "I like being your friend," was what I decided to say, and I think it was the best choice. I smiled.

She smiled back. "Me too."

Despite her confidences, though, I didn't talk to her about the encounters I was having in cyberspace. Bent on rededicating myself, on finding ways to immerse myself in Godly things and to push aside anything that didn't fit that mold, I'd encountered a chat room for people who called themselves Christians, and the way they talked—virtually, of course—startled me, and then intrigued me, and then fascinated me. They weren't afraid of questioning things that I'd always thought I'd go to Hell just for asking about. I'll never forget one exchange that I watched, more than participated in.

> **imok:** my friend doesnt come to church anymore everyone says he's going to hell for sure now

> **awom:** he is if he doesnt acept jesus as his savior and bear witness

> **imok:** so is everyone who doesnt accept jesus and bear witness going to hell?

> **awom:** thats what the bible says and its the word of God

> **imok:** what about Moses whers his soul

> **awom:** he went to limbo or purgatory or someplace before he can get into heven beyond that we wont know til we get there

> **imok:** what about everyone who lived after jesus was here but couldnt hear his message like eskimos

> **awom:** theyll have to do some penance God will decide not us we just have to worry about our own souls

> **imok:** I cant accept that my friend is going to hell hes a good person and loves God

> **awom:** then why didnt he stay in church

There was a pause here. I waited, staring at the screen, wondering if some bolt of lightning had taken imok out. Then,

> **imok:** he wanted to but hes gay and couldnt change so they wouldnt let him

> **awom: BEWARE!** Rom 1:26–32 dont get trapped in approval!

I couldn't get my cursor up to the X in the upper right corner of that screen fast enough. I closed my eyes and repeated those scriptural references Reverend King had made me memorize last summer before he would baptize me. The section from Romans, though the longest, had stayed with me the best, because it implied that although I wasn't homosexual (ha), there were ways to get caught by Satan. I chanted silently, moving my lips to the words.

For this reason, God gave them up to vile passions. For their women changed the natural function into that which is against nature. Likewise also the men, leaving the natural function of the woman, burned in their lust for one another, men doing what is inappropriate with men, and receiving in themselves the due penalty of their error. Even as they refused to have God in their knowledge, God gave them up to a reprobate mind, to do those things which are not fitting: being filled with all unrighteousness, sexual immorality, wickedness, covetousness, maliciousness; full of envy, murder, strife, deceit, evil habits, secret slanderers, backbiters, hateful to God, insolent, haughty, boastful, inventors of evil things, disobedient to parents, without understanding, covenant-breakers, without natural affection, unforgiving, unmerciful; who, knowing the ordinance of God, that those who practice such things are worthy of death, not only do the same, but also approve of those who practice them.

Certain phrases stuck in my brain: "without natural affection" and "worthy of death" and "approve of those who practice them." My inability to disapprove of Tim's feelings for me was a problem, because he had felt they were a problem. He had confessed them as sinful, ensnaring me in the process. I wanted natural affection, whatever that was; at least, I didn't want unnatural affection. And I did not want to be worthy of death—or worse, unworthy of it, since it was the only way to Heaven. Would not being horrified at Tim's feelings for me qualify me for that curse? Would it make God give up on me?

Only much later did it occur to me that "imok" and the gay "friend" might be the same person.

To my surprise, I found that I missed having suppers with the King family. Lorne and Clara were both people of few words, and I had never been a chatterbox. Plus Clara was always exhausted. So mostly all there was to listen to was flatware on plates, chewing, swallowing. These sounds actually began to disgust me. And then I hated myself for feeling disgust.

I missed Aurora. Her cheerfulness, her lighthearted teasing of her father, and her sometimes irritated but not disrespectful exchanges with her mother had kept the meals lively. I had even grown comfortable enough that I had once asked the reverend about his attitude toward desserts. There was a scrumptious chocolate cake with fudge frosting, and he had a piece in front of him. But all he did was inhale from it once and then ignore it.

"It's practice, Jude," he replied when I asked. "A piece of cake may be harmless enough, but if I can maintain the strength of will to avoid this little temptation every day, that will make it easier for me to turn away from the big ones. The important ones. The ones that lead you out of purity. Do you know what purity is, Jude?"

"Well . . ." I knew what the word meant, but I couldn't see how it applied here.

"Purity is the exclusion of everything that would contaminate. Something is pure when the only characteristics it has are good, and anything else is excluded. I want purity." He gestured toward the cake with a hand. "Resistance is the way to maintain it. So I practice resistance."

I was still a little vague, but not knowing what else to ask I said, "But—why smell it?"

"Smell yours." I did, the little that was left; it smelled wonderful. "Can you understand that smelling how good it is makes it that much harder to resist?"

I could. And I wondered if I would ever have that kind of strength. If I would ever need it.

One morning Reverend King and I were in his office while I helped him search for something. I was surfing around, Googling different phrases, and he wasn't following me very well. He decided to make a phone call while I searched. Half listening to his side of the conversation, it dawned on me that

I'd already found something like what he was looking for, maybe a month ago, and I might have bookmarked it. So I clicked on the menu bar to look.

Scanning the various URLs visually and following with the cursor, I saw the phrase "hot gay" and jumped, and the cursor clicked on it. The window that popped up made me gasp audibly. It was a screen full of thumbnail videos of men, naked, and doing things I'd never seen anyone do before. And some things I couldn't have imagined.

I don't know how Reverend King ended his conversation; all I know is that he hung up immediately and slammed the laptop screen down. Not knowing what else to do, I just sat there, speechless and in shock. The reverend sat in the chair next to mine, elbows on knees, and knitted his fingers together. After a couple of deep breaths he spoke.

"Jude. Look at me." I did; it wasn't easy. "I never meant for you to see that." I nearly responded, *You don't say.* I swallowed hard. He went on. "You need to understand what that was all about. Obviously you could tell what was going on, but you need to understand why it's on my PC." He leaned back, looking at me from beneath hooded eyes. "Have you ever seen a detective show, or read a book about detective work?"

That was pretty broad, so I just said, "Yes, sir."

"Then I'm sure you've seen situations where the detective has to learn as much as possible about the criminals he's after. He has to get inside their heads. Understand their motivation, what's driving them. And he has to become familiar with their habits. These are the things that help him catch them. Stop them. Arrest them. Can you see that?"

"Yes, sir." I could, although in this case . . .

"That's what I'm doing. And then I use it in my mission work."

"What mission work?" It was a little easier to look at him now.

"Every once in a while, I go down to Boise to try and save some souls. And you couldn't ask for easier pickings of souls in trouble than a bunch of gay men, hanging out in a bar. So, to make sure I'm not shocked when I see them together—because

sometimes they hug and kiss right in front of me—I expose myself to even more shocking behavior. To prepare myself."

I remembered that Aurora had mentioned, last spring, that
her father sometimes went to Boise on Saturday nights to witness. It never occurred to me that this was why. In an odd way,
this reminded me of him smelling the cake to make resistance
harder, but that hardly seemed applicable here. I was still confused.

Reverend King looked at me for a minute, thinking. "Have
you ever gone fishing for souls, Jude?"

"What? Me? No, sir. I mean, I've talked to people about
Jesus, the Church, you know."

"I'm thinking it might be good training for you. And it might
help you in your particular circumstances."

I blinked at him. "What circumstances?"

He leaned forward again, speaking softly. "I have some idea
how you've been struggling. I know you were in spiritual pain
last summer, when you knew Tim Olsen had talked about you
to me. You denied having similar feelings. And I believe you've
done your very best to tell yourself they weren't real, they didn't
mean anything, they aren't really what they might look like."
He paused. "Haven't you." He wasn't asking.

I couldn't speak. I could barely breathe.

He nodded. "Yes. I thought so. And I think it might help you
to see where men who don't fight those feelings end up. You'll
see the depravity, the disgusting unnaturalness, the exposed
lust. You'll practically be able to feel the sin around you. But
you'll be protected. You'll be safe. You'll be with me. And God
will be with us."

I swallowed again. Was he saying what I thought he was saying?

"Will you do it?" His voice was quiet and hypnotic. "Are you
brave enough? Do you love Jesus enough? Are you determined
enough to leave anything like that behind you?"

I grasped at the only straw I could see. "I can't go into bars.
I'm too young."

"I know places that will let you in. They won't serve you

liquor, but that's not why we'll be there. We'll be there for souls, Jude. We'll bring souls to God. Together. You and me."

Another straw appeared. "Lorne would never let me."

"You just let me talk to Lorne."

Panic! "You wouldn't . . . you wouldn't tell him . . ." I wasn't sure how to say it.

"It's enough that I know. I'll help you in a way Lorne can't."

Somehow he knew. He knew that what I didn't want Lorne to know was that there was even the slightest possibility that those feelings Tim felt were something I understood. And I figured Reverend King must have been able to tell because of his research. Because of all the work he'd done with these people. Lorne had stopped thinking about it after my denial last summer, I was sure.

"Open the PC, Jude." Slowly, gingerly, I lifted the screen up and away from the keyboard. The photos, plastered all over the screen, sprang back to life, and my attention was riveted. The men, as though caught in some version of Hell, were still pumping away at each other, or still licking, or sucking, or pulling. One guy shot cum and hit the camera lens, and then the sequence repeated and he did it again, and again.

When the reverend spoke again I jumped. "Do you want to be like those men, Jude?"

Almost reluctantly, I turned my gaze to his face. He was looking at me, not at the screen. Despite the familiar swelling in my pants, I believed I did not want to be like those men. Any of them. I shook my head. "No, sir."

"Then come with me. You saw more on that screen than you'll see on our mission, I promise you. So you've seen worse than we'll encounter. But you'll know that this"—he jerked his head toward the screen without breaking his gaze on me—"is what they do. This is the perverted, lustful, sin-driven behavior that we will save them from. We will bring souls to Jesus together, Jude, my boy." His voice rose, and he smiled. "Are you with me?"

I couldn't say yes. I didn't know what I should do. But I nodded. He slapped my back. "Praise the Lord! Now, young man, close that browser and start again. I'm still waiting for a very different type of information."

This mission, this soul-fishing expedition with Reverend King, took place in early August, on a steamy, hot Saturday night. I hardly slept the night before, partly from trepidation about our little adventure, and partly because I was keenly aware of my personal mission; I was determined that I would either prove to myself (and Reverend King) that I wasn't gay, or that I'd identify this particular sin in myself for sure and use this work with the reverend to cure myself. I mean, if teaching math to Pearl had helped improve my own math skills, wouldn't convincing gay men to purge themselves and dedicate their lives to God help me do the same?

Lorne had not been enthusiastic about this plan. Understatement. I didn't hear the conversation that took place the Tuesday before we went, but I knew when it was taking place. I was in a state, worried that Reverend King would feel he had to tell Lorne just how badly I needed to do this work and why, even though he'd more or less promised he wouldn't say anything. Personal needs and commitments always come second to serving God; I knew that. So when Lorne talked to me about it, I watched for the slightest sign that he knew I was endangered by this darkness myself.

"Jude, do you have any idea what this will be like? Do you know how depraved these people are?"

Was he trying to tell me I'd fall into that pit, or was he just concerned? I couldn't tell. "Reverend King has...um, described it to me." I didn't mention the Web site I'd seen. "I know it's ugly. But that will make the message of Jesus shine that much brighter!"

He gave me an odd glance, and I was afraid I might have overdone it. He said, "I don't like it. I told him that. I don't think a young boy should be exposed to that."

Was he now saying I couldn't go? If I didn't, there might be no other way for me to get the strength to purge myself. "Reverend King said it would be good for me to see that. Help me understand why it's so bad." I got an inspiration. "Do you remember when I was little and I sucked my thumb all the time?" He looked taken aback; it was a curve ball, for sure. "Mom used to spread this nasty gunk on my thumb at night before I went to bed, and if I sucked on it I got that yucky taste in my mouth."

"Did it cure you?"

Here was my chance to find out if Reverend King had said anything. "It helped. But in that case, I was a real thumb-sucker. In *this* case . . ." I shrugged my shoulders as if to say it wasn't necessary to say more.

Lorne's face told me that I'd made a point, even if he still wasn't happy. *Thank you, Jesus!* If he'd known, I felt sure his expression would have been very different. In the end he had to satisfy himself that he'd officially registered his disapproval and that Reverend King was responsible for the safety of my body and soul for the duration of this adventure.

Later that night, though, I heard a conversation that made me wonder two things: whether Lorne had always agreed with the idea and had been testing me; and whether he did, in fact, know how much I needed to go. I'd gone to bed, and I heard Lorne and Clara come upstairs but didn't pay much attention until I heard Clara's voice rise a little and say my name. I got up and crept as close to their closed door as I dared and heard Lorne's response.

"Reverend King wants him to go, Clara. Do you really think he'd take the boy if there was any danger?"

"There are so many kinds of danger!" Clara's voice rose higher as she spoke. "And there's no earthly reason to expose Jude to this . . . this depravity. He knows it's a sin, and he's a good boy. You know he wouldn't do what God doesn't want. Not in anything important. He doesn't need to have his nose rubbed in this!"

"There's no better way to get convinced that your mission is righteous than to see the extremes of what happens in the darkness. I'm telling you, Reverend King and I both feel he needs this." Clara must have opened her mouth to argue, because Lorne's next words were curt, final. "There's to be no more discussion about this. He's going."

I lay awake for some time trying to decide how much Lorne knew.

Saturday night arrived, finally, and I was to have supper at the Kings'. Lorne drove me over and, no surprise, used the opportunity to lecture me.

"Jude, I want to make sure you understand how important it is that you stay right with Reverend King and do everything he tells you. And nothing he doesn't."

It wasn't clear to me exactly why this was so important, but it was what I intended to do anyway. "I do. I understand."

"You'll be there to witness for Christ, to bring lost souls to the light if you can. But don't get too ambitious. It's likely these people won't want to hear what you have to say, and they're capable of all kinds of horrors."

"I get it. I'll be careful." I allowed myself to show just a little anger. Too much might spoil things, but the right amount would seem convincing to Lorne, and it might help quell some of my terror. I needed this chance. I'd fought for this chance, once I understood what it could mean to me. But it scared the willies out of me.

I could barely eat the early supper I had at the Kings', sitting alone at the kitchen table with the reverend while Mrs. King fed us sandwiches, potato chips, and sodas. I think the soda helped; I might have upchucked otherwise.

Aurora wandered in and out of the kitchen a few times. I knew she was IMing with Andy Bruckner upstairs and didn't want him to think (that is, didn't want him to know) that she was anxiously awaiting his every response. Coming downstairs was her way of making her folks think she wasn't up to anything—we both assumed they wouldn't approve of this exchange—and of forcing herself to give Andy's replies some waiting time. She knew that her father and I were going to Boise on a mission, and she knew it was the same kind of mission he'd been on many times in the past, but Reverend King had already warned me that neither his wife nor his daughter

knew the exact nature of the mission. He said it wouldn't benefit them to know, and it would worry them a good deal. Silently,
I pondered the comparison between this house and mine. The
wife of this powerful, righteous minister of God couldn't take
that he was going to look for lost souls among the homosexuals
of Boise; my brother's wife not only knew but had been allowed
to express at least some disagreement. Was Lorne foolish, or
was Reverend King's relationship with his wife less open than
Lorne's with Clara?

I didn't say much on the long drive to Boise; between not
having much of an idea what to expect and never having set
foot in any city before, everything inside me felt like it was shaking. Reverend King made me sing through a few hymns with
him, and he must have repeated what he called the "ground
rules" three or four times: stay right with him; don't respond to
taunts or suggestions; try not to talk at all, just listen; don't reveal disgust or repulsion; don't take anything anyone offered;
and don't be afraid. "Keep in mind, Jude," he admonished me
in different ways about twenty times, "these are lost souls. Satan
has them in his grip, and they don't even realize it."

It was about nine thirty and fairly dark when Reverend King
pulled his Jeep into the gravel parking lot of a place that must
have been just outside the city limits. Neon lights flashed and
music thumped, audible at all times but louder when someone
opened the door. The neon sign that caught my attention had
rainbow colors progressing around a form shaped like a male
torso in side view, round ass on one side and erect dick on the
other. I couldn't take my eyes off it, even when Reverend King
placed a hand on my shoulder and we moved forward. With his
other arm he hugged a Bible to his chest. "We represent Jesus,"
he said just loud enough for me to hear. "We're doing God's
work. We're saving souls." It almost seemed like he was talking
to himself. Encouraging himself.

As we approached, I found it easier to stop staring at the
neon torso. Three couples were standing in separate clumps
along the front of the building, the lights flashing on them and
creating odd shadows and odder color tints on faces and cloth-

ing. All three couples were kissing and groping, a sight I never expected to see with my own eyes. My breathing was shallow and odd, and my jeans felt distinctly snug at the crotch. I was riveted, not repulsed the way I had believed I would be. The way I believed I *should* be.

Inside, the noise was fierce until I got used to it. We stood there looking around, until a man who was maybe thirty approached us, his movements slinky. He wore a black-and-white checked shirt, open down his chest, tight black jeans, and black cowboy boots. He looked me up and down. "Hi there, Reverend. Isn't he a little young for you?" His voice, loud enough to be heard over the music, had an odd lilt to it.

I couldn't decide whether I wanted to look at the man or watch Reverend King's reaction. I tried to do both and nearly made myself dizzy.

"Trevor." Reverend King's tone was flat, unreadable. "The boy is here to learn. He's observing tonight."

The man's face pursed into an odd smile, and he waved a hand in parting. "Whatever you say, Rev."

Reverend King extended his hand to Trevor, one of his folded yellow paper pamphlets in it. Trevor threw his head back, laughed, and walked away. Into my ear, Reverend King said, "The men who've seen me before pretend that I'm here for the same reason they are. They're trying to dilute the Lord's message so it has less effect on them."

I tried to make sense out of this, but my eyes were bouncing from man to man on the dance floor, some of their moves distinctly imitating acts of sex from that site Reverend King had bookmarked. I felt his hand on my shoulder pushing me forward again, and we made our way to the bar. Reverend King ordered a ginger ale for each of us.

The bartender, like Trevor, looked at me as he spoke to the reverend. "The kid shouldn't be here, Reverend. You tryin' to get me in trouble?"

"The boy's here to learn. He needs to start reclaiming souls for God, and he needs to see how badly everyone here needs it."

The man's eyes flicked back to Reverend King. "All the same, I'm gonna ask you to finish your drinks and leave. All I need's the law bouncing in here tonight, and I could get arrested for contributing to the delinquency of a minor. So could you."

"I understand. We won't stay long."

As the bartender turned away, looking dubious, a dark-haired man in a shiny red shirt and a tan cowboy hat leaned on the bar beside me. He looked from me to the reverend, his smile twisting a little more with each glance. Before he could say anything, Reverend King spoke. "My friend here and I would like to extend an invitation to you." One of the man's eyebrows rose. "We'd like you to come to Church with us. Tomorrow morning, or any Sunday morning. Here." The man's eyes stayed on the reverend's face as he reached out a hand to take the pamphlet. Like the one Trevor had refused, it was a copy of the yellow brochure listing all six of those quotes I'd had to recite before my baptism, and I knew that in point-counterpoint style it provided the means to overcome this particular sin according to scripture. It also had information about our Church services and a few Bible studies.

The man unfolded the paper, glanced down at it, nodded. "All the usual," he said and folded it up again. He held it out to Reverend King, who didn't take it back. The man dropped it on the bar, where a ring of moisture from my glass of iced soda darkened a corner immediately and then spread slowly deeper into the paper. The man, his eyes still on Reverend King, asked, "What's your shirt made of?"

"Cotton." Reverend King's voice sounded victorious; they were obviously both in on something beyond me, and I didn't have a clue where the question came from.

"Your underwear?"

"What?"

"Mixed fibers, by any chance? Can't do that. According to Leviticus, you'd be ritually slaughtered. And are you having bacon with your eggs before church tomorrow?" I glanced at Reverend King, who just shook his head. "Using birth control?

Masturbating? Killing your child if he curses you? How much do you think you could get selling your daughter to a slave trader in Calgary?"

"Stop!" The tone was not victorious any longer, but angry. "You are pointing to scripture that suits you. It is not only in the Old Testament that the Lord condemns homosexuality."

"Then at least"—and the man picked up the brochure again—"you must agree that all these quotes from the Old Testament must be discounted. They're either mixed in with other sacred laws that you yourself ignore, or they refer to male prostitution, or to victorious soldiers raping the vanquished ones." He started making strategic tears in the moist paper, eliminating the Old Testament excerpts.

I felt the reverend stiffen. His voice calm now, he said, "That cannot be proven. And there are enough other condemnations to support—"

"Can't be proven? What *can* be proven? Nothing in your sacred texts can be proven." The man's voice was as calm as Reverend King's, though they both had to raise the volume to compete with the music. "And we do know that the word *homosexual* didn't exist until the last couple of centuries. Everyone who was alive, when the books you're so fond of were written, believed that everyone was straight, and that some people just decided to be perverse and take part in activity that no one else understood. Homosexuality as we know it today didn't exist. So it couldn't be condemned *or* condoned."

"My son, you are obviously struggling. You've given a lot of thought to this. Please come to us tomorrow morning and begin your journey from darkness into the light."

The man replied as though Reverend King hadn't spoken. "We also know that in the Middle East, at the time when these books were written, it was believed that all the essentials for a new human life came from male cum. 'Wasting seed' was like murder. It was—what was that word again? Oh, yes: an abomination. It didn't matter how you wasted it. It was wasted any time you didn't plug it into one of your wives, or one of your female slaves, or whomever you were told to use as a human oven. Judah's son Onan got slaughtered by God for dumping his seed on the ground rather than have mandated sex with his brother's widow. Fine bunch of people you're emulating."

"Please." Something in Reverend King's voice caught my attention, and I looked away from the man in the cowboy hat for the first time since he'd said, "All the usual." The reverend's face looked pleading at first. But then I saw something like what I thought I'd heard in his last word. I saw fear. "Please," he repeated, "come to us tomorrow. Let us show you the way. Let us help Jesus to help you out of this sinful existence. We can show you how to read God's Word in the way that will save your soul."

The man snorted. Then he looked at me. "What's your role? Are you his prop? Or is he trying to save your soul, too?"

As if his words had sucked the air out of the world, all the voices in the room hushed. The music was still playing, but everyone's attention turned to the door, in which two burly policemen stood. They glanced around the room slowly and then swaggered toward where we were. Someone turned the music off.

One of them, while looking at me, spoke to the bartender. "Leo, ya gotta keep your patrons inside. We got another call." He jerked his chin at me and then turned to Leo. "And what's this kid doin' here?"

"Drinking soda's all I know," Leo practically growled.

My mentor put on his richest tones. "Officer, I'm Reverend King from the Grace of God Church in Newburg. My young parishioner and I came here to invite these misguided souls to attend our service tomorrow." He handed the officer a brochure. "I'd be honored if you would join us as well."

The brochure disappeared into a ball of wrinkles in the man's broad hand. He took the reverend's arm, and the other cop took mine, and they marched us outside, gravel crunching under our feet more audibly than before, with no music to distract our ears.

"Reverend, take that boy home to his mother where he belongs. And if I see you bring him back here, you'll find out what the expression 'Hell to pay' means." He gave Reverend King a rough push toward the parked cars and turned to me. "What's your name, son?"

I had to clear my throat. "Jude Connor."

He handed me a pen and the wadded up brochure. "Write your home telephone number on here for me." My hand was shaking so badly I wasn't sure he'd be able to read what I wrote. "I know where Newburg is. I'm gonna give this fellow"—and he inclined his head toward Reverend King—"just enough time to get you home, and then I'm gonna call. I wanna speak with your parents. Got that?" He looked at the reverend. "*You* got that?"

My throat felt too dry to explain that I didn't have any parents. We watched the cops go back into the bar, probably to finish explaining to Leo that passersby didn't appreciate seeing men out here necking. Or maybe to get a drink, since no one in there was likely to report them. I turned back toward Reverend King, and he sighed loudly.

"They just don't understand." He shook his head. "This wasn't your fault, Jude."

I didn't know what he was talking about; *what* wasn't my fault? But I agreed when he said we'd best get on home. The plan had been for me to stay the night at the Kings' because of how late we'd probably get back, but that was out of the question now. The cop might not call, but if he did I needed to be at home.

We drove for a few minutes before I asked, "Will you come back, do you think?"

"Still lots of souls to save, Jude. Doesn't look like you'll be back with me, though. At least not until you're older."

"Have you ever saved anyone's soul from a place like this?"

"Not yet."

"Has anyone ever come to Church at all?"

He glanced at me and back at the road. "This was a test for you, too, and you never know when a soul will respond to the Word. Would Jesus want us to give up, Jude?"

"No, sir."

Maybe half a mile later he said, "Jude, I want you to understand what that man at the bar was doing. It's just too easy to pick things out of the Bible and hold them up and say, 'This makes no sense.' When the book of Leviticus was written, it was delivered to people who thought their civilization needed slavery to exist. And women were considered much less important than men. We know better now. So I want you to ignore what he said. His words are like pebbles cast against bulletproof glass, and the Bible is stronger than his weak criticisms." He heaved a breath. "So it isn't productive to argue back and forth with people who cherry-pick scripture to suit themselves. Because for each reference you quote, they'll have one they've twisted to throw back at you. Don't get caught in that trap."

I was thinking that maybe we should consider what else should be discounted, like maybe it wasn't such a sin to have sex before marriage or be gay—mutinous thoughts, to be sure, and I would never have voiced them. Instead, thinking of the missing Veronica Voelker, of the chat room banter that had frightened me, and of Gregory Hart, I asked, "What if someone in our congregation was gay?"

Just before I decided he hadn't heard me, he spoke. "During my missions, I've had several lost souls tell me that homosexuality is not a choice. Whether it's a choice when it starts or not, I can't judge for another. But what I say is that when we've seen how the power of Jesus can purify us, it is a choice to *remain* that way." He drummed the steering wheel a few times, whether in thought or frustration I couldn't tell. Then, "Paul's second letter to the Corinthians, Chapter 12, has some verses where he referred to lack of humility as a thorn that was in his flesh. He called it a messenger of Satan and said it was there specifically to harass him. Three times he asked God to remove it, and always God refused, because it was there to remind Paul that he was human, he was imperfect, and to keep him striving for purity." One more hard WHAM on the wheel. "If someone believes he's homosexual, then perhaps that's just God's way of letting Satan plant a thorn in his flesh. And it should drive that person to God, Jude, because that thorn could drag him all the

way to Hell faster than he knows what's happening. Only
through Jesus and the Father can this person hope for salvation. Only through the Grace of God."

I thought the discussion was over, and I'd gone to staring out
the window into the night, wondering if that thorn was in me.
Then, in a voice I could barely hear over the engine drone, he
said, "The homosexual who can't return to the natural ways
God laid out for us must remain chaste. He may have to remain
chaste for life, if that's what it takes."

True to his word, the policeman did call my house. Lorne
and Clara were upstairs, and as quietly as possible I was washing
my face in the bathroom when I heard first the phone, and
then Lorne landing on the floor in his bedroom. He staggered
into the hall, paused for a second as I opened the bathroom
door, and then thundered downstairs with me at his heels.

"Hello? . . . Yes, this is Mr. Connor . . . Yes, I knew he was . . . Is
there a problem?" He wheeled around and saw me standing
there. I shook my head; no problem. "Yes, he's right here, safe
and sound . . . No, I assure you, it was really a Church mission . . .
WHAT? No! Of course not . . . Yes, I understand. Good night,
officer."

Lorne ran a hand through his tousled hair. "Are you all
right?"

"Yes. We were in this bar, talking to this . . . person about the
Bible, and two cops came in. They took me and Reverend King
outside and told us to go home. They said they'd call here, so I
figured I'd better come home after all, in case they really did."

Lorne gazed sleepily at me a moment. "They had some idea
that Reverend King was doing something with you that he
shouldn't."

I blinked. Then I shook my head again. "We just drove down
there, went in, had a soda, talked to the guy, and left when the
cops said to."

Hand back in his hair, Lorne said, "Yes. Yes, of course. But I
think there won't be any more of this particular kind of mission
for you. You're going to bed now?"

I nodded, to both the question and to the statement, and then followed Lorne back upstairs. But I lay awake for a long time, going over in my mind the things the man in the red shirt had said. Eventually, sleepless, I turned on a light and got out my Bible, which still had that pamphlet from a year ago tucked into it. I looked up all the verses, only this time I read a lot of the stuff around them. The more I read, the more convinced I was that it wasn't just the red shirt guy who was pulling things out to suit him. It was anybody who pulled things from the Bible out of context. Including Reverend King.

So Clara had been right in one way; this mission had made me feel really weird and had stirred me up in ways she probably wouldn't have wanted me stirred up. But in another way, although I had in fact had my nose rubbed in something, I believed it was good that it had happened. Because if I was right that everyone used the Bible to their own ends, which ends were better? That noisy, unsettling bar where the owner was nervous about the police? Or eternal salvation, all the love God could offer, and being with my mother again? Reverend King's ends had to be better. They just *had* to.

Chapter 12

The next morning, for the first time in my memory, Clara didn't go to church. She didn't even get up to see us off. Over our breakfast cereal, Lorne told me she hadn't slept at all. "It's so hot. And she has such a hard time sleeping on her back." He rubbed his face, and by the looks of him I'd have said he hadn't slept much himself.

Reverend King looked chipper enough; it must have been that on his usual mission work to the bars in Boise he got home much later than when the police sent him home under suspicion of wrongful acts with a minor.

But I'd been right about Lorne; he collapsed on the couch almost as soon as he'd finished lunch. I took a sandwich and some iced tea up to Clara, who looked wilted onto the sheets. Then I left; I hadn't slept well myself, but it was depressing in the house. The cool shade of the pine trees along the edge of the meadow stream, mostly dried up though the water was by this time of year, seemed much more appealing than the stifling atmosphere in the house. Right about where Pearl had shoved the skunk cabbage in my face I found a soft bed of old, decaying hemlock needles in the fork of a tree's roots. I stretched out there, fell asleep, and stayed that way until I felt something kicking my foot. Startled, I sat up quickly.

"Where've you been hiding?"

Pearl. I rubbed my eyes and tried not to be irritated; this was more her territory than mine, after all. "I haven't been hiding. I've been busy." I didn't want to admit that even if I'd had more time to myself, I wouldn't have sought out her company. I was rededicating myself, and consorting with pagans wouldn't further this goal.

"Yeah? Doing what?"

Who was she to demand explanations? I pulled myself up a little and leaned back against the tree, still sitting on the soft forest floor. "Let's see. In the mornings I've been helping Reverend King do Internet searches for scriptural stuff and finding other Church sites. In the afternoons I've been helping Clara with the housework."

"Oh, right. She's preggers. How's that going for her?"

Why couldn't this girl speak like a normal person? "She's okay, but she can't sleep."

"Weather? Big belly? All that stuff?"

"All that stuff." Whatever that meant.

"Wait here." She turned and hobbled away. *Wait here?* It was very much like that day I'd ridden out to the Harts', to be greeted by Pearl at the door. Wait here. I lay back down again to see if I could regain that blissful oblivion I'd been enjoying. I did drift off a little, but before long Pearl was back. She sat down beside me on the ground.

"Here." She handed me a little brown bottle with a black rubberized squeeze bulb in the cap. "Have her put about thirty drops of this in a glass with a tablespoon of warm water half an hour before she wants to fall asleep."

I looked at it dubiously, opened the cap, and sniffed. It was like shoving a fistful of someone else's dirty socks into my face. "Yuck! What *is* this stuff?"

"It's valerian root tincture. It will help her sleep. The only side effect is that she might have more vivid dreams. It's not toxic to her or the baby this late in the pregnancy, if she takes only as much as I said, and it's not habit forming. It works."

I studied Pearl's face long enough to be sure she wasn't putting me on. But then I stretched my hand, with the bottle, back toward her. "Clara won't take this. She wouldn't even try any of the things I harvested last spring, even though Lorne and I ate them. Plus how am I going to explain where I got it?"

"Oh, right. I'd poison my neighbor for no reason."

"But I'm not supposed to be spending time with you."

She stood, leaving the bottle in my outstretched hand. "You're not. It's been . . . what, two minutes tops? I'm leaving."

"Wait! Where did you get this?"

Her words were thrown over her departing shoulder. "I made it. What do you think?"

She made it. I sniffed it again, and again recoiled. How could I give this to Clara? Using the dropper, I put one drop on my finger and took it into my mouth. It didn't taste nearly as bad as it smelled. Capping the bottle, I looked at it, thinking. I decided to try it myself first.

I slept very well that night. I took the valerian right after I brushed my teeth, which was closer than half an hour before I got into bed, but even so it didn't take long. I barely had time to wonder how it was that Pearl knew so much about plants and herbs, and to speculate that it might be her way of dealing with the fact that she'd been nearly killed and certainly maimed by one of them. With a picture in my mental vision of her on her boulder, surveying her meadow, I began to feel a softening effect of the general atmosphere all around my body. My mind relaxed, then my limbs, and I drifted gently to sleep. And, just as Pearl had said, my dreams were pretty vivid, but they weren't bad. Just intense.

At the Kings' next morning I did a little research on this stuff, and basically everything Pearl had told me was true. I printed out some pages with particularly useful information and took them with me when I bicycled home for my afternoon work shift.

Clara was sitting in the middle of the kitchen floor, sobbing, when I got there. Around her were puddles of water and the shards of a milk glass pitcher. I stood in front of her, very worried. "Are you okay, Clara? I mean, I see what happened, but what about you?"

She nodded, still sobbing, and then held out a hand so I could help her up. She held me awkwardly and sobbed some more while I patted her shoulder and wondered what to do. As her sobs abated, she spoke through them. "I can't do anything. It wasn't even heavy. It's just that I'm so tired I can't even see straight. I missed the table."

I helped her to a chair. "I'll clean this up, Clara. But there are so many pieces. . . ."

"Oh, I know. There's no way to mend it. It was my grandmother's." More sobs.

I picked up the larger pieces of the bluish white glass and set to work with a sponge mop and some damp paper towels. Frankly, I had never liked the thing anyway. Several minutes later, the mess was gone. So was the pitcher. I sat in the chair facing Clara. "I have something that might help you."

"Help me?"

"Help you sleep. It's one of my herbs. You remember how I was learning about herbs?" She nodded. "Well, there's one called valerian. Hang on." I fetched the printouts, which I'd dropped onto the counter when I saw Clara on the floor. "Here. This explains about it. I've taken it myself, and it's wonderful. It really helps."

I gave her a minute to read, and she tried, but she set the papers down. "Tell me what it says, Jude. I can't focus with my eyes or my brain."

"It's been used all over the world for centuries for insomnia. It relaxes you; that's all. It's not a drug, and it's not habit forming. And," I stressed this knowing how concerned she would be, "if you take it in small doses it can't hurt the baby. It probably wouldn't hurt it anyway, but I know you want to be careful about any of this stuff."

She closed her eyes, took a deep breath, and looked at me. "You're sure?"

"Yes. I'll get the bottle so you can see it." It was in my room, hidden in my underwear drawer. Since I was doing the laundry these days, I figured no one was likely to go in there. Back in the kitchen I handed the bottle to Clara. "It tastes lots better than it smells. Kind of sweetish. You put about thirty drops into a tiny bit of warm water right before you want to go to sleep. Then—poof! You're asleep."

"Poof?" She looked scared.

"That's just an expression. It's very gentle. Very gradual." I watched her open the bottle, smell, and recoil as I had done. "Listen, let's try this. You take some and go lie down. I'll check on you every fifteen minutes, and I'll make sure you're awake before Lorne gets home."

"I don't want to sleep that long. I want to be able to sleep tonight. Can I take it again then?"

What did I know? "Sure." Would she try it? I wasn't sure why I cared, but I did.

She set the bottle on the table. "I don't know."

I shrugged. "Just a thought. It worked so well for me, and I know it can't be good that you're not sleeping."

She blinked slowly as though that was all the energy she had. "It can't be good for the baby, either. Suppose I fall someplace more dangerous than the kitchen floor?"

My head jerked up. "You fell? I thought maybe you just . . . I don't know."

She let out a long breath. "I fell. I dropped the pitcher and slipped in the water." Arms on the table, she lowered her head on them. I waited. Then, slowly, she sat up. "Will you get me some warm water?"

I helped her upstairs after she took the valerian and positioned the fan for her where she wanted it. Lying on the bed, she looked fragile and almost sick, sending my mind back to images of my dying mother on this very bed. And then I knew why I cared: as a small child, there was nothing I could have done for my mother, dying of cancer. But as a young man, thanks to my quasi-friendship with Pearl, I could help pregnant, sleepless Clara. I pulled the shades down over the top halves of the open windows, told her to relax, and said I'd be back in a few minutes. She nodded without opening her eyes.

In the kitchen I set the timer for ten minutes. If anything bad happened, I'd never forgive myself. Plus, if she really fell, that might mean something bad *could* happen. I'd been planning to vacuum today, but I didn't want to make that much noise. I cleaned the kitchen sink instead and then, with two minutes still left on the timer, I crept upstairs.

Clara was breathing softly, deeply, very much asleep. I stood there watching her for maybe three minutes, more images of my mother flashing through my mind. It was everything I could do not to wake Clara up and get her to a hospital. But the difference, when I allowed myself to think clearly, was vast. My mother really had been on death's door and had looked like it. Clara looked peaceful, almost happy. I went to clean the bathroom.

I checked on her several more times, and then at four I touched her shoulder. I had to shake her just a little, but then she woke up. "It's four o'clock," I said. "Do you want to sleep some more?"

She smiled, stretched gently, and shook her head. I helped her sit up and then stand. Again, she held me, in a real hug this time. "Thank you, Jude. God bless you."

Back in the kitchen, I made each of us a glass of iced tea, and we sat at the table. She said, "Where did you get the valerian?"

I looked sharply at her. "Are you sure you want to know?"

"Yes."

"I was in the meadow on Sunday afternoon, asleep under a pine tree. Pearl Thornton found me. She asked how you were, and when I told her you were having trouble sleeping she went home, fetched this, and left again. I took it to be sure it was all right, and it was."

"You took it first? Even though you brought it home for me?"

"Sure. I didn't want anything to happen to you."

She closed her eyes and then swiped at the tears that leaked out. She took a deep breath. "I don't know if we should tell your brother about this."

"Probably not." Another secret. I'd been piling them up over the last couple of years. If Lorne ever found out about the valerian, I never knew it.

I went into the meadow that afternoon before Lorne got home. On top of Pearl's boulder I left a folded paper under a large rock. It said, "Thank you." Then next afternoon, just to see if she'd found it, I went to the boulder. Waiting for me was, "You're welcome."

I took just enough time after finding the note to look around for tansy plants. They were everywhere. Tall, gangly stems with bright pom-poms of yellow on bracts nearly as wide as my palm stood proudly all around me. Cheerful poison.

Clara's baby was born on September twelfth, a girl that she and Lorne named Christina because she had been conceived during the twelve days of Christmas. Christina Catherine Connor. It felt weird to have a niece; I wasn't old enough for that. So to make things less formal I decided to call her CC.

Clara's labor had been long—a day and a half. Lorne had stayed there with her, but I was sent to spend the night at the Kings'. In "my" bedroom there. I'd almost stayed there the night the Boise mission trip was cut short. I'd spent endless hours in this room but none of them overnight. It felt weird. And I had a dream. It wasn't the first dream I'd had that had caused me to waste seed in my sleep—which I didn't hold myself accountable for—but the others had all been pretty vague, and it hadn't even been clear to me in the past exactly what had caused my physical reaction. But this time there was no doubt.

It was the man in the red shirt. Flashes of shiny red mingled with expanses of bare flesh and dark hair, and I swear I could feel his hand on me. It held my dick, or it poked into my ass, or it rubbed hard on the space between. It squeezed my balls and it pinched my nipples and went back to my dick again. The man's mouth was hot on mine and seemed to take half of my face into it.

When I opened my eyes I was sitting up in the darkness, panting, eyes wide and straining. I waited just long enough to make sure no one had heard any sounds I might have made, and then my own hand was on my dick. I finished the task right there in that bed in the home of the pure and righteous Reverend King himself. Then I turned my face into my pillow and smothered a scream. Clara had been right. And this dream was the proof; I shouldn't have met that man. Now he haunted me. There was a brief moment of false hope when I thought maybe the intensity of this evil dream was from the valerian, but I had given the vial to Clara. I hadn't taken more than the one test dose.

I got out of bed and knelt on the floor, head collapsed onto folded hands still dirty from what I'd done. I whispered my plea.

"Please, Jesus! Please, please help me. I didn't want that dream! I didn't! I'm trying so hard. You *know* how hard! You know everything! Can't you give me a sign? Can't you tell me what I have to do that I haven't done? Do I need to get baptized again?"

I listened for a few seconds. Then, "Please?" Silence. "Please!" Face pressed into the side of the mattress, I fought tears as a squealing whine came out of me and was muffled on the bed.

To prove my intentions to Jesus, I stayed there on my knees until sunlight found its way over the mountains to the east.

Everyone said what a good baby CC was. The name caught on, and pretty soon there was no one who wasn't calling her that. Having come up with the nickname myself helped me in my next step toward rededication: helping Clara take care of the baby.

Looking back at that time of my life, I think of it as my gray period. Gray sky, gray mountainsides, gray buildings, gray baby toys, gray me. I moved like a zombie through the days: get up, go to school, come home and do chores, bike to the Kings' for supper if I needed the computer for homework, bike home and collapse into bed. When the weather got colder, Clara was able to bring CC and drive me to the Kings' when I needed computer time, and Lorne would pick me up. I missed my bike ride home, though; it had drained even more energy so that I wasn't as tempted to enjoy being alone in bed.

I used Reverend King's dessert example to limit my computer time. Using the Internet for homework was like his inhaling the sweetness of what he would then deny himself. I denied myself time on the computer for anything other than schoolwork, unless Reverend King needed me to do something for him.

That November I turned fifteen. Gray birthday, despite Clara's best efforts. By then I had even less time and energy for temptation, because I'd taken an after-school job for the holiday season at Newburg's only real gift store, Emily's Emporium, where they had a lot of Belinda Thornton's sweaters for sale. My entire salary, after buying a few gifts, was to be my gift to CC for Christmas. I knew that if it was for CC, Lorne and Clara couldn't turn it down.

It kept me exhausted, but in terms of keeping my thoughts about sex in check it helped only so much. But I reasoned with God, through Jesus, that I could give up only one thing at a time. I promised that as soon as it wasn't so much of an effort for me to stay away from personal computer time, I would move on to the issue of wasting seed. I argued, during these prayerful negotiations, that my seed was hardly wasted anyway, since I wasn't supposed to be getting anyone pregnant at this point in my life.

Despite the gray, I had expected to feel something on Christmas morning when Clara opened that box I'd packed full of the cash from my job, along with a note explaining what it was and where it had come from. It was a nice note, saying something about this being a token compared to the gift God gave to the world on Christmas, but like the little drummer boy in the song, I would give what I could to this new baby. I'd been hoping that the expression of surprise, of excitement, of happiness, of something on Clara's and Lorne's faces would bring some light back into my heart. They did their part, expressing all those things on their faces and with their words, and with Clara's hug. But the light didn't do its part. I almost felt as though the Light—you know the one I mean—had failed me.

There was one present for me under our tree that had a weird effect on me. I don't know how it got there, although there were a number of ways it might have happened. It was from Aurora. She gave me a white T-shirt with the words **Computer Angel** across the front in black block letters and a pair of angel wings outlined on the back in thin black lines. But it wasn't the T-shirt that moved me. It was the card inside, under the tissue paper, that I didn't see until I'd taken the box upstairs to my room. It was a miracle I didn't overlook it. She must have made it herself. The card had a little girl angel drawn in the front, a sad expression on her face. Inside were printed the words, **I miss you.** Aurora had signed her name and drawn a few teardrops. I fought to keep from adding to them.

My gray period lasted into about the end of February, right about the time I began to weaken in my resolve to resist the computer. I still wasn't spending nearly as much time at the Kings' as I had the year before, but when I was there it became easier and easier to spend "just a few minutes" browsing Christian chat rooms. I told myself it was okay because it was related to Church. I'd never participated much in these things, probably because I had a tendency to gravitate toward conversations that were questioning doctrine, and you never know who's out there, who might figure out that "fortress" was me. It was a handle I'd coined because of the hemlock fort and the famous hymn—an odd combination of frustrated desire and godly power.

The gray was also lifted by Aurora, whose company I had missed as much as she seemed to have missed mine. She was off Andy Bruckner and onto one Lawrence Matvey, and I heard all about Lawrence's charms and the irritating quirks that didn't do much to diminish said charms in Aurora's eyes. I didn't much care what she talked about. Just being with her livened my life. Brought color back in. I think now that part of it was that I felt as though I could express myself more safely with her than with anyone else. True, I had to watch the subject matter, but at times I felt like her closest girlfriend as we gossiped and laughed and made up stories about people. Sometimes we would pray together, too, and that always left me feeling happy in a weepy kind of way.

As if I needed any more temptation to be at the Kings', Reverend King decided to do a weekly blog on the Church's Web site, and he was always asking me to find Web sites that pertained to some topic or that helped answer questions that came from people responding to the blog; he wanted to add links to make it seem as though he understood the Internet better than he did. He began to pay me for my time, which meant that Lorne started to take it seriously and helped make it possible for me to do it. I decided to take all this as a sign from God that the computer was all right after all. But then, it was like God had said to me, "We've knocked this one down, kid. Now, what about that other matter?"

I started exploring chat rooms for conversations about religious ramifications around masturbation, assiduously clearing my cache, my browser history, and all cookies before powering off the computer. I was searching desperately for some mention of what the red shirt guy had said, about how everyone in the Middle East used to believe that the woman didn't contribute anything to new life, just "baked" it, which would have meant a case could be made—in those days, anyway—for not murdering unborn babies by masturbating. Or by shooting off anyplace that wasn't an "oven." And two guys doing it together would have meant two deaths, by that logic. Condemnation, big-time, but for perceived murder, not necessarily homosexual activity. But it was hard to search for this type of argument, and the chat rooms were mostly filled with what sounded like kids

trying to get a hold on themselves by not taking hold of themselves. If you know what I mean. So I told myself that I was following up on "that other matter" by reading what everyone had
to say, because there were a lot of voices out there that were
very explicit on just what one shouldn't do and why, complete
with scriptural references. I was living up to my end of the bargain in this way.

So I left the gray period and entered the time of sex. I just
couldn't not "do it." When I wasn't wasting seed, I was thinking
about it, reading about it, doing research on it. And Reverend
King added to the critical mass by devoting more than a few of
his blog topics to related issues: premarital sex, homosexuality,
adultery, masturbation, homosexuality, and—oh yes, homosexuality. I became convinced that it was his favorite sin, and
that jibed with the fact that he was still going to Boise for his
mission work. It seemed to me that the frequency of these trips
had increased. He didn't mention them to me again, but the
number of Sunday mornings on which he looked like he
needed sleep grew. Most of the time he still delivered a rousing
sermon; he just looked like Hell doing it. Sometimes I would
look around for Gregory Hart, wondering if he knew about the
missions. If he had access to a computer anyplace. If he knew
about the most frequent blog topic.

By Good Friday all effort to make a sacrifice of personal computer time was behind me, and I was embarked instead on my
search for moral purity—that would be all the online time researching issues related to sex, of course. A couple of weeks before the Easter weekend, one Saturday morning I was at the
Kings', bent on researching some particularly interesting images that had been in a dream the night before, and I was waiting for my laptop to finish booting when Aurora appeared at
the door to my room. She looked awful. I knew I should ask if
she was okay, but I was anxious to get underway with my research. She solved my dilemma. "I need to talk to you."

Staring at the screen, which was indicating that the computer was nearly ready for me, I replied, "To me? About what?"

I glanced at her in time to see her look down the hall to make sure she wasn't overheard.

"Something I heard last night."

I sighed, resigned but also curious. "Take a seat."

She shook her head. "Can we go out for a walk?"

She had my attention now. "Meet me on the back steps." I grabbed my coat, headed downstairs, and within a couple of minutes we were headed down the road that led to the river. I let her take her time, though I was dying to prod.

Finally she said, "I heard my folks talking about something. Arguing, really." She stopped. I waited her out. "It had to do with . . . you know."

In my book, "you know" would always mean sex. But in hers? "Okay. Go on."

"They don't."

"Don't what?"

"They don't do it."

Like most kids, to me the idea of grownups going at it was not very appealing, but you sort of had to admit they must do it. My brain fired in several different directions and landed nowhere. All I could say was, "Why not?"

"Daddy won't do it."

An image of berry pie launched itself into my brain. "You mean, like the desserts?"

"Yeah. I guess so. He said that God spoke to him and commanded him to be chaste after I was born. God said their marriage must be pure."

"Pure? Pure from what?"

"He used the word *carnality*." We walked in silence for a few minutes while I contemplated this news. Then Aurora said, "I feel so guilty."

This stopped me in my tracks. "What? Why? What have you got to do with it?"

"I kept pestering. For years, I kept asking for a baby brother or sister. And then after CC was born and you were never here anymore, I asked again."

"So . . . you're guilty of what, exactly?"

"They were shouting! They *never* do that. It's only because I brought it up." I couldn't help myself; I laughed. "Jude! This isn't funny." She moved ahead of me.

I caught up with her, and we were quiet again until I couldn't stop myself from telling her what I thought. It wasn't very comforting, but if I couldn't help in any other way, maybe I could get her to stop blaming herself. "Look, Aurora, if God told your father not to have sex after you were born, then this isn't something that's just coming up now. This has been going on for fifteen years. It has nothing to do with you."

"But I—"

"Did it sound like your mom wanted to have a baby?"

"Yes. She talked about all the baby showers she's organized, all the new mothers she's helped, how wonderful that feels, and how much she wanted another child."

"Still, you didn't put that idea into her head, you know. CC isn't the only baby we've had a shower for in the last several years."

A few steps later, "I guess not."

We were nearly at the river. "Do you think they know you heard?"

"No. I moved away while they were still shouting. I couldn't take it."

The water looked cold. Really cold. It was early April, so that made sense; but around here, the mountain snowmelt kept water feeling icy well into warm weather. We stood there staring at it, and I felt Aurora shiver. With my gloved hand I reached for hers.

Pure, I thought; the marriage must be pure. My mind ranged back over the past few months, and it seemed to me that the more I had thought about not wasting seed, the more I had wanted to do it. And if I hadn't thought about it at all, I'm sure it would have happened a lot anyway. And Reverend King was so adamant, so literal about the law, the rules, that it was hard to believe he'd do anything like masturbate. So that left a question bouncing madly around in my brain: Did he not have any kind of sex experiences at all? Did he really do *nothing?* I shook my head; impossible. But—what would he do? Did he really love God that much? So much that he gave up *sex* for him? He'd told his wife that God had commanded him to remain pure.

An awful jerk went through my body, and I yanked my hand away from Aurora's without meaning to. Was this my sign? The one I'd prayed for? Was this what I was supposed to do? I sat down hard on the ground. No way! No fucking way! I was no Reverend King. I couldn't do that! And into my memory came the sermon about happiness, and about what we might be asked to give up for God. I had begged not to be asked to give up my friendship with Tim. And it had been taken from me by force.

I felt Aurora's hands on my arm. "Are you okay, Jude? It looked like you fell."

Barely able to speak, I managed, "Yeah. I'm okay. I just need to sit here for a minute."

She sat beside me, leaning her shoulder against mine. Her warmth was comforting, but not nearly comforting enough. Eventually she shivered again, and we headed back.

"I don't know how I can just be normal after this," she said. "I mean, like, I have to pretend I didn't hear all that. Pretend everything's normal."

"Everything is normal, though. Nothing has changed, except that now you know." And now I knew, as well. I knew what I had to do. My very soul was in danger. I'd heard this warning before, but it had never struck home. Now it had, and I had to act.

As soon as we got back to the house, I knocked on Reverend King's closed office door. He boomed, "Come in." I stood before his desk and looked directly into the intense darkness of his eyes as though I gazed at God himself.

"I need to confess. I have not been pure. I have been abusing myself and thinking about men at the same time. I need to repent and rededicate myself to Jesus. I want to deserve my baptism this time." Shaking badly, I grabbed at the edge of his desk.

He stood and went to a closet in the corner, bringing out a draped object. He set it up in front of the closet door and removed the cloth, revealing an extremely realistic and painful image of Jesus on the cross. The face, lifted upward, was pure agony. I had to stifle a gasp; in our Church, we held this kind of representation to be sacrilege; it was leaving Jesus on the cross, denying his death and resurrection. Reverend King held out a hand and led me to a spot before the statue, and we both knelt. If he was doing this, it must be all right. Maybe he was letting me in on a secret known only to God's chosen saints. In any event, I accepted it without question.

I lost track of time. He prayed aloud, I joined in when I knew the scripture he recited, he prayed more, I prayed, we both cried and sobbed and wailed, and when it was over I lay on the floor, curled into a fetal ball while the reverend's hand warmed my shoulder. As he withdrew and sat back, he said, "You are like a son to me, Jude Connor. I love you like the son God decided should not be of my body. You were delivered to me, fatherless, motherless, and I have loved you as my own son. He sent you to me for both our sakes, so that I could earn the son I wanted, and so that you could earn the eternal love that you can reach only with my help. For I will lead you on the path. I prayed for you, Jude. I begged God to send you to me. Praised be God in his mercy, in his love, in his understanding of the way of all life. He knows us better than we know ourselves, and he provides for us that which we most need for the salvation of our souls. You are my son, Jude. You are mine, and I love you."

I began weeping all over again, and he held me until I was calm. Reverend King was the father God sent me to replace the one I lost. Only this father could help me out of this darkness that my real father might not even have understood. I was blessed indeed.

I was baptized in the river on a blindingly sunny day in early May, as witnessed by a very small group of saints. Lorne and Clara were there, and Natalie King. No one else. The river was cold. So cold.

Chapter 13

I began what I now think of as my proselytizing period. I was newly washed. Lorne and Clara had both been aware of my struggles (to some extent, anyway) and had forgiven me. Clara surprised me as I emerged from the freezing water by taking me into her arms, dripping ice though I was. She whispered in my ear, "I'm sorry, Jude. I was wrong. You needed to go on that mission last summer, and I tried to stop it." She hugged me hard and swayed side to side for a minute while I worked out what she meant: The mission to Boise had forced me to confront the sin that was taking hold over me, had brought it to the surface where it could be dealt with.

As the saying goes, there's no one as obnoxious as a new convert. I felt newly converted, newly reborn. Rededicated wasn't a powerful enough word. I faced a problem, though: in our tiny little town, there weren't many people who weren't in the Body, and those who weren't were so sick of hearing about it that they practically ran from anyone they knew to be especially prone to witness at them. Until now, I hadn't been one of those people the unsaved ran from, but that changed. It changed because God had seen fit to align things for my salvation, and because God had chosen me to be Reverend Amos King's son. Obnoxious was definitely the right word for me. I didn't see it like that, of course, but I believed God had given me permission to do just about anything in his name.

My new sense of purpose—of permission—took me first to Tim Olsen. I was on a high that has rivals only in the areas of psychosis and illicit drugs, and it didn't occur to me to be anxious or nervous as I biked to his house early one Saturday morning. (I slept little in those days—too excited, too full of plans about bringing God's Word into the world.) His mother answered my knock. "Hello, Jude. We haven't seen you in some time. Tim's just having breakfast. Come in. Would you like anything?"

"No, thank you, ma'am. I just have something I need to tell Tim."

Tim and I hadn't seen each other outside of Church or school since the time I'd come here to study with him while his sister watched that Disney DVD in the next room. I didn't even know whether his parents had been told why his baptism had been delayed. Reverend King and Mr. Voelker had known, but they might have told the Olsens merely that Tim needed a little more preparation. And so I also didn't know if they'd been aware of my part in that little drama. I didn't care, either; others' discomfort wasn't going to interfere with my doing God's work. Tim's nervous eyes followed me as I came into the kitchen and sat myself down across from him. He held onto the spoon resting in his cereal bowl, frozen.

"I want you to know I forgive you," I began, smiling my new "love of God" smile. "And you were right, not to get baptized before you were ready." His eyes begged me to stop, flicking between me and his mother, who had busied herself at the sink, a few feet away. "I never told you this. I never told anyone. But I felt the same way. We were both wrong, and I know that now. Thank you, brother." I held out my hand. The spoon clanked against the bowl and slowly he reached his hand out to take mine, barely allowing a touch. "God be with you all." I nodded to Mrs. Olsen as I rose to leave, not knowing or caring what kind of damage I might have done to Tim's day. Tim's week. Tim's life.

By the time school let out for the summer I had developed a reputation among my classmates and teachers. A couple of people called me the Damascus Kid. In Bible Study I always spoke up when the leader asked for thoughts about a particular passage or a particular life situation. When I noticed looks exchanged between some of the other kids, I brushed them aside, reminding myself not to feel arrogant in my enlightenment, to keep that thorn in mind, the one the real Mr. Damascus wrote about, to remember that I was human, imperfect, and humble. If I felt exalted, it was not me but the spirit of God within me.

What I didn't understand—among so many other things— was that humility is like class; as soon as you think you have it, you've lost it.

One big change that my new state made not only possible but also essential had to do with people I had avoided before: Pearl and Belinda Thornton, and Gregory Hart. Now it was incumbent upon me to seek them out and bring them to the Lord. Never mind that better persuaders had tried very hard to get Belinda back into the Body, that others had pressed Pearl on this issue, and that Gregory was already saved. Those details were irrelevant to me.

Another thing I missed, in my lack of understanding around my own obnoxious pursuit of holiness, was the lesson of the sun and the wind. Remember that children's fable? The sun and the wind have a wager on who can get a traveler to remove his cloak. The wind howls and howls, and the traveler holds on ever tighter to the cloak until the wind gives up. But the sun surrounds him with warmth, and off comes the cloak. The protection. The resistance.

I was the wind. Blustery. Heedless of damage I might be causing. Set on my course with a determination that blinded me. I wasn't the one doing this work, after all; it was Jesus, acting through me. The effect on me was that I felt almost no trepidation at all about approaching people in a way that they might not like. There was a buffer zone, or a one-step-removed protection, between me and what I was doing, and that protection was the spirit of Jesus himself.

It was in this frame of mind that I bicycled over to the Thorntons' trailer one Saturday in early July. I could have gone across the meadow, lovely right now with flowers and greenery, but that way seemed pagan to me now. Perhaps I was afraid of its influence, not quite strong enough yet in my new life to resist the purples and the yellows and the trickling stream and the soughing of the breeze through the pines—and the intriguing, puzzling times spent with Pearl.

Belinda was behind the trailer, weeding a patch of vegetables surrounded by chicken wire. Colorful streamers of cloth attached at random intervals to the flimsy fence flapped lightly, catching sunlight. It was an immensely cheerful scene that I was too single-minded to appreciate. Too blinded by my own light. I called from a slight distance so I wouldn't startle Belinda, who was bent over with her back to me. She stood up awkwardly when she heard me, stiff from her weeding posture, her hand clutching crabgrass and pigweed that dropped dirt bits from their violated roots. These she tossed into an old apple basket, and then she slapped her hands together, dislodging soil as she turned and moved in my direction.

"Jude Connor. How the heck are you? Pearl's not here at the moment. Off with her own plants someplace, I expect."

"That's okay. I'll see her another time." I took a deep breath as Belinda, her face pleasant but puzzled, got closer. "Um, I, uh, I actually wanted to ask you something."

She stood a few feet from me, hands on hips. "Me, is it? All right." And she waited.

"Um, I would really, really love to see you in church tomorrow. I would be happy to come by and escort you, if you'd let me." Her face changed, a warning in her eyes, but I plunged ahead. "I know you used to go, and you got—discouraged, but there's so much happiness waiting for you if you'll only come back. God's love—"

She turned abruptly toward the little garden, the sweep of her arm taking it in along with the woods beyond, the open fields in the distance, and the hills to the south. Facing me again, both arms out to indicate everything around her, she said, "This, Jude. This. All this. *This* is God's love. I would sooner be here in a blizzard than cooped up in that building where *you* find God's love. I can't see it in there. Those people, who use their self-imposed piety to condemn anyone who sees God outside of that little box, are not my people. It's too bad, too. Because, you know, I'd share my church with them. But they don't want it. So I worship here, Jude. You worship where you want. I worship here."

Well, this was the first time I'd witnessed to someone who had an answer other than "I'm not interested, okay?" Those who push God get used to people turning away, because they just don't want to talk about it. But this, this equal and opposite force, I was not prepared for. I couldn't exactly say "God isn't here."

I tried my best. "God is in our hearts, not just in our church."

"Then God is right here with me, in my heart. And here, with the rest of God's creation, is where I'm most aware of that presence in my heart. I've been in that church, Jude. I know the kind of love you're talking about. I even believed I felt it once. But it wasn't real. Not for me. If it's real for you, fine. But it made me feel as far away from God as if I'd murdered someone."

Ha! I had her. "But you tried."

"What?"

"You tried to do that. With tansy."

She slapped me. Hard. And then she pinched my ear painfully between her thumb and fingers and pushed me down onto the ground as I gasped in pain, until I knelt. "You cruel child. I had thought better of you. Let me tell you something, Jude Connor. You may think you're doing God's work, but if you think you can do God's *job,* you're insane. And pathetic. Do you think I need you to remind me about anything? Every time I look at my child, God reminds me that I nearly destroyed that beautiful soul. I nearly brought that sparrow to earth before it had lived. Before it knew how to fly." Releasing my ear, she grabbed my hair and forced me to face the garden. "Do you see those streamers? Those are my prayer flags. When they get shredded, I replace them. Because they remind me that even rags that we might be tempted to cast off can be beautiful and useful. They please the eye, they celebrate the weather, and they discourage forest creatures from grazing in my garden."

She released my hair suddenly and pushed so that I fell fully on the ground. As I scrambled up she spoke again. "This, Jude, this is why I left that Godforsaken church of yours. They pretend to be all love and forgiveness, but never for one second did they stop condemning me for my mistake. Have you ever made a mistake, Jude?" I just blinked, which she must have taken for a yes. She wasn't wrong. "Did you confess that mistake and repent it? And did you receive forgiveness? And were you allowed to go on with your life? Because I was not. I became their Goddamned doormat. They wiped their feet on me every time they saw me. I was no more than a child myself, scared out of my wits, and believing that the sin I had committed in conceiving a child would bring hellfire down on me. What I did next was because of them. I don't deny my own guilt but I did it because of their so-called love.

"And after Pearl was born I realized they were going to treat her the same way. It was for her sake, as well as mine, that I shook the dust off *my* feet and left. And there's nothing you or anybody else can say, offer, threaten, or do to make me go back to a place where God isn't. *That's* your church. A place where God *isn't.*"

We stood there a few seconds, me not knowing what to say, Belinda heaving breaths of emotion. Then, "You'll *forgive* me, I hope, if I go inside my home for a bit so I can rant and rave in private. The garden doesn't need that negativity. And if you ever come here again, Jude Connor, you leave your 'witnessing' in the street." She marched away.

Rubbing my ear and then my face, I skulked back to my battered black bicycle. I was angry, ashamed, confused. I couldn't go home in this mood. Throwing caution to the winds, knowing but not caring that Pearl might be in the meadow, I walked my bike partway in, left it leaning against a tree well off the path, and strode blindly forward until I was well past Pearl's boulder. Then I turned and went uphill for a little way, up where I'd found the western springbeauties over a year ago. I stood on an outcropping of rock and glared at the distant hills where Belinda found God, as though they were in league with her against me. I hated what she'd said about my Church, about the people there. Now I felt angry with myself. Was my faith so shallow that I had no words to return when Satan raised his hideous head and damned the Body itself?

Separating my grinding jaws I released a wordless howl. Then another. And a third. Then I collapsed on the hot, uneven stone platform I'd climbed. Without speaking, I asked Jesus what I had done wrong. What had gone amiss? Why couldn't I feel him with me, lean on him, let him speak through me?

Inside my own head the answer from Jesus came: Because she was right about the way she'd been treated. The saints have been cruel and unforgiving and relentless.

But, I reminded the Jesus in my head, they're only human!

His answer: I expect more from God's chosen, from the saints. I expect them to treat others, even the unsaved, with love.

I wonder now how many people have argued with themselves, believing that one of the voices was Jesus. Or Satan. Or the Virgin Mary. That's where I was that day. I argued back: But Belinda Thornton represents Satan! She damned us!

Jesus's response: Even Satan had a purpose. He showed mankind that there's a difference between good and evil.

I rubbed my face again, calmer now that I understood Satan, and forced myself to thank Belinda Thornton, at least from this safe distance, for helping me to see that I was once again following in the footsteps of Mr. Damascus. He'd been in this position, too, where he had difficulty feeling love while knowing it was everything: *If I have the gift of prophecy, and know all mysteries and knowledge; and if I have all faith so as to move mountains, but don't have love, I am nothing.* I was sure I could move mountains with my faith, and I felt I was gaining on the mysteries and knowledge. So I just had to get love.

But it was harder than I would have thought—as I sat pinned by my confusion to that rock—to let go of the things Belinda had said to me. My strategy was that whenever I remembered the pain of her pinch or her strike, or her words, I'd send rays of love in her direction. Or I would try.

But I was still feeling stunned by the power of her response. Where had she found the courage, the strength of mind to respond to me like that? Did she have some kind of totem, or medium, that facilitated her connection with Satanic powers? I thought about what I knew of her life, which wasn't much, but there was one thing I did know. Pearl had told me that she knew about Gregory, and about Todd Denmark, and about Tim's delayed baptism because her mother and Gregory were close friends. Alarms jangled in my brain. Close friends? If Gregory were witnessing to Belinda, that would be one thing. But from the way she'd responded to my invitation, I felt sure they wouldn't be "close friends" if that was happening.

I tried in vain to remember any of their conversations that might have filtered into the kitchen where Pearl and I had sat with Dolly. Maybe I couldn't remember the words, but I did remember the laughter, the camaraderie that floated its way into my unconscious. That was undeniable. And it was undeniably wrong. If I couldn't argue with Belinda's reasons for not wanting to spend time with people who constantly condemned her, I could point out to Gregory the error of fraternizing with the unsaved. Reverend King—my godfather—had said so in his sermon about happiness. He had said that if we had something that we had to keep secret, our brothers and sisters will know we're hiding something and confront us. If we want to avoid that, we can hide our secret from the light, but it will trap us and send us to Hell. In my newfound love for Gregory Hart, I couldn't let him be sent to Hell for something so easy to change as spending time with Belinda Thornton. And as a full brother in the Body, I had the right to confront him. With love, of course. And I wouldn't mention that other thing; one had to assume that since he was in the Body, he was not giving in to the darkness of—well, of what I'd seen on that PC screen. No; Gregory Hart was *certainly* not doing that. Before I could consider that this might mean he'd given up sex for God, just like Reverend King, my mind slithered away from thoughts of what Gregory might or might not be doing.

It was late afternoon by the time I headed back to where I'd left my bicycle. Head down, thinking deep thoughts no doubt, I heard Pearl before I saw her. She was on her boulder, turned mostly away from me and facing down the slope into the distance, and she was singing. The lilting tune was one I'd heard before, I knew. That first time I'd seen her here, a few years ago now, she had been singing it. And perhaps it was my recent visit to Tim's house, but I suddenly realized that I'd heard it from the next room when I'd studied with Tim at his house. I froze and strained my ears.

I was certain that rag doll was in Pearl's arms again, and her words, which I could barely make out, made it sound as though the lullaby were to a baby—"baby mine"—who had been ridiculed, made to feel inferior. The lyrics were all about how wonderful the baby really was, if only the world could see that. It was a sad song.

I waited for her to finish, which took some time because she seemed to be singing it through a number of times. This gave me a chance to decide what to do. I determined to exercise my new commitment to love. I would ask Pearl to do what her mother would not. Jesus had been with me up on the rock; maybe he would touch Pearl now.

She heard my footfalls and turned toward me, surprised, and scrambled down off the boulder. As I drew near, before I could speak, she beat me to it. "Ha. My turn. *I'm* not supposed to talk to *you*." She wheeled round, doll legs lifting with the force of her turn, and trudged away.

"What? Why not?"

She ignored me. I caught up with her easily and repeated my questions. She repeated her silence. By the time we got near where I'd hidden my bicycle, I felt stunned and angry. Watching her retreating back, wondering what Belinda had told her, I struggled to feel love. I tried, I really did. But mostly what I felt was shame.

The summer was well into July before I had the guts to talk to Gregory Hart. Part of my problem was that the approach wouldn't be as simple as with the unsaved. I couldn't very well open with, "I'd love to see you in church tomorrow. What time shall I come by to get you?" I'd had several . . . make that many, many imaginary conversations in my head with Gregory recently. Sometimes they took place in his kitchen with Dolly there. Sometimes I'd corner him in his barn. Sometimes we'd be walking up to Denmark Cliffs together. I liked that one best: stopping from time to time, admiring scenery and talking about the glory of God and how it would feel to be in paradise, and how easy it would be to jeopardize that by making the wrong decisions here, by not doing what the Bible and Reverend King made so clear. It wasn't unlike hiking up this hill, I would tell him; the path was narrow, and it wasn't easy, but you knew it would lead you up, up to Heaven itself.

He was always very impressed with my use of imagery. In my imagination.

Our actual meeting happened almost by accident, though of course at the time I deemed it providential. I was cycling back from delivering CC's outgrown baby clothes—some of which had been donated to Clara by other saints—to a new mother, when I passed a field where Gregory was operating a backhoe. At first it wasn't clear to me what he was doing. The field hadn't been plowed or planted this year. I slowed as I saw him, came to a stop, and stood by my bike watching as he worked with gentle, patient determination to coax a huge boulder from the ground. He used the bucket; he pulled with a chain; he got out of the backhoe and examined the situation; he got back in and worked the machine some more. I watched him for perhaps fifteen minutes, feeling a rush of satisfaction when the rock monster was finally vanquished, subjugated, forced to bend to the will of man. With God's help, of course—a qualifier that I believed to be validated when I saw Gregory get down from the machine once more and kneel by the side of the boulder, head lowered.

It was as though Jesus himself had issued me a personal invitation, promising me more of that protection he'd given me lately. I laid my bicycle on the ground beside the road and strode into the field toward Gregory, expecting to find his heart already opened and softened and ready for my message.

I waited, hands crossed in front of me, for him to finish his prayer and realize I was there, expecting him to be surprised. After all, I hadn't had the nerve to speak to him in some time. Or, at least, not to approach him. But as he stood, he just nodded to me and moved toward the backhoe.

I was the surprised one, but I couldn't lose this opportunity. "Brother Gregory!" I called, which must have sounded like a familiarity he hadn't granted me, all of fifteen years old that I was; but I was in the Body, I was Reverend King's godson, and I was on a mission from Jesus.

Left foot on the edge of the machine, he halted and turned his face to me as I hurried toward him. He said nothing.

For want of anything sensible to say, I opened with, "I see you offered thanks to God for helping you rid the field of this obstacle."

He blinked as though he didn't recognize me, then said, "It's a dangerous thing, assuming you know what's in another's mind."

I looked for a twinkle in his eye, a twitch of the mouth to indicate humor. Nothing. I was off track already. "What will happen to it now?"

He lowered his left foot back to the ground. "Tomorrow I'll work together with *Mr.* Tomkins"—a slight leaning on the title—"to push it off to the side so it won't get in the way of plowing next spring."

I shook myself mentally; this wasn't what I wanted to discuss. "Do you have a few minutes?" He said nothing, just looked at me. "I, uh, I wanted to talk with you about Belinda Thornton."

Now I'd surprised him. At last. "*Miss* Thornton? What about her?"

I sighed inwardly. Fine; he was chastising me for over-familiarity. I would bend. "Have you asked Miss Thornton lately if she'd join us in church?"

There was a brief laugh, no humor in it. "No. I wouldn't insult her like that." He fell once more into silence—no asking why I wanted to know, nothing to help me move the conversation forward, nothing by way of a clear indication whether she had told him of my own insult to her. But I didn't mind; I had him where I wanted him. He had shifted the huge rock with God's help. And with God's help, I would shift him.

I sighed meaningfully. "It pains me to say this, brother, but I have to advise you that it's against God's purposes for you to have a personal relationship with someone who refuses to be saved. And I know that you maintain a personal relationship with her." I wasn't sure where to go from here; my turn to fall silent. At some point the audacity of what I was doing and saying began to creep up on me. I pushed it away, though; the only person, other than the Thorntons themselves, who knew about Gregory's fraternizing transgression was Dolly (who might have said something but not very forcefully, and who relied on Gregory for everything and would be unlikely to challenge him to any great degree). It was up to me to take action. I was the only one who could.

He was shaking his head, looking perplexed and kind of sad. "Jude, what happened to you? You used to be a real person. You've been a bit of a stranger to me and to Dolly in the past couple of years, but you were still real."

"That's just it!" I nearly shouted, grateful for the chance to explain. "I wasn't real at all. I was outside of the spirit, even after my first immersion. I had a mistaken idea of what it meant to love God. Now I can see the path before me."

He turned toward the backhoe again, got ready to climb in, and turned his head toward me. "You know, when you come up out of that water, you're supposed to be full of love. Instead, you're full of some ugly, fake version of yourself."

Stunned, I gaped at him while he got the machine started

again and began to fill in the hole where the rock had lived. I walked in a dusty fog back to my bike.

That evening, I rode over to the Kings' to help the reverend with responses to his Church blog, my mind so focused on trying to sort out my feelings that I couldn't remember the ride by the time I got there. Part of me was furious that Gregory Hart had sent me packing, and that he'd insulted me personally. Part of me was reminding myself through proverbial gritted teeth to turn the other cheek, to return only love. And I was trying to figure out whether to talk to Reverend King about this confusion. I hadn't told him about Belinda's fury or Pearl's snub, so I didn't see a good opening to talk about Gregory. But I was saved from too much angst when Reverend King barely looked at me other than to hurry me into his office. Evidently he'd received an e-mail message from someone recommending that he post a link to a Christian-based Second Life community, saying he should encourage the saints to join, and he wasn't sure what it was about.

"Jude, I know you can help me figure this out." He handed me a printout of the message. "What on earth is this thing? I don't much like the sound of it, but I need to understand it better."

I'd never heard of Second Life, and I told him so. "I think I should follow this up and see if I can get a handle on it for you. I'll go upstairs and—"

"No, do it here. I want to watch so I can ask questions."

He watched over my shoulder, asking questions I couldn't answer, until he gave up and waited for me to do some digging. I used search engines, I scoured reviews of books about it, and eventually I pieced together a rudimentary understanding. Pushing the chair away from the computer so I could face Reverend King, I struggled for a starting point. He waited patiently until I found one.

"Okay, what I think is going on here is that there's this virtual space, kind of like a Web site but much more, where people take on some new personality. They talk to each other . . . I mean, their imagined personalities do. There's a way to make money, I mean virtual money that's good only in this online community. You can have a house, and buy things, and have friends and conversations. It's like life, only it's all online. And you don't have to be yourself. You can be anything you want. You have an avatar."

"A what?"

"I guess it means like a fake personality. A virtual one. It looks as though you can choose a name, and you can create your virtual body and make it whatever you want."

We stared at each other for several seconds, both trying to assimilate this collection of implausible information. Then he said, "Why?"

I shrugged. "I guess it's like a chance to start over. To be whoever you want to be. And this message is talking about a community that's organized around a Christian . . . um . . . I'm not sure what. I guess an online church."

More confused looks. "Is there a preacher? A pastor? Someone leading them?"

"I guess so. Though, of course, since anyone can be anyone they want, I suppose anyone could say he was the pastor, as long as everyone accepted him."

He rubbed his face and ran his fingers through his hair. Then, "Can you tell me who the pastor is in this community?"

I shook my head. "I'd need to pay to subscribe to this . . . group, whatever, just to get into it and see how the pastor looks, how he acts, what he says. But from what I've been able to find out, it doesn't seem as though anyone in the community could tell who anyone really is, unless they let on. Unless they tell you. I suppose the person behind the pastor avatar could even be a woman or a girl, even if the avatar is a man."

He nodded. "Thank you, Jude. I knew you could help. Now, it's getting rather late. I think you should pedal on home for tonight. Let's just pray before you leave." He got the draped figure out of the closet, and we went through a ritual that had become common for us. We knelt. "Almighty Father, Jesus our

Lord, I ask your guidance in responding to this misguided individual. I ask for your words to come through my fingers to help me reply with love and inspiration. I thank you, once again, for sending my son Jude to me and giving him the talent and the intelligence to be such a wonderful servant in this capacity, to help me further your cause in this avenue of twenty-first-century technology. And I pray that you will be with Jude tonight as he journeys home, keeping his body and his soul safe in your power and your love. Amen."

I had some trouble falling asleep that night. Only barely tempted to waste seed, I couldn't stop my mind from wandering through that virtual place where I could be anyone I wanted, do anything I wanted. I'd heard my godfather use the word "misguided" to describe the person who'd told him about Second Life. It hadn't been clear to me why, although it did seem as though having just anyone set themselves up as the pastor would be a little troubling. But that wasn't what kept me preoccupied. I tried to focus my mind on picturing the virtual Christian community to help me understand how it would be misguided. But every time I turned my thoughts that way, I got gently, seductively distracted by the possibilities.

If I joined that community, I could tell them *I* was the pastor. I could tell them I was the Damascus Kid, the reincarnation of Saint Paul himself. I could tell them I was Moses, or Solomon, or even Jesus. But then I was struck with the sacrilege of these thoughts and struggled to bend my mind back to things like what baptism would mean there.

Resolve weakened again. I could tell them I was Saint John the Baptist; how much trouble could I get into for that? Maybe there was a Salome of the seven veils already there! I pictured her, her dance slow and sultry as it matched the sway of music from exotic instruments. She would have harem pants, tied at the ankles, a bare midriff, and diaphanous drapes of material barely containing heavy, silken breasts. Her veils would seem to flow out of her hands, rainbow colors describing soft arches through the air as she turned and twisted, movements becoming more frantic to mate with the increasing tempo of the music. Finger cymbals were buried in her hands somehow, and she used them to accent particular movements as her intense dark eyes burned from beneath black eyebrows, the straight nose falling toward a full, ripe mouth that fell partly open as her movements intensified, until everything came together in a tremendous climax and she stood, bosom heaving, one arm raised, mouth open, triumph and lust on her face.

The music wasn't all that climaxed at that point. I hadn't even realized I had done so, but my hand had been working as hard as hers, and it was all I could do not to cry out in triumph with her. Then, horrified, I realized the triumph was all hers, and I'd done what I'd struggled so hard not to do. I'd sinned yet again.

On my knees beside the bed, one hand still a little sticky, I prayed. "Dear Jesus, forgive me. I see now what Reverend King was upset about. I see what's wrong here. I see what it can lead to." I was so intent on absolution for my sin that it wasn't until I'd gotten back into bed that it occurred to me to see some silver lining in what had just happened. The idea of a woman—wrong though it was to let myself imagine that scene—had caused me to climax. Amazing! Halleluiah! Aloud, I whispered, "Thank you, Jesus!" Then I rolled over and proceeded to have a dream in which I was the dancer with the veils and the cymbals and the breasts.

Reverend King and I didn't talk about Second Life again, but he used it as the basis for his sermon that week. He opened with, "Are you or are you not a child of God Almighty?" Shouts of agreement rose from all around me and from within me as well. "Does God Almighty make mistakes? Or does he know best?" More predictable responses, mine among them. "Then would you want to be someone you're not? Would you fly in the face of our Heavenly father and tell him he didn't do a good enough job on you? Tell him that you could do it better? Would you?" His voice had been rising—not unusual, although this time it was reaching a level of pitch and intensity that carried with it the seeds of something desperate, something frantic. It was like he was afraid of something, and if he could just shout it down it would retreat. It would leave him alone. I added my voice to support his whenever appropriate, as though I could shore him up or help fend off whatever threatened him. I wanted him kept safe so he could keep me safe. Ours was now a symbiotic relationship, and if he fell then so would I.

I was a kid, younger than my years in many ways. And my idea of supporting someone, of loyalty, meant agreeing with everything he did or said. So I had to agree with Reverend King. Period. That meant I had to agree with him about Second Life, so I did. The blog entry I posted for him made the same points he'd made in his sermon; but in the sermon he hadn't actually referred to anything specific. He hadn't mentioned Second Life. In the blog, he was very clear, and he added this:

> "We in the true, the real Christian communities
> have a sacred duty. We are commanded to help
> each other. We are God's eyes and ears on earth,
> and we see and hear not only those times when
> our brothers and sisters need help because of
> some sin they've fallen into, but also when they
> need help with daily life. We are commanded to
> love and to help each other. I implore all Chris-
> tians to consider what this virtual community
> does, and what it does not do. You might believe
> that your avatars love and support each other. But
> I must ask: What real help—what genuine succor
> are you offering? What actual good are you
> doing? If you have that love, that help to offer,
> then give it. By all means! But give it to each
> other in life, in times of trouble and joy. Provide
> material assistance to those who need it. Really
> need it. Not to some imagined person who isn't
> even a person. Do you think God would deem
> that worthy as an answer to the commandments
> he sent through his only son? The son who

suffered—*really* suffered—so that we might really
live? How much good would that suffering have
done for humankind if Jesus had been an avatar?

"Love each other. Help each other. Follow in
the footsteps of Jesus Christ. But do so on the real
earth, in real life. If you have time to spend creating false communities, then you have time to
spend doing genuine Christian acts. Make your
love real. The only other life is the one in
Heaven. Don't waste this one as a false being."

This made a tremendous amount of sense to me. As I read it,
something warm and expansive filled me and swelled (though
I know this sounds contradictory) in humility, because this
man—this man who understood God so well—had begged God
for me. Had prayed that I could be his spiritual son. And God
had said "Yes."

That expansive warmth faded of course, as these things always do. I could have understood that. I could have felt all right
about that. But it was replaced with something organic, fecund,
even gritty, on the night that I posted this inspirational entry, as
I was drifting into sleep. It was something that approached me,
rather than the other way around. It was a shape shifter. An
avatar.

At first the image was that of my godfather, whose example I
so much wanted to follow, whose praise and pride I so much
wanted to deserve. So I let it approach. But as soon as it knew I
welcomed it, it began to change. First there was the hat. The
cowboy hat the red-shirt man had worn. It looked great on Reverend King at first, but then the face began to change, growing
softer, prettier, as the red shirt became more of a blouse, filmy
like Salome's veils. I watched in fascination as the face become
more and more like mine. Then he/she danced lightly away
from me, surrounded now by other shape shifters, whose forms
and faces and clothes changed shape and color, and whose in-
teractions with each other grew more and more unpredictable.

There was no sound. No voices, no music, nothing. And the

silence itself pulled me into the crowd like a vacuum. I was aware of the others, dancing and swirling around me, yet never touching me or each other. Light came from nowhere, and yet each figure was clearly visible, blackness all around and between them. The faces that flashed in and out of my vision smiled, eyes happy, creating silent laughter. But gradually this changed, too, and the smiles changed into grimaces still trying to be smiles but also trying to keep pain from showing. Their motions grew frenetic, and I knew that they knew that if they stopped moving, if they stopped smiling, they would have to acknowledge the agony they were in. And since I was among them, the same was true for me. Suddenly aware that I was also in a frantic dance, also smiling that grimace desperate to repudiate pain, I lashed out with my arms and yelled. At last! Sound! I yelled again.

"Jude!" Lorne was shaking me. "Jude, wake up! Snap out of it!"

I sat up in the bed I'd had since I'd left the crib behind, panting, eyes darting around the room, trying to shake off Lorne's hands, but he held me, arms moving around my shoulders until we were in a tight hug, which I returned. I leaned against him, breathing audibly against the place where his shoulder and neck met. My eyes squeezed shut, creating flashes of light that obliterated what was in my mind's eye. After a minute or so I pushed away. "I'm okay. Just a bad dream."

From where she leaned against the doorframe Clara said, "Want to talk about it?"

I shook my head. "No, thanks. I'll be okay. I'll just sit up for a bit and read my Bible."

This seemed to meet with everyone's approval, and they left me alone. I did turn on a light and open the Bible. I just didn't know where to read. The words blurred as my mind focused back on the dream images. Awake, light on, I tried to figure out why they'd been so frightening. Why they were still scaring me. I didn't get very far then, at age fifteen. Now I think the horror was the feeling of separation, of isolation, brought on by lying. By pretense. There was physical separation—blackness—between the avatars, and there was verbal separation, with no sound, and then there were the lying smiles. The grimaces that pretended to be something they weren't. Just like avatars. But at the time I just sat there puzzling, and suddenly there was sound. It was Gregory Hart's voice, berating me again for not being real. For being full of some ugly, fake version of myself.

Finally I opened to Psalm 23. It seemed appropriate. *Even though I walk through the valley of the shadow of death, I will fear no evil, for you are with me.* Looking back on that scene, seeing myself huddled over the book where I sat on that tiny bed, I know that in my mind the "you" in "you are with me" was Reverend King.

Chapter 14

August brought a shift in the physical part of my life that followed an emotional shift already underway. I felt kind of sad for Lorne, that Sunday afternoon when he took me out into the backyard to sit on lawn chairs away from the house. I felt sorry for him, because he thought what he had to say was going to be difficult for me to hear. I decided to let him think that, because I wasn't sure I wanted him to know the truth. His message was that he and Clara needed my bedroom for CC.

This was actually okay with me. Maybe it wouldn't have been, before Reverend King became my true godfather. But ever since that had happened, Lorne had been shrinking. Not physically; it was that he seemed less of an authority figure, less knowledgeable, less wise. Less and less like someone I could look up to. I still loved him; he was still my brother, and he'd been very good to me. But he was only my brother.

He took a deep breath before he spoke, his eyes moving from my face to the ground near my feet. "We haven't been able to save enough money to move anyplace bigger, and CC will be a year old in September. If she doesn't move out of our room soon, she could get too dependent on us. Plus"—and here he looked at his hands where they dangled between his knees—"with CC in there, we don't have much . . . um, privacy."

This was my only difficult moment, really, wondering what decisions had been made about precisely where my bedroom would be. Then Lorne said, "I've spoken with Reverend King about the offer he made after Mom died. He's agreed." He looked at me, silently asking for a response.

I nodded. "I understand. I sort of thought this would happen sometime anyway. It's okay."

"You'll have your computer anytime you want it." I did my best to make my smile bittersweet. "And we want you to come over for Sunday supper." I looked up, not quite sure how I wanted to respond to that, not sure how I felt about it. "You'll always be my brother, Jude. And you'll always be welcome in my home." He sat back, rubbed his face, and then looked vaguely toward something off to one side.

"It's okay," I said again.

"Just before she died"—and he coughed once—"Mom made me promise to take care of you. I think right now, having you live at the Kings' is probably the best way to do that. But if you ever need anything . . ." His voice trailed off, and he stood and turned away from me. I went to him, he turned, and we hugged hard. Into my hair, voice husky, he said, "You're a good boy, Jude. I'm so proud of you. Mom would be, too."

At that moment I wouldn't have trusted my own voice.

I packed that night and Monday morning, and when Lorne got home from work, he drove my few boxes of possessions and me to my new home. If this had happened a year ago, Aurora would have been pleased and excited to have me, her special friend, always available for computer assistance or dishing about her girlfriends or sighing sessions over her latest crush. But as things stood, I'd become such an instrument for spreading the Word that she had little patience with me. She didn't like being reminded that Jesus would never have gossiped, or complained, or gone all moony. So she treated my exodus as just one more day in her life. I'd be in the house more than I used to be; so what?

Her mother was another story. She was waiting outside when we drove up, and as soon as I was out of the car she wrapped me in a welcoming hug. "Jude, it's going to be so wonderful having you here! We're all just as pleased as we can be."

Placing my things carefully, almost reverently, took me up to supper time. The laptop lived on a desk that had shelves above it, and I moved my mother's photograph three times before it was in a spot where I could see it from nearly anywhere in the room. As for the leather bag with my father's marbles, I put that on another shelf altogether; he'd left her, after all, so even though I valued the collection it didn't deserve quite the same place of honor. While I was positioning it, though, handling it repeatedly, something felt odd about it. And there was an odd sound. I pulled it from the place I had determined would be its home and set it on the desktop. The bag was closed with a leather thong that was woven in and out of holes just below the top edge, and the thong was tied. I pried it apart, wondering how long it had been since I had opened it, and saw a piece of lined paper, folded to fit. I stared at it. Where had it come from? Who would have put it there? Certainly I hadn't.

Only one way to find out. I pulled it out and opened it hastily. When I saw my mother's handwriting, I nearly dropped it again. Here's what it said.

> *Sweet Jude, when you read this I'll be gone. God is calling me, and I must go. But I want to leave you with something you can keep, so I'm writing these words down. I've said them to you while you slept many times. I love you so much, sweet boy. It may seem that I loved Lorne best. But remember he was older and I could lean on him some. You're the one headed for greatness. God has great plans for you. He will care for you and guide you. I won't be there to do that, and it breaks my heart. So I must give you to God now.*

I would have thought I'd already shed all the tears I was going to shed over my mother's death. But maybe it wasn't for her death I cried this time, but for her love. I felt the sharp pain of not having her with me, watching over me as I slept and showering that love on me. If only I'd known it then. I also felt the painful joy of that love. I wonder, today, if I would have appreciated that love as much if she'd lived. Paradise isn't paradise if you've never been anywhere else; it's just same old, same old. You have to lose it to know its value. You have to get kicked out.

For supper that night, as a celebration for my coming to live there, Mrs. King made my favorite dessert—that chocolate cake that we'd had the time I'd asked Reverend King why he didn't eat his. I ate mine.

Later, in what was now officially my room, I barely felt tempted to do anything I shouldn't. Being here, and then finding my mother's note, were signs, I was sure, that my life was taking a turn for the better. Here, I could resist evil. No more wasting of seed. No more avatars. God's will was being done in tandem with my mother's, and Gregory Hart had been wrong. This *was* the real me.

I ran out of people near me to witness to. But as they say, when God closes a door . . . In the past, following the online conversations about God and scripture and all things Christian, I'd been a lurker—someone who hangs out but never speaks up, so no one knows he's there. So the window that God opened was that I now felt brave enough, buoyed by the protection of Jesus and Reverend King, to jump in.

Cautiously at first, and then more and more brazenly, I posted comments in discussion threads about God, religion in general, Christianity and my own Church in particular. I quoted chapter and verse, arguing ferociously on the side of righteousness, absolutely sure of the infallibility I sent in the form of zeros and ones into the ether. As the Damascus Kid, my epistles took digital form. The ether was insubstantial, but the truth was not. I was a truth pusher. A dealer of truth and righteousness and absolutism. It was black-and-white; why couldn't these people see that?

I was glad I'd chosen the handle "fortress." It spoke worlds.
As "fortress," I was as unassailable as the Word of God. Being
Reverend King's godson bolstered my bravado even further. He
trusted me to use this tool, the Internet, to help him; and now
I was using it to help God, and to bring truth and light to the
confused and blind of the world.

One evening in mid-September, having raced through a history homework assignment to get back into a thread I'd been
focused on, and after scanning the eight or so comments that
had been posted since my last one, I saw one from "hemlock."
I'd never seen "hemlock" in any of the many threads or blogs
I'd been participating in. But it wasn't the unfamiliarity of the
handle that grabbed my attention. It was what he'd posted.

**hemlock: i heard that the original Bible didnt use the word
homosexual. it didnt exist then.**

I didn't even need to grab my yellow pamphlet to quote the
retort I typed.

fortress: romans, 1:26–27 says *for their women changed the natural function into that which is against nature. likewise also the
men, leaving the natural function of the woman, burned in their
lust for one another, men doing what is inappropriate with men,
and receiving in themselves the due penalty of their error.* **do you
see the word homosexual in their? no. but is their any question what its talking about? no.**

**hemlock: you mean there not their. kinda not the point tho.
when you hear about gays today they might be in these really
committed relationships they might really love each other.
thats not what Paul was talking about.**

**fortress: dude, changing the natural function into whats
against nature is not an option. if theres a relationship like
that, its against nature. its against God, okay? What part of
"vile passions" dont you get?**

Maybe three minutes went by with no more posts. I wandered into another thread and laid down the law there as I saw fit before venturing back over to where I'd left off with "hemlock." And I saw this:

hemlock: all I know is love is love. sometimes you cant help who you love. sometimes you just love, that's all. and you cant stop it.

fortress: r u saying your gay?

I didn't see anything else from "hemlock" in that thread. But then one day he/she turned up in another thread.

hemlock: does anyone know hebrew?

No one responded, so I did.

fortress: why?

Silence. I went and posted elsewhere, and when I came back there was a response, time-stamped several minutes after my question. Was "hemlock" trying to avoid me? Waiting until I gave up and went elsewhere?

hemlock: I want to know what abomination really meant.

I clicked open my bookmark to an online dictionary, and then I responded.

fortress: hateful. disgusting.

Again, "hemlock" waited several minutes before replying.

hemlock: but whats the translation from hebrew?

imok: it meant against custom or tradition nothing to do with hate or disgust in the OT. like, eating shellfish was abominable. not evil, just against custom and tribal law.

fortress: prove it

imok: look it up I did

"Jude?" Mrs. King's voice from the other side my door tried to yank me back into the literal world. "Time for bed, dear. Have you finished your homework?"

I jumped to the door and opened it so she wouldn't think I was doing anything wrong in here. "Yes, ma'am."

"Brush your teeth, then, sweetie. I'm off to bed. Good night."

" 'Night." I watched her walk down the hall to the room she shared with her husband. The husband who, in one respect, was no husband. The husband whose physical expression of love was limited to hugs and the occasional kiss. The husband who refused to make love to his wife.

I had one more shot to fire on line.

fortress: what part of "vile passion" dont you get?

hemlock: what part of love dont YOU get?

denimboy: Jesus says love God with everything you are. Who- ever you are. Whatever you are. That means you have to know who and what you are. And then you have to love God with all of you.

Who was this "denimboy" character? I couldn't remember seeing him before. I sat there staring at the screen, my brain doing a random access seek for anything I could throw back at him. Maybe a full minute went by. "Hemlock" beat me to it.

hemlock: even if your gay?

denimboy: Even if you're gay. And then you have to love your neighbor as much as you love yourself. Which means you have to love yourself, or it wouldn't make sense.

denimboy: Even if you're gay.

My head swam. This couldn't be right. And then I had a kind of epiphany about "denimboy." He could be the man at the bar! The guy in the red shirt and the cowboy hat! He must be the one who'd refused Reverend King's pamphlet, the one who'd thrown scriptural contradictions at him. Or at least, he was someone very much like that man. Reverend King had cautioned me against getting into a scriptural pissing contest with someone like this. I had to respond. I *had* to. But I couldn't do it with scripture; he'd just throw junk back at me.

fortress: denimboy, you need to see the light. you need God's forgiveness. will you come to my church? just once? dont be afraid.

denimboy:

LOL! Typical. But fortress, I've seen some of your posts, and I've been to your church. It's a crock of shit. It's like Invasion of the Body Snatchers. You have to pretend you're someone you're not just to be there. I'd tell you to go to hell, but you're already there.

Desperate to refute this response that was so much like what Belinda Thornton had said to me, I held tense fingers over the keyboard for several seconds.

fortress: please! dont do that to your immortal soul! do you think God would make someone gay and then say it was evil? God doesnt make people gay, b/c being gay is a sin and God doesnt create abomination. choose Heaven. choose God.

I waited, staring at the screen until my eyes burned and I blinked. I waited some more. No response from anyone. I was afraid to disobey Mrs. King, so eventually, reluctant and afraid to miss a chance to witness for Jesus, I powered my laptop off.

It had been several weeks since my confrontation with Gregory to stop fraternizing with the enemy. That is, Miss Thornton. But I was still burning with fervor to do something about it. Pearl had avoided me all summer and also at school, once that started again; and while I wouldn't have admitted either of these internal responses to myself at the time, not only did I kind of miss her tart, edgy personality, but also I wanted to punish her mother for making *me* the ostracized one now. But I wouldn't confront Gregory head on again. That had gotten me nowhere. And it's not easy to coach someone in spiritual matters when you can't even call him by his first name.

My new strategy was to get to Gregory through Dolly.

Not living any longer with Lorne and Clara, I had much more time on my hands. There were no daily chores of housework or caring for CC. Also, as if giving me a home and a computer and a whole new life weren't enough, Reverend King surprised me with another gift. I'd just come home (Home! Yes! Home to the Kings') on the old, rickety black bike that had been Lorne's so long ago, the one I'd had the day I'd run away and Gregory had rescued me. It was not only rusty and noisy, but also it was now too small for me. And one day just before school started again, when I came home after some proselytizing mission I'd been on, as soon as I got in the house Reverend King met me in the kitchen.

"Not so fast there, young Jude. Back outside with me this minute."

I'd long ago gotten over being intimidated by the man, though I never treated him lightly. I could tell by his tone that his stern words were in jest; I couldn't guess why. I followed him out as he led the way to the garage.

"Stand here," he told me, pointing to the ground. He went

into the garage and came out wheeling a sleek, shiny, titanium-colored twelve-speed bicycle. "Can't have my godson riding around on that dangerous old thing any longer! This is now your chariot." He stood there, one hand balancing the bike, the other held out in a gesture of expansiveness. It took me a minute to get over the shock of having something new, something beautiful, and something that was really all mine, and then I threw myself at the man, nearly knocking the bicycle out of his grasp. He laughed as I hugged him. I laughed so I wouldn't cry, feeling both intense happiness and some kind of pain all at once.

The new bicycle, along with my freedom from chores at Lorne's, meant that I could spend even more time witnessing, inviting sinners to Church, and exhorting saints to rededicate themselves in areas where it seemed to me they were lacking in sincerity or obedience to the letter of the law. I was all about the letter of the law. Traveling always with a Bible—never leave home without it, I often told people—I could pull it out at any time and open it to any of my favorite verses. I had verses that spoke to any kind of sin; you name it. So of course I found lots of verses to quote about why maintaining ill-advised relationships with those who were not in the Body would not only waste time you could be spending to evangelize, but also how it would jeopardize your soul. And this was Gregory's sin.

I couldn't have said where Dolly had gotten the reputation of being a scripture pusher, but she had it. But it didn't seem as though she had coached or even chastised Gregory about his friendship with Belinda Thornton. It was true that Dolly depended on Gregory for just about everything in her life, and it was possible that she chose her battles carefully when it came to chastising him. Thinking along these lines, I felt pity for Dolly. And I decided to be her savior. So to speak.

She had said to visit anytime, and that's what I started doing. On a Saturday not long after school started, I pedaled out around mid-afternoon. I had a plan. I'd memorized several places in the New Testament where the scripture indicated that our quality time should be spent with the other saints, and that the time we spend with the unsaved should always be with the objective of bringing them into the Body. I wanted to know if Dolly knew of these scriptures and what they meant.

I wheeled my new bike out behind the Harts' house, less eager to leave this one in plain view than I had been with the old one. I knocked on the back door. I'd never knocked here before. Dolly's voice came through the window. "Who's there?"

"It's me, Dolly, Jude Connor."

"Oh! My word. Just a minute."

I felt a mild jolt of disappointment that Pearl wasn't there to answer the door for Dolly. But Dolly was as pleased as ever to see me, despite how long it had been.

"I'm afraid all I've got is store-bought cookies today, Jude, but you're welcome to some. It's so good to have you visit again! What brings you out this way today?"

"I'm sorry it's been a long time. I, um, I've been kind of busy."

"I heard you got baptized in May." Her face looked expectant, as though she were hoping I would explain myself; she knew I'd been immersed before, over a year ago now.

All I said was, "Yes, ma'am. I felt the need for rededication."

"So soon? But I suppose boys will be boys." Again, that expectant look, despite the blank eyes.

I wasn't sure I wanted to leave it like that, but I wasn't about to give her details. Instead, I used the event as a launching pad. "It's not uncommon, you know. Rededicating yourself, I mean. And sometimes you realize that the first immersion wasn't right, because you weren't quite right with God when you did it." She nodded vaguely, and I plunged ahead. "You come to see that you need to be purer, to follow the Word more closely. It's not always necessary to do another baptism. Sometimes it's more like you just have to be clearer on the best way to do what God wants." I waited. Would she open this door?

She sat quietly, hands in her lap, smiling. Then, "Yes. There are lots of ways to show love, and there are ways to do it with ulterior motives. It's better when it's pure, but we're all human and sometimes we let distractions get to us. Things we think are important, but that aren't really. Is that what happened with you, Jude?"

"In a way. I mean, yes, I got distracted." If you can call wet dreams about men distracting, then I was distracted. "And I had some help, from Reverend King, figuring out how to get back on the path again."

"We do need each other, don't we? I hear you're living full-time there now. How do you like that?"

"Oh, it's great. I mean, I miss Lorne and Clara and CC, of course, but it's so inspiring to be living with Reverend King. And it makes it even easier to stay on the path. It's important to be with the other saints. It's important not to be distracted by things—or by people—who aren't with us. Do you know what I mean?" I watched her intently. Would she take *this* bait?

"I do. Though I hear you've been spending quite a bit of time talking to all kinds of people, not just saints. I hear you're becoming quite the little evangelist."

I nodded, though she couldn't see. "But I've been talking to saints, too. Because sometimes we need each other to point out when we're, you know, getting distracted. And I've been looking for scripture to use, so it's not my words; it's God's words. Actually, I've been looking for a particular kind of verse. Maybe you can help me."

She laughed lightly, prettily. "Jude Connor, you're living with the reverend himself. Why don't you ask him?"

Good point. My mind fluttered around, helpless, until I said, "Oh, sure, I could do that. Maybe I will. But I hate to bother him with little things, you know?"

She lifted one shoulder and dropped it. "Well, you can ask, surely, but I'm not likely to know what to tell you. What kind of verse do you need?"

I blinked. How could this be the case? Maybe I didn't know how Dolly had come by the reputation she had, but I knew she had it. "Um, I need to talk with one of the saints about spending a lot of time with someone who isn't saved. Someone who doesn't even want to be saved."

She scowled lightly. "Why?"

I scowled back. "Well . . . because we're not supposed to do that." Hadn't I just made that clear a minute ago? "We're supposed to spend time with each other and help each other stay dedicated. When we're with those outside, it's supposed to be to bring them to the Light. Our true friendships must be within the Body."

She took an audible breath, apparently thinking hard. Then, "What is friendship to you, Jude? Who are your friends?"

I did not mention Tim. I named a few kids who were also very intent on spreading the Word, kids who often went with me on those hunting-and-gathering missions, knocking on doors on Saturday afternoons to invite people to Church, and I mentioned Aurora, though she and I weren't as close as we'd once been.

"And why are these children your friends, particularly? Do you have the same interests? Do you think the same things are fun? Do you confide in each other?"

"We witness together. That's the most important thing."

Her eyes took on a sadness. "Once upon a time, I was kind of hoping you and Pearl might be friends."

"Pearl?" Was *that* why Dolly had set up those math sessions? It wasn't to get Pearl into the Church after all? I was astounded, and it must have showed in my voice.

"Why is that so surprising? You're neighbors—or, you were—and you're good at something she needs help with, and I think you have a lot in common."

I scowled harder. "Like what?"

"Pearl can be a little rough on the outside, but she has a heart of gold. You do, too. At least I used to think that when I saw more of you. I wouldn't know, now. But Pearl has so much to offer."

I nearly sputtered. "Pearl's not saved. And she doesn't want to be."

"This saint you want the scripture for. Is it someone who's spending time with Pearl?"

I took a breath. How much should I say? I decided not to show all my cards yet. "No."

She shook her head a little. "Well, I'm afraid I can't help you with scriptural references. I'm just not that well versed."

"Don't you have a Braille Bible?"

"I do, but it's difficult for me to skim through it looking for references to jump out at me. I could use the concordance, but—honestly, I just don't feel the need."

I had to say it. "I always thought you knew the Bible really well. Everyone thinks so."

"Do they? That's interesting. But wrong, I'm afraid. Perhaps they have that opinion because so often when people come to visit me they're at a loss what to say. So they usually read from the Bible, or from some other inspirational book. They probably convince themselves that's what I want."

"It's not?"

She shrugged. "I've never requested it. Well, maybe once or twice."

This information floored me. "What *do* you want?"

"I'd like people to talk to me. I'm enjoying this conversation quite a bit. Or I'd like people to read all kinds of things to me, not just religious material. I don't want to live in a church. I don't want to be lectured or chastised or told how to live my life. What I want is connection." Silence. Then, "Are you here to chastise me, Jude?"

"What? No! No, ma'am."

"So asking me about what verses you might use, that wasn't a test?"

I shook my head. "No! It wasn't. Honest."

"Because you wouldn't be the first." I just stared at her. "Sometimes people read to me from the Bible about things they'd like to be able to say to me directly, but they use verses instead."

"What would they say? How can you do anything wrong?"

She laughed again. "All kinds of things, I'm afraid. For one, I subscribe to recorded readings for blind people. And I don't usually get recordings of religious books. Usually I get books that teach me about other things in life. Things outside of my limited world, outside of this limited little community. So I get fiction—novels—and I get books about philosophy different from ours. Books on other kinds of religion, other ways of thinking about God. Other ways of loving. Often I'm listening to this kind of book when one of the saints stops by to visit." She chuckled. "The other day I was listening to a book about how reason and science are going to make faith obsolete when someone stopped by. I only wish I could see! I had to imagine the expression on her face."

This was too much. Faith, obsolete? I didn't know whether I felt more shocked or betrayed. "So why do you even stay in the Church, if you don't believe?"

"Oh, Jude, don't misunderstand me. I want to understand about lots of things. That doesn't mean that I don't believe. My word, if I didn't believe in God, if I didn't think that some-where, sometime I'll be better off than this"—and she gestured toward the wheelchair—"if I didn't believe that someday I would see the face of Jesus, I couldn't live. And quite honestly, I think humanity needs to believe in something greater than themselves. For me, that's God and his son, Jesus. For others, it might be a different image. But it's all about love, Jude. Love, and hope."

"But—this is the only way! Ours is the only right path!"

"I understand that you need to believe that, Jude. You go right ahead."

By now I felt not just betrayed, but also patronized. As though my fervor was a source of amusement for her. "Dolly, how can you—there's only one truth! There's only one God, and the only way to God is through Jesus!"

She sighed. "Truth. It's an important word, Jude, an impor-tant concept. But what does it mean, really?"

"It means Jesus. *I am the way, the truth, and the light.* Every-thing Jesus said was part of the overall truth."

"But he points us toward love above all, Jude."

"Well . . . yes, but there's truth all through the Bible!"

"Yes. But we need to understand what that means. It doesn't help to say it's everywhere. Is it true, for example, that we shouldn't kill each other?"

"Yes, of course it is."

"Why?"

This was crazy. I repeated to stall for time. "Why shouldn't we kill each other?" What was it about the Ten Commandments that I could use to demonstrate truth? "We're commanded not to." It was the best I could do. Unfair, pitting a single-minded, naïve teenager against an intelligent woman who had so much time to listen to philosophical treatises. This was nothing like participating in my Internet discussion threads.

"Yes, but why? I don't think it has to do with murder. I think it has to do with love. Murdering someone you love is a very different thing from killing a stranger. Perhaps *you* couldn't do either of those things. I don't think I could. But love makes it even harder to contemplate or to do. That means that it isn't avoiding murder that's most important; it's loving each other so much that murder becomes impossible. The same, I think, applies for most of the commandments. Jesus, the way, the light, and the truth, told us he came to fulfill the law. Love fulfills the law."

This was not what I had expected to be talking about. My silence must have said worlds. Especially to a blind woman, accustomed to interpreting silence.

"Jude, I've overwhelmed you, haven't I? I apologize. It's just that there's no way at all I could talk with most of my visitors like this. I'm not sure why I needed to say these things to you, but it's for sure I felt called to do it."

I swallowed. "Who *do* you talk with like this?"

"Gregory, mostly. Sometimes Miss Thornton or Pearl."

Aha! There it was. So it wasn't just Gregory who was fraternizing. And, though I hadn't known it before, I *should* have come here to chastise Dolly after all. My fingers itched to reach for my Bible and point me toward some of the verses I hadn't needed her help to find, verses that would cut into her heart about how disobedient she'd become. But if I did that, she'd know I'd lied about needing help to find them. There would be another visit, I decided, and at that time I could pull those verses out, letting her think I'd asked Reverend King about them as she'd suggested. The thought of actually asking him flashed through my mind, but I wasn't ready to reveal to him the level to which the Harts had sunk. I wanted a chance to elevate these people myself. To quote my mother, God had plans for me.

So my first visit to Dolly hadn't gone exactly as planned. For one thing, there was no way she was going to be my ally when it came to fraternizing with the Thorntons. Also, I'd discovered some rather disconcerting information: Not only was Dolly not as familiar as she should be with her Bible, but also she was given to reading things that I felt sure Jesus would have told us to destroy.

Sitting in church the next day with Lorne and Clara (an arrangement that was part of my new protocol), my eyes on the back of Dolly's head where she sat between two of her sisters in the Body, I refocused my mission. The Damascus Kid was not to be dissuaded. He had God, Jesus, and Reverend King on his side. I decided to use what I'd learned about Dolly's habits and dangerous ways of thinking as chinks in the door to accomplishing the rededication of both Dolly and Gregory: two souls I would return to God. Yes, I was definitely headed for greatness.

I visited again a week later, cycling through a cold drizzle, my Bible in a double layer of plastic to protect it. This time, Gregory was home, and when I got there he led me into the living room. Dolly was settled beside a pot of tea and some cookies, and Gregory had evidently been reading to her himself. A book was turned over and open in the chair he resumed when I came into the room.

"Jude!" Dolly smiled toward me as sweetly as ever. "Such a treat, seeing you again so soon. I'm so glad you're here. Gregory was just reading to me from a new book about the Bible. I'll bet you'll find this very interesting. Do you want some milk to go with the cookies?"

"No, thank you, ma'am." I didn't want to make this too casual. I was here on a mission. That didn't stop my eyes going to the plate of cookies, which looked like Pearl had made them.

"Well, just help yourself, whatever you'd like. Set yourself down, child, and listen up. This is fascinating stuff."

Obedient, biding my time and prepared to wait for the right opening, I sat. Gregory settled some reading glasses on his face, cleared his throat, and picked up where he'd been interrupted by my knock.

Dolly had been correct in that it was about the Bible. But it was hardly good Christian material. The more Gregory read, the more obvious it became that the author was not a believer. I strained my eyes to see the cover and saw the title: *Misquoting Jesus*. What Gregory was reading was blasphemous, to my fundamentalist ears. It told about how very many errors must be in the Bible, in the New Testament in particular, because of how the scriptures had been copied times beyond measure by various individuals, some of whom didn't know what they were doing and made errors, and some of whom thought they knew what they were doing and deliberately changed things. It even said that an entire section of one of the gospels had been added long after the original author was gone.

It had never occurred to me to speculate what it meant that different gospels said different things. I'd always taken the whole as holy and hadn't troubled myself beyond that; it was the infallible Word of God, after all. But this book made a big deal about it. I sat there, aghast, wondering how much trouble I could get into just listening to this sacrilege, not having a clue where to start in terms of refuting it or debunking the author.

Gregory came to the end of a chapter or a section or something and leaned back, eyeing me over the tops of his reading glasses. I looked back at him, then over at Dolly, whose head was nodding gently, then back at Gregory. I was just getting ready to say something like whatever versions of the New Testament had come to us, they were the ones God wanted us to have. But Gregory beat me to the punch.

He closed the book. "Dolly tells me you're concerned about me."

I blinked. I hadn't said that. Not in so many words, anyway. "What do you mean?"

"Don't be coy, Jude. You approached me last summer about my friendship with Miss Thornton, and then you show up here talking about someone who is consorting with a non-saint, supposedly looking for verses to support your position. How naïve do you think we are? Say what you have to say, boy. You don't need Bible verses, though I'll warrant you already have them."

I hadn't decided, while sitting there listening, how or even if I would say anything to the Harts today. I hadn't been prepared for Gregory at all, and certainly not for a situation in which I was outnumbered. I shrugged. "She doesn't want to be saved. She doesn't want God in her life. That makes her a dangerous influence. Reverend King said so."

"Reverend King?" Gregory sat up straight, his eyes narrowing a little. "What did he say, exactly?"

"Oh, it wasn't about you. It was about me. But it was the same thing. Or nearly, anyway. It was when I walked Pearl home a few years ago, alone. Reverend King told me it was dangerous to spend time with someone who had refused to be saved. Saint Paul said, 'Don't be unequally yoked with unbelievers, for what fellowship have righteousness and iniquity? Or what communion has light with darkness?' "

Dolly laughed; it threw me. I mumbled something else about not casting pearls before swine, but I'm sure she wasn't listening. She said, "I knew it! I just knew you had your verses all lined up already. You're a sly one, Jude Connor! Very resourceful." If her voice hadn't sounded gleeful, her words would have got my back up. Glee; I didn't know how to respond to that in a conversation such as this one.

Even Gregory smiled. "Interestingly, I would guess that excerpt probably remains very much intact as it comes to us today; it wasn't likely one of those that got mangled. It would have been very like Paul to be black-and-white about this, to cast others into darkness if they didn't agree with him completely. He was a radical fanatic when he was Saul and still was as Paul. No shades of gray for Mr. Damascus." Gregory's eyes flashed at me, and I knew that he was aware of the title I'd earned in the past months. "Seductive, isn't it? Being absolutely right and knowing it?"

He was goading me, and I couldn't stop myself. "But it *is* black-and-white! God's Word is clear."

"God's Word is anything but clear, Jude. You want truth? That's truth."

I made a note to myself that nothing I said to Dolly could be counted on not to be repeated to Gregory. "You're wrong! You're absolutely wrong."

"There's that word again. Absolutely. God save me from that, from wanting that."

Astonishment upon astonishment for me. "Don't you want to be saved?"

"Oh, but I am saved, Jude. I took the oaths, I died to the world, and I was raised again in Christ. You're too young to have been at my baptism, but I had one." His tone was nearly sarcastic.

"Maybe you need to do it again."

Gregory laughed this time. "Not on your life! Not if what happened to you happens to me." I tried to protest, but he went on. "You're a smart boy, Jude. You're a seeker. Don't stop looking. Don't let anyone convince you to stop asking questions. Approach Jesus as a little child—open heart, open mind—and always asking why."

All I could do was shake my head, violently enough that my neck snapped sharply.

Gregory sat back again. "Dolly and I would love it if you would visit again. If I'm not here, that's fine; Dolly loves to talk about how we should live according to God's word. Since you seem to love that too, please . . . come back and talk with her." He snapped the book shut. "And now, would you like milk with your cookies?"

In a kind of trance, or maybe stupor is a better word, I did have cookies and milk that afternoon. And I did go back. And I did talk with Dolly. And I'm not sure that I know why even now—certainly I didn't know then—but I didn't consult with Reverend King about those conversations. I think I was still set on my mission to get the Harts to see that they needed to rededicate themselves. I think I saw myself as saving them all over again. But that's not what happened.

One day Pearl was there before me, in the kitchen with Dolly. Gregory was in the barn working on some piece of equipment. When Pearl saw me, she told Dolly she had to leave. But Dolly said, "Oh, sweetie, no. Don't go. I know what your mother said, and I understand it, but I'm here with you. It will be all right. I'll talk to your mother if you like, but please don't go just yet."

So Pearl sat there, glaring, arms crossed on her chest, as Dolly and I performed our own brand of exegesis on some Bible verses, which had become our custom. Pearl said little or nothing, and I almost forgot she was there. Dolly and I had our routine. I would come prepared with some scriptural references about some aspect of life, and we would talk about them, and even argue about how to apply them to our lives. She told me that she enjoyed this thoroughly; it was a far cry, she said, from just being read to endlessly as though there were nothing to discuss.

I began visiting after school some days as well, not just on weekends. I was convinced that I was having an effect on Dolly; also, Pearl was there more often now, and I added one more soul to the list of those I would help to salvation. I didn't see then that what was really happening was that Dolly was getting me to view scripture critically. I didn't see that I was enjoying learning a new way to think about using scripture to live by. I didn't see that the edge between the black and the white was blurring, and that not only was I perceiving shades of gray, but also I was fascinated by them. I was fascinated by how to understand scripture in the duller light of real life. I was slowly becoming less blinded by the light. I was becoming less blind.

Another thing I didn't see was that all the attention I was paying to the Harts, and especially to Dolly, made me less aware than I might have been otherwise that I saw less and less of Reverend King. He had taken to going on his mission work to Boise more than on just the occasional Saturday night. Now he was going two or three times a week. And one more thing I didn't see until later was that Natalie King grew less and less cheerful.

But being the near-child that I was, focused on my own life, I allowed myself to become immersed in the mental stimulation and the sheer fun of my discussions with Dolly. And Pearl and I renewed our almost-friendship. After a couple of visits when we were both there, she began to enter into the discussions, and sometimes we argued bitterly, ending the visit in rancor and something approaching animosity, eager for the next meeting and the next confrontation. I loved being angry with her, and I'm sure she felt the same about me. She was a dyed-in-the-wool heathen, and I was a stubborn little fundie, and there were sparks and there was life. We loved it.

I never did chastise Gregory for consorting with Miss Thornton. But I did begin to call him "Gregory."

Chapter 15

One cold Saturday afternoon, a dull sky darkening overhead, Pearl and I left the Harts' at the same time, moving in silence to where both bicycles waited. It was almost too cold to be riding by this point in the season, and there had been a few snowfalls, but the roads were free of ice and there were still days like today that promised bitter cold weather but didn't quite deliver it.

She eyed my new bike, even though she'd seen it several times by now. "Where'd you get that?" As always, her voice had an edge.

I almost didn't want to say it. "Reverend King."

"Thought so. You're his little pet now, I gather."

I knew she was goading me, so I refused to react. "He's my godfather."

She barked a kind of short laugh. "Found any dead horse heads lately?"

"Huh? Oh, the movie. Don't be absurd. Being my godfather means he keeps me on the straight and narrow. And I help him with his Internet stuff."

"D'you help him with his reclamation project?"

"What reclamation project?"

"The one where he goes to Sodom Boise and pretends he's there to save souls."

My back did stiffen at that one. "He never pretends anything! And he *is* there to save souls. I know more than you about it. I went with him once." Her eyes widened. Ha! Something she hadn't known. My chin rose in the air a little, even though that made it even harder to look at her; I had grown taller in the past few years, and she had not.

"Really. Meet anyone interesting? Bring anyone to church? Pull someone away from the brink of eternal damnation?"

For some reason, this cut into me, perhaps because for all those trips to Boise, I wasn't aware of anyone who'd been convinced even as far as curiosity. I looked down at my bike and got into position to mount it, saying, "You don't know anything about it." Without a glance back I rode off.

I turned toward the Kings', toward home, but for some reason my bicycle veered off in the direction of the bridge where the tires on my last bike—and Pearl's current one—had been slashed by Bruce Denmark. Dismounting, I wheeled the bike off the road and into a snowy copse where it couldn't be seen from the road, and I trudged down the hill, feet slipping on ground that was partly covered in ice, partly in snow, and partly still just dirt. Perhaps it was Pearl's goading about Reverend King. Perhaps it was remembering how my own Boise mission had stirred up so much sinful lust. Perhaps who knows what. I headed for the fort.

It looked peaceful. Serene. The shape of the fallen tree was more obvious with the contrast of snow outlining its edges, at once making the image both clearer and softer. I approached slowly, almost reverently. And then I ducked inside.

I heard myself gasp, felt the jolt of surprise shake my body. Despite the failing light, the sheltered area seemed homey. There was a log that must have served as a kind of seat, and on a makeshift table of a flat board laid across two upended logs there were two plastic cups and a little ceramic vase with dried flowers and leaves in it. Hanging on the branches overhead and on the sides were little yarn shapes, brightly colored, irregular, and odd-looking. It took me no more than a few seconds to know who had been here. Pearl Thornton had assumed owner-ship of the hemlock fortress.

I wanted to heave everything outside, to return the logs to the woods and let the forest do what it would with the vase and the yarn shapes. If I couldn't have Tim and the fort, Pearl couldn't have the fort. It was mine. It was sacred. Somehow. I stood there, breathing audibly, clenching and unclenching my fists and my arm muscles, and I then reached for the board across the logs. As I lifted it, the cups and the vase toppled off. Ignoring them, I stomped outside, and with one hand flung the board sideways as hard as I could away from me, away from the fort, away from what was Tim's and mine. A sudden stab of pain made me curl my arm back toward my chest protectively, and I saw that there was a gap in one of the seams of my genuine-imitation leather glove, and into that gap a large splin-ter of wood had forced its way. It looked like a thorn.

A thorn. I gazed stupidly down at it, my brain cramped into painful knots of non-thought, and I breathed harshly through my teeth as my eyes began to water. Finally a thought formed: Pearl did this to me!

But then I heard another voice, the one that had spoken in my head on the hillside after I'd invited Belinda Thornton to Church. This voice said, *You did this to yourself.*

Penitent pilgrims sometimes put a pebble into their shoes deliberately to make their journey more meaningful, to offer their pain to Jesus in a token gesture of return for his suffering, to remind themselves constantly what their journey was for. In this spirit, I didn't remove my thorn. I could barely see now, in the dusk, where the board had landed, but I found it and brought it back. I carried it inside and carefully settled it back onto its rustic platform. I felt around for the vase and the cups—couldn't find the dried flowers—and set them on the board. And with one more shaky breath and one last look around, I left.

* * *

Monday at school I watched furtively for a chance to speak with Pearl. I had some vague idea about telling her to stay away from my fort. But my vigilance was in vain; she didn't come to school. She didn't show up again until Wednesday. But when at last I managed to approach her with relatively few witnesses, the conversation didn't go quite the way I'd planned. To open, I kept my voice low but friendly. "How's the bike?" It would have been the bike that had transported her to the bridge, so this was where I began.

She glowered at me, of course. "How do you think? What a stupid question. As if you didn't know."

If she'd stopped after "What a stupid question," I would have plunged ahead. Instead, my back up a little at her tone, I asked, "What am I supposed to know, exactly?"

Her suspicious eyes scoured mine for deception or artifice. "You haven't heard?" I shook my head. "Tires were slashed. Sunday night sometime. The bike was behind the trailer, and the tires were slashed." Now her tone had more fear than confrontation in it.

"Bruce again?"

Her movements jerky and angry, she rearranged her book bag. "Bruce says he didn't do it. He says he hasn't slashed any tires since we left our bikes at the bridge that day. Says he's turned over a new leaf, or something."

That day at the bridge. When I'd shown her my fort, my fort that she'd taken over. I nearly said something about her trespassing. But—no. "D'you think it's the truth?"

She snorted. "He's too stupid to lie."

"So . . . who, then?"

"I've got my suspicions." She struggled once more with her bag and walked away.

Dolly came down with the flu the next week. Gregory found me in church and told me to stay away for the time being; she was too weak and possibly contagious. But the Saturday after that, a stormy, snowy day, he called the Kings' and asked for me. Dolly was going stir crazy, he said, and would I please come over and read to her? He had to work on something in the barn. He said he'd pick me up and bring me home afterward. I could tell Mrs. King wasn't especially enthusiastic about this proposal, but she probably couldn't bring herself to refuse a visit to a sick, crippled woman. Plus, she was deep into preparations for a Church supper the next night, and the reverend had taken Aurora to a special girls-only Bible Study that met each month. He was the guest speaker today.

Dolly and I talked for a few minutes about Pearl's bike tires. It seemed the reason she had stayed out of school for a few days after it happened was that she and her mother were both afraid. An assault on the bike where it leaned against the back of the trailer was getting personal—much more personal than Bruce Denmark would ever have been.

Then I read to Dolly from *The Sparrow,* about a Jesuit priest in the future who leads an interplanetary expedition to locate the source of exquisite music coming from outer space. We stopped long enough to share some peanut butter cookies Belinda had left the evening before. Dolly said, "Go and get Gregory. He's got a heater out there, but I'm sure he's cold as ice and should come in."

The afternoon was quite dark, partly due to the storm and partly because we were only weeks away from the winter solstice. Gregory was working as close to his heater as he dared. He looked almost relieved when he saw me.

"Dolly says to come inside and have some cookies," I told him from a slight distance. He said he'd be right there and bent back over his work, and I returned to the house. Dolly and I had consumed a few cookies and were deep into a discussion of the book when Gregory came in, shook snow off himself, washed his hands, and then sat down with us. Dolly had talked me through how to make spice tea, and it was warm and almost festive. Then the phone rang.

Gregory went to answer it. "Hello? . . . No, she hasn't been here." This caught my attention and Dolly's. Gregory looked over at us, and to me he mouthed, *Pearl?* I shook my head, understanding him to ask if we'd seen her. I turned to Dolly.

"Dolly, have you seen Pearl this afternoon?"

"No, dear. She hasn't been here since I got sick."

There was a little more silence, and then Gregory spoke again. "Don't worry, Belinda. And for Heaven's sake, don't go out in that car of yours in this weather. I'll get some folks on the road. We'll find her. Stay home where we know how to reach you."

He hung up and turned to us, his face pinched. "Pearl's missing. Belinda says she was in the meadow earlier, or she headed that way. But she's not there now, and it's nearly dark. Belinda is sure Pearl wouldn't have tried to go anywhere in this weather, especially after what happened to her bike." He took a breath and looked at me. "Jude, I'm going to make a few phone calls, and then I'm going to ask you to come with me to look for her. You'll be able to look around a lot better than I will while I'm driving, especially in the storm. You okay with that?"

I nodded. What else could I do?

First Gregory called Mrs. King, who agreed to contact her husband and have him begin a search. Then Gregory made two more calls to other people who had storm-worthy vehicles, and they both agreed to help. He was about to call a third when the phone rang under his hand. It was Reverend King. Natalie must have told him the problem, because the conversation went immediately to the task at hand. They talked about who was searching already, which brothers the reverend would call, and what areas each vehicle would cover. I listened, confused; why would they need to cover so much ground for a crippled girl who had no access to transportation other than her legs?

It wasn't until Gregory was backing his truck out of the driveway and into the road that it occurred to me to be surprised at the readiness of these saints to go out into a nasty winter storm late on a Saturday afternoon and search for a heathen for whom they wouldn't ordinarily spare the time of day. Gregory handed me his cell phone. "Call Belinda and let her know we've got eight search parties out looking in different areas."

I took the dull silver thing and stared at it. "Um, I don't know how to use this."

"Shit. Sorry." He took it back and went through the routine to make the call, then handed it back to me. "Here. And ask her if she's thought of anyplace else the girl might have been likely to go."

Within seconds I heard Belinda Thornton's voice. I told her what Gregory had said. She thanked me and said that no, she had no more ideas. Her sigh was ragged.

"Did you call her friends to ask?" I wanted to know.

There was no sound for a few seconds. Then, "Pearl has no friends, Jude."

Gregory said, "Tell her I'll be in touch again soon."

"I heard," she told me. "Jude, please. Please find her."

Her voice was breaking with emotion. My own eyes watered a tiny bit. "We'll do everything we can," I said, not quite knowing what that would mean.

"Press the green button on the left once and close the phone. Hang onto it." I did as I was told. We drove as fast as Gregory dared, I think, which surprised me; weren't we supposed to be looking?

"What area are you looking in?" I asked.

"I'm going to talk to people who might know what happened to her. Don't talk now."

I sat there silently, watching the headlights reflect off of what was nearly a wall of falling snow before us, wondering how on earth I would see Pearl if she stood only a few yards from the edge of the road.

Gregory pulled up to a house I'd never been to before. "Wait here." He left the motor running and slammed the truck door. He pounded on the door of whoever's house this was. I watched and saw Mr. Schumacher open it. Braving the assault from falling flakes, I lowered the window to listen. It didn't help, and when Gregory disappeared inside I had no idea why. Within a few minutes, though, he came out of the house and climbed back into the truck, a storm in his own right, slamming the door with a violence that hinted at what he could do with his size and strength. The truck skidded as he vented his fury on the accelerator, and we were back on the road. Somewhat afraid of this version of Gregory that I'd never seen, I didn't speak until he pounded once on the steering wheel and asked through gritted teeth, "Jude, think! Where would she be?"

My voice shook. "I wish I knew. Miss Thornton has already been in the meadow, and that's what I would have guessed." A few heartbeats went by. "Unless . . ."

His head snapped briefly toward me. "Unless what?"

"Well . . . she sort of adopted a kind of fort that Tim and I discovered in the woods, but I really don't think she'd go there in this storm. Plus, she would need her bike."

"This fort thing. Is it near where you got your tires slashed that day?"

"Yes. She would have gone down the hill beside the bridge."

He headed in that general direction, more slowly now. "Watch the sides of the road as well as you can, Jude."

Eyes straining, I asked, "Why did you stop at the Schumachers'?" And as if he had answered, which he hadn't, my head whipped toward him. "Do you think they did something?"

I could see his jaw grind. "They said they didn't. Both boys were there. But I don't know that I believe them. We're pretty sure they slashed the tires last week, and it wouldn't have been the first time they threatened Pearl."

I watched out my window again, lost in thought and paying not enough attention to what I couldn't see through the snow, which was now thinning a little. And that's when it came to me. "The river!"

"What?"

"Get to the baptism bank, as fast as you can!" It was like God himself had spoken to me. I could almost hear Larry, or Bill, whichever, taunting Pearl about why she couldn't be baptized. I wanted to hurl myself out of the truck, convinced that in my panic I could fly there faster than Gregory could drive.

We skidded to a halt, and Gregory left the headlights on where they pointed out over the water, only a few flakes catching the light now. He grabbed a huge flashlight out of the covered truck bed. I was out of the truck and at the water's edge as fast as the snow-covered ground would allow, looking around me for signs of anything. Gregory was right behind me. We stood there, side by side, heaving breaths that added more moisture to the air and following the light's beam across the water, blackness broken by white where the ice had started to form.

We both saw her at once. Gregory dumped his jacket on the ground and thrust the flashlight at me. I held the light high, casting the beam ahead of the man so he could see where to go. This water had been cold for my baptism last May; what must it feel like now? But I was sure Gregory felt very little for himself. I could just make out his form as he plunged forward, breaking some of the thin ice, and when the water was up to his neck he reached the sodden form of Pearl's dead body. I could hear his groans through the wind. My own eyes were blinded by tears now, so all I can relate about his trip back was that it was slow and accompanied by the low moans he managed through his ragged breathing. He collapsed on the shore, the malformed girl lifeless and frozen. He leaned over her and wept.

In a daze, tears streaming down my own face, I went back to the truck in hopes of finding a blanket. I found two, and half-running, half-falling in the snow I brought them to where Gregory was wrapped around Pearl's body. I threw the blankets over him and picked up his jacket, shaking so badly I had trouble feeling in the pocket for the cell phone. I dialed 911.

It was not easy to coax Gregory into the truck, to convince him he could do nothing more for Pearl. But I had to try; I knew hypothermia would set in quickly. The final straw was when I told him, "If you get sick, what will Dolly do?"

When the police were on their way, Gregory sat up and reached for the phone, fighting to regain some composure and to keep his teeth from chattering. He dialed, and I heard him say, "Belinda. I found her. I'm so sorry."

He handed me the phone. "Call Mrs. King. Tell her to go and be with Belinda. *Not* the reverend. And then I need you to phone her husband and have him tell the other searchers to go home." He stood, a hulking mass under the tent of blankets, and turned toward the truck. "Come on."

In the cranked-up heat of the truck cab, I made the phone calls and gave Gregory back the phone. He took it with shaking hands. "We need to get you home," I told him.

"We'll wait."

I got out of the truck. I had the distinct feeling something really important had to be done, and I didn't know what. I bent over the form of what had once been Pearl Thornton, shadows falling oddly where the truck headlights hit and missed. I knelt. I knew I should pray. I *knew* it. "Dear Lord," I began, "Father in Heaven . . ." I faltered, eyes widening in delayed horror. "How could you let this happen?" My voice rose. "How could you let this happen?"

Odd thoughts ranged at random through my shocked brain. She was a pagan. She refused to be saved. She did not worship God through Jesus his son. She used inappropriate language. Before I knew it, I was on my feet. "That's not enough!" I shouted at the black water, fists clenched at my thighs. "That's not enough reason!"

I turned and ran back to the truck, slamming the door hard, breathing harder. Teeth clenched in fury, I threw my head back against the headrest. And again. And again.

Gregory was leaning over the steering wheel, face hidden by his arms. Once I calmed down and sat still, I could hear his quiet sobs. The only other man I'd ever seen cry was Reverend King. He used to cry from time to time during his sermons, tears running down his face, and yet somehow was still able to speak to the entire congregation in ringing tones that made you want to cry with him, and somehow even the crying would make you feel good.

In comparison to what I'd seen in church, Gregory's weeping felt real. Too real. And there was no good feeling in it.

We waited, staring through the windshield at the swirling snow that did its best to hide the ugliness of what had happened by shrouding Pearl's body in white.

The arrival of the police felt anticlimactic. I barely remember their questions or our answers. I recall only that Gregory had suspected Larry and Bill, and I said I had remembered their taunt, and those things together had brought us to look here. One cruiser took Gregory home; he was shivering too badly to drive and needed to get into a warm bath as soon as possible. Another policeman drove me to the Kings'. I got into a hot bath myself and sat there shivering, adding more and more hot water to counteract the cold that was inside me, until I heard Aurora's voice. Mrs. King would probably have told her what happened. I did not want to talk about it. Not just because it was so ugly, but also because of what I had been unable to do. I had been unable to talk to God and to ask for his forgiveness for Pearl's lack of repentance, unable to pray that he take her soul because of her good heart, to be her advocate. How could I advocate for her with a God who had allowed two evil sinners to kill her in mockery of God's own symbol of salvation?

I didn't know what was happening to me. I felt afraid and numb at once.

"Jude?" It was the reverend's voice. "Jude?"

My voice croaked. "Here. Taking a bath." I ran more hot water. I couldn't get it hot enough. If there was a reply I didn't hear it.

Chapter 16

There had always been a certain amount of talk about the Thorntons among the saints. Not a lot, but you could count on their name to come up with some degree of regularity. After Pearl's murder, I heard her name everywhere. And it was always "Pearl," never "Tansy."

Aurora, somehow, had figured out that even though my relationship with Pearl had been unconventional and not condoned, it had been real and deep. So every time our eyes met, hers were full of sympathy and, often, tears. I wanted her to stop, but how could I tell her that? I didn't want sympathy. I didn't know what to do with it. I felt as though nothing touched me, or if anything did I couldn't feel it. And if I felt it, I might start crying. Plus, I didn't deserve sympathy from Reverend King's daughter; I couldn't talk to God.

I began going to the Harts' again, but now as an escape rather than as a mission to save their souls. It was there that I heard what was happening with Larry and Bill. The investigation had turned up some incriminating evidence, such as tire tracks in the near-frozen mud under the snow that matched their vehicle, a human bite matching Pearl's mouth shape on Bill's hand, scratch marks on both boys, and Bill's DNA under Pearl's fingernails. It seemed she had fought hard for her life to keep them from throwing her into the frigid water, and probably fought again as she tried to get out and was pushed back until the cold and her own heavy clothing made fighting impossible, and she drowned. I found myself wishing I knew some magical herb that would bring her back to life, but the only way I'd ever seen a person die and be reborn was in Christian baptism. Pearl's baptism could hardly be that.

The Schumacher parents admitted that they had joined the Church in an effort to give their boys a moral foundation—as Gregory put it, "Rather too late."

Dolly's blind eyes functioned as far as tears were concerned, that much was certain. I sat with her for hours, holding her hand, which she reclaimed frequently to wipe her face and blow her nose. She asked me to read to her sometimes from Psalms, which comforted both of us. But I really didn't know what to feel. I hadn't even known how I felt about Pearl when she was alive. All I knew now was that it felt as though color and light had gone out of the world, and I couldn't make sense out of that.

Gregory spent a good deal of time with Belinda, making sure I understood that it was important to him that I spend a good deal of time with Dolly. I didn't mind. It was better than Aurora's sad looks, or the horror of Reverend King somehow divining that this thing was separating me from God. Which would also separate me from Reverend King.

I was struggling to feel a connection with God, with Jesus, with any semblance of sanctity. Reverend King had delivered a very moving sermon the day after the murder, about forgiveness that I think he meant for Pearl, and about love, and if he hadn't polished it off by using her heathen death as a caution to be sure we're saved, I might have been able to grasp at some straw of religious conviction again. But . . . no. Still numb. Still isolated. Still lost.

I sat beside Lorne for that sermon, the warmth of his body oddly comforting, and wondered if he remembered, as I did, that "lost" had been the theme of our mother's funeral.

Pearl's funeral was planned for Wednesday, after the coroner had been able to get all the evidence he could from the corpse. On Tuesday after school something possessed me, and I asked Gregory to drive me to Belinda's trailer. We found her in a state of panic.

"Her doll!" she cried, her voice piercing and frantic. "I can't find her doll!" She began to sob. "I have to bury it with her. I *have* to!"

I knew which doll she meant. I'd seen Pearl sing to that doll; I'd rescued that doll from a fall off the boulder. I knew the doll. Gregory and I helped Belinda search, though in a trailer that size there are only so many places to look. We gave up. Belinda fell against Gregory and wept, and he held her. As they stood there swaying gently I fought my own tears, and then again a feeling of something I didn't understand came over me. I put my coat back on and left the trailer, headed for the meadow, and made a beeline for Pearl's boulder. I looked on top; nothing but leftover snow. I scuffed the snow with my boots all around the boulder. I was on my second circuit, behind the big rock, when my foot cleared snow over a pattern of sticks. I had disturbed them slightly, but not so much that I couldn't tell what they were. They were in the shape of a star. A pentagram. We'd been told this was a sign of witchery. I should have been afraid of it; yet, even though I'd never seen Pearl use it, it spoke of her. And there was something reverent about it.

The earth under the sticks was only partly frozen this early in the season, and it seemed recently disturbed. I found a pointed rock and stabbed and scraped until the frozen top layer gave way to softer earth beneath. About four inches down, I encountered a cardboard box, slightly sodden and disintegrating. Inside it was the doll.

Reverently I unearthed the odd body, peculiar color patterns in the clothing, a skin tone matching Pearl's fairly well. For some reason I sheltered the doll inside my parka before heading back to the trailer.

Gregory and Belinda were on the step outside, watching me approach. When I handed the doll to Belinda, she reached for me and held me very close, sobbing and sobbing until Gregory shepherded us all back inside.

Belinda sat on the couch, clutching the cloth surrogate for her odd, misshapen daughter. Gregory and I sat there, silent, present, until Belinda recovered herself.

"Thank you," she said to me. "Where was it?"

"Buried behind her rock. There was a pentagram in sticks over it." Belinda nodded, and I asked, "Why would she bury it?"

"I'm not sure. All I know is that after her bicycle tires were slashed, we were both terrified something would happen to her next. She was a very mysterious girl."

A shiver passed through me. Had Pearl known she was about to die? And had she gone there to bury the doll on the very day that she died, herself? Is that why she'd left the trailer at all, to go to the meadow that stormy afternoon?

Finally Gregory and I got up to leave. I felt the need to say something comforting to Belinda. Maybe it was on my mind that I'd been avoiding Reverend King, and that I hadn't been able to talk with God lately, but what I said was the reverend's usual end-of-sermon invocation "God grant you peace."

Belinda's voice caught, and she said, "Oh, child! *That* we must grant to ourselves."

As soon as we were back in the truck, Gregory asked, "How did you know?"

"About the doll?"

"About Belinda. How did you know she needed us?"

I shrugged. I didn't have a clue.

The funeral was packed. It wasn't at my church; it was at one of the only two other churches within reasonable driving distance. I think it was Unitarian Universalist, but I'm not certain. Gregory took Dolly and me; I didn't tell anyone at the King household, or anyone in my family, that I was going.

Their pastor was a woman. That's all I remember about the service, other than the music. A woman I didn't know sang "Baby Mine" from *Dumbo*. Pearl's song. I finally heard all the words. The ridicule, the judgment, the ostracism. And the value—the nobility—that most people would never see.

Evidently, Reverend King had been prepared to grant me a certain amount of leniency, in terms of spending time with the unsaved, in the immediate aftermath of Pearl's death, but when Gregory continued to spend time with Belinda it must have begun to chafe.

In the past, the amount of time Belinda might spend at the Harts' would not have come so much to the Kings' attention; but the frequency of my own visits gave them a window into that household. When I'd get home after a visit with Dolly, the reverend would ask if Belinda had been there, or if Gregory had gone to the trailer (which seemed to make Reverend King even more peevish). He never told me not to visit the Harts, but I lived in a state of fear that he would. I needed them, needed to be with people who would love me even if I couldn't talk to God, people to whom Pearl had meant so much.

During one visit I told Dolly about the reverend's questions. "Should I lie?" I asked her. "Should I tell him Gregory was here when he wasn't, or that Miss Thornton wasn't here when she was?"

Dolly sighed heavily. "No, dear. I don't advise you to lie. If the reverend has a problem with Gregory, they'll have to talk about it together. Don't you get involved." There was something final in her tone that I didn't usually hear; I didn't inquire further.

On the Internet, I resumed my old lurker status, not contributing. I sought out chat rooms in which the participants were questioning scripture, religion, even the existence of God. And for the first time, I cringed at some of the blind obedience and brainless parroting of the more intense Bible supporters. I cringed, because once I would have responded in the same way. Now, I just watched. And winced.

Another fear of mine was that Reverend King would ask me for more Internet assistance; I was terrified that spending more than a few minutes alone with him would be enough for him to intuit that I was feeling separated from him, from God. He did ask me for some things, most of which I managed to do from the relative safety of my own room. He had become competent, within limits, at much of what he needed to do. He'd learned how to search, and he could open new blog threads and respond to messages. Mostly what he needed from me these days consisted of looking at other sites and giving him my opinion about whether some of the features I saw would be good for his site.

And despite the wintry weather, he began to spend more mission time in Boise.

If her father didn't seem to notice that I was becoming withdrawn, Aurora did. She knocked on my doorframe one evening after supper. "Can I come in?"

I shrugged. "I guess. Do you need something?"

She sat on the end of the bed, but I didn't turn toward her. "I need to know if you're all right. You're not yourself lately. I mean, your new self."

"My new self?"

"The self you became around the time when you got baptized again."

Rather automatically, I responded, "You mean when I got baptized. The first one was just getting wet."

"Fine. Anyway, you got all weird and wide-eyed. A real scripture-pusher. People couldn't talk to you without hearing what they needed to do to get right with God. Remember?"

I sighed. "Yeah. Guess I was pretty intense."

"For sure. Only you're not anymore. Since Pearl died. You seem kind of like your old self, only sad." She waited; I said nothing. "So, are you okay?"

Had she figured it out? Had she sensed my isolation? I turned in my chair to face her. "Why do you want to know?"

She exhaled loudly. "Honestly, Jude! I thought we were friends. At least, we were once upon a time. I want to know if I can help. You've helped me lots of times. Can't I offer something to you? I mean, sometimes it helps just to talk about something. It's okay if you want to talk about Pearl." I blinked. She said, "So would you like to?"

Like most people who both want and don't want to talk about something affecting them powerfully, when asked by a friend if they want to talk, I replied, "There's nothing to talk about."

"Were you better friends than I thought?"

"Probably not. We argued all the time."

"All the time? When did you see her, outside of school?"

I didn't want to confess any of the meetings I'd had with Pearl, so I limited my exposure. "At the Harts'. Dolly got me involved in reading to her. And sometimes Pearl would be there. She's always visited the Harts. And we'd all talk about all kinds of things. And whenever I said anything about God or scripture"—I was almost smiling by now, remembering these scenes—"Pearl would roll her eyes and say, 'Oh, pulleeeze!' and she'd tell me I was all wrong about everything."

Aurora's tongue poked at the inside of her cheek. "Nothing to talk about, eh?" She smiled at me. "Sounds like true love to me!" My head snapped upward. Aurora laughed musically. "Don't worry! I'm only kidding. But . . . it must have been really horrible, seeing her like that." She didn't say what "like that" meant, but I knew: a sodden, lifeless lump on the snowy riverbank. When I didn't respond, she said, "So, do you want to talk with *me* about those things? I'll bet we don't see eye to eye on everything, either. So it would hardly be like Bible Study, where everyone has to come to the same conclusion at the end."

The idea of Aurora putting up the kind of fight Pearl had been capable of nearly made me laugh. But something akin to what had led me to Belinda Thornton the day she was searching for the doll came over me. A feeling that I had to do something I hadn't known I would do, that suddenly was the only thing to do. "Well . . . maybe you should come to the Harts' with me, and we can all talk about things."

Her chin went up a little. "Maybe I should." Then she peered at me from the corners of her eyes. "Do you think they'd mind?"

"D'you think your folks would let you?"

"They let *you*. And we'd be together." True. "Next time you go, let me know?"

I had no choice but to agree at that point, though it wasn't clear to me why she wanted to go with me, and also I was half afraid that if we both wanted to go, we'd both be forbidden to do so. But it had seemed right.

We tried it, that very Saturday. I called to make sure Dolly was there and to ask if I could bring Aurora. Dolly, predictably, was thrilled. "Oh, yes! By all means, bring her. Gregory can give you both a ride home afterward."

Mrs. King, reading through a recipe book at the kitchen table, looked dubious when we approached her, but she only said, "Ask your father."

Aurora knocked on his office door. From within, I heard a quick, sharp sound that I knew meant the sudden closing of the laptop screen. Then, "Come in." She opened the door, and I could see the reverend's face. He looked flushed.

Aurora said, "Daddy, is your computer giving you trouble again?" I glanced quickly at her; had he been having problems he hadn't mentioned to me?

"No. No, sweet girl. Nothing I can't cope with. What is it you want?"

"Jude is going over to visit with Dolly, and I'm going with him. Mom wanted me to let you know." I held my tongue; this was not exactly what Mrs. King had said.

"Fine. Just be back in plenty of time for supper. Is your mother driving you?"

"Yes. Thanks, Daddy!" She punched my arm and made a face. An odd, warm feeling crept up from my chest into my throat. I had missed Aurora. I had missed her a lot.

We weren't at the Harts' for long before Belinda Thornton

arrived. Aurora nearly shocked the pants off of me when she went right over to Belinda and hugged her.

With Belinda there, we didn't exactly have a scriptural discussion. We also didn't talk much about Pearl, though it came out at one point that I'd gone to the funeral, and I looked quickly at Aurora. She raised an eyebrow and threw an arch glance my way. I grinned, and she grinned; it would be our secret from her parents. Another one.

Gregory drove us home in his truck, Aurora beside him, me sandwiching her in. Gregory said, "What a pleasant surprise to have you visit today, Aurora."

"I hope it was okay."

"More than okay. It was delightful. What made you want to come?"

"Jude. Well, sort of. I mean, we used to be great friends, and then he got all serious for a while, and then this horrible thing happened." This didn't really answer the question he'd asked, but the quick look he threw at me over Aurora's head told me it had told him something anyway.

Gregory's tone was teasing. "Yes, our Jude did get rather serious for a time there, didn't he." It wasn't a question, and it could have ended the discussion.

But Aurora picked it up. "Oh, my gosh, yes." She elbowed my ribs once. "I didn't like him at all for a while there. It was impossible to talk to him, you know?"

Gregory nodded. "I do know. I'm just sorry it took a tragedy to shake him out of it." Another quick glance toward me. "You are over it, aren't you, Jude?"

I shrugged. I didn't like this conversation very much. Not being "all serious" anymore was turning out to mean that I had no relationship with God anymore. Which meant not only that my second immersion had also been a dud, but also if I couldn't fix things, if I couldn't get back to where I had been, I was not saved and would surely go to Hell.

I sat bolt upright. Where was Pearl? Was she really in Hell? Could that be possible? Would God really do that? What about how great she'd been to give me valerian for Clara? What about showing me all the wildflowers? What about coming with me to the fort, and being understanding about how I couldn't be seen with her when our bikes were vandalized and we both had to get home? What about the way she was at the Harts', with honest discussion and genuine laughter and powerful affection for Dolly and Gregory? What about all the love she showered on that doll? What about the way her mother adored her? Was all that for nothing?

My head snapped toward Gregory. He sensed it. "Something wrong, Jude?"

"I, uh . . . I don't know." How to ask? Should I just wait and ask Reverend King? Ha. I knew what he'd say. "Um, I guess I don't understand something." Gregory guffawed, and Aurora nearly squealed with laughter. "What? What did I say?"

Gregory managed to recover himself. "Never mind, Jude. What is that one something you don't understand?"

"It's not funny, actually." This helped Aurora back to a semblance of calm. "I don't understand how God could send Pearl to Hell."

All I heard was the truck engine and the tires on the road for maybe half a minute. Then Gregory said, "I don't think that's what happened, Jude."

"But—she wasn't saved. She refused salvation over and over. I tried to talk to her about it myself, so I know. So she can't go to Heaven."

Gregory heaved an uncomfortable breath. "Well, my belief is that God will make a determination based on what he knew about Pearl, which is a far sight more than any of us could ever know about anyone. God is the judge, not us."

"But—" I sputtered for a few seconds. Aurora hadn't said anything, so I turned to her. "What do *you* believe?"

I think this was the only time I heard Aurora quote scripture outside of Bible Study. " 'Judge nothing before the time, until the Lord comes, who will both bring to light the hidden things of darkness, and reveal the counsels of the hearts. Then each man will get his praise from God.' "

This hands-off approach irritated me immensely. "But all that does is make it easy. It goes against everything we're told to tell the unsaved! I mean, why bother to believe at all, why bother to get baptized, why bother to bring others to the Light if being saved or not doesn't matter in the end?"

Gregory's voice was so quiet I almost missed it. "Why, indeed?"

No one spoke for the rest of the four minutes or so before we arrived at the Kings'. The reverend had already left for Boise, so Aurora and I sat with Natalie for supper. Maybe it was the contrast with the energy at the Harts', or maybe it was the last few minutes of silence in the truck, but it dawned on me rather suddenly that Mrs. King was in a mood. It felt conflicted, like there was anxious static and depression together. And, even as I noticed this mood, I realized this was how she seemed more and more often. I tried to remember when it had started; must have come on gradually, I reasoned, or I would have noticed it before. Right?

Conversation was desultory and strained until Mrs. King asked about our visit with Dolly. Aurora perked up, evidently glad to have a topic. "Oh, it was great. I don't think I've ever heard Dolly talk so much. She laughs all the time; I didn't know. And I don't think I ever saw Gregory smile before. Not like this anyway. Miss Thornton was sad, of course, but you could tell she was glad to be there."

Mrs. King had rested her fork on her plate, a piece of parsley-freckled carrot impaled on the tines. Her words escaped almost as though she didn't know she was speaking. "Miss Thornton was there? Again?"

Aurora blinked. "Why is that bad?"

The carrot rose slowly toward Mrs. King's face. "I know your father is very concerned about her, that's all."

I said, "You mean he doesn't want her to go there." And it was the wrong thing to say.

Mrs. King closed her eyes. "Jude, let's not get into that, all right?" My stomach clenched; she looked as though she might cry.

After supper, Mrs. King went to take a "long, hot soak" as she put it, and Aurora and I sat whispering in my room. I asked her if something was wrong with her mother.

"I don't know. Things have been getting odder ever since last spring. Remember? When I told you about what I heard them talking about?"

How could I forget? It was the day, and the reason, that I'd exposed the darkness in my soul to Reverend King, the day I'd become his godson. The day I'd decided to do a second immersion. I just nodded.

Aurora said, "I think she doesn't like that he goes to Boise so often."

"He does go kind of a lot. Does she know what he does there?"

"What do you mean? He's trying to get people to come to Church."

Something told me to stop. Instead, I asked, "But does she know which people?"

Again, "What do you mean?"

There was no backing out now. "When I went with him, he was talking to homosexuals." There. I'd said it. A few thoughts flashed through my brain in about a nanosecond. If he was keeping this from his wife, how could he have told Lorne? But he had told Lorne about me, too. The reverend might have sworn Lorne to secrecy about his actions in return for keeping quiet about my own transgressions.

"What?" Aurora's voice was too loud; she clapped a hand over her mouth.

"It's true. That's what we did. You didn't know?"

Her eyes were huge. "No, and I'll bet Mom doesn't, either. Why would he do that?"

"It's like one of his favorite sins. To talk about, I mean. He blogs about it all the time, and he has this little pamphlet about it." Reverend King had never told me not to say anything about this to anyone. He must have been banking on my own shame, my own sense of guilt, to keep me quiet.

"Pamphlet?"

"It's really just a piece of yellow paper with verses on it from the Bible about homosexuality, folded like a brochure."

"Why yellow?"

"How should I know?"

"Well, you seem to know all kinds of other stuff I don't." She sounded sulky.

"Not all kinds of stuff. Just this." We sat silent for a moment, Aurora absently pulling at imaginary impurities in my bedspread, me watching her fingers to avoid her face. "You probably shouldn't tell your mom." I couldn't have said why this felt important, but it seemed Aurora agreed with me. She nodded. And then she got up and went to her room.

After she left I remembered that Reverend King had actually instructed me once not to tell his wife or daughter why he went to Boise.

I spent Thanksgiving with Lorne and his little family, an expectation that not so many months ago would have irritated me. But being at the Kings' lately felt like trying to get comfortable on a mattress filled with small, squirming animals that occasionally poked a tooth or a claw through the upholstery. The reverend was irritable and tended to snap (and then apologize), and his wife seemed jumpy, overreacting to things that once would have caused her to wave a hand in amused dismissal.

CC had taken a liking to me, probably because she saw me regularly but not frequently; according to her baby timetable, a week was a long time. It was good to hear her squeal in fun, and to hear Clara laugh, and to see how proud Lorne looked. Loving CC's response, I did my best to juggle three fabric blocks until Clara took my little niece away for a nap. As I watched them go upstairs it occurred to me that the moods in my two households had switched. Once, it had been my own home that felt gloomy and oppressive, and things had been lighter and happier at the Kings'. Now, I was trying to come up with an excuse to come back here the next day. I turned toward Lorne, who was collecting some of CC's toys.

"What are you guys doing tomorrow?"

Lorne didn't pick up on my reason for asking. "I'm working. Clara is taking CC to her parents' for the day."

So no one would be here. I considered coming here anyway, but I didn't live here anymore, and I'd be all alone. I decided I'd go to the Harts' again, hoping desperately that they weren't getting tired of me—especially since it was fast becoming the only place where I didn't live in fear of having someone figure out that my faith was in some kind of remission.

After breakfast on Friday, I asked Aurora if she wanted to go with me. She sounded sulky. "Can't. Mom's on this big kick about how I have to start making at least some of my clothes, and we're going shopping for patterns and fabric."

Mrs. King topped this expectation she was placing on Aurora with one she dumped on me. "Jude, it's a warm day for this time of year. I'd like you to see if you can tidy up the garage a little. It's getting so it's hard to get my car in and out." She almost laughed at the face I made. "I'm not asking you to clean it out, just bring a little order to it, will you?"

I started this chore right away in hopes of having enough time left for my visit to the Harts. It wasn't a huge project, but the lawn tools were all over the place, the wood for the fireplace was covered in gardening paraphernalia, and the place would benefit from a sweeping to push out all the dead leaves that the fall winds had sent fluttering in.

After a couple of hours of work, I grabbed a couple of peanut butter sandwiches for lunch, polished them off quickly, and headed out to finish. I had eliminated enough clutter to make sweeping possible when I realized that the reverend's Jeep needed to be moved out of the garage first. I was standing there, hands on hips and staring at the vehicle, when Reverend

King came out of the house and walked past me to the car. Not so much as a "Good afternoon," or a "Nice job, Jude." His scowl told me he was on some kind of mission. So did the squeal of tires as he took off. I just sighed and swept out the garage, locked the house, wheeled my bike into the thin afternoon sunshine, and turned the front wheel toward the Harts'.

Reverend King's Jeep was in the driveway in front of the barn. Not knowing what to make of this, and a little worried, I left the bike in the usual spot behind the house and was about to knock on the back door when I heard raised voices coming from the barn. I froze. One of the voices was Reverend King's. I heard Aurora's name.

Stepping carefully so nothing would crunch and give me away, I crept toward the barn. There was no door on the side, just the big doors in the front and the regular door in the back, so I couldn't be seen from there, or from the house, unless Dolly had company I didn't know about. I hugged the side of the barn near the back door and practically held my breath, listening.

"Your daughter is not in any danger here."

"I'm not talking about physical harm. I'm talking about her spirit, her very soul. I'm talking about the example you're setting, fraternizing with that woman so freely! Miss Thornton's ideas are not suitable for Christian ears."

Gregory's voice took on a droll note. "You're not afraid for Jude's soul?"

"Young Jude can take care of himself. He may be able to teach you and your sister a thing or two."

His voice lower than the reverend's angry tones, Gregory said, "I daresay he could."

There was a pause. Then, from the reverend, "Because of how welcome that woman is here, I've instructed my wife that she is not to visit Dolly anymore, or to allow Aurora to do so. I've only recently discovered how much time Natalie had been spending here." This came as a surprise to me, too. Why hadn't I known this? How had she and I managed to miss each other?

She must have been coming during school hours, was all I could figure. But Dolly had never mentioned it. . . .

Gregory's tone sounded edgier now. "She comes here to relieve Dolly of some of the tedium of her days. I believe she considers it a Christian act."

Now the reverend's voice also had an edge. "Your sister wouldn't have quite so much tedium if you hadn't—"

"Stop!" Gregory had lost his cool. "If you say another word about that, you'll regret it."

"What I regret is not putting my foot down sooner about your *friendship* with Belinda Thornton. I've never been quite convinced about your conviction, your commitment to Jesus. And now I hear that she's over here all the time! I also didn't know that Pearl was here so often."

"And you found this out how?"

"Aurora told me that Pearl and Jude used to have religious discussions. I only hope they did that poor girl some good before she was murdered."

In my mind I pictured Gregory's jaw stiffening. "That 'poor girl' understood love much better than you do. You have no right to tell me who my friends are, and who can visit me or Dolly. Belinda Thornton is welcome here whenever she chooses to come. So are your wife, and your daughter. And my commitment to Jesus is between Jesus and me."

Reverend King spoke so softly I almost couldn't hear him. "If you continue to disobey me, I will forbid you entry into the Church. You will lose your salvation."

"I couldn't care less about any salvation you control."

"And your sister will be forbidden as well."

Something rustled inside, and I cringed, fearing one or both men would come storming out and find me. But then Gregory spoke again, his tones measured and heavy. "Dolly will continue to come to your church, even if I never enter it again. She needs it, and you cannot deny her."

"I think you'll find I can."

"And I think you'll find that if you do, some of your activities will be dragged out of the darkness and into the light where everyone can see them."

A pause. Then, "What are you talking about?"

"You know damn well what I'm talking about, *Reverend*." He spat the last word out.

The silence that followed was so long that I started to lean away from the wall, wondering if maybe I just wasn't close enough to hear. Then suddenly what I heard was footsteps moving—thundering hurriedly toward the front of the barn. I pressed against the building again and watched as Reverend King got into his Jeep and roared away.

I crept back to my bike and lifted it over my head so that I could carry it back out toward the road without anyone hearing me. I didn't think I could face Gregory or Dolly right now.

With no plan in mind, I found myself at the bridge near the baptism bank. Bike stowed downhill a little and behind some young evergreens, I headed for the fort.

I needed to think. I had to figure out what had just happened, and the fort seemed like a great place to do that. But as I approached, I felt as though I was trespassing. Like it wasn't mine any longer. I almost expected Pearl, or her ghost, to be inside. Just outside the entry spot, I closed my eyes. *Pearl, if you don't want me to go inside, please give me some kind of sign.* Nothing happened. I went in.

It was very cold inside; the day was warm for the season, but not warm really, and the inside of the fort hadn't seen sun in years. But when my eyes adjusted to the dimness, I nearly left again, in a hurry: there were more dried flowers in the vase— the vase I had toppled on my last visit, the vase I had replaced on the board without finding the flowers that had been in it. And now there were even more flowers, in the vase *and* in one of the two plastic cups. Would she really have come here since the last time I saw the place? It had been—when? Oh, yes; just before her bike tires got slashed. In fact, her tires had been slashed the same night, after I was here. No way would she have come here since I tossed the place, because she wouldn't have had a bike. And then she was . . . she was drowned. It was every-thing I could do not to run out in a panic. My breathing was all I could hear as I looked behind me. Was she here after all? Was I really not so foolish to have asked permission to enter?

I shook myself free of the creeps and reminded myself that even if I couldn't talk to Jesus, he was there anyway and would look out for me. I would figure this all out later; I had more pressing things to think about, and there had to be a rational explanation for what I was seeing. This helped, but only a little.

Getting back to my reason for coming here in the first place, I sat on the log and let my mind travel back to the confronta-tion I had just heard. So many thoughts and images and fears jumbled one on top of the other that I felt dizzy. There was shame, too. Since my mother's death, I had started and stopped and started and stopped thinking of Dolly and Gre-gory as friends, according to circumstances and whims. Mostly I visited them when I needed something, from one or both of them. The most recent "on again" friendship had begun when I tried to co-opt Dolly into my plan to convince her brother to stop fraternizing with Belinda Thornton. While it's true that this mission had gotten sidetracked by more general religious discussions and by stimulating confrontations with Pearl, I couldn't deny my original intention.

The shame seeped out from between the words I had heard Reverend King say just this afternoon: *I'm talking about the exam-ple you're setting, fraternizing with that woman so freely! Miss Thorn-ton's ideas are not suitable for Christian ears.* I might have said those words myself, not very long ago. Now they sounded coarse, uncharitable, ignorant. What must the Harts have thought of me? And yet they let me keep coming back.

And Reverend King kept letting me go there. *Young Jude can take care of himself. He may be able to teach you and your sister a thing or two.*

Something heavy rolled over me. Or it felt like that. It was a mangled mass made up of pride in my godfather's faith in me, shame that I had allowed myself to be sidetracked from the mission we were supposed to have in common, and some unnamable emotion about the man who believed God had sent me to him to be his son. The man without whom I would be perhaps in worse shape than I was now, without whom I might have ended up in that Boise bar wearing backless chaps and a leather cowboy hat.

This last thought, this provocative image, brought up yet more shame. Because although I had managed to stop willfully thinking of sex with Tim or with that man in the bar, I hadn't managed to control my dreams. These people still visited me in my dreams.

To escape these thoughts, I stood too quickly and hit my head on the tree trunk; I was considerably taller than when Tim and I had acted out our fictions, creating fantasies, and had barely avoided confessing our feelings. Rubbing my head, I sat back down, Pearl's cackling laugh echoing in my ears.

Pearl. It had been through Pearl that I had gotten all my real information. Well, most of it. Lorne had told me how Dolly became chair-bound, but Pearl had told me about the grit behind it. Because of Pearl I knew Gregory was gay. I knew he and Todd Denmark had been together. I knew what Reverend King had been alluding to this afternoon when Gregory yelled at him to stop.

What she hadn't told me was what Gregory knew about the reverend's trips to Boise. What had been his words, that veiled threat? . . . *your activities will be dragged out of the darkness and into the light where everyone can see them.* And then he had said the word "reverend" as though it were an expletive.

I placed Gregory's threat beside what Lorne had said to me years ago, after I had walked Pearl home: *You trust him, because he's known for righteous behavior.* Righteous behavior would not mix with dirt hidden from the light.

The reverend's face hovered in the air as I tried to reconcile this conflict. While I had been in my evangelical period, while I had been the Damascus Kid, it had seemed to me as though people like Gregory, like Belinda, might misunderstand Amos King. We all saw him on the pulpit, casting flaming brimstone in all directions, but only a privileged few—myself included—saw the gentle side, the loving father, the fervent teacher, the servant of God who would allow himself to be demeaned by a sinner like the man in the bar, only to return love and proffer an invitation to join the sainted few. Gregory had to be wrong, whatever he thought. But if he was wrong, then why had the reverend turned on his heel like that? Why had he put up such a feeble defense? "What are you talking about" is hardly a denial of shameful activities.

"Pearl, where are you when I need you?"

My voice startled me. I stood again, carefully this time, and attempted a review. Had I come to any conclusions? Had I figured anything out?

I had not. I was left with conflicts and hidden truths and mysteries. And there was no one I could talk to about any of it. Then a name came to me, and I was scrambling back up the hill to where I'd stashed my bike before any other thoughts could catch up with me. Back on the road, I wheeled as fast as I could to the Thornton trailer. If Pearl had known so much, surely her mother would, too.

The ugly orange-yellow bicycle leaned against the trailer beside the door, as if at any moment Pearl would decide to use it. I threw my beautiful, shiny bike down next to it and leapt up the couple of steps to the door.

Miss Thornton opened it at my knock and blinked in surprise to see me. "Jude! What brings you here?"

"Can I talk to you about something? I'm all confused, and you're the only one I can ask."

She gazed at me for a few seconds, her face tired and gray-looking, and then she opened the door wider. She didn't ask if I wanted anything, but she did make her way to the couch and sat down. I sat in the chair across from her. She was silent, so I began.

"It's about Reverend King. And Mr. Hart." Suddenly I realized I couldn't ask my question without admitting that I had eavesdropped. I shrugged mentally and plunged ahead. "I was going to visit the Harts today, but before I knocked at the house

I heard Mr. Hart and the reverend arguing, in the barn. I didn't hear a lot"—this was actually not far from the truth, I told myself—"but I heard Reverend King say Mr. Hart couldn't come to church anymore, and neither could Dolly, and then Mr. Hart said Dolly would come whenever she wanted to because . . . I'm not quite sure what he was talking about, but he said he would bring some of the reverend's activities into the light." I paused for breath.

Miss Thornton frowned at me. "What were they arguing about?"

Well, they were arguing about you—of course I couldn't tell her that. So I lied. "I'm, uh, not quite sure. But they were really angry. Anyway, do you know what Mr. Hart knows?"

"What did the reverend say?"

"Not much. Just something like, what are you talking about. And Mr. Hart said that he knew very well, and Reverend King left."

Miss Thornton's face relaxed as though she knew exactly what the two men knew. "Well, Jude Connor, it should come as no surprise to you that Reverend King is no friend of mine. Even so, I don't think it's my place to say evil about the man behind his back. I can't be sure what Mr. Hart meant, so I'm not going to invent something. I guess I can't answer your question."

"But—you do know, right? I mean, you have some idea?"

She shook her head. "You're asking me to gossip and speculate about some bad thing someone might have done. I don't do that. But I will say this. Beware of idolizing any human being. We're all fallible, we all make mistakes, and we don't always learn from them. Reverend King is just as human as I am, and he can be just as wrong about anything as anyone else. I know you think that he's some kind of saint—and I'm not just talking about the way you people refer to each other. You think he's special, that he knows more than other people, that he has some direct line to God's ear. Jude, listen to me: no one has that. Not one person has that any more than any other person."

She stopped and looked hard at my face, which was probably

clouded with some combination of anger and fear. "I'm sorry, Jude. I know you don't want to hear any of this. You need to think of that man as somehow above the rest of us, or else why should you follow him. Why should it mean so much that he thinks you're special. If he's not special, then what about you? I know this is hard. But Jude, it's the truth."

I didn't even say good-bye. I just shot up from the chair and out the door, slamming it behind me.

Chapter 17

If I had thought things felt odd at the King household recently, that was nothing compared to the period that began that night. In the past few months, Reverend King had sometimes taken his supper into his office while the rest of us sat in the kitchen, and sometimes he'd sit with us but barely speak, casting a pall over the meal. In all cases, supper was a strained, silent event.

The trips to Boise seem to have stopped altogether. I might not have noticed, except that until recently they had been so frequent. When he didn't go for a week, it was unusual. And perhaps it was that lack of purpose, or perhaps lack of purpose had caused the trips to stop, but he began to spend most of his time in his office. He hardly spoke to me or to anyone. Aurora asked her mother about it once or twice, but Mrs. King just shook her head, seeming to pull back a little, and said she didn't know anything. The times I spent at Lorne and Clara's, times I would have begrudged at least a little not so long ago, were now a respite, a huge relief. I didn't mention the situation to them, because I didn't want to bring it into that homey, gentle environment where everything seemed open and loving. I needed that to stay as it was.

The sky fell the Sunday before Christmas, as if the snowfall the night before was its harbinger. Reverend King didn't sit down with us for breakfast. Instead, his tone defeated, he told us in a gravelly voice to go ahead of him to the church in Mrs. King's car, that he'd see us there. He looked as though he hadn't slept, and there was a thin line of dried blood on one cheek where he'd cut himself shaving.

Obediently, we piled in the Subaru Forester that Mrs. King drove and made our silent trip to the church. Our usual routine was that I would go and find Lorne and Clara at this point, because I would be with them for the rest of the day, and I would leave Mrs. King and Aurora to fellowship with people as they moved toward their pew in the front. Not today. Today, although I really wanted the relief of being with Lorne and Clara, I felt that the Kings needed me. I found Lorne but didn't sit down.

"I think I need to stay with Mrs. King and Aurora today," I told my brother. "I'm not sure what's going on, but things seem strange, and I think Mrs. King is worried about something."

Lorne scowled. "Is there anything we can do to help?"

"I don't know. I don't know what's wrong. I just feel like I should stay with them."

He looked at me as though trying to figure out if I knew more than I was telling, but he nodded. I made my way back and sat next to Aurora. She took my hand and held onto it. Mrs. King gave me a tense smile and then looked straight ahead, sitting rigidly upright, glancing as inconspicuously as possible down at her wristwatch from time to time. We waited.

Reverend King was never late for Sunday service. I couldn't even remember a time when he hadn't been there, other than the occasional vacation. He came when he had a cold. He even came once when he had walking pneumonia. Once he had conjunctivitis and he couldn't read anything, and he stood up there pretending to be blind, reciting scripture from memory and telling us all the enlightening things that had come to him during the time when he couldn't see, because there was nothing crowding out God's voice. But today—today he was late.

On the typical Sunday, the congregation was so busy fellowshipping that they needed to hush each other when Reverend

King came out to take the pulpit. Today, they kept fellowshipping, and kept on, until finally someone out there must have noticed how late it was, and the comments began: *Where is the reverend? Is Natalie here? Should we ask her what might be keeping him?* The drone of this commentary went on for about a minute, and finally there was silence. I looked at my own watch: fifteen minutes late. This was impossible.

Like many others there, I glanced at Mrs. King. Her eyes were shut, her jaw clenched, and I was afraid to say anything to her for fear she'd burst into tears. Then I heard a woman's voice from somewhere behind me, and with a shock I realized it was Dolly Hart.

"I think the reverend might not be able to join us today. Is there a brother among us who could lead us in prayer for his health and safety?"

Silence, then some rustling noises, then Mr. Voelker stood and moved to the front of the church. Mrs. Voelker had moved forward with her husband, and she squeezed in beside Mrs. King and sat there, calming in her stolid presence.

Mr. Voelker did his best, considering the circumstances. He didn't try to explain away the elephant among us; he just did as Dolly had suggested. He didn't look toward Mrs. King at all— no doubt to avoid embarrassing her. He must have believed that if she had known anything, she'd have said so.

When Mr. Voelker finished and the collection plate was handed around, we sang the final hymn that had been planned for the service. I don't remember what it was. Mrs. Voelker drove us home in the Kings' Subaru, with Mrs. King sitting stiff and straight beside her in the passenger seat. Aurora and I sat in the back. She huddled against me and wept as silently as possible. We both knew something was terribly wrong, and the creepiest part of it was Mrs. King's silence. I couldn't help thinking she ought to be worried in a more obvious way. She should have been saying things like, "I pray he's all right. He's never done this before. I can't understand what the problem is." Anything. But it was almost as though she had known he wouldn't show up.

I watched the road as well as I could from the back, eyes searching almost frantically for the Jeep. A flat tire? Out of gas? Even seeing it rammed into a tree or a telephone pole would have been better than this emptiness. I decided that Limbo, though we didn't actually believe in it, can be worse than Hell.

At the house, the Jeep was nowhere to be seen. Mrs. King finally revealed to us without words that she hadn't expected this, that she didn't know what had happened; she practically ran into the house, Aurora and me right behind her, and fled from the kitchen to the office, wrenching the doorknob. The door was locked.

"Daddy!" Aurora's voice was tearful, panicked. "Daddy! Please!" She banged on the door.

My own brain couldn't draw a sensible connection between the empty garage and the locked office. If the Jeep was gone, how could Reverend King be in his office? And why was the door locked? I looked at Mrs. King, and our eyes met over Aurora's head. Her voice lifeless, Mrs. King said, "I don't have a key."

Behind us, Mrs. Voelker said, "Let me try." She used a variety of items, including a hairpin from the mountain of gray-streaked hair piled on her head, and finally the door gave. Mrs. King stepped in front of Aurora, who was about to storm the room. "Everyone, please. I'll go in." I was surprised when Aurora didn't protest, even after Mrs. King went in and shut the door behind her.

Aurora waited maybe ten seconds. "Mom? Is he in there? Is he all right?"

Mrs. King's voice was muffled. "No one's in here." And then more silence.

Mrs. Voelker took Aurora's shoulders and turned her toward the kitchen. "Come, child. Your mother will tell you all you need to know as soon as she can." She threw me a glance to indicate that I should follow. I made a motion to let her think I was doing so, but then I turned to the office, opened the door, and went in.

Mrs. King was bent over the near side of the desk, one hand

propping her up and the other arm across her rib cage. I went
to her. She turned to me and almost fell, her arms so tight
around me I thought she would strain something. I held her,
and she sobbed and moaned, her head on my shoulder. On the
desk I could see a typed letter that must have been from Reverend King. It was short enough that Mrs. King had probably
read it all before I came in. I strained to see it, but I didn't want
to push Mrs. King aside. I would have to wait.

Finally, her knees began to buckle, and I maneuvered her
into the chair beside her. "May I read it?" I asked. She nodded,
evidently unable to speak. Here's what it said.

> *To my loving wife,*
> *I have failed. I have failed you, and Aurora, and*
> *all the saints. I have failed my parents and myself. I*
> *have failed God.*
> *I can't continue this life. I'm not leaving life*
> *altogether, not that. My sins are grievous enough*
> *already. I'm just leaving this life, which has been a*
> *lie for so long.*
> *My sin began with lies I told myself, and once I*
> *had lied to myself I had to lie to everyone. I wish I*
> *could bring myself to tell you the sin that has forced*
> *this separation, the sin I tried to kill and then to*
> *hide. The shame is too great. Ask Jude. He will*
> *understand. Tell him to pray and pray and pray that*
> *this sin does not overtake him as well. If he doesn't lie*
> *to himself, God will see him through it.*
> *I have a monster inside me. It does Satan's*
> *bidding. I tried to bury it beneath lies, to pretend it*
> *wasn't still there. But I lied. So I failed.*
> *I am so, so sorry. This breaks my heart, as surely*
> *as it will break yours.*
> *Tell Aurora I will miss her every single minute for*
> *the rest of my life, just as I will miss you. This is my*
> *penance.*

It wasn't signed. There were other papers beneath it. I glanced at Mrs. King, who was looking up at me, expectantly.

Ask Jude. He will understand.

My brain writhed in my skull. Images tumbled over each other: the reverend kneeling with me before his statue; the yellow pamphlet; the way that first man in the Boise bar had greeted us, the one who had known Reverend King; the Web site with all those fornicating men. This was the sin. And he was right. I understood. And suddenly I understood what it was that Gregory Hart knew about him. "Activities" had been the word. Activities that needed to be dragged out of the darkness. They were still going on. And the Web sites had not been for research.

What I couldn't begin to grasp was what this horror meant to me. I was still staring at Mrs. King's swollen eyes, knowing I had the answer, knowing I didn't want to say it, and hating her husband for making me do his dirty work. And as soon as I told her, she'd know it was not his sin alone, but mine as well.

I opened my mouth. I closed it. I shook my head. I opened my mouth again, and closed it, eyes searching the bookcase behind the desk and finding their target: a pile of the yellow pamphlets. I didn't want to tell Mrs. King. I could have pretended I didn't know.

Sin begins with lies. If you commit a sin, confess it truthfully and make your amends with God and anyone you've wronged, and the sin can be forgiven. But if you lie . . .

Woodenly, I moved around the desk, knowing Mrs. King's frantic eyes were on me, and I picked up one of the yellow things. I moved back, nearly hobbling with the conflict I felt, and handed it to her. She took it, glanced at it, puzzled, as though she knew what it was but didn't understand why I'd given it to her. Then she dropped it onto the floor.

And then she screamed.

The next thing I knew, Aurora was in the room, Mrs. Voelker right behind her. They hovered over Mrs. King, who had covered her face with her hands and was screaming, "No! No!"

over and over again. Aurora fell onto her knees, crying, plead-ing with her mother to speak. Mrs. Voelker came over to me.

"What is it?" Her tone brooked no denial, no avoidance.

I wasn't sure I trusted my voice, and in fact it was hoarse, but I managed to say, "He's gone. He couldn't live a lie any longer. He's gay."

Mrs. Voelker, a pillar of the Church known for her calm and steadfastness, a woman who had rejected her own gay child, barely flinched. Her eyes widened and then recovered, and she turned to the sobbing Mrs. King. To me, she said, "Take Au-rora. Stay with her."

For no reason I could have explained, I grabbed the other papers lying on the desktop, which Mrs. King would not have had time to read yet. Probably my intense resentment at what I'd just been forced to do made me feel I was owed something. I took Aurora's hand. She glanced from me to her mother and back at me, and we left.

We sat on the couch, and I remember wishing I knew how much she should know about her father. How much pain was too much? And would there be more pain if she had only part of the story? I still held the letter. I glanced at it and knew that the lie had to end.

"Did you hear what I told Mrs. Voelker?" Aurora nodded, eyes streaming, seemingly unable to speak. "Here's the letter he left for your mom." I couldn't watch her face as she read it, so instead I looked at the other papers I had brought with me. They looked legal. Scanning quickly, I learned that the rev-erend had been married and divorced before he married Na-talie.

I also learned that he had been born Jeffrey Rollins.

It was too much. It was lies, all lies, everything about him was lies. Who—*what* was he? How could there be meaning in any-thing he did or said, anything he had meant to me? I barely heard Aurora speak through her sobs.

"Why do you understand? What does he mean?"

I turned toward her. Again, how much should I tell her? I hadn't even figured out what I should tell myself. I decided to give myself some time. "Remember how I told you what kinds of people he talked to when he went to Boise?" She covered her mouth with one hand and nodded. "The time I went with him, there were some people who had seen him before. They acted like they knew him, like they knew something secret about him. I didn't know what that meant at the time, but now I do. And now I know why he was so focused on this . . . sin." I had to say the word, even though it probably applied to me as well. "He talked about it a lot; he created that pamphlet about it."

She shook her head violently and stood up. "No! Jude, you have to be wrong. You don't know. You don't know anything! This is my *father!*"

"There's more."

She was shouting at me now. "More what?"

I stood, still clutching the papers. "His name wasn't Amos King. It was Jeffrey Rollins. And he was married once before."

She snatched the papers from me, staring wildly at them, but obviously unable to focus on anything. "I don't believe you! You're making this up!" She threw them at me, and they scattered around us.

I picked up a page, saying, "Your mother hasn't even seen this yet." I reached for another, bent over, and Aurora body slammed me. We both fell to the floor as she slapped at me, grunting with effort, writhing in fury and denial. Somehow I managed to grab her wrists and wrap a leg around hers so she couldn't kick me. I pushed her back onto the floor and knelt with my legs on either side of her body as she tried to escape my grasp. She was crying and saying horrible things. I was Satan. . . . I was a traitor. . . . She hated me. . . . It was my fault he had left. Nothing that made sense. I just held onto her wrists and let her scream until she gave up and lay quietly, moaning and weeping. Then I held her.

I held her while somehow managing to keep my own tears in check. Despite my anger at having him dump the explanation—and possibly some of the guilt—on me, this loss was also mine. I'd lost my godfather. I'd lost the man I had thought loved me enough to help me out of my sin, the only man I knew who understood that sin and could actually do something about it. I'd lost the man who'd prayed for a son, joyful that it was me.

I'd lost a father for the second time in my life.

I had been determined not to follow in the footsteps of my first father. Would I follow the second?

We were still lying there on the floor, Aurora whimpering in my arms, when other people started to arrive. I never knew whether they came on their own because their pastor never showed and they wanted to know what was going on, or if Mrs. Voelker made some calls, but there were streams of them. They gathered around as though they could construct a human fence that protected Natalie and Aurora from the agony of what had happened. They began the construction of a wall that they would shore up—more and more each day, with each prayer, with each meeting of the Body—a Wall to block out and even deny the mystery. To reassert the certainty. To keep out the World.

They mostly ignored me. They protected Natalie and Aurora from me, too, though I'm sure they didn't look at it that way.

I gathered the papers together, somewhat crumpled now from Aurora's treatment of them, and because I couldn't get near Mrs. King, I gave them to Mrs. Voelker. She looked at me, puzzled, and I tipped my head toward the office for us to go in there. She read through them as I watched, shaking her head, incredulous. Finally she looked up at me. I couldn't quite tell what she was thinking, but I was afraid she was putting two and two together. To deflect her thoughts from me, I said, "I'm sorry about your daughter."

I think now that it was a cruel thing to say, though at the time it was just self-defense. She closed her eyes and was very still. I left the office.

The living room was now full of people, and several women were milling around the kitchen, preparing tea and coffee and arranging things that people had brought to eat. Somehow this seemed ridiculous to me, but now I know that it's a universal tradition, smothering grief with food. I still don't understand it, though. I headed upstairs and threw myself on my bed.

My thoughts wouldn't settle on anything, and my ears strained to pick out words from the crowd downstairs. Someone knocked on my door, and I jumped up, badly startled.

It was Lorne.

That's when I lost it. My face crumpled. He wrapped himself around me, murmuring, "It's okay, little brother. It's all right. You'll be okay."

We collected enough of my possessions to see me through a few days. School was out for the holiday season, so I didn't need my computer for homework, and there was still no Internet access at Lorne's, but I grabbed it anyway. As I was lifting it off the desk, my eyes fell on the picture of my mother. *God had plans for me, eh?* I mocked her silently. My glance went next to the bag of marbles, which still had her note inside. I left both the photo and the bag where they were.

In the living room of what used to be my home, Lorne, Clara, and I talked about what to do next. For now I would sleep on the couch; my old room had been completely turned over to CC, and unless it was decided that I would move back here, it seemed silly to do anything drastic. Interestingly, none of us even broached the possibility that I would continue to live at the Kings'; it was silently assumed that was not an option.

It seems Mrs. Voelker had phoned Lorne and suggested he come and fetch me. She'd also spoken to him at the Kings' before he came upstairs to find me. "She said that she and Mr. Voelker would be happy to take you in, Jude. They have that big house, and there's no one but them in it now."

That's right, I thought; their son has married and moved, and they chased their daughter away. Almost bitterly I wondered what they would do to me if they knew about my own struggles. And then my eyes widened: Perhaps she had figured it out and wanted to force the perversion out of me!

Clara said, "That idea seems to alarm you, Jude." I couldn't quite tell if she was concerned about me or was preparing to overcome any objection I might offer.

Lorne's voice was softer. "If you don't want to do that, Jude, you don't have to. It's just that there are so few options."

So few options. "Yeah," was all I could say. My eyes stung, tears blurring my vision a little. CC, in my old room for her afternoon nap, began making noises designed to command attention, and Clara left to go upstairs. I found my voice again. "I don't want to go to the Voelkers'."

Lorne looked at me steadily for a moment. Then, "Can you tell me why not?"

Could I tell him? I could not. "It just seems . . . it seems like a bad idea. They're so stiff and old."

He nodded gently. "I know what you mean, but remember that they're also loving saints with your best interests at heart."

I took a shaky breath. "Do we have to make decisions now?"

To his credit, Lorne laughed softly. "No, Jude, we don't. Let's give it a few days and see. But we really should make a decision before the end of Christmas holiday, so you're settled before school starts again."

I tossed and turned on the couch for quite a while before falling asleep. It wasn't comfortable, and the moon was full, its light reflecting off the snow and lighting up the whole world. All except inside me.

Alone, with no distractions, I relived my day many times, and although I was aware of some disconnect someplace, it wasn't until nearly one o'clock that it hit me what was missing. No one seemed to be particularly concerned about my loss. Sure, I understood why everyone had clustered around Natalie and Aurora. They had lost a husband, a father. But I had lost a god-father. I had lost the one hope I had of escaping this trap Satan had laid for me. And, not only was Reverend King gone, and not only was he not the man I had thought he was, not only had he lied to me as surely as he'd lied to everyone else, but also he had admitted failure in escaping his sin. And if he couldn't do it, what hope was there for me?

I climbed onto the floor, shivering in the cold room, and knelt by the side of my makeshift bed. I whispered this prayer.

"Jesus, Lord," I prayed, "I know I haven't talked with you in a long time. I let what happened to Pearl throw me for a loop, and I felt very apart from you. I still don't understand why you let those heathens kill Pearl, and maybe that's why I couldn't talk to you. But now something else has happened, and like Clara says, all things happen for a reason. So I'm wondering if this is supposed to wake me up now. Get me back to you.

"Oh, I'm not crazy. I don't think Reverend King disappeared just to get me to do something. But maybe you thought it could serve a purpose? Maybe if I lost him, I'd turn back to you? Maybe I should take it as a sign?

" 'Cause you see, I can't do this alone. I can't figure this thing out without help. If Satan is after me, I can't run fast enough even to stay ahead of him, let alone escape. I know you'll find a way to let me know. I know you'll send me some kind of sign to point the way. I just don't know what it will be. But—can it be soon? Amen."

It was the first time I'd talked directly to Jesus, or God, since Pearl had died. It felt right, somehow, even if it also felt desperate.

I spent the rest of that wakeful night imagining where on earth Reverend King had gone. I knew I was dozing a few times when images came to me of him at the bar in Boise, the red-shirt man in his arms, moving to silent music.

The next day was agony. Everything I did, from waiting my turn in the bathroom so I wouldn't get in the way to wondering what to do with myself once breakfast was over, everything pointed to the fact that I couldn't stay here. Not for long. I took this as the first part of my sign from Jesus.

Clara asked me if I'd do a few chores for her, and I was so desperate for something to do that I actually didn't mind. I almost wished that it had snowed again, so I could busy myself shoveling.

That night it did snow. In the morning Lorne and I cleared our driveway, and I told him to go ahead and leave for work, that I'd do the McNultys' side on my own. He smiled and slapped my shoulder, which made me feel good, but when the job was done I just stood at the end of the driveway, leaning on the shovel handle, wondering what I could do next. I was in a trance, staring sightlessly across the street, when a blue truck pulled up and stopped beside me. It was Gregory.

"Jude? You okay?"

"Yeah. Yeah, I'm fine."

"Looks like you're done here. D'you want to come with me and shovel walkways while I do a few driveways? And I'm sure Dolly would love a visit this afternoon."

I glanced over my shoulder back toward the house. What would Clara say? "I have to check."

"I'll wait."

Clara was reluctant. She called to see if she could reach Lorne at the office so she could ask him about it, but he was out somewhere.

"Look, Clara, this isn't a big deal. Reverend King used to let me go over there and read to Dolly all the time."

"Reverend King . . ." Her words trailed off, as if to say that was not much of a recommendation. "How will you get home?"

"I'm sure Gregory will give me a ride. He wouldn't exactly kidnap me, y'know." It was difficult not to sound insolent. What was the big deal? The stupid rumors about him?

"I don't know, Jude, and when I don't know something's right, it's usually better not to do something than to do it."

"I'll be helping people. You know how Gregory shovels for old folks for nothing. It's like Jesus is giving me this chance. Clara, I need to get out of here for a bit, and there's no place else to go."

"What about your friends?"

I snorted. "My friends at this point are all people I hung out with when I was playing at being the Damascus Kid. When we would wander around and talk about the Church to people who aren't saints."

"Why can't you do that?"

I stared at her, wondering if I really was about to cry; that's what it felt like. I managed, "For one thing, no one wants to talk to me anymore. They've heard it too many times. For another, I—" How to say this? How to describe for her what Reverend King had done to me? "I'm not sure I could be very convincing right now."

"That's often the best time—"

I interrupted her. "Clara, please! I need a break!"

I must have sounded odd. She pulled back just a teeny bit. "If you get into any trouble, you call right away. And don't be late for supper."

Relief washed through me, and I nearly crumpled to the floor. "I promise."

Gregory was waiting patiently, which was his usual style. I threw one of Lorne's shovels into the back of the truck beside Gregory's, just in case we both ended up shoveling at some point, and pulled myself up and into the passenger seat.

We worked until mid-afternoon, Gregory plowing with the truck and me cleaning up the end bits when he couldn't quite push them all away, and both of us shoveling walkways. It felt so great to be doing this, helping people, working with Gregory. I began to get a sense of why he did it for free for people who needed help and couldn't afford to pay for it. It made you feel really good.

He called Dolly on his cell phone between our last two jobs and told her he was bringing me home for cookies and cocoa. Even from the passenger seat I could hear her enthusiasm. That made me feel good, too.

Dolly had made cocoa. At first I didn't understand how she could have done that, but then I saw the packets of mix in the trash. My mom had always made it using cocoa from the can, adding her own sugar and using condensed milk, but she hadn't been blind.

Sitting down at the kitchen table with Gregory and Dolly, I was amazed that it seemed so long ago that I had done this. It hadn't been; it had been just last week. But so much had happened that it felt like months had passed. I felt comfortable. Wanted. At home.

Dolly seemed kind of quiet, or sad maybe. But she didn't neglect me. In fact, for only the second time since I had read Reverend King's note, someone seemed to understand what had happened in all this to me. "Jude, sweetie, you must feel as though a horse has kicked you in the gut."

She and Gregory were silent, waiting for my response, actually wanting to know how I felt. "More like an elephant." But that was treating it too lightly. "It's, um, it's hard, you know? I mean, he's not who he said he was. His name, and he was married before. And . . . being gay. Did you know all that?" I looked at Gregory, remembering the confrontation in the barn that he didn't know I'd heard.

"Some of it. I didn't know many details. But I always felt there was something missing, or like there was a hole in the picture, and I couldn't quite focus on it. You know how when you want to look at a star at night, and if you look right at it you can't really see it, but if you look just to the side—there it is. You know what I mean?" I nodded. "That's how it was for me, with him. I just knew something was off, but I couldn't tell what. And whenever I looked to the side, I got accused of backsliding or worse."

Dolly said, "Jude, I don't want to encourage gossip, you know that. But can you tell us what you know?"

"I read the note he left. Mrs. King gave it to me to read, because Reverend King didn't quite tell her what was wrong. He said for her to ask me, that I understood."

Gregory mumbled, "That miserable . . . never mind. Go on."

"He left a pile of papers, too. I looked through them first, before anyone else. They said he had changed his name from Jeffrey Rollins, and that he had been married and divorced once before."

"Divorced," Dolly echoed. "Well, that's something; at least that poor woman didn't have a bastard child. Aurora is legally his. And if they ever find him, there could be child support. Oh, that poor little girl." She reached out and laid a hand unerringly on my forearm. "And you, too, Jude. I can't imagine. I just can't imagine. He was the light in the darkness for you."

My head snapped toward her. Did she know? Did she know

about the trap the reverend and I were both in? I had to guess not, after Gregory's next comment.

"Jude, did you know what to tell them? Did you know what it was you were supposed to understand?"

I looked down at my plate, half a cookie still on it. "Yes."

Dolly made a sound, a cross between sympathy and disgust. She covered her face with both hands for a second and then lowered them. "This is not a cross a boy should have to bear."

Was she talking about the reverend's disappearance? Or did she mean the trap? I glanced at Gregory for a hint, but he was looking at his own plate.

Dolly changed the subject, just a little. "Jude, I'm hearing that Mrs. King and Aurora will probably have to sell the house. I don't know where they'll go, and I dare say they don't either yet, but it seems very unlikely you'll live there again, or go with them. What are your plans?"

I shrugged, not really wanting to talk about it because it depressed me, but also feeling relief that I could be at least somewhat honest here. "The Voelkers have offered to let me stay with them."

Gregory's eyebrows rose, eyes back on me. "Really. How do you feel about that?"

I looked down again. "I don't want to go there. They've both been very nice and all that, but—they're so stiff, and old." It was what I had told Lorne and Clara. But here, I added, "And they kicked their own daughter out for being just what Reverend King confessed he is." I looked up at Gregory. "How could they kick their own kid out like that?"

He shook his head. "I don't know, Jude. I really don't know." Then he glanced at Dolly. She seemed to know it, because she turned toward him as well. Something silent, maybe secret, passed between them.

I couldn't stand it. If it involved me or Reverend King, I wanted to know what it was. "What's going on?"

Dolly pulled her lips in between her teeth and inhaled audibly. Then, "Do you think you'll stay with Lorne and Clara?"

I shook my head. "No room. It's way too crowded. And I

can't exactly share a room with CC." I watched their faces, waiting for an answer to my question.

Gregory went next. "What other ideas do you have?"

I barked a humorless laugh. "None. Really, none." My eyes stung again, and I looked up toward the ceiling so the tears that were forming couldn't fall. When I looked back down, the two of them were staring at each other again; it was almost like Dolly could see. Again, I said, "What is it?"

Dolly turned toward me. "Well, I'm sure Gregory is thinking the same thing I am, that it's too bad you can't come live here with us."

I almost said, "What?" But I'd heard. I'd heard. It wasn't an idea I'd ever considered, but as soon as she said it, a huge sense of loss came over me, piling on top of the loss already there. My eyes dropped to the table, and I'm sure a surge of intense embarrassment made my face flush. I nodded. "I don't blame you."

"Don't blame us?" she asked. "Don't blame us for what?"

"For not wanting me here. I've been pretty obnoxious. I know that."

Gregory chuckled, and Dolly said, "Oh, child! Sakes alive, that's not it at all."

I looked up at her face, blinked, and said, "What is it, then?"

Gregory said, "Lorne didn't think it was a good plan."

"Lorne?" I nearly shouted. "Lorne? This isn't *his* life. It's not *Lorne* who would have to go and live with the Voelkers because he has no place else to go!"

Dolly looked embarrassed. "Now, Jude, you know Lorne has your best interests at heart."

Sick of hearing that phrase, I shook my head. "No, I don't. I don't think he understands what they are."

Dolly's hand landed on my arm again. "Jude, dear, I shouldn't have said anything. This is just going to cause problems."

"No," I said firmly, "it won't. If you're serious, then I'm going to talk to him." I looked from one to the other to see if maybe they'd changed their minds, if they now agreed with Lorne. They didn't; they wanted me to live with them.

I was furious! How *dare* he not tell me about this offer? How *dare* he keep this from me, this best of all possible worlds right now? If it was the Harts or the Voelkers, I knew as sure as I knew I was alive where I would go.

I turned to Dolly. "I could be a lot of help around the house. I know how to do all kinds of chores. And I could read to you, and go food shopping with you, and all kinds of things." And to Gregory, "And look at how well we did this afternoon. I could help you when it snows." Ideas were tumbling in my brain, justifications for following through, for taking this invitation that seemed like the next sign from Jesus. I mean, if Gregory could figure out how to get out of the trap Satan had laid for him, maybe he could help me, too! Reverend King wasn't the only one afflicted in this way, and he'd failed, but Gregory was still here. This made so much sense!

It has occurred to me since how many times people who've prayed for a sign are presented with multiple options, and the one they take as the sign is the one they most want to do. And sometimes, they're right.

We sat in silence for a few minutes. Finally, Gregory said, "Do you want me to come with you to talk to them?"

I shook my head. "I have to do this. I don't know what I'm going to say yet, but I'm going to do this."

I was home in time for supper. I waited until after CC's bedtime, though, before I broached my topic, and it was difficult to act normal through the meal. I even helped Clara wash the dishes. She finished wiping down the counter while I swept the floor, and then she said, "Shall we watch a little television?"

I propped the broom back into its home next to the fridge before answering, struggling to remain calm now that the time had come to speak. "Actually, I have something I need to talk to you and Lorne about."

She slumped a little. "Can it wait? Your brother and I are both exhausted, and I should think you—"

"No. It can't. Not really." I turned and went into the living room, where Lorne had the TV already on but turned low while he read the schedule of shows that were on. I said,

"There's something we need to talk about. Can I turn the set off?"

Lorne looked up at me, a little surprised, and nodded. "All right."

All three of us got settled rather formally. I took a couple of deep breaths. Then, looking at Lorne, I said, "You told me that there were very few options. For where I live, I mean. I can't stay here; there's just no room. I understand that, but it still feels kind of difficult being told I can't come back to my own house."

Lorne looked uncomfortable, and Clara started to say something. I ignored her. "I've made my decision. And it's not going to be with the Voelkers. I don't think I could live with them, knowing they kicked their own daughter out of the house, especially when it was for the same thing Reverend King just confessed." I paused just long enough to let that sink in. "I'm going to live with the Harts."

Both Lorne and Clara sat up straight, and I knew they were going to protest, so I kept talking.

"Miss Hart and I have a great relationship, and she could use some company. I can help around the house. I can clean and cook a little and do errands. I can help Mr. Hart by shoveling walks for the people he plows for. The school bus goes right by their house. It's the best arrangement for everyone."

I felt I'd covered all the bases, that there would be little left for Lorne or Clara to find fault with. But they found some anyway. Clara looked at Lorne, and in that look I could see that they had already talked about this and were in agreement.

Lorne exhaled and looked hard at me. "Those are all good reasons, Jude, but I'm afraid they're not enough. That's not one of your options."

"Of course it is. They'd love to have me. They were reluctant to say anything to me, because obviously they had talked to you and you said no. But they asked where I was going to live, and I told them I didn't know, that there was no place I knew of."

"There's the Voelkers."

"I told you! I'm not living with them. And you already told me I didn't have to, remember? Plus they don't love their own children."

Clara spoke. "Jude, that's not fair. . . ."

My head snapped in her direction. "Isn't it? Do you know that they have photos all over the place of them and their son and his family, and not one of Veronica? She's not only kicked out. She doesn't exist anymore! I'm not living with those people."

Lorne said, "Well, you're not living with the Harts."

"Why not?"

"It . . . it just won't do, that's all."

"Why not?"

"Jude, I need you to—"

"Why not!" I was nearly shouting by now, and I had to calm myself or there'd be a fight for sure. "You can't give me one reason why not, can you?" My voice was quieter, but the defiance was thick.

Lorne held my gaze, a heavy look on his face. "I can give you a reason. I choose not to. You are to obey, and you will not go there."

"It's because you think Mr. Hart is gay, isn't it?" That shocked him; I could tell. He hadn't known I had a clue. "Well, you're wrong. I mean, he's not, anymore. He's saved, and he's in the Body, and if he is gay he's doing what he's supposed to. He's being chaste. He lives with his blind, crippled sister, for crying out loud. How could he act on it, even if he wanted to?"

Lorne stood. "Don't be dense, Jude. If you were in the house, there'd be plenty he could do about it."

I stood and faced him, almost surprised that I was as tall as he was now. "Not without my consent, he couldn't. Do you think I'm some sort of child? And how dare you even think that about him, anyway? Has he ever given you reason to think he'd stray like that?"

Lorne looked as though he was fighting for control of himself, and also like there was something he was trying not to say.

I think he failed in the latter part of that struggle, because he said, "I wasn't going to bring this up, Jude, because I know it will be painful for a number of reasons. But I think you should remember why you needed that second baptism. And you should know that Reverend King warned me years ago about Mr. Hart. I think the reverend spoke to all families with young boys."

I didn't know which point I wanted to respond to first. One inspired fury, and one shame. I now had yet another reason to hate Reverend King. Plus, somewhere in my brain it didn't make sense to me that a man who wanted a man would settle for a boy; they're not the same at all. Also, I wanted to deny what he was trying to tell me, to deny that I had one shred of that temptation still biting at my heels. But I couldn't. And I wasn't going to lie; that was one trap I decided I could avoid.

I didn't know how to respond to the implied accusation against Gregory, so I fought for my own position. "So you think that the Voelkers could—what, pray it out of me? And if they can't, they'll throw me out into the street and have a ritual burning of my belongings to purge their home? If they couldn't get it out of their daughter, how are they going to get it out of anyone else?" I wasn't doing very well at staying calm. "Think about this: Mr. Hart got rid of it. He's learned to live a life free of that trap. He doesn't bend to Satan's will. If I really have this problem still, he would actually be a better role model for me than the good Reverend *Rollins* turned out to be!"

Clara, perhaps to calm things down, spoke very quietly. "Part of it is how much time Miss Thornton spends there. It throws a question onto the Harts' judgment, and if you're there you'd be affected. Influenced."

"Reverend King trusted me to take care of myself on that score. He said so." This was true; he just hadn't said it to me.

Lorne sounded condescending. "You can't have it both ways, Jude. If the man was not a good role model, how can he be right about this?"

He had me, but only for a second. "So anytime anyone does something wrong, that's it? They're condemned forever? So you're all going to write off all the good things about Reverend King and focus only on what made him leave?"

"Jude, the man's whole life was a lie."

"Only the details. He was very true to what he believed about God, and he helped others believe it, too. Are you going to pretend that he didn't help anyone? That he was wrong in everything he did and said? That his sermons were a pack of lies?" Suddenly I was the reverend's advocate. I'm not sure how it happened, but there was immense clarity around this concept: This packet of lies about who he was and where he came from was distinct and separate from the way he loved and helped people. It was separate from how much he adored his daughter. And it was separate from the generosity and love he'd shown me. It was separate from his heart.

Clara stayed seated and silent, letting Lorne take me on. "Jude, God exposed him for a liar and a sinner."

"And I'm named after him! If a good person can do bad things sometimes, a bad person can do good things sometimes. And I don't think you can tell me which he was."

Lorne waved a hand in front of his face as if to clear cobwebs away. "He's not the issue here."

"No, but his sin is, isn't it? The sin he couldn't escape? The sin Mr. Hart *has* escaped!" I was angry, frustrated, and near tears. "And if I have that sin, the Voelkers will only make it worse. Gregory Hart might make it better. Would you not let me have this chance? You might as well throw me out of your house the way Veronica got thrown out of hers. Then I won't have to listen to you at all! Then I can go wherever I want!"

Tears threatening to spill from my eyes, I wheeled toward the staircase. One foot moved forward in a motion that would have carried me up the stairs to my room. But before I took a full step in that direction, reality hit me square in the chest. I nearly reeled with the shock of it. I had no room. I had no home. A calm came over me, the tears dried, and I felt suddenly tall and strong.

I turned back to face my brother. "I will not go and live with people who failed their own daughter and then cast her out. I will go and live with people who have been loving and patient. I will live with people I can help, who can help me. If this makes you angry, I'm sorry for that, but that's one thing I can't help."

Lorne sat down and said something about talking more about this tomorrow. I turned the television back on. As far as I was concerned, this discussion was over.

In the morning, over breakfast, I told Lorne I was going to the Harts' before noon. Clara shot an anxious look at him, and he set down his cereal spoon.

"Jude, if you go against my wishes here, I'll consider contacting social services."

This hadn't occurred to me. I hadn't thought of them since Mom died. My jaw ground as my brain thrashed about for a response. Here's what I came up with. "So you'd give up on me, just like the Voelkers gave up on Veronica."

"It's not the same at all!"

Aha! I had gotten a rise out of him. "It's worse. Do you know what happens to kids who are put into foster homes? Do you think they'd place me anywhere near the brother who wouldn't even let me live in the house I grew up in? If you call them, I'll know you don't care what happens to me at all. And everyone here will know that, too." If he was bluffing, I'd just called him out. If not, then at least I'd be away from here.

Clara tried next. "Jude, please understand we want what's best for you. And that's—"

"If you want what's best for me, then let me go someplace where I stand a chance. Let me go someplace where people care about me. The real me, not just some kid they'd like to turn into a project, some kid they want to use to prove it wasn't their fault what happened to their daughter." I sat back and threw my napkin on the table. "Or go ahead and call social services. I'll be sent to Boise, not to the Voelkers, and you'll probably never see me again." I paused. "Or maybe that's what you want."

Lorne stood, throwing his own napkin down. "Come with me. We can't have this talk here."

We went into the living room, which was messy after my night on the couch and with the beginning of my packing efforts. We stood in the middle of the floor.

Lorne began. "You know very well that's not what we want."

"What *do* you want?" I shot back. "I mean you, not you and Clara. What do *you* want for me?"

He took one deep, noisy breath. "I want you to live a life that glorifies God. I want you to be happy in the knowledge that you are with Jesus, that he is in your heart. I want you to have a productive life full of love and companionship."

"So tell me how any of that is something I can't get at the Harts'. It's how they live." We stared at each other a moment. "You know, if I really have this problem that you don't want to talk about, then the Voelkers don't know what to do about it. They don't know how to help me. They'd have me do the same things Reverend King was trying to do. They failed, and he failed. If you care about me, you won't send me back into that mistake."

More staring. I took a tentative step backward and then turned to my task of packing. Lorne just stood there, watching my hands, taking several audible breaths. He stood there until I was finished packing, then watched me fold up the sheets I had used. He stood there while I went to the phone and called the Harts. Surprised, Dolly asked if Lorne had agreed. I glanced at him. He was staring at the floor. I said yes. She said she would call Gregory on his cell phone and have him come get me as soon as he could.

At a loss for the moment, I headed toward the folded sheets, thinking I would launder them. But Lorne moved, finally, and put his arms around me. We hugged, silent, something tender and painful moving between us.

As I waited for Gregory, trying to play with CC but unable to focus, what I felt most wasn't sadness, though that was there. It wasn't hope—I felt too betrayed for that—though there was a sense of relief. What I felt most was a pull away from Newburg. It came from feeling homeless, rootless, without parents, without friends. My stay at the Harts' would be just a stopover, a safe house where I would make plans for where my life would go next. Somehow I knew that. I couldn't stay here.

Chapter 18

I saw Aurora when Gregory drove me over to pick up the rest of my things, and she acted very formal, very standoffish. Mrs. King gave me a long, hard hug as I left. It felt almost like an apology, though for what I couldn't have said; she'd always treated me almost like a son.

Christmas Day I spent with Lorne and Clara, making small talk and holding out gifts to each other through a fog of tension. At some point it occurred to me that they were trying not to pry, trying to avoid asking questions about my life at the Harts' that I might not want to answer, or perhaps to avoid hearing answers they might not want to know. So I talked about it. I did my best to make it sound as though it was fine but not much more, when in fact I was quickly coming to the conclusion that it was the best thing I could have done. The only thing. I tried not to make it sound as comfortable, as warm, as much like a real home as it was fast becoming. I decided, for example, not to tell them that Gregory was putting in an Internet connection for me, on the condition that I do research for Dolly from time to time, when she wanted to know more about something that had caught her active imagination.

After supper I tried to call Aurora, knowing it was her birthday, but no one answered at the King household. I mumbled something to Lorne that perhaps Mrs. King had taken Aurora to a relative's house, but Clara said probably not, because Mrs. King's family came from Michigan, and it wasn't likely they'd spend money on airfare when they would be looking for a home they could afford and surely must pinch every penny.

When Lorne drove me back to the Harts', I asked him to take me past the Kings' so I could see if they were gone or not; I was thinking maybe they'd already moved away without telling me. But there were a few lights on in the house. Lorne pulled the car to the side of the road and idled the engine.

"Do you want to go in?" he asked me.

"No. They didn't answer the phone. I guess they don't want to talk to anyone."

"They might like to see *you,* though."

I shook my head, and he pulled back onto the road. I sat silent beside Lorne on the way to the Harts', picturing mother and daughter trying to pretend that it was no particular day, trying to overlook the conspicuous absence of celebration. Of father. Of husband.

I saw Aurora again the Sunday after Christmas and after New Year's, at church, from where I sat maintaining my tradition of sitting with Lorne and Clara during the service. I was watching for her. She came in with Mrs. King, but I almost missed them; they didn't sit toward the front, in their customary pew when it had been Reverend King at the pulpit. They sat toward the back instead, and they left very quickly, without staying to fellowship.

The elders took turns leading us for the services, with Mr. Voelker taking the one right after Christmas. I forget who did the next one, but I really missed Reverend King. I think I missed him most in church. His passion and intensity used to prepare me for a week of praising God, expressing gratitude, witnessing for Jesus. He'd quell any doubts that had arisen during that week, any surreptitious qualms about whether I was truly on the right path, fully in the Light, and on my way to Gloryland. He'd given me safety. Confidence. Certainty.

And he'd taken them away again.

One thing I do remember about that second service after he disappeared was the last hymn we sang, "Glorious Things of Thee Are Spoken." The last line followed me for the rest of the day.

On the Rock of Ages founded, who can shake your sure repose?

And in my head, in answer to this line, came *Anyone you trust.*

Aurora didn't show up at school until nearly mid-January. She had to take her assigned seat in homeroom, but on the way to first period I didn't see her. She must have gone to the girls' room and waited, because she got to our English class after me. The room had several more chairs than students. She didn't sit toward the front where she usually did. She took a seat toward the back, off to the side. No one else ever sat next to that chair, so she looked isolated and alone. With a kind of shock, I realized it was where Pearl used to sit.

I blinked and shook my head to clear my brain, my gaze taking in some of the other kids. They didn't look mean, or haughty, or anything deliberately hostile or offensive, but they looked extremely uncomfortable. I turned to find Sarah, one of Aurora's best friends, and there she was in her own usual spot, an empty chair beside her. I saw her just as she turned away from Aurora's direction, and the look on her face was one I couldn't read.

I got up from my seat and went to sit beside Aurora. She didn't look at me, but I saw tears welling in her eyes when I looked at her.

I walked with her to math, neither of us saying a word, and when we got there I didn't go to my usual seat near the front. Aurora made a vague gesture and said, "Math is your favorite. Go. Sit up there." But I took her arm and led her toward Pearl's old seat, which I took myself, and she sat next to me.

We had lunch together, off to the side again.

"I called you on your birthday," I told her. "I guess you weren't home."

She shrugged, toying with the crust on the sandwich she'd brought. Then she said, "I heard you're at the Harts'."

I gave a mirthless chuckle. "Yeah. No room at the inn, you know." She smiled at that, which made me glad I'd said it, even if it sounded a bit sacrilegious.

Before I had time to get uncomfortable wondering if I could ask her whether she and Mrs. King would be selling the house soon, Sarah was there, standing beside Aurora. She nodded at me and said to Aurora, "Is it okay if I sit with you?"

Aurora lifted one shoulder and released it. "Sure."

And that, it seemed, was the beginning of the end, at least in terms of Aurora's being ostracized. There was, of course, no reason she should have been, other than the extreme shame her false, disappearing father had coated her with. And I have to say that from what I've heard about other people's experiences in school since I was in one, I'm thinking the end began for Aurora sooner than it would have in many other communities. It's true that there was a certain amount of hypocrisy evident in a few of the comments I heard (one intensely naïve girl of whom I really suspect no ill intent said, "Aurora, don't worry. We don't hold your father's horrible sin against you," in front of several other kids), but the overall response was supportive; it was compassionate without being condescending; and it didn't take very long. Very quickly, both she and I were back in our regular seats in class.

Still, whether it was evident to our classmates or not, both of us were irreparably altered. There was a film—thin, I think, for her, thicker for me—between us and everyone who hadn't been so personally mangled by Reverend King's duplicity and desertion, and who didn't feel, despite it all, a love for him that we could reveal to no one but each other.

This odd bond between us caused feelings of profound confusion when she told me that she and her mother would move to Michigan after the school year.

Temporary stopover though it might have been, the Harts' home brought me relief that was deep and welcome, that loos-

ened the confining carapace I'd built up around my identity. I
didn't have to be the Damascus Kid here. In fact, although
nothing was ever said, I knew he wasn't welcome.

When I contrast the fun and warmth inside that plain farm-
house with the stiff righteousness that dwelled in the Voelkers'
gingerbread fancy, I feel speechless with irony. And with gratitude. Dolly's laughter lightened the house, defying her own
blindness, and Gregory's humor—beyond me a little at first—
proved to be bone dry, surprising, and often irreverent. I found
myself wracking my brain whenever the three of us were together, searching for witticisms that would set Dolly to laughing, or nearly tripping over my own words to get something
funny out before Gregory could beat me to it—which was
pretty silly, because his wit didn't rely as much on speed as on
timing, a distinction it took me a while to appreciate.

And, as Lorne had anticipated, I did see a lot of Belinda
Thornton. Her visits for a while were still clouded with the
melancholy that hung about her because of Pearl, but she
seemed at least a little brighter before she went home again. I'll
always remember one thing she said on her first visit after I
moved in. We were talking about Reverend King's disappearing, even though I'd tried to change the subject, and she said,
"I'll bet he was one of those kids nobody could ever find during
hide-and-seek."

I wish I could say that the epiphany I experienced when I was
defending Reverend King to Lorne in my determination to
avoid the Voelkers' remained with me, but at the Harts' I
heard, from Gregory and Belinda anyway, things about him
that showed him in a different light from any I'd seen cast on
him before. Dolly would hush them, I think for my sake, before
they went too far, but I heard enough to allow my own pain to
transform their vague comments into bitter truth and condemnation. One Sunday night Belinda called him a snake in the
grass, and Dolly had quietly reminded her how quickly and
without question or comment he had responded with help
when Pearl was missing, and she told Belinda how tenderly
he'd spoken of the dead girl in that first sermon after her mur-

der. Belinda muttered something about too little too late, and
this was all on my mind when I went to what was now my room
later that night.

I had a kind of waking dream, not quite asleep and not really
awake. The scene was the Garden of Eden. God resembled Reverend King, and he stood with me in the paradise he'd created,
gesturing all around at the beauty and the glory, saying, "Jude,
my son, all this is yours. Here you have all you need, all you
could want and more. Everything here is for you, because of my
love for you."

We stood there together, his arm on my shoulders, turning
slowly and gazing about us, until my eyes fell on a tree unlike
any of the others. It had fruits of various sizes and shapes, rosy
but not red, more peachy, soft and velvety on the outside and
hinting at something firm yet giving within.

As soon as the sensuality of these fruits registered with me,
God's voice yanked at my mind. "Oh. Except for that." He tried
to turn me away, but my head twisted in an attempt to keep it in
view. "You can't have that. Don't even touch that tree. That tree
is our sin. Yours and mine."

I think at this point I fell fully asleep, because the scene
jumped to one in which I'm not sure where I was. I was watching the scene as you might watch a play. There was a woman.
Not Eve; more like the Salome I'd dreamed about years before,
with veils and long hair and a full, dark red mouth and breasts
swelling beneath the muted silks. She was talking with a snake
in the tree God/Reverend King had told me I shouldn't touch.

In the manner of most dreams, I sensed the meaning of their
conversation rather than really hearing the words. He was saying she should take a fruit so that she would know. She asked
what it was she would know. And the snake said, "Yourself."

I sat upright in my bed. The word "Yourself" had been audible, at least in my head. I had heard it. I can hear it still.

I sat up for a long time that night, contemplating Satan, re-
viewing the Creation stories as they're told in Genesis. I even
got my Bible out. And at the part where Satan tempts Eve, and
he says she can gain knowledge if she takes the fruit, I remem-

bered something Jesus had said to me the day I insulted Belinda Thornton so badly she had struck me. Jesus had said,
"Even Satan had a purpose. He showed mankind that there's a
difference between good and evil."

This seemed incompatible with knowing "Yourself," until my
own words came back to me—what I, myself, had said to Lorne
and Clara about Reverend King: *If a good person can do bad things
sometimes, a bad person can do good things sometimes. And I don't
think you can tell me which he was.*

So Jesus was telling me that it's possible, because of Satan, to
know the difference between good and evil. And Reverend
King had shown me that this is not a judgment I can make
about someone else. But can I make it about myself? Or was it
that I, too, was a gnarled bundle of contradiction in which evil
and good are all twisted and knotted around each other?

Or maybe understanding that I *was* this bundle meant that I
understood—that I knew—myself?

And how much better would I know myself if I admitted how
I had felt when I looked closely at that tree, and at the fruit it
bore? If I admitted that both my hands had wanted to reach out
toward that tree, grab hold, and not let go? If I admitted that
even now, allowing that image back into my mind's eye, something powerful and throbbing pulled from the center of my
chest and lifted me into the waiting arms of that tree? If I admitted my shame that through all the tragedy of Pearl's death,
and then the crushing shock of Reverend King's disappearance, through all of that, a common worry always somewhere
in my brain and ready to leap out at me at odd moments was
the fear—the sharp, stark fear—that someone might turn to
me and say, "You know, Jude, you're sixteen now. Have you
thought about which lucky girl you'll ask out for your first date?
And which of your friends will double with you? Tim Olsen,
perhaps?"

And then, of course, I would have to admit that Reverend
King himself had helped me come to know myself in this re-
gard, that he had played first God's and then Satan's role,
telling me "Oh no, not that tree, not that sin," and then taking

me right up to it in Boise. Add to this the phrasing of his farewell note, and he completed the circle.

What God, I wondered, would create paradise, and tell his son that all of it was his, except that one really beautiful, tempting, luscious, compelling tree that called to that son in a way nothing else could? Why would God plant a tree in paradise that would be the downfall of his beloved son, and then allow a snake to consummate that fall? Because God, being God, would have known all of it would happen. Would have had to allow it.

I could make no sense out of it. And in my confusion, in my uncertainty, in my fear, I began to hate Reverend King. I think now I hated him so that I wouldn't hate God.

One Sunday supper at Lorne and Clara's (another tradition that remained part of my schedule), toward the end of February, I could tell there was something lurking around some corner, something that would be said but that no one wanted to introduce. Clara put CC to bed, and Lorne and I sat at the table. I started to get up, to begin helping with the dishes, but he laid a hand on my arm.

"We need to talk about something that's missing in your life," he opened. My own mind jumped rather rapidly to responses like, *A father? A mother? A home?* But I was silent. "You turned sixteen a few months ago now." My gut lurched. This was THE CONVERSATION. The one I dreaded. The one I feared desperately. "Have you given any thought to your first date?"

My mouth dry, I managed a croaked, "Not yet."

"Because Clara and I have thought of a few possibilities. And you'll need to go with a brother who can drive, unless there's an adult who can go with you. We have some suggestions there, too."

Oh, I'm sure you do. I decided to sit still and listen. Protest would get me nowhere and might close off some options. I don't remember the names he came up with. Certainly I made no effort at the time to keep them in mind. I remember only that I heard nothing I had any intention of following up on. I listened politely and somehow managed to say that I'd give it serious thought.

In point of fact, despite my fear, any dates I went on for the next couple of years would be nothing of concern. I wouldn't be allowed to single out any one girl, we wouldn't ever be in a position where anything beyond respectful conversation and a few laughs would take place. There would be no hand-holding, let alone any kissing. These arrangements were distinctly asexual in nature. Their purpose was to get to know different people in a couples setting and give yourself time to mature into the kind of person who would eventually be taken seriously as dating material. In no way was anyone of sixteen considered serious dating material.

Gregory pointed this out to me pragmatically when I brought it up the next evening at supper. I admitted how terrified I was, and Dolly laughed delightedly while Gregory smiled out of one side of his mouth. I was almost hoping we would come to a point where the reason for my aversion to this process would arise, but it didn't. Without going near that tree or even referring to it, Gregory convinced me that a few dates would be harmless and might even be fun, reminding me there would be at least one other couple with us. He suggested that for my partner, I start with Aurora.

I laughed aloud. "I once told Lorne there was no way I would start with the reverend's daughter!"

"You're not. She isn't the reverend's daughter any longer."

Dolly said, "She's also not going to be here as of the summer, Gregory. Is it a good idea to date someone who'll be leaving soon?"

Gregory shrugged. "Seems to me it's more than a good idea. The poor girl shouldn't be left out in the dark just because she's moving. And no one dating at the age of sixteen is going to zero in on their future mate. Jude, if you ask Aurora, would it be her first date, too?"

"I think so. She just turned sixteen in December."

He shook his head. "Some birthday that poor girl must have

had. But you're already good friends, so it would be painless. She won't let herself pin any hopes on you, knowing she's leaving. And you'll have a good time. Just choose the other couple carefully."

We worked through the logistics, and by the time I went to my room that night it seemed like such a small thing to have worried so much about. Pulling the blankets to my chin, I realized with a start that Gregory was helping me learn a survival technique that had served him well for his whole life.

Aurora agreed to let me be her first date. We went to a play put on at the school—I don't remember what—with Sarah and her date, whose name I've forgotten. It was fun. And it was no big deal.

It took two months to find a replacement preacher—or, at least, to extend the offer to him. His name sounded so fabricated that the Council of Elders spent quite a bit of time researching his background. They did not want another fake Amos King. No more masquerades. No more deceit. No more lies. They wanted certainty.

Pastor Joshua Wright, along with his wife Rachel and their four young children, bought the King house from Natalie. Special legal arrangements had to be made because of Amos's disappearance, although among his papers he had left a signed letter giving her permission to divorce him with no contest. Natalie and Aurora moved into the Voelkers' nearly empty house, which in my mind vindicated my own insistence that I not go there.

Pastor Wright, as he preferred to be called, was like all the fire and brimstone of Reverend King, without any of the palliative relief. There was a lot of shouting about damnation and hellfire and sin and abomination, and I always left services feeling battered—even on those Sundays when he didn't go into Reverend King's personal abomination, which he seemed to do even more often than Amos King used to do. He also talked about fornication and any kind of sex outside of marriage,

using that topic to condemn homosexuality once more because, of course, it was sex outside of marriage.

Sometimes I wondered if he had been asked during his in-
terview with the elders to have his sermons lean heavily on
these topics. But I think now that wasn't it. Many times since I
left Newburg it has occurred to me that the more fundamen-
tally, the more literally someone takes the Bible's scripture, the
more obsessed he or she seems to be with sex—usually everyone else's. It's always negative, to be sure, but the focus goes
there again and again and again and again until it begins to
mimic the sex act itself in sheer repetition.

In the privacy of his own home, Gregory referred to Pastor
Wright as Pastor Hellfire. He called him Pastor Wrong once,
but Dolly said that went too far. He agreed, adding, "Besides,
it's too easy." And he winked at me.

The pastor and his wife Rachel were often the subject of discussion during Belinda Thornton's visits to the Harts'. It
seemed Rachel had decided to make a project of Belinda, or
failing that, perhaps an example, and she showed up at unpredictable times at the trailer, usually with two or three of her
brood in tow. As spring advanced and the ground began to
thaw, Belinda told us that she would hold off on her gardening
preparation chores until one of Rachel's visits, so she would
have some activity to do while Rachel quoted scripture and
made her case for salvation.

Dolly looked confused. "But . . . how do you know when she's
coming so you can get ready? Outdoor clothes, that sort of
thing?"

Belinda laughed. "Oh, I don't bother. As soon as she gets
there I excuse myself, change into my gardening things, and
then invite her out into the cold with me. She has to stand
there and shiver, mumbling between verses about how blue her
baby's lips are getting, while I stay warm with all my work. It's
wonderful."

I asked, "What does she think of your prayer flags?"

More laughter from Belinda. "You remember those, eh? Oh,

it's too early for those yet. I'll save them for some visit when she's really annoying me. Maybe I'll ask her to say a blessing on each one as I tie it to the post!" Her chuckles faded slowly, and then she said, "I miss Pearl so much. We would have had so much fun over this."

I might not have been allowed to date Aurora with any regularity, according to Church custom, and it was also against the rules—once you started your dating life—to spend time alone with anyone of the opposite sex, for the sake of appearances at least, and for the sake of rectitude at all times. But the two of us had a special relationship. I'd been on a number of these sterile "dates" by now with a number of girls, and even without taking our friendship into consideration, I was convinced I liked being with Aurora more than any of the others. So I had begun to hope, but also to worry. The hope was from thinking that maybe, just maybe, I could be "normal." That is, not gay after all, because of how much I enjoyed being with Aurora. The worry was that if I enjoyed Aurora's company but no other girl's, then what would happen to me when she moved away? I realize that it sounds ridiculous now, but at the time it preyed on my mind.

Thinking that maybe this was another of those signs from Jesus I had begged for in December, I went back to him for guidance. Could he suggest, I asked him, what I might do to figure out just how important Aurora was to me, and in what way she was important? I sent up this prayer one Friday night late in March, hoping it would relieve my mind so I could sleep, but I couldn't. I lay there, too fidgety even to waste seed (which I'd been doing like gangbusters since moving to the Harts'), and finally I decided to get up and go online to distract myself. I was about to get out of bed when my own Internet handle inspired me—answered my prayer, in fact.

I would take Aurora to the fortress. It would be a real test. I was fairly sure she would go, despite having to break the rule against time alone; ever since her father had disappeared, Aurora had allowed the quiet rebel I had glimpsed occasionally in the past to appear more and more often. So I would take her there and gauge her reaction. If she didn't "get" the fort the way I did, the way Tim had, I would know she couldn't be the love of my life. If she did, we could spend enough time there away from prying eyes to see what else we might like to do, even if we didn't do much. After all, the important thing for me right now was just *wanting* to do something with a girl. Plus, I wouldn't want to compromise her honor, anyway.

I don't recall giving much weight to what it would mean if I had concluded that I could love Aurora and then she had moved away. My goal was just to see if my feelings for her could replace the ones I used to have for Tim.

I hadn't been to the fort since the day I'd heard Gregory and Reverend King arguing, so I went there the very next day to check on it, to see if it needed clearing out, to see if Pearl's artifacts had survived the winter and maybe to take them down before I brought Aurora there. It was a blustery day, clouds a painful white buffeted about a rich blue sky overhead, bright sunlight throwing everything into high contrast and no doubt calling to the vivid yellow arrowleaf balsamroot still beneath the earth to come out and play.

I traveled in from the bridge, hiding my bicycle first—I trusted Bruce Denmark's repentance only so far—and then jumping and leaping down the hill until I skidded on some icy mud and landed on my backside rather hard. Not injured, just dirtied and little wet, I continued in a more subdued fashion until I could see the fort.

It was showing its age. When Tim and I had discovered it, the tree had probably fallen the previous winter, so the fort wasn't even a year old then. I had been eleven that summer, so it had been five years now since the tree had been upright. In the snow, last December, the ravages of time had been hidden and softened, the tree outline still firm and substantial. Now, the glaring light of early spring told a different story. The tree was long dead, with branches looking as brittle and fragile as a corpse's bones, and brown, dry, lifeless. But the shape was still there. Perhaps it would still be a good place to bring Aurora. In fact, maybe the thinning of the tree's branches would allow more sunlight in now, open to the sky. I moved forward again, in a hurry now to get close enough to assess the possibilities.

I was maybe twenty feet from the tree, making as much noise as a lumbering bear, when a figure appeared in the fort entrance. I froze. He froze.

It was Tim.

Too late to turn around. Too late to pretend we hadn't seen each other. Too ridiculous to do anything but go forward from here. He still didn't move, so I did. I went up to him, looked into his blue eyes, and smiled. I was taller. This surprised me. I think it surprised him. We hadn't had any contact in the past few years that didn't take place in a crowd and from a distance of many feet.

I smiled wider. "Hey."

His face, more beautiful now even than when he was eleven, went through a few tiny contortions and landed on something that was not quite a smile. "Hey, yourself."

"May I come in?"

"Oh . . . uh, sure."

He stepped aside, not in, and I went past him. There was more light than before in here, but it was still darker than outside. The logs I remembered were still there. On the board that served as a table I saw the vase with dried flowers, the cup with the flowers, the other cup that had been there in December, and there was also a paper bag with a sandwich on it, a candy bar to the side, and an apple beside that. The second cup was filled with soda from a plastic bottle that lay on its side on the ground. There was an old quilt on the ground on the side of the table nearer the door. The log seat across from it was still where it had been when I found it.

I stood there, kind of hunched in the cramped space that once had felt open and full of possibility. The walls were hung, still, with the colorful yarn oddments that had been there last fall, before Pearl was murdered. My brain struggled to make sense of what seemed like irreconcilable contradictions. I needed help. I turned toward the entrance, where Tim stood outside still.

"Tim?" He stepped forward, blocking the light so I could barely see his face. "Um, how long have you been coming here?"

"That's a stupid question."

"No, I mean *since* then. I mean . . . When we were twelve, that was the second summer, and we weren't here much. So, after that. I mean, I didn't come back until I was . . . fourteen, I guess."

"And you showed it to Pearl."

"What . . . How . . . So you guys met here?"

He nodded. "She loved it here. I asked her how she knew about it, and she said you'd shown it to her."

"Did you guys come here at the same time deliberately?"

Tim stepped inside, leaning to avoid a branch and then reaching for it with both hands. He stood there, arms over his head, looking at me, faint light illuminating one side of his face. It was an incredibly sexy pose. "Sure. Lots of times."

"And you'd sit here and, what? Have picnic lunches? Why only one log to sit on?"

Without lowering his arms, Tim shrugged. "I sat on the ground. When it was cold I'd bring the quilt. It was so she could be higher than someone for once." There was a challenge in his tone I could make no sense of.

"But . . . none of us were supposed to have anything to do with her."

"And I can see you took that command to heart as much as I did." His tone was harsh, now. Looking back, I suppose there must have been an odd sort of competition between us, both vying to be Pearl's best friend. If only she'd known. If only I had.

So Pearl had had two secret friends in the Body. Maybe others, for all I knew. But Belinda had said she had no friends. "Did her mother know you saw her here?"

"I'm not sure. I never spoke to her mom. Pearl would come here only in good weather, when she could ride her bike."

I nodded. "That explains why Belinda didn't think about this place when Pearl went missing."

"I heard you found her. You and Gregory."

"Yeah."

"I found her doll."

I scowled. *I'd* found the doll. "What are you talking about?"

"Those assholes must have swiped her right near her house. The doll was just off the side of the road, toward the meadow, on the path she used to get to her rock."

"You found the doll." I felt stunned by something I didn't understand. I nearly missed his use of a word I'd never have expected him to utter. *Assholes.* Pearl's influence, perhaps?

"And I buried it."

Eyes wide in disbelief. "*You?* You buried it? And put a *pentagram* over it?"

He lifted and dropped his shoulders. "It's what she would have wanted. But how did you know? About the pentagram?"

"I found the grave." We stared at each other, confused, taking in all these intersections for the first time. "Pearl never mentioned you."

"She never mentioned you, either, other than saying you showed her the fort."

My voice dull, heavy, I said, "And now she's dead."

Silence, while each of us painted his own picture of that horrible day. He lowered his arms and half turned away from me, and his voice grew soft. "I cried for days. My folks thought I was demented. They didn't even know it was because of her. They never put two and two together."

"Aurora knew I was friends with her. Not Lorne, not Reverend King."

He turned his back to me, one hand in his hair. "That no-good son of a bitch." He heaved a couple of breaths. "I'm sorry, Jude. I know you loved him. But—my God!" We weren't supposed to take God's name in vain, of course, but this use could arguably be called a genuine plea. *Son of a bitch,* though . . . what had happened to Tim when I wasn't looking? I waited through a brief silence, wishing I could see the expression on his face. He obliged by turning to face me once more, but now he seemed mad at me again. "And you came back today... why?"

I shrugged to gain a few microseconds in which to find a way to answer without mentioning Aurora. "I was in the woods"— my arm gestured, for some reason, in the general direction of where I'd found the dogtooth violet—"and I thought I'd just, you know, see how the old place was doing."

He moved, stooping, to the other end of the table from where I was hunched, both of us probably looking ridiculous in this space, and he touched one of the yarn bits and gazed at it while softly working his fingers over its odd shape. Without looking at me, he challenged me yet again. "Well, we came here a lot. Who do you think set up the log table and chairs?"

"I . . . I thought Pearl . . ." But as soon as I said it, it seemed wrong. It would have been difficult enough just finding the right sizes of logs to use for the stools and the table supports, let alone maneuvering them into place, and it was not clear where Pearl would have gotten hold of a board just the right size.

I heard Tim snort. "Pearl? Don't be stupid."

"Stop calling me stupid. That's the second time—"

"Then stop acting stupid." He turned to face me. The table was between us. Anger flared in me, and what I saw in his eyes answered it.

"Stupid?" I was nearly shouting. "You're the one who practically got me crucified instead of baptized!"

"I'm the one who told the truth!"

"And then denied it so you could get baptized yourself!" I think this stunned both of us. I had essentially told him that he had never rid himself of the feelings for me that would prevent his ascent into Heaven, and that he'd lied about not having them.

His voice was so quiet, I almost missed it. "You must have denied it all along."

I turned sharply toward the entrance and took maybe two steps, almost leaving, then wheeled back to face him. "No! Not all along. I had to admit it, eventually. That's what my second immersion was for. If you only knew what I've been through!"

He barked a kind of laugh. "You think you're the only one?"

While I was trying to come to grips with what this might mean about him, about me, about us, he closed the distance between us and grabbed my face with his hands. Again, we both froze. Then we fell to our knees. And then he kissed me.

Oh, God, but I wish I could describe how that felt. It was all wrong, and it was all perfect. It was dynamite and Hell opening up but also fireworks and shooting stars. It was Satan's trap closing on me and the answer to my prayers all at once. It would kill my soul, and I couldn't live without it.

I think I bruised his body in several places getting his clothes off of him. I know he bruised me. Somehow we managed to get the quilt under us before we were completely naked. We didn't have any idea what we were doing, really, but it didn't seem to matter very much.

I remember still the curl of his dick, reaching out for me. The feel of it in my hand. The line of his jaw as his head leaned back, eyes tight shut, waiting for the feel of my mouth taking in that part of him that mirrored mine: two dicks, pointing toward each other urgently, desperately. He pushed away from me, hands on my shoulders, when he came, and I watched as the arch of creamy white seemed to glow in the darkness of our dilapidated fortress. Then, still panting, still desperate, he clutched me first with his hand and then with his mouth, as I had done for him, sucking, kneading my balls with one hand. I pulled away as he had, and with my hand I guided my own arch to follow where his had gone.

All that seed. Anything but wasted.

We kissed, still a little frantic at first, quieting to tender as relaxation overtook us. Afterward we lay as long as possible folded into the quilt, warming each other with our breath, not speaking. But soon the shivering was too intense, so we dressed again and sat close together, still inside the folds of the quilt. He broke the silence.

"I've been coming here all along." It was his answer to my

question of an eternity ago. "I never stopped coming here. It was the only place I could be with you."

"I stayed away for the same reason." I rubbed my face. "The first time I came back, I sat here for the longest time, remembering the day you touched my face."

Nearly whispering, he said, "What is this thing, Jude? Is it bigger than us because it's Satan or because it's God?"

"Satan makes it possible for us to know the difference between good and evil." I exhaled loudly. "This doesn't feel evil to me."

He kicked the quilt off his legs and stood. "We can't do this." His voice sounded strangled. "We can't ever, ever do this again."

Every nerve in my body tensed, then itched, then crawled. What we'd shared had been something I knew I could never give up. Getting to my feet, I shouted, "Why the Hell not?"

He wheeled toward me and took a step back. "Are you out of your mind? This is all wrong! This *is* evil, Jude. I don't know why you think otherwise."

"I'll bet Pearl wouldn't have thought so." I have no idea where that came from, but it hit home.

He winced as though I'd struck him. "No. She didn't."

"You—you talked to her about me? You said you didn't!"

He nodded. "I know. I was . . . I don't know. I wanted to hurt you. But she didn't understand! I can't just turn away from God like that. I can't pretend the Bible doesn't hate this. I just— Hell, Jude, I just don't know what to do about it."

I had thought I knew, once. That day that Aurora had told me her parents didn't make love, that her father was chaste, I'd believed that was my destiny, too. But it hadn't worked for the reverend, and I was more sure than ever now that it wouldn't work for me. "Even Reverend King didn't know what to do. But look at the trouble lying about it got him into."

"But at least he admits it! Now he can do something. . . . I don't know what. But he confessed, and now he can ask God for forgiveness."

"He confessed in a fucking letter." It was Pearl's voice, her words anyway, coming out of my mouth. Her free use of expletives suddenly found new life in me. "I don't even know if that counts. It was a shitty thing to do. He even made me explain it, did you know that?"

Tim's eyes widened. "What do you mean?"

"Even in that fucking typed letter, he didn't actually tell his own wife that he was gay. He wrote, 'Ask Jude. He'll understand.' And then he said to tell me to pray and pray or Satan would get me too. Oh, maybe I loved him once, but I'm sure as Hell not one of his fans now. But I'll tell you something else. He did a lot of good here. He wasn't all bad. He was always kind and generous to me. But I've got my doubts about a religion that made him hide who he couldn't help being, that forced him to lie about what he was at his core. It was the lying that ruined his life, and then his wife's and daughter's, too. Religion made him lie. There's a flaw in that design." Standing up for Reverend King, I was standing up for myself. Standing up to God. It was a first.

Tim was shaking his head, not in disagreement, but in confusion. It only spurred me on. "Why do you suppose God would put a tree in Eden that would give Adam and Eve knowledge, then point Adam right at it and say, 'You can have anything but that.' Huh? And why would God let Satan into Eden just so he could tempt them even more? Don't you see a problem with that plan? I mean, does God know what he's doing, or doesn't he? Because if he does, he sure has a fucked-up sense of humor. And if he doesn't, why the Hell are we worshiping him anyway?"

I was furious, with no idea where it had come from. Something had exploded inside me, unleashed by what had exploded outside of me with Tim in my arms. I stood there, panting, fists clenched, ready for battle with the hounds of Hell if necessary. And I'd said things, taken steps that changed my attitude toward God, that were truly blasphemous. I was both terrified and euphoric.

Suddenly my mental focus shifted. "What are you gonna do now? About today? About what we did?"

Tim was still recovering from the shock of my tirade. He shook himself a little. "I—I'm not sure." He ran a hand through his hair and then clenched a fistful of it. "God, Jude, I'm gonna have to confess this. Otherwise it'll be a millstone around my neck, and Satan will drag me down with it."

There was a time—and not very long ago—when I would have felt the same. I would have agreed that we both needed to confess and be forgiven. But suddenly I wasn't in the same place as Tim anymore. "So you'll put me in the wrong again. That will be the second time."

"We both put ourselves in the wrong! You can't lay this on me."

"Then don't lay it on me. If you confess, you don't say a word about me."

"Jude, you gotta understand! You have to confess, too, don't you get it? I can't get forgiveness for you."

"So just get it for yourself, then. But leave me out of it this time, will you? Because if you don't, I'll never, *never* speak to you again."

"But—Pastor Wright will get it out of me! You know he will! And if I don't confess, I'll go to Hell. So will you. I don't want you to go to Hell, Jude. I—" And he froze.

What had he been going to say? I love you?

I made a snorting sound. "That's too bad, 'cause you've just told me you don't want Heaven with me, either." He looked like he might be about to cry. And suddenly he wasn't the person I'd thought. He was a terrified sissy, and on some level he liked the idea of confessing to Pastor Hellfire.

I moved to the entrance, turned just before I left, and said, "You know, in your own way, you're as big a coward as Reverend King. Pearl would be ashamed of you. I think that will help me get over you now." And I left. I didn't look back, but in my mind's eye Tim was in the entrance to the fort, holding onto something for support, watching me walk away for good, this time.

I cycled hard, back to the Harts'. Gregory was in the barn, tuning the engine of some equipment he was going to use the next week to start preparing somebody's field for spring planting. He took one look at my face and asked, "You okay?"

"Not really. I will be. Do you have a hatchet I can borrow?"

He looked at me as though he weren't sure he wanted to trust me with it, but he pointed to his tool rack. It was in a leather holster: perfect. "I'll take care of it," I said. "Don't worry."

Tim was gone by the time I got back to the fort. I would probably have been better off with an ax for this task, but on a bike that would have been too difficult to carry. And it would have attracted too much attention.

I stood there in the diminishing light, looking at the tree. I was near tears, but I wasn't flagging in my determination. Aloud, I said, "Pearl, this is for you. This place is yours, now. I can't have it anymore, and Tim can't have it anymore. It's yours alone."

I stood on a large rock at the base of the dead trunk so I could reach high enough, and I hacked and hacked at the place where the trunk had split until the blade cut through the mangled wood strips that held the upper tree to the part of it that reached into the ground, the part that had once given it water and nutrients in return for the energy of sunlight. The upper tree shuddered and fell onto the brittle branches beneath it, snapping and twisting them. I walked around the corpse, looking for larger branches that still held the trunk off the ground, hacking through enough of them until finally the part of the tree that had made a shelter out of otherwise meaningless space was nearly on the ground. Only the logs Tim had put inside kept it from resting on earth now. I decided to leave them as a monument to Tim's kindness, letting Pearl be taller. If even Satan and Reverend King had their good points, Tim did, too.

I sat on a stump several feet away, exhausted not just from my efforts but also from a sense of loss that left me physically weak. In a tornado of feelings, I recalled how this afternoon I'd cursed and practically called God a fool. I'd told the only person I really wanted that I'd never speak to him again, and I'd destroyed the place that held all the tenderness between us. I'd reached some kind of critical mass, having that moment of bliss with Tim, then hearing him call it evil. It was like he'd called *me* evil.

Before I knew it, tears were streaming down my face. I sobbed and moaned, not caring if anyone might be near to hear me, and then cried harder when I realized I no longer believed even Jesus could hear me. Because if God was a fool, how could Jesus be anything? And in an odd way, Jesus was the loss, not God. He'd been my personal connection with eternity. It was Jesus I had loved, Jesus who'd taken care of me. Only now did I make this distinction. Only now did it matter. Because in losing God, I lost Jesus as well. It was as though on some level I'd never really believed in Father. But I had believed in Brother.

I cried harder still when I realized I'd lost Lorne. On top of everything else, Lorne would be gone. He'd have to turn his back on me with all the other saints. Because I was now beyond reach of the Church.

It was fully dark by the time I got back. I hung the hatchet back on its hook and wondered if I could just stay out here, turn on the heater that Gregory used in cold weather, and die slowly. I didn't know how I was going to go inside looking as I must look, feeling the way I felt. I didn't know how I could face anyone. I wasn't sure I could even speak. And I expected that I would now be thrown out of yet another home.

On autopilot, I trudged to the back door, opened it, and called, "Home, Dolly."

She was at the sink, awkwardly reaching up and out to drain noodles she'd just cooked. Maybe if I were blind I'd figure out how to do things like that without being able to see, too, but she frequently amazed me. "Land sakes, Jude, about time. I thought you'd miss supper for sure. Wash your hands and see what else needs doing. Gregory'll be here in a tick."

Dolly said Grace over the meal, and we began the rituals that had seemed so comfortable to me the last time I'd sat down to eat with these people. But now, I felt hot and anxious when my eyes caught Gregory's, and Dolly's chatter no longer seemed reassuring and homey. Now it was grating, chopping up the minutes and stretching time with words that she strung together for no reason that I could follow, words that seemed to follow each other in no particular order, without any real meaning.

About five minutes into the meal she stopped, sensing a problem as only she could, and Gregory, chewing thoughtfully on a mouthful of bread, looked at me. I looked at him, looked down, and looked back. His eyes were still on me. "What?" I said, rather too loudly.

Two more chews, then he swallowed, still looking at me. Then he glanced down to follow the movements of his fork on the plate before him. "Just wondering how long it'll be before you tell us what's eating at you so hard."

I stabbed at something on my plate and tried to say, "Nothing." But my voice cracked on it, and not much came out.

Gregory let an uncomfortable amount of silence go by, and Dolly stayed quiet. Then he said, "What was the hatchet for?"

I cleared my throat. "Had to take down a tree."

"What tree would that be?"

I set my fork down, gave him a heavy look, and leaned on my words. "A hemlock." I wanted him to get the reference to the tree we'd moved together years ago, also a hemlock. I couldn't have said why, but I wanted to hurt him. Perhaps if I gave him a manufactured reason to kick me out, it could be for that, rather than for the real reason.

"Dead or alive?"

I took a shaky breath. "Dead."

He bent over his plate again. "Good. Otherwise there'd be pitch to clean off the hatchet." We all ate in silence for maybe thirty seconds. Then, "Where was this dead tree?"

"What difference does it make?"

His words formed slowly, in a relaxed way. "Well, you see, a tree is seldom just a tree. It has a long life, if it gets big enough to need a hatchet to cut it down. It just might have had a chance to make some new baby trees, shelter small creatures, support their lives, maybe mean something to someone. Maybe mean a lot."

He didn't look at me. Dolly still didn't speak. No one spoke. And in the silence his words sank deeper and deeper into me, and around the words rose a profound sadness. I pictured the hemlock fortress as it had been when it meant a lot to Tim and to me, that first summer. And the words "hemlock" and "fortress" skittered around my brain until they landed in a pattern I should have seen long ago. Something that was so obvious that I hadn't seen it. If my Internet handle was "fortress," then who could "hemlock" be but Tim?

I had cut down that hemlock. I'd pronounced it dead.

I closed my eyes and leaned back in my chair, breathing shallow, ragged breaths. Something in me stiffened, and I stood suddenly, sending the wooden chair over backward. I ran to my room and slammed the door. I wanted to lock it, but no rooms in the house had locks, so Dolly couldn't accidentally get trapped in any of them.

I sat on the edge of my bed, head in my hands, breathing oddly. Within minutes there was a light knock on the door.

"Go away!" I shouted, my voice high and squeaky.

The door opened, and Gregory came in. He sat on my desk chair. "I think you need to talk, son," he said. "And I'm here to listen." He waited.

"I don't want to talk about it."

"Why not?"

Why not. Reasonable question. There were so many answers, though. I chose the most immediate one in terms of my situation here. "You'll have to kick me out."

Gregory's eyebrows rose slightly, and he nearly smiled. "Oh, I think that's not very likely. Why on earth would I kick you out for cutting down a tree?"

I rubbed my face, struggling for the right words. I exhaled deeply, almost a sigh, resigned. "I've lost my faith." I waited. So did he. Finally I couldn't stand it. "Don't you see? You'll have to turn your backs on me. You and Dolly. You can't have me living in your house."

His head shook slowly, side to side. "Oh, Jude, believe it or not, I do remember what it felt like to be young, to have everything be black-and-white, life and death, to feel such intensity about everything. So I'm going to take you seriously, because I can see how seriously you mean it. But in case it helps you unburden yourself, know that no amount of faith you can leave in the road behind you will make me throw you out of my house. You'd have to do something much, much worse than that. So." He leaned back a little, obviously ready to listen. "Talk to me. You can start with the tree, if that's easier, or someplace else if you want. But talk."

I stood and went to the window, which looked out onto the fields and woods behind the house. In the distance I could see where the dark shapes of the mountains looked like black holes against the night sky, which wasn't as dark as the earth beneath it. In the morning, the earth would be flooded with light, but now it was darker than the sky. Darkness, light; evil, good. It seemed so simple, so undeniable. So final.

"If I stay in the Body, I'll have to lie. And I'll go to Hell. If I leave the Body, I'll be condemned to Hell."

"What would you have to lie about?"

My jaw worked and then opened. "The same thing as Reverend King."

"Why will you go to Hell?"

I spun around. "Did you hear what I just said?"

"I believe you just told me that you're gay, and that if you stay in the Body you'll have to lie about that. Seems to me if you did that, and if the only reason you lied was so you could stay in the Body, you'd be in Hell already."

What was he saying? How could I make sense of this? "How do *you* do it, then?"

"Ah." He heaved a breath. "Well, I'm in a kind of private Hell, it's true. But it's different from the one you're afraid of."

"How?"

"Your Hell is one you expect will be brought on you by going against God's Word, and it would last through eternity. I expect mine will be over when I die."

He had my attention. I sat down on the bed, facing him. "You mean what happened to Dolly?"

His body stiffened visibly. "What do you know about that?"

My eyes dropped involuntarily. "I heard you were with . . . someone . . . when it happened."

I heard his slow exhale but still couldn't look at him. "I was. I was young, but that's no excuse. But I don't stay here with Dolly because of guilt. I stay here because I love her and she needs me. She knows what happened, and she knows why. She has forgiven me. Otherwise, we couldn't live as we do. But I haven't forgiven myself. That's my problem, though; not hers, and not yours. It's one born of momentary selfishness and immaturity, not some eternal damnation. Mine speaks to frailty and will live only as long as I do. Now, tell me about yours."

What to say that he didn't already know? "Mine separates me from God, just like it says in Isaiah. It separates me from the saints. It makes things dark and ugly and heavy."

"That's the way they want you to feel."

"What? Who?" My eyes flew back to his face.

"The saints. You know the restriction about spending time only with each other? About not spending time with Miss Thornton or Pearl? About how much danger you'd be in if you did that? It was right, wasn't it? You spent time with Pearl and Miss Thornton, and now look at you. You're a regular scion of Satan." He winked at me. *Winked!*

"This is no joke! I'm in the trap, don't you see? I'm in the same trap as Reverend King, and even he couldn't get out of it because he lied. I was hoping you could help me get out of it because you don't!"

He chuckled. It wasn't at all the response I expected. "It's true I'll do my best not to lie to you, Jude. But I'm in a trap anyway. It's not the same trap"—he raised a hand for silence when I started to protest that it was—"because what you're calling a trap I would call a way of being. The trap is when you try to be what you're not, and you lie to convince yourself and others that you're something you're not. That's when you get caught. So don't lie. You're gay, Jude. So am I. So what?"

The expression on my face, the sputtering when I couldn't find words to respond, made him laugh outright. "I'm sorry, that was flippant. Gay is not something you can be open about and stay in the Body. I'll give you that."

I'd never in my life heard anyone just come out and say that before: *I'm gay.* Even I hadn't actually said the words. And for all the spiritual agony I had gone through with Reverend King, he had never said to me, "You're gay, Jude." Hell, he couldn't even say it in a typed letter of confession. With Gregory, it sounded no more upsetting than if he had said, "You live in this house. So do I."

"I could change."

"No. You can't. That's one thing you can't do. You could modify your behavior. You could even marry some poor girl who believes you love her the same way she loves you. But the union would shrivel over time because of the lie. Because the lie would be about who you are, and about love. If you believe you can pray your way out of this, forget it. Even Amos King couldn't do that, and that was one prayerful man."

"So I can't change, and I can't lie." I shook my head. "How can I get away with that?"

Gregory let out a long breath before he answered. "If you want my advice, here it is. Do whatever you need to do to get along here until you're out of high school. If college calls, do that. But go as far away as possible. If college doesn't seem right to you, then just go as far away as possible. You can't stay here and be gay. Even if you leave the Church, you'll be reminded every time you turn around that everyone here thinks you're condemned to Hell. You were right about that. You're going to have to leave, Jude. I'll help however I can, but you'll have to leave."

My heart felt cold. It's true that as I'd been preparing to leave my temporary quarters at my old home after Reverend King had disappeared, I had felt a pull away from Newburg. But then I'd found a home here, and in the short time I'd been at the Harts' I had settled into it in a way I would never have expected. It was home. Really home. Now Gregory's words, while not pulling me away, were pushing me.

I stared at him. "Why didn't you leave?"

His eyes closed for just a second. "I'm not a free agent."

"You mean Dolly?"

He stood and went to the window I had just gazed through. His words were quiet; I barely heard them. "I can move the hills. I can uproot trees. I can reshape the land. And I couldn't help her." He turned to face me. "I couldn't help either of them. I can't bring Pearl back to life, and I can't give Dolly back hers. I can't fix anything important. But I can provide. That, I can do. And she needs the Church. I need the Church *for* her. Things are a little different with you here to help, but in the past the women have brought food, done grocery shopping; they've driven Dolly places when I couldn't. I couldn't pay for all that. We don't have the kind of money that would pay for the help we get through the Church."

"But—if we're gay, and we can't change, what will happen to our souls?"

"Yours and mine?" He chuckled again and sank into the chair. "Our souls will be just fine, Jude, as long as we bring love into the world whenever possible, and as long as we do our best to avoid hatred."

This went against everything I had ever been taught, because it left so much out. All the rules, all the rites and rituals, all the thou-shalts and thou-shalt-nots. Baptism itself, the very portal to salvation, was made pointless. "How can you say that?"

"I'd be willing to wager, Jude Connor, that on any Sunday morning you could select any three saints at random and take them into three separate rooms and ask them to define God and define Jesus and define the Holy Spirit, and each of them would come up with something different. And each would be convinced they knew."

"That can't be true! Not any three people from our Church. We've all been taught the same thing; we hear the same sermons."

"Even so, each of us hears things through our own filter. Have you ever heard the expression, 'The Devil is in the details'?" I nodded, though I'd never understood it. "The more detailed a description you get from any of those three saints, the farther away from each other they will get. In the end, each will describe God and Jesus and the Spirit according to their own needs. God will be who they need him to be. Jesus, too. The Holy Spirit most people don't understand at all."

"Of course they do! We all do!"

"So what is it, then? What's the difference between God, Jesus, and the Spirit?"

I would have thought this distinction would just roll off my tongue. We all refer to the Spirit frequently. But—what was it? "See," I said, "this is what I meant. I've lost my faith, don't you get that? I can't talk to God anymore, or even to Jesus. I always used to be able to talk to Jesus. I always felt close to him, and now I don't. I can't even answer your question!"

He was unfazed. "The Bible tells us that Jesus is both the son of God and God incarnate. So anytime you're talking to one, you're talking to the other. But we perceive them differently, don't we? You could say that God decided that the only way he could communicate with us directly, effectively, given our limitations, was to do it on a personal level. So he came to earth as Jesus, and we called him God's son. Jesus allows us to have a personal relationship with God, who seems like this big, imposing, impersonal character. Right?" He waited for my nod, which I accompanied with a shrug. "But then what's the Spirit?"

I had no response. Gregory waited several seconds and then said, "The Spirit, Jude, is what connects God and Jesus. It's what makes them the same. And it's what connects us, in our physical state, with God. The Spirit is what will join you to God, not following all the rules or believing in some specific way of interpreting the things in the Bible."

I started to shake my head, but he didn't give me a chance to interrupt. "Do you remember what you said in the truck that day you and Aurora both came over? About God sending Pearl to Hell? She's not in Hell, Jude. Aurora quoted scripture that says it's not God's intent for us to condemn each other. The message of Jesus was all about love. That is the be-all and end-all. If you live a life of love, no God anywhere is going to send you to Hell. You don't have to be in any church's Body to be saved."

My voice was shrill with pent-up protest. "What you've just said goes against everything! Are you telling me I've been doing it wrong all my life?"

"I'm telling you they've been telling you wrong. I'm telling you it's more important to listen to Jesus than to any reverend anywhere."

This was incredible. "Do you know what they'll do to you if I tell them you said that?"

He smiled. "What are you going to tell them? Why should they listen to you, anyway? You're gay."

I got to my feet. He didn't. He kept talking, though.

"You're gay. There's no way you can understand the Bible, because you refuse to change. You're gay, and you're going to Hell. You know that, right? You can lie, but that will make God send you to Hell. Some day you won't be able to take it anymore, and you'll follow in the footsteps of Reverend King, leaving behind you a trail of blood and pain that will never stop, because it will be with you always. You're a disgrace to your family. They will cut you out of their lives as though you never existed. You've already lost both parents, and now Lorne and Clara will turn their backs on you. CC will never know who you are. Aurora and Mrs. King will deny you exist. Dolly will bar the door—"

"Stop!" My hands had formed fists at my sides, and I was just about to raise them, though what I thought I was going to do to Gregory I couldn't have said. Then he stood, and for the second time in my life he held me. I leaned into his powerful frame and held my breath so I wouldn't cry.

His arms around me, he said, "This is what you'll have to face, Jude, if you stay here. This is what your life will be like.

You have the wings, boy. You have the freedom. You need to go. Stay long enough to be as ready as you can, and then fly away from here."

He was right. I knew he was right. But I hated that he was right.

Chapter 19

If Tim confessed his own part in our mutual transgression, I don't think he said anything about me. Pastor Hellfire never approached me, and I have to believe he would have if he'd known, or even suspected.

I spent the rest of my high school time exactly as Gregory had suggested. Living in his house made it possible, because I could let down my guard at home. I let it down only so far, to be sure, but I could relax.

I went on dates, I attended Bible Studies, I went with groups on evangelizing forays when I couldn't avoid it, through areas outside Newburg where there were more heathens to be found. I went through all the motions, but I kept a low profile. And it never stopped feeling wrong. It never stopped hurting.

I missed Aurora painfully. She and her mother disappeared as soon as school was out that June. We exchanged e-mails for a while, but I knew she was still corresponding with a few other friends, and not knowing what she might repeat, I couldn't say what I wanted to say to her. So my messages felt false, and I'm sure that registered with her. The frequency lessened and then the messages stopped. It didn't take more than a few months, I'd guess about the time she got involved in her new school.

Sunday suppers were still at Lorne's house, but CC was every bit the attention hog most children are, and the gap between what I said to Lorne and what I could have said was filled by baby noises and then toddler interruptions and just plain talk about CC. If I'd spent a lot more time there, it would have become obvious that I wasn't talking much about my life, and I certainly didn't tell them about the time I was spending on the Internet trying to come up with a plan to move away. I didn't ask for their advice on anything.

In my last year at high school, I waited to tell them that I was even thinking about leaving, until Dolly had helped me zero in on a few college possibilities. I decided to study math, partly because I loved it, and partly because I could get into a decent school with math as my major.

Clara had the reaction I expected when I revealed my list one Sunday. "Jude, those schools are all so far away! Why can't you go to Idaho State in Pocatello? It would be so much closer to home. And there are Church members there for you to be with."

"I want a better math department." I didn't even know about the math department at Idaho State, because I hadn't looked into it. It was, as Clara said, so much closer to home. And I was eighteen. As long as I didn't ask them for money, there was nothing they could do about how far away I went.

When I got three acceptances, I settled on Washington University in Seattle. Gregory encouraged me to be in a city, one with a real metropolitan attitude. I was too chicken even to consider someplace like San Francisco or New York; Seattle seemed about as metropolitan as I could handle, and the school was willing to give me financial help. I'd have to work, that was certain, and maybe even take longer to finish, but it was a plan. It gave me hope. It was my Light at the end of the tunnel.

On one of my final days in Newburg I decided to do what Gregory had invited me to do years ago. I would hike up to Denmark Cliffs.

It was a warm, breezy day in June, the week after my high

school graduation. What I wanted was to go there with Gregory, but before I thought of going, before I'd even come to the kitchen for breakfast, he was already out. Dolly told me he was going to spend an hour or so helping Mr. Randall and his son put up some fencing. So I decided to go on my own; better get used to being alone, I thought. I made sure Dolly didn't need anything I could help her with, and then I packed a lunch, threw it in my backpack, and rode my bike out to where Gregory had told me the trail started, just past the barn on the Johnson property. I wheeled the bike into the woods a little way, hidden from casual view, and started my trek.

The trail wasn't steep at first, just meandered in a broad swath of packed dirt that looked as though cattle probably used it sometimes, judging by the hoofprints and the occasional cow patty. But then there was a fork. One side, the one on the right, went along the flat toward pasture land. On the left, the trail went into the woods and immediately twisted around a curve, uphill, and out of sight. That's the way I went.

Climbing steeply for a good five minutes, I felt a little winded already. But I kept going, loving the way it made the muscles in my thighs and calves burn, relishing the way my chest had to expand to take in more air. It was as if I'd been granted permission to take up more space. To take all the space I needed.

The trail began to grow narrow and faint. I wondered if people sometimes decided to try it and grew discouraged by the slope. Another ten minutes or so of hard work brought me to slightly more open space, fewer trees. Although there were a few flowers here, the show was hardly like the meadow. But I recognized springbeauties and even a few lady slippers, the orchid of the mountains. I heard chickadees and jays and caught the occasional flash of yellow and red of the western tanager or the parakeet-yellow goldfinch flitting from dark green hemlock to sunlight-green aspen.

Ahead the trail went into denser woods again, level briefly, but I could see the steep uphill beyond. I put one foot in front of the other, let the birdcalls wash pleasantly over me, and let my mind wander where it would.

Clara was pregnant again, due in November, a few days after my birthday. She had talked about what fun it would be to celebrate my birthday and the baby's together while I struggled to smile and agree, knowing I'd probably never meet this child. Whenever I was at the house these days, I stared at my brother as much as I could without attracting notice, searing his face into my memory, fighting the catch in my throat at the thought that I might never see him again, wondering how much he would hate me if he knew who I was. I was still undecided whether to let him know before I left, and the ambivalence and potential consequences colored every second I was in his company.

Dolly. I would miss Dolly so much. She'd been such a wonderful friend, always cheerful, always ready to listen, never judging. From her copious reading material she had located a few books for me to use over the summer, books designed to give the beginning college math student a head start. I would use them when I got to Seattle, well ahead of when classes would start; I wanted to feel at least a little familiar with my surroundings before I had to plunge in for real, and Dolly had helped me figure out how to locate cheap summer housing on campus.

Belinda Thornton and I never grew close, though I always enjoyed her company. I'll never know for sure what it was that kept us apart. Perhaps it was jealousy over Gregory's free time.

Pearl. Pearl's grave. I'd visited that little plot more frequently than I'd been to my mother's grave in the past year. I'd sit down beside the headstone, carved with the quote "You're so precious to me, baby of mine," harking to the song Pearl used to sing, and I'd talk to Pearl. I'd tell her what was going on in the meadow, or along the riverbank, what was growing, what was blooming. I told her she'd been right, that I was gay, and that I was leaving. I asked her to keep Gregory company, to watch over him, because he had to stay.

And then Tim. I was supposed to climb this path with Tim, but Lorne had put a stop to that, and now it would never happen. Tim had started dating a girl named Shelly more fre-

quently than any other girl, and the talk was they'd end up together. I remember thinking how much Shelly resembled Mrs.
Denmark: pale hair, skin luminous now with youth but likely to
become ashen with years. I felt sorry for Tim. I felt sorrier for
Shelly.

Thoughts of Tim no longer brought up the painful longing I
used to associate with him. I was over him. He was going to lie,
and I couldn't help but believe he would fail. He wasn't a
strong person, and one day the pressure would be too great.
He'd crack, just like the broken hemlock of our fort.

I'd been hiking perhaps an hour before the woods opened
suddenly onto an expanse of rock ledge, mostly flat but uneven
underfoot. I dropped the backpack and inched toward the
edge. There was a deep valley below, the river I'd grown up beside—the one I'd been immersed in twice by Reverend King—
flowing far below, cutting a watery wound into the earth. My
head felt light and almost dizzy, and when my eyes found the
raptors circling not far below I nearly lost my balance trying to
follow their stately movement, distant woods blurring behind
their carefree bodies. I stepped back and then dropped to the
ground, crawling out on my belly to watch the birds. There
were red-tailed hawks, peregrine falcons, and even an eagle or
two. They soared effortlessly on thermals rising from the warming landscape, watching for prey, fearlessly beautiful. Gregory's
words came back to me: *You have the wings, boy. You have the freedom. Fly away from here.*

I felt stimulated and yet peaceful. But peace is a funny thing.
I felt it powerfully that day on Denmark Cliffs, looking down at
the raptors soaring below just as Gregory had described. I've
come to see peace not as an absolute, and not even as relative
to circumstances. I think peace comes from accepting what is
and responding to that in your own way. Openly. Honestly.
Without bitterness or joy, fear or expectation. This doesn't
mean you never feel these things; it just means peace has nothing to do with them. It's outside of them. And Belinda was
right: It comes from within.

I fetched my backpack and sat on the ledge, as close to the

edge as I dared, and consumed my own food as I watched the birds hunt for theirs. The uncanny feeling that Pearl was beside me kept returning. I think it was that finally I understood what she'd told me the day I showed her the fortress. She'd said that Pagans find holiness through nature, allowing it to show them where the guideposts are between the physical and the spiritual. I could see that path in my mind's eye, and she was right. It led to God.

I sat there until early afternoon, longer than I had expected to, sometimes watching and sometimes just gazing sightlessly into the distance, wondering what my life would be like when I was someplace I could be myself. Wondering what I would be like when I could open up a little. Wondering what was under this artificial shell that the Church had done its best to convince me was my real self. I barely knew who I was. Whether that was the case with others my age, I couldn't speculate. But the future held so much promise, so many possibilities, and they no longer depended on the secret safety of a shelter in the woods. I couldn't wait to get started, and yet I hated the way I was leaving, because I was leaving a lie behind, a lie most people would never know was a lie. And as I sat there, excitement and peace alternating moment by precious moment, I decided I would stop lying to Lorne. He could say what he wanted to Clara or anyone else, but I would not leave myself as a lie with my brother.

On my way down, I got to the place where the woods had opened briefly, where I'd stopped to listen to birdcall, when I saw them. They were coming into the clearing from the other side, coming up the trail, walking slowly and very close together, eyes on the ground. Gregory's hand rested on Todd's shoulder lightly as they walked, and they didn't see me at first. I stood very still, fully in view if they looked up. I could hear Gregory's low voice but not the words, the sound tender and intimate, and I could see the smile on Todd's face. Then Gregory looked up.

They stopped about twenty feet away and looked at me. Todd's face showed concern but Gregory's was gentle and kind, his hand still on Todd's shoulder. He smiled at me. I grinned back, my face involuntarily expanding into what I can only call beaming. Todd smiled too, then, and they walked past me without a word.

I waited until just before I left for school to reveal the truth about myself to Lorne; I didn't want to have to face him, or Clara, or anyone they might tell, for any longer than necessary. Although I knew I had to tell him, although I was on my way to tell him, my mind skittered away from the reality of it as I drove to my old home in the used car Lorne had helped me find, a car he had worked on and made as perfect as possible, knowing even as he did so that I would get into it soon and drive far away.

Lorne and I sat in lawn chairs behind the house, iced tea glasses sweating in our hands. Clara and CC were off someplace, I don't remember where. He'd asked a few things about how ready I was, whether I was nervous. I remember thinking they were questions he could have asked if he'd barely known me, something that was more the case than he knew. At some point I realized the time had come, and that there would not be a better chance. I didn't even take a breath first, as though it would be better if I were surprised by my own voice.

"I have to tell you something."

He took a sip from his glass and smiled, a solicitous older brother letting the youngster think he'll say something important. "Sounds serious."

"It is." I waited for his smile to fade. "I don't want to be a coward about it. I didn't just want to disappear and not tell you, and I didn't want to do it in a letter." I had seen the results of that approach, after all.

My turn to take a sip, though it was more like a gulp. A scowl began to form on Lorne's face. I did take a breath at this point, and then I plunged ahead.

"Remember that second baptism? After the first one didn't take?" He nodded once. "The second one didn't, either."

I waited again. So did he, for a few seconds. He closed his

eyes, compressing the lids two or three times. Then, "Jude, what are you saying?"

Another breath. "I'm gay." And another. "I'm gay, Lorne, and there's nothing I can do about it." I wanted to add that there was nothing I *should* do about it, but I knew he wouldn't agree with that. And I was still searching for the guts to believe it myself.

Lorne leaned forward and set his glass on the ground. It tipped and spilled tea, ice, and a lemon wedge onto the grass. He stood. "I was afraid this day might come. Come inside and pray with me."

I stayed in my chair. My head began to shake "No" of its own volition. I couldn't stop it, and it jerked from side to side faster and harder until I finally got control, clenched my jaw, and stared hard at my brother.

"Come inside." His voice was harder, even commanding.

"What for?"

"We'll kneel together, you'll confess this to God through Jesus, and then we'll go to Pastor Wright together."

Still I sat. "Pastor Wright will never know about this unless you tell him. I'm not talking to him about anything. I'll pray with you if you like, Lorne, but not about this."

Lorne's scowl crumpled into confusion. "So, what—you're just going to *be* like this?"

I snorted. "You might as well ask me if I'm just going to leave my birthday in November. I have about as much control over that."

Now his head moved side to side. "That's not true! Jude, please. If you pray hard enough, if you're sincere—"

I stood at last. "Don't you get it, Lorne?" My voice rose despite my effort not to shout. "Do you think I haven't done that? Good God, man! Do you think Reverend King didn't do that? He spent his entire life praying for that! Are you going to tell me he wasn't sincere enough?"

Lorne calmed slightly. "Is that what this is about? You think that because he was a homosexual, you are, too?" He made some sound between "Oh!" and "Ah!" and then said, "I *knew* this would happen! I just knew it. We should never have let you go to the Harts'.'"

I turned my back on Lorne to keep from striking him, one hand clutching my hair, the other planted firmly on my hip where it couldn't do any damage. Facing the meadow, I shouted, "You idiot!"

Then I half sobbed and turned to Lorne. "I'm sorry. I didn't mean that. You can't know what it's like, though. You can't possibly understand." I took a step toward him. "The prayers, the endless prayers. The kneeling for hours—sometimes all night—by my bed, begging and pleading and crying and ranting. And then having dreams about being with another boy, or a man I don't even know." I took a long, shaky breath. "This has nothing to do with Reverend King, or with Gregory Hart, or with anyone but me. You can't know what I've been through. You can't change what I am. No one can."

It was so hard not to try and get Lorne to see that what I was—a gay man—was something God seemed to determined to have on the earth. That it was deliberate, that it was okay. That it was not a mistake. But I knew what his response would be, because I knew what my response would have been before Reverend King disappeared. And it would have left no chink for reason to get in. If I had tried to reason with Lorne, between the lines of any response of his I would have heard, *I know what I believe. Don't trouble me with facts.*

Into the silence, Lorne's desperate voice said, "Then I don't know how to help you!"

"Then just promise me this. Promise me you won't cut my face out of every picture I'm in. You won't search the house for anything I might have left behind and set a ritual bonfire to destroy it all. To destroy me. Promise me you won't tell people you don't have a brother." Between my own lines, I was begging, *Don't make me another Veronica Voelker. Because I exist. Oh, I exist very much!*

Nearly in a whisper, Lorne said, "But Jude . . . you'll go to Hell!"

I shook my head again. "You're limiting God. Don't try to

tell him how to treat me. And don't try to tell him he made a mistake in creating me. Don't judge me; that's his job."

We stood there, only a few feet apart, a gulf of pain between us. I couldn't say now which of us threw the first lines out to bridge it. Maybe both of us together. But I do remember that even as we stood there in a tight hug, I knew that his sobs were not from relief. I knew that they were sobs of fear. Fear for me.

Gradually I pulled away and turned to leave. Head down, his back to me, he said, "I won't tell Clara." Then he half turned his body, his face toward me. "And you'll always be my brother."

I took a tearful leave of Dolly the day I left Newburg, promising to write often, even if it was "only e-mail," as she put it. Gregory helped me load my car and gave me a long, hard hug just before I got in. I felt almost like the terrified eleven-year-old boy I had been the first time he hugged me, the day I ran away from home.

"Let me know if you need anything. Anything at all," he said, his eyes moist. And then, his face intense, he added, "You be yourself, boy."

I stopped briefly to say good-bye to Lorne, Clara, and CC. Lorne looked uncomfortable, but I could tell from the way Clara acted that he hadn't told her about my revelation. She extracted promises similar to Dolly's before I was allowed to drive away. Anxious as I had been for over a year to get away from Newburg—from the stifling Pastor Wright, from the painful memories this town held for me—I pulled to the side of the road just outside the town line and got out of the car to gaze for a moment at the modest white sign whose black letters announced, **Town of Newburg.** Just beyond it, within the town limits, was a larger sign, in a kind of dark blue with white letters, that declared, **Grace of God Church Welcomes You!** I sighed, turned my back on both, and drove on.

I had another destination: the Boise bar.

Boise was out of my way by a good distance, but there was something I had to do before I left my old life behind. I had timed my departure from Newburg so that I would hit Boise after dark, not caring that it would mean giving up enough money to spend a night in a cheap motel.

The pit of my stomach felt sick as I pulled into the gravel parking area; it looked smaller but otherwise not much different from the night Reverend King had brought me here. The neon signs were probably the same ones, and perhaps even some of the necking couples were the same men.

I was not yet old enough to have something other than the ginger ale Reverend King had bought for me. I kind of wished I could; it might have steadied my nerves. But I also wanted my wits about me, and I'd never had a drink in my life.

At least three men approached me as I headed toward the bar, hoping Leo was still tending it. I cast my best half-smiles at them and kept moving. And Leo was there.

He didn't recognize me; no surprise. I asked for a ginger ale, and that made him look again, but still no glimmer. As he set it down I asked, "I'm wondering if you've seen a friend of mine who used to come in here. He was the pastor at Grace of God Church in Newburg."

Leo's gaze intensified. His chin rose for a second as he said, "You that young kid the reverend brought in here once?" I smiled and nodded, and he made a harrumphing sort of noise. "I ain't seen the *good* reverend in years. Why're you looking for him?"

I sipped from my glass and shrugged. "I'm not, really. Just thought I'd stop in and ask. I'm on my way to college, and I hadn't seen him for some time." I wondered if Leo had a clue what Amos King's real name was. The man would always be Amos King—Reverend King—to me.

Leo went to serve another patron and then came back to me. "I heard he disappeared."

I nodded, eyes on my glass. "Yeah. I don't know where he went. Just thought I'd see if he'd been here at all."

Leo watched me for few seconds. Then, "Take some advice, kid. Steer clear of men like that." He took a swipe at the bar with a grubby white towel and moved away.

I downed a little more of my drink, left some money beside

the glass, and did my best to avoid the eyes of several men who watched me head for the door. If I hadn't been so torn between disappointment and relief, perhaps I would have considered spending a little time. But as it was, I felt very near tears for reasons I couldn't have explained. *What did I expect,* I asked myself as I kicked up gravel on the way to my car, *that he'd be in there dancing with my red-shirted devil, the Satan who had haunted my dreams?* I felt like a stupid little kid whose daddy had forgotten his birthday. I slammed the door of my car and leaned my arms and my head on the steering wheel.

I was halfway to Seattle before I realized that I hadn't looked for a place to spend the night—and that I didn't remember much of anything I'd driven past. Instead, I'd been seeing the black hair, the piercing eyes, the strong jaw of Reverend King. I'd been watching his expression change from the customary holy confidence through various stages of surprise and shock until the features landed on a pain that was at least in the same league with the pain he had caused me. The changes on his face were in response to what I was telling him, how I was condemning him. Because despite the good I know he did, for me and for others, I couldn't deny that what floated to the surface as I left my life behind, as I tried to leave him behind, was pain. Desolation. Betrayal and lying and dismissive cruelty. Only half consciously did I realize I was speaking aloud, shouting at the reflection on the inside of my windshield, which in my mind was his face, not mine.

"You lied! You lied to me, to your wife, to Aurora, to everyone! You made us feel like we would go to Hell if we weren't like you! And just *look* at what you are!"

"*You're* not righteous. *You're* not trustworthy. You weren't leading us toward God and Light and Truth and Beauty. You were running away from yourself, and you were leading us straight to Hell!"

"You're gutless, that's what you are. Gutless coward! Didn't even have the guts to speak for yourself! Made *us* confess all the time, though, didn't you? Christ! You even made me confess *for you!* Made me practically reveal what only you and I knew about me! A secret you had promised to keep!"

There was a moment of slight surprise for me at this point, when I realized I couldn't quite remember him promising to keep my secret. And then it occurred to me that perhaps when he'd written that I should pray that this evil wouldn't trap me, he hadn't meant the evil of homosexuality. Perhaps he'd meant the evil of lying.

I began shouting again, but it was just more of the same, and eventually I ran out of steam. At some point in the night I pulled off the road and napped for a couple of hours. I found a roadside diner for breakfast, and I drove on, hands firm on the wheel, mind frozen into a grim determination to live a life that was mine. A life that was true.

At the End: The Fallen

It's been over a decade, and a whole lifetime, since I left New-burg. And this new life has been much more difficult and even more rewarding than my imagination knew to make it. I've loved and lost and loved again. I have a great career designing Web sites, doing freelance work on a flexible schedule. A friend from college wants to hire me full-time. I might do that. Or I might not.

Stan, my lover, is the perfect complement to me. He's soft where I'm tough and tough where I'm soft. One place I particularly rely on him has to do with the scars, not quite healed—maybe never will be—from where Reverend King ripped my world apart, tore horrid, gaping gashes in my relationship with God. Stan has an uncanny knack for knowing when I'm in a mood that has those old pains at its source, even if the current circumstances don't reveal that. He knows. And when he sees that happening, it doesn't matter if I've just said something cutting and hurtful to him. He takes me in his arms and won't let go, even if I struggle, until he's shined enough light into my darkness that I can see what's real once more. And what's real is that there's still love, there's still God. What's real is what we have, Stan and I.

Stan is not especially religious, but now that my own way of approaching God has become more open, this isn't important to me. Maybe one day we'll move in together. I met Stan in college, my junior year and his freshman, and I fell in love with him on the spot. But he wasn't ready. He wasn't ready to be gay, and he most certainly wasn't ready to have a male lover. We were friends, though, and we stayed in touch after I graduated. He moved to San Francisco after he finished school. As he put it, he wanted ". . . just to see what it was like to be someplace where no one would care if two men stopped to admire a shop window and exchange an affectionate kiss." But the city was too expensive, and he came back to Seattle, finally ready for what we could offer each other.

He loves to hear me talk about my days as a saint. Sometimes it makes him giggle, and sometimes it makes him cry. He says he gets near orgasm when he pictures Reverend King up in the pulpit, black hair flying, soulful tears running down his face, that resonant, resounding voice booming out to the saints and up to the vaulted ceiling.

Last week I saw him. The reverend. It was in Partners—think Madison Pub, with its shiny brass and polished wood and its patrons in designer labels, and take it down a notch or two, which makes the cover charge easier to take for people like me and my budget-conscious lover. Seattle is a great city, but it ain't cheap; all the California dropouts have increased the cost of living. So I was meeting Stan in Partners.

Stan wasn't there yet—no surprise, I'm usually early and he's usually late—and at first my gaze glanced off of Amos King and moved on. I was on a search-and-match mission, not out to identify anyone who wasn't Stan. But when my eyes had done a full circuit and hadn't spotted Stan, something jangled in my brain.

I almost didn't recognize him. He was alone at a small table, what looked like an untouched glass of something straight-up and clear like gin or vodka in front of him, and his eyes followed the retreating backside of a waiter on his way back to the bar, the twin cherry-tomato mounds thinly covered by black fabric. The reverend was kind of hunched over the table, arms folded in front of him.

A voice in one ear said to me, "Turn away. Don't even look at him. What do you think you can say that he wants to hear, or that will make you feel any better? Leave him alone." But in the other ear I heard, "You can't predict someone else's reactions. Approaching him *might* push him over some edge, or it might pull him back from one. Do what seems right to you. *For* you. And do it with love."

He barely glanced up as I approached his table. I almost missed him saying, "Not interested. Please leave me alone." But when I didn't move, he looked at my face.

"Reverend King?"

He sat back in his chair, his full attention on me now. Or, at least, his eyes were on mine. I'm not sure where his attention was. In better lighting I think I would have seen several different expressions dance in succession across his tired, sagging face. His arms unfolded slowly, and at first I thought he was going to hold out a hand for me to shake, but instead he covered his face.

Well, I couldn't leave him like that. Maybe his direction—toward or away from that edge—wasn't clear, but there was definitely an edge someplace. So I sat down. When his hands fell away from his face, the expression was settled. He looked depressed. Lonely. Haggard. "No one has called me that in years."

Suddenly the cherry-cheeked—and I don't mean his face—waiter was there. "What would you like?" he asked me.

"I'm meeting someone in a few minutes. I'll wait to order then." To the reverend, I said, "You should go ahead. I mean, your drink."

He shook his head. "I don't drink."

"Then, what . . ."

"If I can see it, if it's right here in my reach, I can resist it."

Christ, I thought; what a way to live. But he had always been like that—never touching the desserts in front of him. Practicing resisting temptation, and maybe trying to prove how righteous he could be. To impress God. But in this case, with men, maybe it was more like if it was real, he could see the flaws, the impurities. It was his fantasies—pure and free of blemish—that he couldn't resist. Before I could stop myself, I said, "Same with the men?"

There was a brief silence in which I wanted to lacerate my back in penance. What a dumb-ass thing to say. Hurtful.

"Yes. Same with the men."

"Why?"

"What?"

"Why resist?"

His eyes closed. "You know very well."

I took a few shallow breaths and then one deep one. "I'll tell you what I know." I tried to keep my voice as soft as possible, which was hard with the music thumping. "I know who I am. I know myself. And because I do, I can love God. With all of me." His eyes opened but looked away from me, at nothing as far as I could tell. "Love yourself, reverend. God does."

"And here's what I know. I had the answers. Now all I have are questions."

What I wanted to say was maybe having questions is the right place to be. That life isn't an algebraic equation. Then what I wanted to say was all those things I'd shouted at my windshield as I'd driven from Boise to Seattle years ago. All those things that would tell him the painful truth about what his lies had done to me. I wanted to tell him what I thought of him now, what a coward he was, what a pathetic excuse for a child of God he is now and always has been. I came so close to dumping all that on him.

Instead, all I said was, "Tell me, reverend. Are you afraid to die?"

He didn't look at me as I stood to leave.

I chose a table where I could see who came in, ordered my usual ale, and carefully avoided looking toward the fallen saint. Before my drink arrived, the figure of that sexy, sweet man who was meeting me appeared, and my groin took its usual ecstatic lurch. I smiled and lifted my chin in Stan's direction.

A READING GROUP GUIDE

THE REVELATIONS OF JUDE CONNOR

Robin Reardon

ABOUT THIS GUIDE

The suggested questions are included to enhance
your group's reading of Robin Reardon's
The Revelations of Jude Connor.

DISCUSSION QUESTIONS

1. After Jude's mother dies, with his father already having deserted the family, his brother Lorne—a very young, uncomplicated man—fights hard to keep what's left of his small family together. He even pushes back against the charismatic and powerful Reverend King, who suggests that Jude come to live with him and his wife. Can you trace the changes in Jude's life, and in Lorne's, that lead to Lorne's eventually agreeing to this arrangement? Does Lorne actually let go of Jude, or does his life just get complicated enough that he can't manage all the moving parts?

2. In the open fields between their homes, Jude overhears Pearl singing the song "Baby Mine" to a doll her mother made for her, a doll that bears a certain resemblance to the misshapen Pearl. This song, from the movie *Dumbo*, is sung by a mother assuring her unique and "different" child that he is perfect just as he is. Do you think Jude knew who it was Pearl was really singing to when she sang to her doll? Do you think Pearl knew?

3. Pearl is ostracized by the Church, not just for her background and her disbelieving mother, but also because of her own willful refusal to believe. She's also an outsider by virtue of the color of her skin and her misshapen form. How does she respond to this marginalization? What does she do to establish an identity she can be proud of?

4. When Jude learns about Dolly's accident and Gregory's connection to it, he assumes Gregory stays in Newburg out of guilt. Gregory more or less confirms this for Jude as he tells Jude to leave. But in many ways Gregory fits

in with his environment, with his roots in this community. If not for the accident that maimed Dolly, what do you think Gregory would have done?

5. Some of the men in the gay bar in Boise, where Reverend King took Jude, knew who the pastor was. King said he was there to save depraved souls. Do you think it's possible he meant to do only that? And even if this was true then, later it becomes evident that his trips to Boise had a different agenda. At what point do you think the reason for his trips began to change?

6. For most of the story, anything the church congregants have to say about Pearl leaves Jude with the impression that they consider her a heathen. And yet when she goes missing in the blizzard, Gregory has no trouble recruiting church members to help search for her. What does this say to you about the Church?

7. Dolly is seen by the other congregants as someone who knows her Bible well and reads it constantly. But as Jude gets to know her better, he discovers her attitude toward scripture is far more lenient. What does this tell you about Dolly? How would you describe her belief system?

8. During Jude's eavesdropping on the argument between Reverend King and Gregory Hart in the Harts' barn, Jude learns that the pastor's wife, Natalie, had been spending quite a bit of time at the Harts'. Later, when the truth is discovered about Reverend King, Natalie is devastated. How much do you think she already suspected? And if she suspected, why?

9. When Jude and Tim meet in the hemlock fort years after their first summer together, Jude discovers that he was not the only one who'd had a secret relationship

with Pearl. Not only had Tim and Pearl spent time in the fort, but also Tim had been the one who found Pearl's missing doll and had given it a Pagan burial. What is Jude's reaction? Is he jealous, or merely confused? And what does it mean that Pearl never mentioned either boy to the other?

10. Pearl has treated Jude with obvious disdain throughout their friendship. Yet it seems she treated Tim very differently. Why?

11. When Jude confesses his "sin" to Lorne, his brother's response is painfully predictable to Jude: "Pray with me." If—despite his efforts to that point in his life, and despite Reverend King's failure—Jude had succumbed to the belief that through Jesus, God can accomplish anything, what do you think his life would have been like? If he had allowed his love for his brother, and in fact his love for the Harts, to keep him in Newburg, what would the man Jude have looked like in thirty years?

12. *I know what I believe. Don't trouble me with facts.* This attitude seems ingrained in the minds of people who deny that homosexuality is as natural, as normally-occurring as heterosexuality. Many, but not all, of these people claim religious scripture as their source for what's true, facts notwithstanding. For those who don't lean on religion as the source of their misguided condemnation, what do you think the source is?

13. How many times over the course of the story does Jude lose a father figure? Toward the end, he partially gains one of them back. Which one?

TELL THE WORLD
THIS BOOK WAS

Good	Bad	So-so

GB✓
slow start
but good
message